Novels by Rick Stiller

Fiction

Dealer

Nellis Gray
The Redemption Series – Volume 1

Young Adult

The Morgan's Knot Serial Fantasy

Morgan's Knot
Island of the Children
Ice Island
Islands of Concrete and Steel
Islands of the Mind
Islands in the Sky
Islands of Dark Miracles

Visit: www.rickstiller.com for more of his books, photographs, and music and www.morgansknot.com for the latest on the Morgan's Knot series.

Sunny Breeze

The Redemption Series
Book II
By
Rick Stiller

ISBN - 978-1-7326505-1-0

Visit www.rickstiller.com

For John Deckert

Sunny Breeze

Tate Sloan straightened his crimson tie as the first limousine pulled under the portico of The Mansion House, an aging resort on Dolphin Bay - classic, majestic, and long past its prime. His stunning wife, Mavis, leaned to whisper, "Marvin Standler, CEO of Brinksman Investments."

He shook his head in awe, *"Famous for massive leveraged takeovers that wring every last penny out of a company, before dumping the remnants and the debt for the vultures. Brilliant and intimidating!"*

A doorman, dressed in formal black tails despite temperatures hovering near ninety in the shade, opened the rear door with a bow. Before Standler's boot heel hit the pavement, Mavis marched down the red carpet to offer her hand and a kiss on each cheek. Her elegant gown, a sheer wisp of teal silk, accentuated long lean lines and daring cleavage, but her carriage implied much more. "Marvin, I'm so glad you could join us today!"

"I'm always pleased to spend time with you and Tate," replied the weathered billionaire from Montana. "Especially when it's about making money."

Tate shook his hand with a practiced, toothy smile, "I think we've got a deal you can't resist."

"Find me some top-shelf bourbon and I'll listen."

Mavis took his arm as the car pulled away, "You're a busy man, so you know we wouldn't waste your time."

Standler tipped his cowboy hat to brush back thick silver hair curling over the collar of a well-worn leather jacket. He patted her hand and leaned close, "I've got plenty of money but I'd fly these thousands of miles, just for a whiff of your scent."

"I do like real men," laughed the beautiful blond, "but this is about more than just money."

"Any chance I could steal you away from your quarterback husband?"

Mavis kissed his cheek, "My daddy taught me to believe that anything's possible, if you want it bad enough."

Tate greeted Ned Flint, an arrogant aristocratic hotel and shipping magnate, as he stepped from a silver Bentley, "Ned, I'm so glad you could make it."

Flint gazed around at the aging resort, "I do hope this is not an indication of the quality of your proposal?"

"That's exactly why we're meeting here. This was the height of glamour, not so long ago, but we're going to be talking about the world we're going to invent for tomorrow."

The Sloans guided more than two dozen potential partners into a formal library off the lobby, offering privacy amidst the hushed sophistication of fine Early American furnishings, vibrant bouquets of flowers, and thousands of rather dated leather-bound volumes lining shelves floor to ceiling. Guests were invited to indulge in a full bar and sumptuous buffet, which allowed time for introductions and re-acquaintance.

Tate glanced over Ned Flint's shoulder, watching Mavis work the crowd with flirtatious hugs and seductive whispers, taming and inflaming the infantile egos of a roomful of the most powerful and reclusive tycoons in the country.

Beneath the seductive silk clinging to her voluptuous body, behind the enchanting smile and crystal blue eyes that hypnotized intelligent men and infuriated every woman within sight, there resided a she-devil born to mold the world to suit her vision and purpose.

She first noticed Tate on a television interview, when he was a promising freshman quarterback destined to lead Oklahoma to a National Championship before he graduated. He looked comfortable and relaxed, responding to questions from the press with clever one-liners guaranteed to be featured on sports shows across the country. He was a dazzling, athletic, all-American con-artist playing the part with an 'Aw-shucks' countrified shtick, and what he lacked in sophistication was overshadowed by the magnetism of his personality on the screen. In spite of his boyish arrogance, his humor and his physical presence even charmed fans of the opposing teams, and he was just what she was looking for.

Each of these exceedingly wealthy investors was predictably quirky; most made no bones about wanting to bed her and each managed to touch her body, caressing her ass or brushing against her breasts, with two exceptions. Bernie Baker, eighty-five if he was a day and, certainly, long past potency, reached for her crotch and got a sharp bite on his ear for his roughish audacity. Tight-lipped Flint scanned her body the way an architect appraises a building; analyzing proportions, lines, and curves with a critical eye. Rumors suggested he was gay and she was not surprised to see him standing very close to Tate, his hand caressing her husband's muscular shoulder, sharing seductive confidences. She was amused by one of the richest men in the world fawning over her husband instead of her, and wondered whether the elder man's advances aroused her macho mate.

Mavis discovered her ability to flirt and seduce men of all ages when she was a precocious child, and had no compunction about using her beauty to tame the ferocious lion that guarded their egos and their wallets. Tate would play his part, because Flint's expertise would prove invaluable.

Erwin Nash, with several PhD's and youngest of the guests, created Primary Pharmaceuticals to market his arthritis drug, 'Rhythmus', and was currently bringing a genetic coding device to market. Famous for boasting that he had more money than most developing countries, he attempted to French-kiss Mavis and ran his hand down her spine to squeeze her ass, "Whatever you're selling, darlin', I'm buying."

The tall blond smacked his cheek, playfully but hard enough to leave a stinging scarlet outline on his face. "Even with all your money, honey, you couldn't begin to afford the upkeep."

Harvey Sacks, CEO of the country's second largest financial group, Harvard graduate, and certainly the most refined of the group, took her hand and kissed her fingers, "It is my pleasure to have a moment with you."

"I'm pleased you decided to join us. I know your schedule is always full."

"For you, I would make an exception."

"I hope we can make your trip worthwhile, besides Florida's sunshine and sultry breezes."

"M'dear, we both know that you inspire something primal in every man in this room and I doubt that many of us would be here, if you were not presiding."

"That's about as honest as I've ever heard it put," smiled the beauty, patting him on the chest with a kiss to each cheek. "You keep that motor running, honey, because I want you to be part of this."

Tate raised a finger and Mavis joined him behind a covered display case. "Gentlemen! I'd like to thank each of you for taking the time join us today. I hope your bellies are full and our staff will make sure that your glasses remain topped off."

Mavis smiled, "Our proposal involves multiple layers, so Tate will give you the overview of the first project and then we'll move on to the rest of the story."

Tate pulled the drape from the case, revealing an intricately detailed model of a resort development stretching across Breezy Key from a marina village on the bay to the white sand beaches of the Gulf. The town was centered around a curving complex of shops, galleries, and restaurants bounding a grassy commons with a stage at the center, shielded from the elements by a band shell sculpted to resemble an open clam. Another retail complex, with overlapping thatched roofs interlaced above a shaded promenade, snaked along the top of the dunes.

A maze of tightly packed houses, stretching for a mile in each direction along the key, ranged from tiny bungalows to multistory mansions. The expansive marina sported extensive docks and two swimming pools surrounding an entertainment complex. Forest and fences, at either end of the model, concealed clusters of housing blocks and other buildings.

"Allow me to introduce you to SunnyBreeze, a new concept in upscale resorts," said Tate. "This town will be what dreams of paradise should be - lush and tropical, perfect in every detail, offering every luxurious amenity and service any guest might desire.

As you can see, there are no hotels or tacky motels plogging up the beachfront. Each of these opulent homes will be available for rent eleven months of the year. They range from cozy cottages, that newlyweds might enjoy for a honeymoon, to eight-bedroom mansions suitable for entire families. Our designers have arranged the houses into neighborhoods, where a corporation could rent a cluster of homes for retreats or large meetings or an extended family could host a reunion.

At the center is The Commons, which houses a conference center, themed restaurants, fashionable shops, and exclusive galleries surrounding a grassy park and an amphitheater for evening concerts and films. The only major road through town has been rerouted into a series of gentle curves to reinforce a speed limit of fifteen miles per hour. Fronting the dunes and the most beautiful snowy white sand beach in the world are restaurants catering to families with kids, casual clothing stores, and a rental shop to serve the beach crowd. We want this development to be so family friendly, it'll make Walt Disney look like Dirty Harry."

Laughter and the question, "What about the adults?"

He pointed to the sweeping lines of the venue on the bay, "While the beach sector is extremely family-oriented, young adults and folks without kids will find plenty to do at the marina. This complex can host more than a hundred yachts, offer charter deep-sea fishing excursions, rental boats, and the most incredible bait and tackle shop in the state, with everything a fisherman or boater might need. Add two salt-water pools, a swim-up bar, three restaurants, and a disco featuring hot bands, we've got the adults covered."

"Who's your clientele?" asked Flint.

Tate grinned, "The almost rich."

Snickers and amusement from the moguls gathered around the model.

"And by that you mean?" asked Erwin Nash.

"I mean our society is rapidly moving towards dividing itself into two classes – the rich and the rest."

Again, laughter.

Duffy Timmons bellowed, "But that's the way it's always been!" Mavis replied, "Only more so!"

Tate pointed to the model, "This is for the brain surgeon or the overpaid lawyer or the young entrepreneur, who wants to take the family on a vacation, where everything is taken care of and everyone's happy, to make up for his neglect the other fifty-weeks a year. We can put the whole crew in one house, which is far more intimate than a half-dozen rooms at the Hilton, and there'll be plenty of activities to keep every age group busy." He paused, "Oh, and we'll be happy to charge them for everything."

"Tell us about this housing," said Bernie Baker. "You've really got them crammed in there. This looks like a miniature version of Manhattan."

"That's absolutely right, we've created five-foot lot lines within these blocks but every house is positioned, for utmost privacy and easy access, and isolated by flourishing green belts into little communities. We want maximum capacity at all times to keep the machinery running in peak form…but I'm getting ahead of myself.

Our Corporation will hold title to the entire tract, extending ten-year leases to buyers, who will pay for the construction of each unit by our contractors, to maintain cohesion and quality control. Their percentage of the rentals will result in complete repayment of their investment in six-years and four-months, plus one-month of off-season use of their home. After ten years, every structure will be torn down and replaced. The owners can choose to re-up or walk away."

"That's assuming nearly one-hundred percent occupancy," said Flint.

"No, that's calculated on eighty-six percent," replied Sloan "but those figures do not include insurance, property taxes, management fees, community dues, landscaping and maintenance, or a host of other revenue streams."

"They'll be lucky to recoup half, when you get done with them," laughed Bernie Baker. "That's the oldest con in the book."

"That's Florida real estate!" replied Tate. "Every line in our sales pitch is absolutely true and meets the requirements of state, county, and local laws and ordinances. We have a pack of lawyers making sure that we're covered in every direction."

"What about all these shops and restaurants?" asked Standler.

Tate grinned, "All owned and operated by the corporation. I should also note that there's a grocery store, over here on the south wing of The Commons but it won't sell anything substantial enough to make into a real meal. Deli sandwiches, drinks, snacks, and anything else you might want after a few hours on the beach, but we do offer an incredible variety of dining options."

"Do the homes have kitchens?" asked Timmons, a chiseled chunk of a man, who made his fortune in timber and was far more comfortable in the forest than the boardroom.

"Of course, but our guests will have to drive twelve miles to find a real grocery. We're betting that they'll be more inclined to walk the kids down to the pizza parlor and fill 'em up. Our high-end restaurants will cater meals or banquets to any house in the complex and we'll have several bars, in addition to the disco, and a fabulous liquor store."

"Who's going to build it," asked JD Calhoun, real estate tycoon and power broker for southwestern Florida.

"Simons and Sons," replied Tate.

"Why? I've got everything you need ready to roll."

"Because, we want to maintain quality control through every phase of development and that can't happen by hiring independent contractors. The only way to guarantee that level of performance is to have everything flowing through a central command."

"Mavis' old man is gonna make a killing on this, we put up the dough and he claims the profits. What's he contributing?"

"His entire construction firm will be focused on this project until it is complete."

"Well, I've had dealings with Selby Simonson before and once was enough. I'm not getting screwed by that bastard again." He stood up, "I don't know about the rest of you suckers, but I'm outta here."

Calhoun's bodyguard stepped out of the shadows to guide the grumbling old man outside.

"What do you want from us?" inquired Standler.

Tate flashed that practiced grin, "Your money and your commitment."

"We all expected that, at the very least," roared old man Baker.

"We want directors, who believe in this project and the philosophy behind it. We invited each of you because you bring not only wealth and position but the expertise and experience to make this and every future project into the finest resorts on the planet. As we'll explain, there's another layer to all of this but our corporation will own the land, receive lease payments and an increasing percentage of the rents in perpetuity, and take a sizable commission on every transaction that occurs on the property. Oh, and the homeowners will build us a brand-new resort every ten-years!"

Most of the crowd applauded.

Flint pointed, "What about these buildings hiding off in the corners?"

"These will be used for housing staff, administration, utilities and maintenance, as well as a school."

"A school? For who?"

Mavis stepped forward, "Perhaps, I should interject a little bit of the 'rest of the story', as Paul Harvey used to say."

The drapes closed and a slide screen rolled down behind her, displaying a chart shaped like a Hershey Kiss without the foil wrapper. "As each of you knows, the divide between the have's and the have-not's is expanding at a geometric rate. We, as a group, are blessed to reside in this tiny blue patch in the very tip of the top one percent and, for that, we should be grateful."

Smiles and nods, as most of the men in the room were mesmerized by her every move.

"The greater concern is this gigantic mass of the population, forty-six percent and growing, who are working harder and harder and falling behind faster than at any time since the Great Depression. With the rapid advancements in the development of robotics, forty-percent of those mid-level jobs will be eliminated within ten years."

She turned to point at the chart, "This huge bloated bulge at the bottom represents the poor and the destitute, and millions of middle-class families are dropping in every year, while the skinny in-between portion represents our market, those who need to flaunt extravagance to prove they've made it. They're in trouble too, but most of them are too arrogant and dazzled by their unwarranted success to realize what's happening." She lit up her glamour magazine smile, "But we'll be happy to take their money."

"Your point is?" inquired Standler.

"How long do you think the struggling masses are going to tread water, before there's a revolution?" She didn't wait for a response, "I don't know about you, but I'm a news junkie. I need to know real facts about everything that might affect our enterprises but I also want to understand what's happening in the real world for the other ninety-nine percent.

Every news cycle is filled with examples of our society's unraveling and it's time to pay attention. The toxins festering at the bottom, out of sight in the ghettos, where uneducated young men know they have no chance to save themselves, so there's no reason not to let it all hang out, until they or someone else gets killed. Young women get pregnant and have numerous children to collect from the government, because they have no education and, other than working as a prostitute, no other way to survive!

Or the typical middle-income family, with two kids and two working parents. Dad's taken a second job, cleaning offices at night, and they still can't make ends meet. That's paying the rent and putting food on the table and nothing else. They work their asses off to provide for their kids but they don't have a chance, because the minimum wage is just that, the bare minimum that someone could survive on, but just barely, and it hasn't risen in decades.

Or white cops killing people of color without any real provocation…and these are not isolated incidents in the deep South, it's happening all over the country! Or people, driven mad by frustration and isolation, who arm themselves and go hunting for children or an audience watching a movie in a theater or defenseless parishioners in churches, in futile and senseless attempts to rekindle the Civil War! Someone has to be responsible for their fear and frustration, someone has to act to save humanity!

I'm a firm believer in the Second Amendment, my daddy taught me how to shoot before I could ride a horse, but American manufacturers produce eight and half-million guns a year. That's enough to arm every man, woman, and child in the state of New Jersey this year and next year and every year after that forever! Who are we arming ourselves against? No one seems to know but it's obvious that our national paranoia demands more guns!

We have, by far, the largest prison population in the world and, at more than seven per thousand, that's more than Russia and Cuba combined! I look around this room and I know that at least a few of you are heavily invested in our private prisons and you wouldn't have ponied up the bucks if you weren't assured of a tidy profit. Keeping those institutions running at absolute capacity is crucial to the bottom line…but at what cost?"

"Making the streets safe for white people," snickered Jeffry Marsh, slum lord and porn producer.

Mavis stopped to stare at the bigot, for a long uncomfortable moment, certainly testament that gaining great wealth does not ensure class. "We're back to that kid in the ghetto shooting someone or the dad, working two jobs, who gets clobbered by a crisis and is forced to do something desperate to save his family from starvation. This whole scenario is worthy of Dickens!"

She marched to the front of the little stage, "We've partitioned off huge chunks of our major cities to segregate the poor and the desperate to live like caged rats in appalling conditions. As more and more people fall off the edge into poverty, we'll pack more and more of them into hellish hovels, smoldering and decaying until they explode in frustration and, when the uprising comes, they'll be armed with all those millions of guns U.S. companies have been producing. We're getting ready to repeat the darkest chapters of history, where the very concept of civilization was lost to arrogance and greed, ignorance and hate. If you'll look back through the moments before each great cataclysm, in every case, there was a brief period where history might have followed a different tack, had the powers that be made more informed decisions."

The crowd was silent, until old Bernie Baker exclaimed, "That's preposterous! I lived through the Depression and we got by."

"You got through it because your old man owned half of Manhattan and, what he didn't own, he bought at pennies on the dollar in foreclosure!" replied Mavis. "The point is, you're the men who run this country. You choose the candidates, you chart the bills that are proposed in Congress, you own governors, mayors, councilmen, and judges, and you have your fingers on the levers that drive the economy. You manage our world, and maybe you didn't cause this fiasco directly, but who's going to manage this mess that's spilling across the nation, because it isn't going to solve itself?"

Murmurs and muffled comments.

Erwin Nash blurted, "In theory, a world-wide recession would provide an opportunity to acquire an even larger share of industry and commerce."

"Even without a full-fledged depression, there's no future for these people! And, if there's no future for the vast majority of the population, then there's no future for us either. We're doomed to hide behind well-fortified mansion walls, while the world rots and festers around us."

She strolled behind the model and pointed to the southern complex of buildings. "These buildings will house a school to educate a very select group of young people about our place in the world and our responsibility to manage the masses, who won't be able to fend for themselves."

"And who will these young people be?" inquired Harvey Sacks. "Democrats?"

"This isn't about politics, it's about survival," replied Mavis. "We'll take your children and our children and promising young talent from the local population."

"Our children attend prestigious schools by tradition, why would we send them here?" asked Standler.

"Because, as we all realized, the only thing we learned, in those musty old museums, was how to use our contacts to keep what we've got.

The world is about to change and if we don't get out in front of it, by taking control, we'll all suffer the consequences."

"First, what are you proposing?" asked Flint. "And second, how does all of this tie into SunnyBreeze?"

"I'm suggesting that our society, world society for that matter, is about to divide itself into those few, who have acquired great wealth and power, lording over those, in this bloated bubble at the bottom of the chart, who will be forced to serve, starve, or rebel. Certainly, no one wants to return to the days of land barons and peasants but that's where we're headed."

Tate interrupted, "The re-education of our society will take a generation and we'll need an ever-expanding legion of true-believers to spread out like missionaries, preaching the truth about the new reality."

"You sound like you're selling religion," laughed Sacks.

"We are! We're going to replace them all!" replied Mavis. "What if we could do away with poverty and ignorance and petty crime?"

"And how are you going to do that?"

"By employing everyone who's willing to work, in one giant enterprise that will supply everything our citizens need to thrive."

Tate grinned, "The problem is and always has been the inefficiency of our system. The middle class is history, so let's do away with capitalism. We already own everything of value, let's replace it with a new reality."

"Which is?"

"We've got a job for everyone and in return for your effort and your loyalty, we'll provide intelligently designed housing, adequate and nutritional food, medical care, security, and a real education for every child. This looming calamity could be transformed into true and absolute equality for the common citizen. Our people will set up systems to keep everything running smoothly and we'll maintain control."

"That's communism!" shouted Baker, his fist clamped to his withered chest, as if the very idea might steal his last breath.

"Our economy is based on archaic precepts, spawned during the Victorian ages. It's time to think about building the next two or three hundred years," said Mavis. "Do you want to oversee the transformation that's sure to come, or should we let it fall into anarchy and inefficient nationalized industries?"

"How's all this tie in with SunnyBreeze?" asked Timmons.

Tate replied, "Think of our new development as a testing ground for the future of urban housing, control of commerce, and re-education."

"Of who?"

Mavis pointed to the green stripe on the chart, just below the thin blue line, "These folks, the working rich, stand in the way of this whole process. They'll be the last to admit to contributing to the dysfunction of our society, so they should be the first to be indoctrinated, here, as well as dozens of other retreats that we'll build in stunning locations around the world." She grinned, "And don't worry, we won't be invading any of your exclusive haunts."

"Who's going to be doing the indoctrinating?"

Tate pointed to the back of the room, "James Robert Combs!"

The imposing former basketball forward strode to the front. Most of the guests had presumed that he was a member of the staff, dressed in a dark suit with a milk chocolate complexion, and sitting in the shadows at the back of the room. But everyone was familiar with Jimbo Combs, life-coach minister who built a glass temple in Tampa, seating ten-thousand for inspiring sermons that rambled on for hours. His programming was beamed to hundreds of thousands of disciples in every country on the planet and he was the master of evangelical entertainment.

The huge man kissed Mavis on the cheek and hugged Tate like a ragdoll, before turning to the group with that enormous smile, "I'm really pleased that all of you could attend this meeting and I promise not to hypnotize anyone or pick your pockets!"

The crowd laughed, for he was famous for taking large audiences under his spell, to convince them that they could perform extraordinary feats, like breaking boards with their hands or walking barefoot across a bed of blazing coals without injury.

"I think you all know my reputation for being a convincing kind of guy...to the extreme!"

Again, roaring laughter.

"Then let me convince you that I believe what you've just heard is a very clear vision of the near future. Mankind has evolved into the most prolific parasite this planet has ever known. The population is exploding, resources are overtaxed and dwindling, and the environment is telling us to clean up our mess, before we all face catastrophe.

I travel all over the world and meet with every kind of human being you could imagine; from miserable underprivileged tycoons, like you, to impoverished children in Ethiopia, who don't have clean water or sanitation or nutritious food or adequate shelter, let alone a school or a future.

The vast majority of people are clamoring for a drastic change in the way our system works. Either someone is going to provide them with a viable and credible alternative or they're going to create one for themselves…and history demonstrates that revolution is always messy, counter-productive, and the poorest suffer most…but dawdling aristocrats are the first to face the guillotine!" He paused and scanned from face to face, "I've read dossiers on every one of you and I predict that ninety-percent of your industries will become completely irrelevant and your vast fortunes worthless, when those on the margins of society revolt."

Everyone was attentive.

"One of my techniques, in inspiring people to take charge of their lives, is to plant a seed in their imaginations. And, yes, I use hypnosis to insert an idea or a challenge inside their brains that itches like a mosquito bite until they act on it and once they start, they can't stop themselves from accomplishing something totally beyond their capacity. I do this with thousands of people every year and it works every time!"

Applause.

The huge former basketball star raised enormous hands in appreciation with a shrewd smile, "So, let's imagine what the outcome might be, if I could share my message with every guest that stayed in every one of these magnificent homes, through subliminal transmissions?"

He pointed to the model, "Simple math - if we average five-thousand new guests each week, I'll be able to convince more than two-hundred-and-fifty-thousand people each year, not only to support our cause but to go back to their communities to spread the word for us. And that's just this resort. Think about having dozens of these around the country and then the world!"

Many in the crowd cheered, some were intrigued, and a few antagonistic.

"I doubt that many of you are genuinely altruistic but I have no doubt that you are all savvy enough to recognize that, at this juncture in our history, you are the people who should take charge of this next chapter in our evolution…not self-serving politicians or theoretical economists or brash young entrepreneurs, who have no grasp of how our world descended into this state. Each of you possesses the power and knowledge to help guide mankind through this looming disaster. You will design the future!" He paused, "And I've been ordained to devise and implement the re-education process."

Chapter Two

One Year Later

Young Johnny Warmington's blue eyes glistened in expectation, as he eased the skiff into the stubby dock poking into the bay behind Jessie's studio. The boy's father was killed by a drunk in an auto accident, when he was three, and Jessie stepped in as surrogate and best friend. They shared a passion for fishing and headed out as soon as Johnny got home from school, so they'd have enough time before the magic evening light, when Jessie liked to paint his landscapes.

The wiry artist wandered down the path, carrying two poles, a tackle box with lures, line, a couple of sandwiches and a thermos full of ice-cold lemonade. "How was school?"

Johnny cut the engine, "Aw, it was okay, I guess."

"What's with the 'I guess'? How'd your math test go?"

"I aced it," smirked the boy, baring oversized buckteeth in a crooked grin.

"See, I told you that you could do it and you did!"

"Showing me how to use those little formulas sure helped."

"Pleasure," said Jessie, climbing into the boat to stash his gear. He always let Johnny pilot out of respect and, besides, the kid had been motoring around the bay without incident, since before he could stay up on a bicycle. The boy hand lettered the name 'MissU' on the stern, in honor of the father who could not be here to share their adventures. The artist settled on the bench seat, "Where we going today?"

"I was watching the gulls when I got off the bus, and they're all headed down the Little Bay. We should check it out. If the shiners are running, the tarpon will be in to feed."

"Great, we haven't been down there in a while, let's go!"

Johnny yanked the rope on the little Johnson outboard and the dingy putted along the lee side of Breezy Key, through the narrows at

Pelican Turn and out into the bay. Flocks of white gulls dove on shimmering schools of minnows rippling across the surface ahead of a dozen swells erupting with thrashing tails, as tarpon and sleek barracuda darted through dissolving clouds of silver sparkles.

Jessie rigged two lines, while Johnny guided the little boat upwind to follow the frenzy back upriver, and cut the engine. The boy grabbed his rod and flipped a lure out ahead of the turbulence on the water then reeled in rapid spurts, whipping the jig into a flitting dance.

On his second cast, the tip of the pole dipped, the reel whined and his line zipped across the bow. A shimmering tarpon leapt from the water and Johnny reeled in the slack, as fast as he could turn the handle on his spinning rig. Silver flashed in the afternoon sunlight as the fish jumped directly at the boat, spitting the lure before he hit the water.

"Rats!" exclaimed Johnny, "I had him!"

Jessie cast his line on the opposite side of the school, "Check your hooks, they might be mangled after that monster chomped down on them."

The boy hauled his line in to inspect the jig, finding two hooks mutilated. He opened the tackle box to grab some nail clippers, replaced the lure with a quick knot, and dropped it into a wash of tiny silver fish before Jessie could cast again.

"You sure are getting fast with that Palomar knot."

"You're right, when you're in a hurry, it's the easiest," replied the young angler, ripping his line to make the bait flicker and jump. The pole bent and line whizzed out of the reel, heading straight upstream.

"Patience," cautioned the artist, reeling his line out of the way. "Play him a little and, maybe, you can tire him out."

The boy kept the line taut but made no attempt to reel it in, watching the lead move across the bow, from port to starboard, in a slow steady arc. Suddenly, the line went slack and Johnny reeled fast.

"He's coming straight in and he'll dive under the boat, if you don't guide him around."

The boy leaned his rod over the port side and the reel spit water as he wound in line. Again, the tip of the rod dipped and the fish jumped straight up, not twenty feet out and darted closer, leaping over the bow, bouncing off the gunnels to fall into the bilge water, flopping at Jessie's feet.

"I've got to say, I've never seen that technique before," laughed the artist, grabbing the fish to extract the lure.

The boy hooked a finger under the gill flap and lifted the fish, "This little guy can't be more than ten or twelve pounds."

Jessie pulled out a pocket camera, "Hold him up and give me a smile."

Johnny grinned through two frames and dropped the fish overboard, "Grow another foot and we can try this again."

The commotion on the water died away, as the boy brought the boat upwind. He pointed at a cloud of smoke billowing from the key, "What's that?"

"Let's go see," replied the artist, stowing their gear.

The slender skiff puttered down the center of the bay, until banks of lush mangroves, a tangle of buttonwood, glasswort, Christmas berry, sea-blite, saltmarsh cordgrass, cabbage palms and cypress, opened into a barren patch that stretched to the highway along the beach. A flock of angry nighthawks dove on a herd of massive bulldozers scraping every scrap of vegetation into giant bonfires, spewing blistering columns of orange flames and black smoke into the air. Little packs of rabbits, raccoons, and possum scurried across the desert, unmolested by two foxes, a bobcat, and a coyote fleeing the noise and destruction.

"What are they doing? They're destroying the jungle!" yelled Johnny.

Jessie pulled out a pair of binoculars and scanned the scene, "They've got survey stakes lined up all the way down the highway and they're already building some sort of huge complex right in the middle." He turned to scan the shoreline, "And there are orange stakes for more than a mile along the bay."

"But why would anyone do that?" asked the boy.

"My guess is that they're going to build a very large resort or condominium project."

"But who gave them permission?"

"They bought the land and have every right to build whatever they want, within the limits of the zoning commission. Unfortunately, I'm pretty sure they'd have all their permits in order, before starting this much work."

"So, they can just destroy the forest and chase all the birds and animals away? That's not fair."

"No, it's not. The sad part is they call this progress." He handed the boy a peanut butter and grape jelly sandwich on white bread and a cup of lemonade. "Here eat this, I know you haven't had anything since lunch and it'll be a while before your dinner."

Johnny cut the engine and let the little boat drift with the incoming tide. "I don't think I like progress."

"I know exactly how you feel. I live here because I can be close to nature all the time and I'd like to make sure they don't completely destroy the keys," said the artist. "On the other hand, demand for housing in Florida is constantly expanding, because retired people want to spend their final years in the sunshine."

"They could go to Arizona or Hawaii or someplace else," replied the boy, through a mouthful of sandwich.

Jessie pointed to the demolition, "When this project is finished, they'll be able to house thousands of people."

"And every house or apartment is going to make lots of money for whoever is doing this," replied Johnny, waving his sandwich, "but that won't buy new homes for all the critters they're chasin' away."

"I agree absolutely," replied the artist, pouring more lemonade. "Tell you what, I'll check with the folks at the Planning Commission and see what I can find out."

"Okay, but I still hate it."

~

Jessie drove the battered blue Volkswagen van south, through several unruly miles of scrappy jungle along the beach road, interrupted by an occasional gas station or homestead. He braked, allowing a cougar to scamper across the pavement as he approached a flagman holding up traffic for a parade of giant earthmovers trundling across the highway to deposit sand on the dunes. The pause gave him time to scan the progress of transforming vibrant scrub forest into a barren moonscape. Roadways were being graded and a large depression excavated, with the diggings piled into a small mountain, about a mile into the project. As the bus puttered down the two-lane, he noticed surveyors placing stakes for another mile. He checked his mileage counter, "Two miles, that's impressive! Someone's sinking a boatload of money into destroying this wonder."

Thirty minutes later, he pulled into the parking lot of City Hall and walked down the stairs on the side of the building to the basement offices of City Planning. He found a stout leprechaun prowling around a repository overflowing with plans and documents stacked on every surface. Twinkling green eyes gazed up from beneath bushy gray eyebrows, "I be helpin' you with somethin'?"

"I was curious about the project down on the key."

"Ah, SunnyBreeze. Yeah, that's gonna be huge."

"What's it going to be?"

"Big resort housing project. Basically, they're building a new town, except it's all for rent. No hotels or motels."

"Wow, that's original."

"Yeah, there's gonna be a complex of shops and restaurants in the middle and a big marina down on the bayside, with docks for more than a hundred boats."

"Who's behind it?" asked Jessie.

The elf looked up, "Officially, it's all owned by SunnyBreeze Enterprises but I hear the money's coming from out west someplace, Texas or Oklahoma, maybe. I don't get to sit in on private commission meetings, I just handle the paperwork down here, so I'm not privy to who's doing what for whom, if you know what I mean?"

"I do," replied Jessie. "Thanks for the help."

"You take care, Mr. Cotton," smiled the strange little man. "I bought one of your paintings, of pelicans flying through a sunset over the bay, at the art festival last year. I've got it hangin' in my living room."

"I know exactly the one you're talking about. It's called 'Reprise'," replied the artist. "I'm honored that you're enjoying it."

"Wouldn't trade it for nothin'," laughed the diminutive archivist. "I ain't no authority but I know what I like."

"Say, what's your name?"

"Sammy Ball."

"Pleased to meet you," said the artist, reaching a hand, "and, thanks a lot for your help."

"Be seein' ya'."

Jessie climbed the stairs to the pavement and noticed several men in dark suits, walking along the sidewalk with two of the Commissioners. One of them was gesturing emphatically with his hands and the artist hesitated in the shadows, recognizing a maturing Tate Sloan, quarterback for Oklahoma in the Orange Bowl game for the national championship that Jessie's Wisconsin team lost years ago.

He waited until the small posse entered a white limousine that slipped into traffic, before stumbling across the parking lot to climb into the bus. A tangle of repressed memories, long since locked away, rushed from a shadowy corner of his soul. He drove mindlessly back towards his cottage, suppressed visions overwhelming any consideration of the information Sammy Ball provided.

The roar of the crowd echoed through the tunnel, as Jessie and coach Farrington led the team onto the field, behind a regatta of fluttering red banners bearing giant white 'W's. The polls predicted victory and Las Vegas favored Wisconsin by seven. Media hype vaulted him into star status and the fans expected the super-hero to lead the team to triumph over the hicks from Oklahoma.

The pressure built through weeks of final exams, press conferences and media events, two-a-day practices, and endless strategy sessions. His focus was absolute, his mental and physical preparation complete, but something seemed off. In spite of the excitement of the moment and a huge adrenalin rush, he felt as if special effects had added a glow to his peripheral vision and his legs felt heavy, as the team trotted out into brilliant sunshine glimmering off the perfectly manicured turf amid deafening cheers screaming above both school bands playing at full throttle. The entire stadium pulsed and vibrated as red and white stomped and screamed, vying to out-shout the crimson and cream.

Oklahoma won the toss and Tate Sloan marched the Sooners down the field with crisp efficiency. Five plays, eighty yards, touchdown!

The first four plays were scripted by the coaches and practiced, until the sequence was second nature to the entire squad. Jessie set up the team but Henny Matson, the center, was nervous and snapped the ball before he finished the count. Fumble! Oklahoma recovers at the Wisconsin thirty-two.

Sloan hit his wide receiver in the flats for eight, flipped one over the line to his fullback, who rumbled for another seven, then dropped a bomb on his tight-end streaking across the back of the end zone. Touchdown!

Jessie hit the brakes, as the van screeched into an intersection, barely avoiding honking traffic beneath a red light. Bewildered, he glanced around to regain his bearings and took a deep breath to settle himself. Wisconsin, tough and polished, played in slow motion, while Oklahoma's runners and receivers dashed up and down the field like pros playing against a sandlot team. Their defense picked up twelve penalties for roughing the passer or unnecessary roughness. By the start of the fourth quarter, Jessie was spitting blood, gimping on a swollen knee, nursing a broken rib, and barely able to focus through a severe concussion…but he played on, determined to fight until the final gun.

The exalted expectations came crashing down, when the other team won in resounding fashion. The fans and press were unmerciful in blaming him for the embarrassing defeat, while his teammates and once cheering fans avoided him on campus. Damning stories and opinions continued in the press and on television and radio, until he barricaded himself inside his apartment near Lake Mendota on North Carroll. Struggling with deep depression, he packed his gear into the bus during a blizzard in the wee hours of a bitter February morning and headed south to warmer climes without a word to anyone, including the love of his life, Kate.

The ramifications of his escape to self-preservation still rumbled through these many years since. He never found the courage to go back and the guilt constructed a little shrine in his gut, transforming shame into a pain that gnawed on his conscience to this day. His isolation taught him that hindsight is peppered with 'what-ifs' and, in his new life, there was no way to answer those questions.

He drove down Poinsettia Avenue and parked in the drive of the little garage that he renovated into a studio with attached living quarters. His existence was simple but comfortable, his life dedicated to capturing the beauty of nature on canvas every day.

The front door had a latch but no lock, as he did not possess much that thieves might want, and, other than truant kids, there was little crime in the area. But there was also Miss Gracie, a Shepherd/Doberman mix, who adopted Jessie on a cold rainy night when he was particularly blue. She pawed at the door, until grumpy and annoyed, he opened it to find her wet and dirty, without a collar, staring at him with the most soulful brown eyes she could muster. He started to close the door but she pushed past him and curled up on the throw rug on the floor in the kitchen. She had been his roommate and best friend ever since.

Gracie trotted up, standing to rest her paws on his shoulders for a hug and a lick.

"Hey, girlfriend, how are you? Do you need to go out?"

She trotted out the door and disappeared.

He poured cold tea into a glass, added some ice and a squeeze of lemon, and wandered out to settle into his favorite chair on the little veranda overlooking the bay. Gracie wandered over to sit close enough for a rub behind her ears.

He gave up drinking long ago, after a raging binge landed him in front of a judge who admired his artwork but left little doubt that, if he ever showed up in that courtroom again, His Honor would have little sympathy.

His punishment entailed giving free art lessons in the park, during the month of June, for the community's poorest children. Naively, he expected a handful of kids. Thirty-seven showed up the first day, and more the next, and every one eager to learn how to create art. He had to scramble to stretch his supplies but each child left the park with something they made from their imaginations with their own hands, and every one of them was smiling and laughing, feeling pride and confidence, perhaps, for the first time in their lives. In spite of the stress, he realized that he had allowed himself, forced himself, to enjoy the interaction with other people again. Working with enthusiastic children, who were so open and honest in their efforts, filled his heart with a joy that he had not experienced in a very long time.

The shaky start evolved into an annual event, with classes in painting, sculpture, photography, music, and dance through early summer, culminating with a weekend art festival to display the children's creations and a concert to feature young talent under the banner, 'Art's Important'.

Between commissions on sales and the generosity of the community, the classes and the celebration became self-supporting. Grocers and restaurants provided lunches for the staff and every student throughout the month. Idled school buses transported the children to and from the park and volunteers orchestrated the logistics of coordinating workspaces, tools and supplies for each discipline, musical instruments for those without, and herding children through four weeks of events.

In spite of becoming a local celebrity, he preferred to spend his time immersed in the beauty of this place, in the visual music of nature and the rich society of birds and animals, who populated this wonderland long before humans started leveling great tracks of a perfectly balanced ecosystem to build parking lots surrounding concrete buildings.

The intensity of his perpetual production dulled the regrets and demons that flashed through his dreams, welling up through a cloudy hole in his memories, from halftime through the next few weeks. Snapshots and out of context comments rattled relentlessly inside his head, building in volume and venomous passion, until an impenetrable door or window would burst open to provide escape into morning.

He opened his pocketknife, the handle worn to comfort, the blade razor-sharp, and held a tart green apple up to the light. "I should have painted you but my stomach thinks otherwise." He cored and quartered it and munched each wedge slowly, savoring the sweet-tart crunch. Three pelicans swooped out from behind the Banyan trees along the shoreline, streaking effortlessly above little whitecaps rippling across the surface of the bay, highlighted by the morning sun's brilliant radiance etching dark thunderheads rising in the west.

"Might be time to make sure things are battened down. Let's go check the dock."

Gracie trotted down the path and out across the gangway to the covered slips, where Jessie's runabout, Kate, bobbed in a moderate chop.

Jessie grabbed two lines to cross tie her to the steel piping. A little extra spring at the stern should keep her bow from thrashing against the structure under the dock, if the squall pushed in from due west. The wind kicked up as he latched the lockers and walked over to squat next to Gracie. His eye found his next painting in the clouds building over the keys, ominously dark underneath but glowing with dazzling sunshine etching roiling peaks in shades of gold. "This storm's comin' fast, sweetheart, let's head for the house."

They climbed the little hill and dashed inside just as large pellets splattered rain across the veranda and gusts from the west whipped the shrubbery and bent the oaks and banyans to the ground.

A late afternoon storm was not unusual, dumping an inch of rain before dissipating over dry land. They took shelter in his studio, where he could work while waiting out the torrent outside. Gracie's ears pricked up and she stared at the ceiling, the rattle of hail pounded the skylight.

Jessie looked up from adding a highlight on a deep red hibiscus bud, "It's okay, girlfriend. It's just a storm and there's nothing much we can do about it until it decides to move inland."

The dog cocked her head and raised her golden eyebrows over a black mask across her eyes, which always made him wonder whether she had a question or was she waiting for him to catch up? She usually knew what was going on long before he did.

Four hours later, the rain eased and a beam of sunshine shot through the stained-glass windows framing the entry. He walked over to open the French doors, salvaged from a magnificent dilapidated mansion that was being torn down instead of renovated, and gazed across the bay to a double rainbow arcing across a clearing sky. "There's hope."

Gracie wandered outside and turned back to Jessie. He followed her to a large limb torn from the ancient oak, waves still lashed the gangway, and a fresh gulley had been carved down the hill by the runoff. The rain gauge was topped out, "That's amazing! At least five inches in three or four hours?"

He walked back into the studio, a former double car garage with a workshop along the side that he transformed into a second bathroom at the front and a quirky personal office in back. Thirty or forty colorful canvases hung from bare brick walls or leaned against an odd collection of completely mismatched antique furniture, arranged around a pair of large easels under a long skylight on the north face of the roof. Dolly, a well-endowed mannequin, dressed in a scandalous 1920's flapper's dress and a frizzy blond wig, sat at a small table before an empty tea cup overseeing his work, her graceful fingers pointing with an unlit cigarette in a long holder.

He flipped the radio on and the announcer said, "This short but monumental storm dropped eight inches of rain across parts of the city, downed trees and power lines are blocking roads from Federton to Venice, and the tide pounded the beaches. We're getting reports of considerable erosion and…" he paused. "This just in, a large pit at the SunnyBreeze construction site overflowed and cut a swath through the beach road and the dunes to empty into the ocean. Midnight Pass Road is impassible!"

"I was just down there, I know exactly what he's talking about!"

Gracie looked up at him and cocked her head inquisitively.

"I'm no engineer but it seems fairly logical that, once they've taken out all the vegetation that holds the key together, if they get the drainage wrong, it'll be a disaster waiting for the right storm to wash it all away."

Mavis looked up from the report binder, sensing the plane weaving, the wingtip rising ever so slightly, then dipping, as the flight from New York glided around massive thunderheads, bubbling into a brilliant blue sky, on descent from cruising altitude.

The intercom crackled, "Ladies and gentlemen, this is your captain speaking. We're getting ready to land, so I would ask that everyone find your seats and that the cabin crew stow their gear. There's a massive front approaching Dolphin Bay and the control tower has cleared us to land directly. For those near the starboard windows, you can see incredible clouds building off to the west and they're moving east at more than thirty miles per hour. Buckle up, seat backs forward, we're going in."

The plane dropped through plunging air pockets and soared on rocketing updrafts but the pilots powered through the turmoil to put wheels on tarmac, with only a jarring bounce or two. Battered by a vicious gale, the fronds on the palm trees waved frantically after jolting licks of blue lightning danced across a roiling gray cloudbank, racing across the horizon to devour the last desperate glimmers of sunlight.

Jasper, a young, enthusiastic SunnyBreeze driver sporting a black suit jacket over a rainbow pastel SunnyBreeze tee-shirt, with gleaming white jeans and tennies, greeted her at the luggage carousel with a genial smile, "How was your flight?"

"Great, until the last twenty minutes that rivaled some of the best roller-coasters I've ever ridden."

"I'm sorry."

"Hey, I learned a long time ago, you travel, you roll with the weirdness."

The young man grabbed her bag and guided her to the waiting limousine, just as the first giant drops of rain splattered on the pavement. He helped her into the car and ran around to take his seat, "Where to?"

"SunnyBreeze."

Before the long car started to roll, the heavens opened with a torrent and visibility dropped to nothing. Jason hesitated but Mavis said, "This can't last long, it's usually a fifteen-minute deluge and then it disappears over the everglades."

The driver leaned forward, trying to focus through the whiteout, "I don't know, this one feels different."

"Hey, if you don't feel comfortable, then pull over. You're in charge of this vehicle!"

"I think I can handle it, if we take it slow."

"Fine, take us home. I'm not your boss, I'm your passenger, so treat this ride like any other, with grace, gusto, and good judgement."

The driver shook his head, "That sounds like a take on our most Reverend Combs."

"He does have a way of planting things inside your head. Maybe, if he was with us, he could summon the Lord to move this storm away but I'm doubting that even he could accomplish that!"

Jason barely chuckled, intent on staying between the lines on the road. The car inched south on Highway Forty-One, every intersection a snarl of cars, plowing through rushing rivers to avoid serial collisions and the unlucky few, who ended up nose down in the ditch. His knuckles were white with the strain of gripping the steering wheel but he wrangled the stretched Cadillac through traffic, floods, downed limbs, and splintered trees to turn west to the bridge at Pelican Turn.

Lightning rippled through churning black clouds, thunder fractured the roar of a pummeling wind, and spray from the relentless rain formed a dense fog that swirled above the surface of the bridge, as they crested the hump and started down to the beach road, into the wash of titanic waves exploding over the dunes. The tires skidded on a bog of wet sand that swamped Midnight Pass and he slowed to time his moves between surges blasting across the roadway.

"You've done a great job, we're almost there."

"I can't believe we made it through this storm," replied Jason peering through a fogged windshield, flapping wipers, and pelting rain to follow dark patches of asphalt, until they passed the first retail shops above the beach and he hit the brakes, swerving to a stop.

"What's wrong?" asked Mavis, leaning forward for a better view.

He wiped the condensation on the window and turned to her, "The road's gone."

"The what?" She almost climbed over the seat to watch violent waves demolishing the dunes and chewing an inlet into The Commons.

"Do you have a phone in the car?"

"Yes."

"Dial 941-555-2121 and give me the handset."

She waited for a moment, "Tate, we've got a problem. Yeah, I'm in the limo on Midnight Pass just outside The Commons. The road's gone, the surf ripped a huge hole in the dunes, trenched the pavement, and now it's working on the amphitheater." She paused, "No, I'm not joking, get your guys down here, now!"

Within minutes, a caravan of two Jeep Waggoneers and a Land Rover maneuvered through the devastation on Breezy Key, as the rain finally eased. The cars stopped to clear a Highway Patrol car blocking the road on the other side of the divide, and parked on a fringe of grass along the edge of the highway.

Tate Sloan, Milton Fore and his chief architects, along with several engineers, walked over to greet the project foreman and his crew when the mayor, two commissioners, and several County officials showed up. Mavis ditched her heels and climbed out of the limousine, clutching a large pink umbrella, to hug Tate and shake hands all around.

The crowd wandered back and forth along an inlet from a lake overflowing the amphitheater of The Commons through the dunes to the Gulf. At the junction with what used to be the road, the channel was nearly fifty feet across and twenty feet deep and the nose of one of the company's large graders was wedged in the bottom of the hole.

Rupert Dent, chief engineer for the project, paced back and forth inspecting the patterns in the sand on either side of the ditch. He stopped just west of the waterfall spilling from the lake, "I'll be damned."

Sloan walked over, "What?"

Dent knelt down pointing to diagonal lines flowing away from the edge of the trench. "This channel was carved by water running to the sea but that was preceded by water rushing inland. See these lines, they point in the direction the water was moving. The receding flow eroded the sand below this level."

"So, you're saying the Gulf punched a hole in the key that just happened to connect up with rainwater pooled in the amphitheater?"

"That's exactly what I'm saying," replied the engineer. "With a little more power, it could have cut right through to the bay."

"How quickly can this be repaired?" asked Mavis.

"We'll get organized and put everyone on it in the morning. We should have things buttoned up in a couple of days but we'll have to bring in a crane or two to salvage that machine."

"What about repaving the road?" inquired Mayor Bert Kane.

"No problem, we'll take care of it, we've got plenty of materials stockpiled to pave our roads," said Sloan. "It was an act of nature but we'll make it right, at no cost to the taxpayers."

"Fair enough," replied the mayor, "but you make sure to get your guys on the stick, before the inspectors show up and start asking questions. They'll shut the road down for months to do some damned study, before they get started on the repairs. Hell, we're heading into tourist season and my constituents depend on the revenue and so does this city."

"We'll take care of it," said Dent, "but you keep the dogs off us for a couple of days, so we can get things done right."

"Deal."

Sloan pulled Dent aside, "I've got our first group of prospective buyers coming in, a week from tomorrow. Can we have things together enough to show them around?"

"You bet, boss. I'll see that everything is shipshape in time for your show-and-tell but you're in charge of keeping Mother Nature out of my way!"

~

Jessie settled into his favorite chair on the veranda, with the morning paper and a cup of thick coffee, lifting his nose to the fragrant scent of oleander hanging in the still air. Gracie made a feeble dash after a squirrel that darted up a battered Banyan tree, mocking her with his chatter.

"You didn't really want to catch him anyway, did you, old girl?"

She'd gobbled her breakfast and a nap seemed a better choice than hunting an ornery tree rat. She stretched out next to his chair and rested her chin on his foot.

"Comfy?" asked Jessie, leaning to rub behind her ear. He opened the paper to read the headline, 'Stock Market Plunges!'

"Crap! Just what we need, more doom and gloom. This doesn't hurt the big guys, it's the working folk and the retirees who are depending on their meager

investments to see them through. As long as we've got Republicans controlling the purse strings, the middle class is screwed."

A smaller headline read:

Beach Road Reopens

Mayor Bert Kane was on hand this morning to officially reopen Midnight Pass Road, which was breached by a tidal surge during the violent storm on Wednesday. He praised the construction crew from Simons and Sons Construction, who are building the SunnyBreeze development, for stepping in to make the repairs. "If we'd gone through normal channels, we'd be waiting on surveys, studies, and approvals until who knows when. These folks did an extraordinary job in providing access to our residents three days after the disaster struck. That's more than admirable and the community owes Tate Sloan, Rupert Dent, and their people a debt of gratitude." State and County engineers approved the repairs and traffic returned to normal at nine o'clock this morning.

"That bastard can turn a turd into a diamond. He might be a jive-ass but he's always been smooth in front of the press, I'll give him that much. Married that rich girl straight out of college and started his own company, with her daddy's money, and made a fortune with his process of injecting inert gases into oil wells to loosen up the sediments, instead of a slurry of nasty chemicals and foul water. It's cleaner, safer, and he gets a piece of every well that uses his technology. He'll be collecting on that one forever."

He took a sip of coffee, *"So what's his angle with SunnyBreeze? He's way too out front on this for it to be a little side project. I'd be more inclined to believe it if he built a giant house for himself right in the middle of that desert, but a resort? Not so much. There's something bigger going on behind the scenes."*

Gracie lifted her head, gazed up at him with those patient brown eyes, and settled back into her nap.

Chapter Three

Waiters eased through the crowd gathered in the ballroom of the Mansion House, offering sumptuous canapés and flutes of champagne to select investors from all across the South. A jazz trio played soothing new age music, as background for unchecked egos challenging each other to the ultimate game of one-upmanship. "Mine's newer or bigger or more expensive...or..."

The lights dimmed and a spotlight flashed on Tate Sloan - dark suit, red tie, standing alone on the stage wearing his best good-old-boy grin.

The crowd cheered and applauded, until he raised his hands, "Thank you all for being here. We have a lot to cover so, if you'll take a seat, we can get started! I'm sure the staff will keep those glasses full!"

The crowd shuffled around for seats at long tables draped with white linens, vibrant bouquets of flowers, and tastefully printed folders with 'SunnyBreeze' embossed on the cover and a silver and gold Cross pen to take notes.

"Most of you know me, I see lots of friends in this crowd. How's things in Little Rock, Chester? And how's the Missus, Freddie?"

Chester yelled, "I couldn't stand it if things got any better!"

Freddie hollered, "She's fit as a fiddle and twice as sweet!"

"I'm thinkin' most of us male people should be jealous of your little woman, Freddie, but I promise she'll love what we're going to send home with you!"

The crowd roared.

"For those of you who only know me as a famous football player and front man for my favorite charities, let me give you a little background to put things into perspective."

Tate paced the stage as the crowd settled in, smoothed back tousled hair, and placed a battered cowboy hat on his head. He dropped the polished diction of the Business Tate and eased into the soft slur of his Southern Plains accent, "I was born in Senders Creek, Oklahoma, population two-hundred eighty-seven, including me. My ol' man ran a small herd on a tiny spread next to that creek, which watered the fields during good years, flooded us out more than once, and withered to nothin', when the rains didn't come.

I was the eldest of five children who had to sneak off to school, because my daddy didn't see much point in education. He worked hard but, when the drought hit and it was hand-to-mouth for five straight years, he drank a lot, which brought out his anger and frustration. He beat us kids and my mom, until the Sheriff finally hauled him off to jail for thrashing Elvis Spooner half to death over a card game where he was down fifty bucks, which was a week's worth of groceries for us.

I played eight-man football in high school and got a scholarship two weeks before the Sheriff came back to evict our family, so the bank could foreclose on the ranch. I never saw my old man again; he died awaiting trial, and my mother considered whoring down at the truck stop to feed me, my brother, and three sisters until the booster club figured out how far I could toss a football. I moved them to a house in Norman and everyone in my family got an education, including my mother who has a degree in nursing."

He took off the hat and placed it over his heart, "Was accepting money, as a student-athlete, ethical?"

The audience was silent, enthralled, despite knowing that he was a consummate pitchman.

"Probably not," he grinned, "and I hope you'll keep it our secret!"

The audience applauded.

"No, it was wrong…but I was a desperate kid from the sticks who couldn't let my family starve. Where I come from, that's what loyalty is all about and that's why we've invited all of you to be the very first to have a shot at owning a piece of our new development, SunnyBreeze!"

He whipped the cover from the model with a flourish and tilted it for an overview, "I want to share this opportunity with each and every one of you!"

"Ooo's" and "Ah's" wafted across the room.

"SunnyBreeze is a unique concept because we intend to build an entire town, two miles long and more than a half mile wide between the Gulf and the bay around a central Commons, where the entire population can gather for concerts and special events, in addition to the finest dining in the state, upscale shopping, and exclusive galleries. The beach compound is designed to be family friendly in every way, with entertainment for every age group.

We'll also have a state-of-the-art marina, with docks for more than one hundred yachts, as well as charter services and rental boats. Those looking for more sophisticated entertainment will find adult swimming pools, several bars, restaurants, and a discotheque featuring prominent acts throughout the season."

A confident grin acknowledged the applause.

"One thing that makes this little town unique is that there will be no hotels or motels. Instead, we'll build custom-designed homes, ranging from quaint cottages to eight-bedroom mansions with every amenity, clustered into neighborhoods with individual identities. Every unit will be available for rent eleven months of each year and the owners will have use for a full month in the off-season."

A screen rolled down from the ceiling and a slide popped up, with lazy palm trees and pink flamingos behind a chart illustrating the basic calculations. "Another unique aspect of our plan is that every house will be demolished and replaced every ten years."

A call came from the audience, "Then how do the investors recoup their investment?"

Tate smiled and lit up the graphic with a pointer, "Let's take this two-million dollar, eight-bedroom luxury model as an example. First, the SunnyBreeze Corporation, which represents every investor, will maintain ownership of all the land in SunnyBreeze, leasing out lots for ten years. The owner's investment is confined to the structure, so that diminishes the exposure.

Our auditors have combed through these figures and we wouldn't be here if they hadn't given it their blessing. So, for each property, we will guarantee that if you allow us to build one of these homes to our specs and your expectations, it will repay your investment in six years and four months and that includes one month of personal use each year. The balance is pure profit."

"That's fantastic," said Harold Lloyd in the front row. "It's also slightly unbelievable!"

The audience laughed but Tate responded directly, "That's what I thought too, until I understood how the Corporation is really a holding company, with all of us as shareholders. We all profit from every activity that happens on the entire property."

"What happens after ten years?"

"You have the choice to reinvest your money in an even more fantastic home or walk away with a tidy profit. That's entirely up to you because there are no strings attached. Our architects have designed this community into eighteen-hundred individual properties so, when the last one's claimed, we'll close membership in our little club."

"What if we want to get out before the ten years is up?"

"With the profit potential, the only reason that you'd want to get out is because you're in dire straits."

Laughter.

"With the response that we're getting to this exclusive opportunity, I have no doubt that we'll have anxious buyers to sublease any property." He paused, "I should mention that this is only the first of a string of exclusive residential resorts, that will be located in the most beautiful locations in the world. SunnyBreeze and all the other properties will be little slices of paradise - where everything is perfect, from your residences to our beaches, restaurants and entertainments, all with the impeccable service that you would expect of exclusive facilities."

Applause.

"Ladies and gentlemen, we're going to build a town where people like you and I want to spend our vacation. This will become an environment where your every expectation is met or exceeded and we all know that there are successful people, all over this country, who would jump at the chance to enjoy our little slice of heaven." He grinned that publicity smile, "And we'll be happy to let their enjoyment pay us handsomely!"

Cheers.

"We'll have buses waiting to take you out to the development shortly but, in the meantime, our sales associates will be happy to answer any questions. C'mon up and take a look at our model, it's beautiful!"

~

The Lear touched down in Austin and, within minutes, a helicopter whisked Mavis to the family compound, buried in the forest overlooking Lake Travis. Chen Chen, her father's houseman and overseer of all of Selby Simonson's properties, braved the wash from the rotor to guide his 'Precious Lotus Flower' down the few steps and into a plush, covered golf cart for the ride up the hill to the starkly modern mansion impaled into the hillside.

"Did you have a good flight?"

"No problems," replied Mavis, with a kiss to his cheek. The ancient Chinese consigliore had been with her father since long before she was born. Neither ever revealed how they came to share their bond, far more complex than boss and employee, but she assumed that it started during the war. Through five wives and as many divorces, everything in the house, the stables, the ranch, and anything else that Selby acquired, ran like a Swiss watch. Chen anticipated everything and expected perfection from a staff of hundreds.

"What kind of mood is he in this evening?"

"The oil fields are productive and the markets are rebounding," replied Chen. "His favorite mare produced a colt the other night, sired by White Lightning, so your father has high hopes that he will be fast."

"Good, I'd rather spend time with him when he's up, than when he's pissed off."

"I think the stars are aligned for you, young lady. Besides, he's always pleased to spend time with you, you are his pride."

"I'm the son he never had."

Chen grinned, "I don't think anyone who isn't blind would confuse you with anyone's son."

Mavis laughed, "You know what I mean. I might have all these curves but he trained me to be just as tough as he is."

"That's because he expects you to take over when he's finished."

"He'll never retire."

"No, you're probably right but, little by little, he will hand responsibilities over to you. He has a vision of what the future holds and he expects you to see it through."

"I know…but it's still kind of daunting to face the prospect of filling his expectations, let alone his boots. He's always been larger than life."

Chen's eyes crinkled into slits, concealing secrets and stories, knowledge that Mavis needed to understand before both her men died. "He's brilliant, cantankerous, and ambitious but he is just a man, like any other, who got lucky more than once in his life."

"I'd love to know how you two met," replied the beautiful blond, with a fetching smile.

Chen pulled the golf cart up at the kitchen door, "That story will have to wait for another time."

He hopped out and trotted around to take her hand, grabbing her bag, "He's expecting you for drinks in the study and I'll have dinner on the table in thirty minutes."

"You know I'd never be late for one of your meals!" laughed Mavis, with another kiss to his ruddy cheek. The clack of her heels reverberated off the flagstone floor and arched ceiling of the long hallway.

Chen watched after her, shaking his head in admiration. His Precious Lotus Flower blossomed from a charming but precocious child into the personification of grace and beauty, masking the temperament of a lioness just entering her prime. The future of everything her father built over the years depended on the strength of her will and depth of her character.

She found her father leaning on the hearth of a grand fireplace, flickering orange flames silhouetting chiseled features in a weathered face, thick silver hair swept back above piercing eyes, charcoal crystals glimmering in firelight. In spite of his age, he was lean and fit, ready to lead the roundup or punch another hole in the Texas dirt or take over another company. His energy was boundless, his appetite for life ferocious.

He turned as she walked into his arms, "Daddy, it's so nice to be home."

"You're looking gorgeous. How was your trip?"

"Your private jet service makes things easy. I could get used to that."

"We're expanding from twenty-two to thirty-six planes that will be stationed to cover a growing customer base." Selby Simonson smiled, "The bonus is that anyone, who can afford a ride on one of our planes, is a potential client and all of their information is being consolidated into a database that will prove useful in so many ways."

"I'd love to pitch them on SunnyBreeze!"

"That's exactly the point, these are the future leaders that we need to recruit into the fold, if there is any hope of containing the coming economic and social disaster."

"Jimbo Combs is working on the indoctrination program," said Mavis, accepting a fine malt Scotch with a single ice cube. "If anyone can transform stark reality into auspicious pipedreams, he's the guy."

"I had the pleasure of dining with Reverend Combs at the Twenty-One Club in New York many years ago, when he was transitioning from brash front-court enforcer to high-end motivational huckster. He is a most entertaining fellow - confident, totally prepared, and extremely humorous. He claimed that he grew up in the tiny town of Riverside, nestled into the soggy isolation of a bayou called Peace River, best known for giant mosquitoes and hungry alligators, as well as tarpon fishing. He informed me that tarpon can gulp enough air to roll across the surface of the water to escape a predator."

"I sat in on one of his retreats where, in a matter of a few hours, he convinced several thousand people to walk barefoot across fifty-feet of burning coals and no one refused or suffered an injury."

"There's some basic physics and sophisticated trickery behind that totally astonishing feat." Selby grinned, "So, did you walk?"

Mavis cocked her head, "Of course! I even cheated and snuck into another line, so I could go twice. It was a blast."

"You never cease to amaze me."

"That's good, because I've been trying to live up to your expectations since I was born!"

"You've succeeded!" He hugged her again, "How are things with the project?"

"On the upside, Tate gave the first sales-seminar today, for three-hundred prospects, and we've got five more scheduled in the next two weeks. I wouldn't be surprised if we didn't sell out before we finish the sales pitch!"

"And the downside?"

"As you probably read in my report, most of the topo-work was complete, roads laid out, and the amphitheater in the Commons was being graded, when a major squall came up and raised a surge that opened up a trench fifty-feet wide and twenty or thirty feet deep from the Commons to the beach. It took out the only road through the key in the process."

"What did the experts say?"

"That it was a fluke and, geologically, there was no soft or undermined area that invited the storm to cut through the dunes in that particular spot. It could have happened anywhere along the coast and, if there's a repeat, it will probably pick someplace else to chew on."

"How'd the County react to the damage to the road?"

"Tate jumped all over that and got the mayor to hold up the inspectors, until our crews could make the repairs. They worked day and night and had the road open in less than seventy-two hours."

"That's why we've got Rupert Dent running the show. He knows how to get things done right and on time."

"No argument there. I love Tate dearly but he's the front man not the brains."

"You trained him well," replied her father.

"He was easier than your retrievers! Flying to San Francisco for dinner or Paris for the weekend gave him a taste of real wealth, he was hooked from the git-go."

"You are sumptuous bait," laughed her father.

"Underneath all that testosterone, I found a really decent person who genuinely loves me for me. He might not be cultured or sophisticated, but he knows how to play his part and does what he's told."

"I set him up with TMS Oil and stocked it with the best engineers in the business, thinking it would provide a decent living for you two, but he was bright enough to find that one little niche that needed an intelligent solution and his crew developed it. The fact that you convinced him to license the process put the finishing touch on a fairly brilliant enterprise."

"I just used Bill Gates' model."

"Adapting someone else's idea is no sin," laughed Selby. "How was the attendance at the sponsor's meeting?"

"We only had one get up and walk out in a huff, last time, but everyone seemed ready to jump in on the second phase."

"I should have warned you about JD Calhoun."

"On the upside, he didn't come back."

"We're infringing on his turf and he doesn't appreciate the competition. He's got his fingers in every land deal in every county along the west coast of Florida and he's hooked in with the mob. Don't underestimate his connections or his greed."

"We had to grease a few city and county officials to get everything smoothed out," said Mavis.

"I can guarantee that Calhoun is taking a percentage."

"I'll put up my antenna."

"There's another cadre, who don't take kindly to rich folk indulging their good intentions by enabling the little people. Their goal is to destroy the government, eliminate all regulations that might inhibit the raping of the earth, hand education over to evangelical extremists who believe their god put Adam and Eve on the Earth six thousand years ago, all science is suspect, and history is open to interpretation and revision, which will make it easier to control a nation of ignorant vagabonds."

"We're not without fault."

"I know we've desecrated the earth but you have to agree that we've made great progress in building a clean operation."

"You're right, but we also know families who have poured enormous fortunes into promoting hate, bigotry, and nationalism. They're determined and they're dangerous but even their well-financed campaign of lies can't convince good people to vote against their own interests. Someday, desperate Americans are going to rise up in rebellion and the greedy tycoons, who stacked the deck against the little guys, are going to be the first to face the firing line."

Her father held up his glass, "That is very astute."

"From what I've seen, it's the truth," replied his daughter.

The fire crackled and Selby turned to his daughter, "Is Ned Flint on board?"

"He's hot for Tate, so he's spending a lot of time on site, offering very useful advice."

"The man knows his stuff." He paused, his eyes probing and curious, "Are they involved?"

Mavis smirked, "I'm not sure but, knowing my horny-toad husband, I should be suspicious."

"I had hoped for another generation, to pass all of this on to."

"Oh, you'll get your grandchildren. If Tate can't serve his purpose, there are plenty of suitors."

"I feel sorry for any man foolish enough to believe he could tame you."

"That's your fault, you trained me to be independent and, besides, you're the only real man in my life," replied his daughter, with a kiss to his cheek.

"So, how'd the pitch at the executive investor's meeting go?"

"I worked the crowd over and we got almost twice the projected budget to cover the land and to complete the facilities and infrastructure. The dwellings will be paid for by the buyers, so we could begin the second resort in six months or so."

"Stash the cash and get this one right, first," said Simonson. "What about converting the faithful?"

"I think we got a few more people who grasp what's coming, a middle group that's still in denial but, maybe, paying a little more attention to what's happening in the world around them, and more than a few who don't see any problem with destroying the Earth or pushing the masses off a cliff into poverty. Some of those are adamantly against everything we're trying to do," replied Mavis.

"As you pointed out, there's no cure for blind ignorance nor hope for those who won't face the truth. A thriving middle class is history and it's our responsibility to prevent society from disintegrating in the coming catastrophe."

"Amen to that," said the daughter, pouring two fresh tumblers of rare 30-year-old Jura 'Camas an Staca' Scotch. "I did get a very positive reaction to Milton's incredible design for the school, in spite of continued grumblings about generations graduating from the same old musty institutions that taught all of them how to manage what they inherited, rather than forging a new dynasty. That's why family fortunes disappear by the third generation."

"I understand that it will take a long time to educate a core, large enough to manage the future, but I'll be interested in the progress you make during the first few years, as you refine the curriculum."

"Even if all of our projections are wrong, our graduates will have the skills and the knowledge to lead the world into the next chapter in the story of humanity."

Simonson stared at the flames leaping from the logs on the grate and took a sip of Scotch, "I feel no guilt for the wealth I've accumulated. I can honestly say that I never screwed anyone to get where I am. I might have twisted a few arms and leveraged the competition out of my way but I always tried to make my ventures work for the people who were actually doing the job. The employees have to have ownership and pride in their accomplishments."

"There's no pride in poverty," replied Mavis.

"And that's the point, isn't it? The system's stealing humanity's self-esteem, the dignity of place in society, and crushing their dreams. Too many millions have lost hope that tomorrow can be any better than today."

"Which leads to nationalism, xenophobia, and chaos."

Jessie missed fishing with Johnny, on the afternoons he attended soccer practice during the week. His mother, Bobbie, nixed any thoughts of playing football, so Jessie attended soccer games on Saturdays. He was amazed by the nine-year-old's stamina and coordination, moving the ball downfield at astonishing speeds and dribbling through defenders, who looked slow by comparison. He would make a terrific running-back or wide-receiver in American football.

The artist parked the bus on the gravel drive behind the bleachers and found a seat behind the parents of the children on the home team, who were screaming and hollering, as if the boys were vying for the finals of the World Cup.

Bobbie Warmington, a middle-aged matron who overcame her husband's death to work two jobs and raise three kids on her own, climbed the seats to sit next to him. "How are you, darlin'?"

"I'm fine. Yourself?"

"Aw, we're getting by, if just barely."

"You're working two jobs and raising three kids, I wish there was more I could do to help," said Jessie, folding a hundred-dollar bill into her hand.

She opened her palm and looked up at him, "You mean so much to Johnny, you don't have to do that. We don't need charity."

"That's not charity, that's Johnny's commission."

"For what?"

"Something he said one day, while we were fishing, got me started on a painting that I called 'Amity'. I sold it a few days ago for more than I thought it was worth, so that's his share."

"That's mighty generous of you, Jessie. I'll put it away for a rainy day."

"Great."

"Have you heard about SunnyBreeze?"

"Yeah, Johnny and I were fishing the Little Bay and came across the destruction. I realize that the population's exploding but they don't have to destroy a whole ecosystem just to satisfy the snowbirds."

"Well, they're already taking applications for housemaids and restaurant help, so I went over to fill out a form and found out that they're going to build a very exclusive private school on the property. They're also going to give away at least a dozen scholarships to smart but needy children from the community, so I'm signing the kids up, just to see what happens."

"A school? Really? What's a school got to do with a residential resort?"

"I have no idea but the lady said that they were already getting inquiries from all over the country."

"I guess there's nothing to lose, at this point, but I'd sure want to know a whole lot more about the curriculum and the staff, before I sent my kid to any school."

"If it gives them a shot at going to college, I'm sending them," replied Bobbie, her eyes following Johnny scampering down the center of the field, dribbling the ball and dodging defenders, as he swept right to launch a massive kick that sailed behind the goalie and hooked the corner of the net. "Goal!"

The bleachers creaked and groaned as the parents jumped up and down cheering, while Johnny's teammates piled on him at the far end of the field, as time ran out. The boy ran over and hopped up the steps to Jessie, "I'm glad you came to my game."

"I wouldn't have missed it for anything and that goal was absolutely incredible!"

Johnny smiled, "Can you drive me home?"

"Sure, if it's okay with your mom."

He turned to his mother for a congratulatory hug. She looked up at Jessie and winked, "I don't see why not."

They followed the crowd out to the cars on the lot and climbed into the bus. Jessie asked, "Why'd you want me to drive you home?"

"Because I haven't seen you since last week and I missed you."

"To tell you the truth, I missed you too. Want to go fishing this afternoon?"

"Sure. I saw a pod of dolphins out on the bay this morning."

"Is everything alright at home?"

"Yeah, I guess," replied Johnny, as Jessie followed the other cars out onto Blue Ridge Road.

"What's the 'I guess' part?"

"Mom wants to sign us up for some new school over at that SunnyBreeze development and I don't want to go."

"Well, first, according to what your mother told me, they're only offering a handful of scholarships, so who knows how many other kids' parents will apply? The other thing is that they won't have it up and running until next fall. A lot can happen between now and then."

"I guess you're right," replied Johnny, glumly, "but I don't like what they're doing to the land and the animals and I don't want to have anything to do with those rich people."

Jessie pulled over, dropped the gearbox into neutral, and pulled the brake. "You're a very bright kid, so who knows, you might get accepted and that could be really good or not, depending on lots of things. The first is your attitude. I'm not saying that you should or shouldn't go to that school but what I am saying is that you should never turn up your nose at any opportunity. Check it out and make an informed decision based on real facts, not assumptions."

Johnny stared at his knees, "What are assumptions?"

"Assumptions are when you decide that you like or don't like something or someone, even though you don't really know anything about them. You're making things up, instead of finding out for yourself."

"Okay."

"You know I'm right. Don't get yourself all worked up about something that might not even happen and, in the meantime, let's find out what kind of school it's going to be, what kind of curriculum they plan on instituting, who's going to be teaching, and what kind of extracurricular activities they'll offer. It could turn out to be really cool, or, maybe, not. Let's at least find out, so you can make your own choice."

"That's fair."

"The other thing is that you should never judge other people by their background or their race or their religion or beliefs, for that matter, and I'll give you two reasons. One is that you don't know anything about where they came from or what they went through to be standing in front of you today. Show enough grace to find out about each individual person and you'll be treated the same way. Just because they have wealth doesn't make rich people good or bad. Sure, there are some snobby rich folk in this town but I know more than a few who pay for the 'Art's Important' camp and don't expect anything more than happy kids in return. We both know there's just as many poor people with a bad attitude. The point is that everyone is an individual and they should be respected until they give you a reason not to."

"What's the second thing?"

"That every person you meet in your life will be able to do at least one thing that you can't."

"Like what?" inquired a curious Johnny.

"Like speak another language or do math in their head or build a beautiful piece of furniture or grow vegetables that will nourish people or ride a horse, it's endless. No one can do everything well but, if you put the right group of people together, wonderful things can happen. Look at your soccer team. You couldn't have scored that winning goal, if your mates hadn't blocked out the defenders on either side. They didn't score but they made it possible for you to make the shot, that's teamwork."

The boy smiled, "I see your point."

"The question is whether you'll use these thoughts to calm yourself down and gather some facts, so you can make a good decision with your mother." He paused, "And don't assume that you know anything about a stranger, because you don't. They could be your next best friend or they could be bad people. Keep your eyes and ears wide open, you'll learn a lot."

"Is all of growing up going to be this hard?"

"Yeah, pretty much."

"Can I stay a kid?"

Jessie wrapped an arm around his shoulders and ruffled his ginger hair, "You're doing great, just take it one day at a time, one problem at a time, and you'll do fine."

"Promise?"

"I have confidence in you and, besides, you're my best friend."

"You too."

~

The little engine whined as the prop pushed the boat through the narrows and out into the southern bay. There were no shiners rippling across the surface of the water or gulls swooping out of the blue sky in search of an easy meal.

"Doesn't look promising," said Johnny, guiding the boat along the eastern shore. "In fact, I don't see any birds flying."

"Maybe they know something we don't," replied Jessie, scanning the horizon for weather. "Keep going and let's see what they've done down at SunnyBreeze."

"Okay, but I promise, it's going to be a bummer."

The dense wall of mangroves and scrub palm ended abruptly, opening to a vast wasteland contoured to channel rainwater away from a dense thicket of structures. Gently curving asphalt roads divided the smooth brown landscape into tiny communities and hundreds of utility boxes marked coming construction.

Johnny pointed south, "Look, it goes on forever!"

Jessie shook his head in disgust, "It's an abomination."

"And we can't stop it."

"Keep going, let's check out their marina."

The skiff idled south until a dredge, shooting a continuous stream of wet sand up onto the barren shoreline, blocked most of the channel. A crane perched on top of a barge hammered rows of pilings into the soft sandy bottom.

"This is going to be huge," said the boy.

"I think I heard that it's going to dock one-hundred boats. That dredge means they're planning to bring in some big luxury yachts with deep drafts."

Johnny pointed to machines carving curving terraces into the land behind a sturdy seawall snaking along the bank. "Clubhouse?"

"I'm sure and a whole lot more, think restaurants and bars and pools. This is where the swingers will hang out."

"Swingers?"

"When I was young, 'swingers' meant young adults out to have a good time," laughed Jessie. "I guess I'm showing my age."

"So, this really is going to be a resort?"

"Yes, check in and everything's provided, so you don't have to leave the compound until you head for home."

"And they get to keep all your money."

"That's exactly the plan! Even better, they'll set it up so the guests don't even have to reach into their pocket. They'll just charge everything to their accounts." He grinned, "How old did you say you are? Forty-two?"

Johnny giggled, "I guess I see how everything in this little town ties together, from the houses they rent, to where and what to eat, to all the activities…they're all right here, within walking distance." He gazed around and sighed, "I really hate what they're doing but somebody's pretty smart to figure all this out."

"Somebody's going to make a lot of money out of this scheme and, if this works, many more," said Jessie, as Johnny turned the little boat north. He opened his tackle box and pulled out a sack of marshmallows. "What'd you think about going by to check on George and his family?"

"Yeah," said the boy, checking the water along the bank. "Tide's just about in, we can make it up in there and back, no problem."

He turned up a narrow creek that meandered back into the woods and opened into a pair of connected ponds. Johnny cut the engine as soon as they entered because Jessie's warning echoed through his mind. *"Keep our back to the door, so we've got a way out and…don't ever get between George and his mate or the little one. He's libel to go right through this little boat. Show some respect."*

Jessie opened the sack, "You remember, don't you?"

"Yup."

"Call 'em in."

Johnny clapped his hands three times, paused, then clapped three times again. A ruddy snout and a pair of dark eyes bobbed to the surface across the pond, checking the intruders. "Hey, George, how's the family?"

The long tail swished gracefully and the massive alligator swam effortlessly, causing barely a ripple in the pond, and the mother and little gator rose up in the narrows. Johnny and Jessie tossed marshmallows and fearsome jaws opened slightly to trap the white bubbles, gently gnashing each one, like someone joyously nibbling on tiny bits of chocolate, savoring every morsel, until only pale dribble escaped the side of their snouts, and they'd move on to the next.

When the bag was empty, Johnny clapped again and George opened his terrifying mouth very wide, slapped his tail against the surface of the water, and disappeared. "I'm still astonished that we can interact with a primal primitive beast, as if he's the neighbor's puppy."

"You said that we need to show respect but I'm always just a little bit scared that he's going to still be hungry and I figure I probably look like a good snack to him."

"That's why we leave ourselves a way out," laughed Jessie. "Besides, it doesn't cost anyone anything to show respect for each other or Mother Nature's most wonderful creations."

"That's kind of the best and worst…we realized how bad the destruction is across the bay but we get to do something really cool that no one else would believe."

"Let's keep it our secret," said Jesse, stroking with an oar to back the little boat out of the pond.

~

Before the final sales meeting snared the quota of investors, who snatched up every available slot, streets were being paved and utilities buried underground. Foundations for the shops in The Commons and the marina complex erupted from the moonscape and dredged sand from the little bay filled this side of Sloan's little mountain. A growing forest of pilings would allow an armada of luxury yachts safe harbor.

"Things are really moving along," said Mavis, as Tate pulled the golf cart up to the edge of the amphitheater pit. A gang of workers hustled around a giant boom pouring concrete footings for the stage and band shell.

"It isn't hard to imagine this entire plaza covered in green grass, with fountains bubbling under huge royal palm trees, surrounded by banks of hibiscus in a rainbow of colors," replied Tate, hopping out to inspect the work.

"And hundreds of families with money to burn," added Mavis, turning to watch a line of concrete mixers spewing their loads into curving forms that outlined the base of the three-story showcase of shops and restaurants. "I can see this whole complex just from the shape of the footings. Big columns rising between lush planters shielding the circle drive and parking from the pedestrian walkways and so many opportunities to spend money."

"How'd your meeting go with Howard and the accountants?" asked Tate, wrapping his arms around her waist to be close enough to be heard over the din of machinery.

"The initial investments for the land, design concepts, and preparing the site will all be repaid within sixty-days, assuming the vast majority of our new partners don't bounce their checks."

"That's incredible."

"What's incredible is that we should have enough to cover all the construction costs, twenty-million to build and staff the school and the personnel residences, more than half the startup for the next project, and a tidy little profit for our troubles."

He kissed her passionately, "We should celebrate."

"I heard they just opened a new steakhouse at the Fontainebleau. Why don't we fly down there for dinner?"

"This seems very familiar," mused her husband. "Did you steal daddy's plane?"

"Let's just say, I've got connections," replied Mavis, ignoring the stares of the workers, as she humped his muscular thigh. "You know the prospect of power and success make me horny."

"I think we can take care of that problem."

"Daddy wants to know why we haven't provided him with grandkids."

"If memory serves, the last time we had this discussion, you were hell-bent on saving the world."

"Still am but I think the guilt he dumps on me and the relentless ticking of my biological clock are starting to make me consider a broader range of possibilities."

"With our looks, we'll have beautiful babies, who will be blessed to be born rich."

Chapter Four

Sammy Ball locked up the archives, climbed the stairs, and tottered across the parking lot to climb into his apple-red 1964 Volvo PV554, all original, with the exception of extended pedals and an elevated seat to accommodate his tiny stature. It always reminded him of a slimmed down version of the heavy American coupes from the 1930's.

He eased out of the parking lot, west across Tarpon Way and north on Highway Forty-One to his tiny bungalow on Alameda. Cammy, his tabby-cat, started meowing long before he unlatched the door. He picked her up for a hug and opened the glass slider to the porch to let her out, pausing to gaze through a grove of tall palms, across the lawn and the bay, to a liquid orange sun melting behind Treasureman's Key. The only thing missing from Jessie Cotton's 'Reprise' was the wedge of pelicans.

His wife, Penny, died several years ago and he used the insurance money to pay off the mortgage. His modest salary barely covered the other expenses but he was thankful to have his own little piece of paradise with a magnificent view and nature all around.

Prices for everything were rising rapidly but he had not received a raise in almost seven years. The city fathers claimed that the coffers were nearly empty and froze all salaries, until funding could be stabilized, but sales and property taxes were at an all-time high and, with so many people moving in from the north, there was plenty of money stashed away someplace. His dilemma was common to almost everyone he knew, except the good ol' boys, who were screwing everyone else.

He found a wedge of Camembert and some French bread, and poured a small glass of Merlot before wandering out to sit on the porch to watch the last flares of the sunset and a lanky blue heron trolling the little pond for tiny fish or frogs.

"You work for city government for thirty years and still can't make enough to get by, so I have to choose between eating or taking my meds. That's just not fair."

His neighbor, Rex Tatum, traipsed across the lawn to rap on the screen door, rousing Sammy out of his thoughts, "Hey, man, how are you?"

"I'm hanging in there, same as always," laughed the plump Irishman, taking a seat. Rex was a janitor over at the high school, had been for twenty-something years, and suffered as yet another dedicated member of the working poor.

"Can I get you something?"

"Naw, I'm fine. Just wanted to stop by to say that Hank Miller's getting a meeting together to talk strategy."

"Hell, he can talk all day long but the people who control our salaries aren't going to cave in to common sense. They're in it to get re-elected by claiming they're holding the budget and keeping property taxes low and they sure as hell aren't going to mention all the roads and bridges and buildings that are falling down out of neglect, let alone hundreds of city employees about to starve to death."

"I don't know, man, we're never going to get anywhere until the rest of the population understands how bad things are for all of us. We have to make some noise."

"They'd just as soon fire us," laughed Sammy, tipping the glass to savor the last drops of Merlot.

"We need a spokesman with enough stature to make people listen."

"Well, it sure as hell isn't Hank Miller."

Rex stood, his posture slightly stooped from mopping too many floors for too many years, "I'm going to the meeting. I'll let you know what happens."

Sammy rolled out of his chair, "Listen, I'm sorry I'm being such a grouch but I don't see these guys making much of a difference."

"It's only going to work if we get everyone to stand together, all for one and one for all - win, lose, or draw."

"Well, we sure don't have much left to lose."

"Come with me," pleaded Rex. "You're just what we need."

"You're full of shit, you know that."

"Grab your coat and let's go," said Rex, heading out the screen door.

~

Two-dozen city employees gathered in the back room of the VFW over on Summit, despondently sipping beers, as Miller droned on about drumming up good will in the community.

Rex bought Sammy a beer at the bar and the little man perched on a barstool, taking in the depressed and defeated vibe in the room, as a crabby overworked, underpaid waitress with flaming orange hair balanced trays of refills from bar to table and empties back. After five minutes of pointless drivel, he raised his hand.

Miller looked up, "Yes?"

"Has anyone put together a complete list of all the city and county employees?"

"Well, no."

"Why not? If you want to make changes, you need mass. You need to convince every one of our coworkers to stand together for a one-day strike to get the press to take notice and raise awareness throughout the community. You want action, then take action!"

"But...?"

"Do we have an accountant or an attorney in our midst?"

"No."

"Well then, get one of each in a hurry! We need experts to go over the city budget to find out where our money is going and to advise us on what our rights really are."

Someone yelled out, "Right on!"

"Has anyone had a chat with the cops or the firemen?"

"No, we..."

"Then, anyone got an in with either force?"

Harvey Harris raised his hand, "I work in the motor pool. I'll ask around."

"Great," said Sammy. "Who are we missing?"

"How 'bout the hospital workers?" asked Benny Young, who worked on the maintenance crew responsible for public landscapes, a demanding job in a tourist town.

Sammy raised his beer bottle in agreement, "Okay, let's schedule another meeting for a week from tonight and all of you contact anyone you can think of who might have a stake in this. We're not going to get anywhere unless we get everybody who's under-employed by the city on board."

The meager crowd cheered and applauded. Benny Young ambled over and leaned on the bar next to Sammy's stool, "Listen, man, my sister works in the kitchen over at the hospital, and there's probably a hundred-fifty people taking care of everything in that building, that isn't doctoring or nursing."

"Talk with your sister and see if we can get a list with contact information."

"I'll see her tonight and let you know what I find out," said Benny, reaching to shake. "You're the first guy who's managed to get this crew motivated to actually do something more than whining about the system that's screwing them."

"Let's change it!" laughed Sammy.

Rex punched Sammy in the shoulder, "I knew I shouldn't have brought you along." Then he grinned, "Hell, worst that can happen is we all get fired!"

"No, man, we just want to be treated fairly," said Benny. "I don't see why we should be struggling to make ends meet when we all work our asses off to make this city shine."

"Remember exactly what you said, because I want you to say that to the reporters just the way you just said it to us," said Sammy. "That's the soul of this struggle. We give our best. All we ask is to be treated fairly."

～

Benny Young jogged into twilight along Tuttle Avenue on his way to his sister's house, as streetlights flicked on, one by one. His job kept him in shape but he missed running competitively, having won state titles twice in the middle distances during high school.

A gray police car pulled up next to him and the officer riding shotgun yelled, "Where you runnin' to boy? Where's the fire?"

Benny kept his pace, "I'm going home."

"Where's home?"

He stopped and walked over the car, hands on hips, breathing hard, "What's it to you? I haven't done anything, other than jogging, which, as far as I know, isn't illegal."

"We got a report of an attempted rape, over on Hawthorne Street, and you fit the description," replied the officer, opening the door to get out of the car.

Benny backed away, "Why, because I'm black?"

"Are you being a smartass, boy?" yelled the cop, leaning close, his hand on his gun.

"No, Sir! But it does strike me as odd that, if I was the guy you're looking for, I'd be running away from Hawthorne Avenue instead of towards it."

"Are you resisting arrest?"

"What am I being arrested for?"

"Being a smartass!" sneered the cop, dropping Benny to the pavement, with a knee in his back, to snap the cuffs tight on his arms. He dragged the prisoner upright and the other officer hauled back and punched him in the stomach. Benny dropped to his knees, blood spurting from his mouth. "I'm a city employee, you morons. Check my ID."

The second cop hit him again and Benny toppled face down on the concrete.

Before Benny moved any part of his body, he struggled to clear his brain enough to remember being hammered by that fat cop over on Tuttle but he was sure that he had no idea of where he was or how he got here. He inventoried the damage - the taste of blood in his mouth, massive pain and lacerations on the right side of his head, and severe bruising in his abdomen. His hands were not shackled but his wrists were bruised from the handcuffs. His fingertips sensed the cold rough texture of concrete, scented with the acrid aroma of mold, the draft of air conditioning ruffled the hairs on his arm, and he could hear the slow steady breathing of one other person above and behind him.

He opened his eyes to find himself lying on the floor of an empty yellow room with white trim, which certainly wasn't jail. He rolled over to face the steel-toed boots of a very large man, hairy arms folded over a dark blue dress shirt, patiently staring at his prisoner. He could be one of the cops who beat him but the memory of their faces was blurry at best.

"'bout time you woke up."

"Where am I and who the hell are you?"

"I'm the guy who's going to decide what happens to you, nigger."

"What do you want?"

"We want you and the midget to stop stirring up trouble."

"How could you possibly know about any of that?"

"Never you mind or I'll have to figure some cruel way to make you disappear."

"Wait a minute…let's get back to the 'what do you want' part."

"You're going to convince the little guy and the rest of the rabble-rousers to shut it down, before things get out of hand."

"Or."

"By morning, we'll know everything there is to know about Benny M. Young and all of your kin." His jowls puffed out when he sneered, "The neighbors will probably wonder why you and your whole family suddenly left town, but that will remain a mystery."

The brute stood up, knocked the chair out the way, and kicked Benny in the ribs. "Are we clear on all this, nigger?"

Benny groaned, "Yes, Sir!"

The huge man pulled a bag over Benny's head, lifted him over his shoulder, and carried him outside. He opened the side-door of a van, dumped a barely conscious body on the metal floor, then tied his hands behind his back with a zip-tie.

Benny crashed around the back of the van, as the driver floored it, then hit the brakes hard, barreling around corners and bouncing over curbs at full throttle. Thirty minutes later, the little truck screeched to a stop, the back door opened, hands dragged his bruised and battered body out and dropped him on the pavement. Footsteps retreated and tires squealed, as the roar of the engine faded away.

He struggled to sit, wiggling his head back and forth to dislodge the black hood, which fell behind him just as headlights flashed around a corner. Too unstable to stand, Benny curled into a ball and rolled off the pavement, as brakes screeched and tires skidded to a stop, a few feet past where his body was lying a moment before.

The door opened and the click-clack of high heels preceded a tall willowy woman, who brushed thick blond hair out of her face, as she stooped down to him, "Oh, my God, are you alright?"

Benny rolled to sit up and the light from a streetlamp revealed the wounds and bruises on his face. "Look at you! What happened to you, who did this? Oh, look your hands are tied. Stay right there, I've got a penknife in my purse."

Before he could respond, she scampered around the car to retrieve a small shiny blade. "Hold still, I'm fairly handy with a knife but I sure don't want to hurt you anymore than you already are."

She pursed her lips and squinted her pale gray eyes, as she sawed at the plastic band, until it popped open. Benny rubbed his wrists, "I guess you're my guardian angel, appearing out of the darkness to save me."

Her whole body started shaking, "I almost ran your butt over! I didn't even see you, until I saw the flash of your shirt in the headlights as you rolled out of the way! I could have killed you!"

He stood up and rested his bruised hands on her shoulders. She was beautiful in a very natural way, as if her radiance required no effort. "Now calm down, we're both okay."

"I'm usually pretty tough but it's not every day you almost kill a guy, who looks like someone else already tried." She took a deep breath, "What happened to you and who would do this?"

Benny grinned, in spite of the staggering pain in every cell in his body, "It's a long story, let's just say I never imagined that violent vigilantes and rampant racism still exist. I used to think that stuff got straightened out with all the riots and marching, during my parent's generation, but I learned tonight that if you say the wrong thing to the wrong person, people take offense and want retribution. Freedom of speech is just a campaign gimmick, it's only true if you say what you're supposed to say."

"I agree," said the blond. "Our family stories included marching in the anti-war demonstrations during the Sixties, and getting gassed and beat up for exercising their patriotic rights."

"I'm thinkin' it ain't finished," coughed Benny, wiping blood from his lip.

Kate fished a crumpled Kleenex from her pocket and handed it to him, "Can I take you to a hospital or something? You look terrible."

"Where are we?"

"Well, I'm a tourist, so I'm just following my map. I think we're just south of Federton and we're pretty close to Highway Forty-One. I pulled out of a gas station and got turned around. I was trying to find my way back."

Benny scanned the horizon above the trees and spied a band of light reflecting on puffy clouds floating across the sky. He pointed, "That way, see the lights?"

"Yeah, c'mon, I'll give you a lift and you can get me pointed where I need to go."

He held out his hand, "Thanks. You probably saved my life. What's your name?"

"Kate, Kate Crocket. Happy to help," replied the woman, reaching under his arm to help support him, as he hobbled up the slight rise to ease into the passenger seat of a bright red rental. "What's yours?"

"Benny Young. I work for the city doing landscaping. What do you do?"

"I'm a reporter for *American Style* and I got sent down here to check out SunnyBreeze. Heard of it?"

"Yeah, big development down on the keys. I think someone said it was going to be like two miles long. There was something on the news about them having a flood that busted through the highway during a storm, a while back. I guess they got it up and running in record time. Beyond that, I don't know much."

"Well, I guess I'll have to let you know what I find out," said Kate, following the dark road towards the glowing sky. "So, where do you want me to take you?"

"I can't go to a hospital, so I guess my sister's place down in Bellevue. She can fix me up. Just stay on Forty-One and I'll get you there." He grimaced and glanced at his bloody fingertips, "I sure hope I'm not bleeding all over your rental."

"Don't worry about it, I'll get you there as fast as I can."

He leaned back in the seat, "Where are you staying?"

"The Beach Club on Breezy Key. The magazine's paying for it, because I sure couldn't afford the bill for a broom closet in that place on my salary. Not that I'm complaining, I love getting assigned to check out cool new places, on their tab, but it's kind of disappointing when the fantasy's over."

"Where are you from?"

"Originally, a little town called Manitowoc, in upstate Wisconsin, but I live in Atlanta now."

"That's gotta be a site milder than Wisconsin in winter."

"Amen to that," smiled the reporter. "Although, there are times during the winter up there, when the sun's out and the air is still and dry, that it really doesn't feel cold at all. And it is chillingly beautiful."

"If you say so."

"I do."

Kate followed his instructions and turned into a driveway in the middle of a neighborhood of small but tidy homes. She climbed out and hurried around to help him swing his legs out to stand. "How 'bout I help you to the door."

"How 'bout you go knock on the door and tell my sister, Alva, to come help. You don't need me bleeding all over your nice dress."

She knocked on the door, which was opened by a petite black woman, flipping a soggy dishtowel over her shoulder. "Can I help you?"

"Yes, I've got Benny in my car and he's been hurt."

Alva rushed to the driveway and wrapped an arm around her brother, "What happened to you? You look terrible."

"Feel worse," said Benny, stumbling up the walk. He stopped and turned back, "Thank you for saving my life. I owe you one."

"Just pass it on," replied Kate.

"Go back out the neighborhood the way we came in. Go south and turn west at the stoplight, that's Buena Vista, follow it 'til you hit Forty-One. Go north around the marina until the highway splits off to the west, cross the bridge and you'll end up at the circle in St. Michael's. Head south and your hotel should be about a mile down."

"Thanks," replied Kate, turning away. "How can I get in touch with you, I want to know that you're okay."

His sister smiled, "My name is Alva, call me at 477-1404."

"Thank you, I will."

~

J.D. Calhoun sat back with a satisfied groan and gazed across the water to Flamingo Key, from the stern deck of his ostentatious yacht, 'Winner', which bobbed gracefully in a halo of reflected lights skittering across the dark waters at the Dolphin Bay Yacht Club. His doctors kept telling him that he had to lose some weight and get his cholesterol down but he just couldn't resist a charbroiled slab of Angus beef, slaughtered and aged on his ranch just east of Naples, and grilled to bloody rare by his personal chef.

His young wife, Sonia, a Brazilian bombshell, embraced her role in his business dealings by flirting with pudgy and stodgy Mayor Kane and chatting with Nina, his wife and Calhoun's daughter, with sophistication and humor that her husband could never muster. He was a good ol' boy, who worked his way up from grunt laborer to dominating construction from Tampa to Sanibel Island, as well as virtually everyone holding political office within his realm.

J.D. leaned over to the mayor, "Tell me, how are things coming with SunnyBreeze?"

Kane shrugged, "From what I hear, they've got all hands on deck, trying to make deadlines on the construction. They're supposed to be ready for the first guests by Easter."

"It'd be a shame, if they didn't quite make it," laughed the real estate tycoon. "I've built my share of projects and they've gotta be cutting corners along the way, if they're going to make the deadline for the opening."

"Our inspectors have to sign off on everything and there hasn't been anything to take issue with yet. It's all precisely to code."

"What about the highway?"

"We had our engineers out there through the whole process and they claimed it was better than before the surge carved it up," replied the mayor. "Simons and Sons is one of the biggest construction companies in the country. They do everything in house."

"Yeah, I know. I've had dealings with Selby Simonson before. Hell, his daughter and son-in-law had the gall to pitch me as an investor! Why would I invest in my competition?"

"I take it the results were somewhat less than satisfactory?" inquired Bert, with a cocked eyebrow.

"Let's just say that Simonson's construction company does everything exactly to the letter of the specifications in the contract and absolutely nothing more. And I'm not the only one who has bad history with that bastard." He looked up, as his bodyguard, Al Delveccio, appeared, and motioned the huge man to approach the table.

The seams in Delveccio's linen sports jacket bulged to barely accommodate a muscular torso and thick biceps. Coupled with dark darting eyes and a permanent scowl, he was a menacing presence, even when he was standing still.

He bowed and said very quietly, "Excuse me for interrupting," before leaning to whisper in Calhoun's ear. "The message has been delivered."

Calhoun nodded his approval and Delveccio disappeared inside the cabin. A few moments later, the twin engines rumbled to life and J.D. stood up, "I'm afraid we're going to have to be on our way. I sure do enjoy spending time with my favorite daughter and I'm proud of the work you're doing, Bert."

The ladies hugged and Calhoun shook his son-in-law's limp hand, "It appears that the rebellion has fizzled."

"I appreciate your help," smiled the mayor. "I'll have my secretary send that check for the Children's Fund over next week, if that's alright with you?"

"Certainly," grinned Calhoun, hugging Nina. "I appreciate your generosity!"

~

The following morning, Kate drove back to St. Michael's Circle to buy a broad-brimmed straw hat to protect her fair skin, during the interview and tour of the construction at SunnyBreeze. She parked the car and walked around the broad walkway, circling a fountain with a bronze dolphin leaping through an arching gush of water. She found a store window displaying beachwear and, after trying on several straw hats, picked a light green one with a broad rim and a little burst of yellow flowers sprouting from a deep pink ribbon around the crown. She admired herself in the mirror, "Perfect."

The reporter had a little time to waste, so she wandered around the rest of the shops and stopped in front of the window of a small gallery, featuring an absolutely stunning impressionist painting of a cresting wave about to collapse on the shore beneath threatening clouds billowing through an extraordinary sunset, with a flock of gulls flying into twilight. She focused in on a little red pail and shovel, half-buried in the sandy foreground, misplaced toys that would be fondly remembered for a lifetime. Her eyes scanned across to the artist's signature, 'Jessie Cotton', and her hand covered her lips, as she gasped, "Oh, my God. It can't be."

She glanced at her watch and hurried to the rental. She started the engine and turned the radio off, staring absently, remembering her Jessie, who collapsed and withdrew into a deep depression after Wisconsin's defeat at the hands of Oklahoma. Try as she might, she could not draw him out of his funk and, then, one night he just disappeared with most of his stuff into a blizzard and she never heard from him again. It took more than a year to admit that he was not coming back and for her broken heart to heal enough to date other guys but it was never the same. *"Stop it, you fool, there are probably a thousand guys named Jessie Cotton in the world. Isn't it strange enough that you're about to interview the quarterback who won that game and changed your life forever?"* A tear rolled down her cheek, *"But what if it's really him?"*

A shiny black jacked-up pickup with giant tires, pulled into the slot next to her car, rousing her from her thoughts. She backed out, followed the road back across the bridge to pick up Forty-One south, then Pelican Turn across to the beach road.

After several miles, a dense jungle of scrub oaks, scrappy pines, sea grape, and palmettos opened into a vast construction site with workers and machinery bustling around the project like ants swarming to build a new nest before the first frost. She pulled into a circular drive around The Commons and parked facing a half-finished band shell looming over a broad stage.

Tate Sloan opened her door before she could get out, "You'd be Kate Crocket, from *American Style,* if I'm not mistaken."

Embarrassed, she grabbed her hat, purse, notebook, and recorder and stood, fumbling to shake his hand, finding him far more handsome than the photographs in the magazines. "And you're Tate Sloan."

"Everyone knows who I am," laughed Sloan, taking her arm to lead her along the drive, where massive structures were beginning to take shape. "This is The Commons, which will house a conference center, fabulous restaurants, tony shops, and trendy galleries…as well as an ice cream parlor, an arcade, and a bike rental for the kids. We'll have long planters, overflowing with voluptuous flowers, and big columns separating the driveway from the pedestrian mall. Everything about the environment will be lush and beautiful."

He pointed across the highway, "We're building more family-oriented restaurants and shops on a boardwalk above the beach and we'll also have a large marina complex on the bay side of the property, that will cater to a more sophisticated crowd."

"Something for everyone?"

"Only more so," laughed Tate, hopping into a gold golf cart with a silver awning and two SunnyBreeze flags flapping in the salty breeze.

Kate climbed in and held on to her hat, as he sped around the circle. She pointed to the band shell, "Entertainment?"

"We'll have concerts, shows, and movies out here in the evenings and rock bands playing in the disco over at the marina. No guest at SunnyBreeze will ever be able to say that they couldn't find entertainment any time of the day or night."

"I heard that you won't have any hotel or motel rooms available."

"That's absolutely right," replied Sloan. "We're building eighteen-hundred custom, high-end homes with every amenity any guest could possibly want. We'll have tiny bungalows for the newly-weds up to eight-bedroom mansions for families and large groups in secluded neighborhoods with unique identities, so corporations could bring in the entire executive staff for a retreat or a family could hold a more intimate and private reunion than staying in some overcrowded hotel. Plus, we'll have the staff and facilities to cater any kind of function."

She noticed that every truck they passed bore a 'Simons and Sons' logo. "Is all the construction work being done by Simons and Sons?"

"Yeah, it's a turnkey operation. Our architects developed the plans and they make it happen on time and on budget. We couldn't get that kind of consistent quality if we subcontracted it out to local companies."

Kate gazed around at the town growing out of barren sand, "I need to shoot a few photos for the article, do you have any models yet?"

"Yes, we have the first four going up right here," said Tate, pulling up in front of a two-story unit. "C'mon, I'll show you what we're trying to accomplish."

He started up a textured concrete walkway and stopped at a junction that split off in several directions. "Each cluster of homes will offer privacy from the others and every home will have a secluded garden. This particular unit will have eight bedrooms but it will also have two kitchens, one on each floor, so it can be rented to two smaller parties, as well as a large group."

The four buildings fit together in a rectangle, each entry and most of the large windows faced away from the other homes, and the interior courtyard was partitioned with curving walls that created intimate and private spaces for each residence. The exterior finishes were slick and modern and flower beds were already being prepared for landscaping that would soften the angles.

Brilliant light washed through the scene from the southeast and Kate backed away to fire several shots that included parts of three of the structures, then moved in close for a few details of a massive slab door with ornate brass handles. "I see what you mean, these buildings all fit together."

"That's the brilliance of the site plan. There are blocks designed to form homogenous communities and continuity of interior spaces, yet every home will have a unique exterior." Sloan pulled the door open to allow her to enter a large foyer, with a massive chandelier suspended from a soaring ceiling, above the curve of a circular staircase and another beautifully finished door that was propped open.

They walked into a cavernous great room with huge windows along one side overlooking a walled garden, a large granite fireplace with a matching bar flanking the far wall, with space in the paneling for a large screen television and speakers, and a kitchen, at the back, designed to accommodate a hungry crowd.

Tate walked over to an empty console, "This will become the control center for the whole house. You can run everything from the A/C to the TVs to the lights and security monitors, as well as an instant connection with the main desk. There's a duplicate panel in the master bedroom, which is just through here."

She followed him into a wide hallway that opened in a spacious master suite with a spectacular bathroom. Skylights provided smooth soothing illumination and tall narrow windows would frame small picturesque vignettes outside. "This is going to be lovely."

"The finishes will be first-class throughout every unit. We want every guest to think they've landed in paradise!"

Tate leaned against the molding of a window and Kate fired off several frames for the story, "I love that expression."

"What expression?"

"That you're delighted with what you're creating and excited to share it with other people."

"That's why you're here, isn't it? You're going to be one of the first writers to tell your readers about what we're building and how special we intend it to be. This will be an ultimate destination."

"How's the deal work?"

"Well, the property is owned by the city corporation but each property is privately leased. When the owners are away, each unit is available for guests. Everyone is equally represented by our sales agency, which handles all the reservations, and we're already almost fully booked for our soft opening next spring without any advertising at all."

"I'm guessing this might be spring break for a more sophisticated crowd than the usual rush of college kids."

"I don't believe that our rental fees will seem particularly outrageous, when you take into account the facilities, amenities, and level of service that our visitors should expect. I'm hoping that there's no wish or dream that our staff can't provide."

"That's a big promise," laughed Kate, as they walked out through the great room and around the curving walkway to a tiny two-story cottage that was completely hidden from the first house by newly planted mature trees hanging over a tall stone wall.

Sloan pointed, "That will be covered with moss and a little waterfall will trickle down the surface to cool this terrace. And, yes, that is our commitment, to make everyone's stay as perfect as it can possibly be. The fun part is that I'm absolutely positive we can deliver on that promise."

He opened a door with a beautiful glass panel etched and frosted into a scene of unicorns frolicking in the forest. "This is our smallest unit and I'm hoping that lots of newlyweds will enjoy the warmth and intimacy of the space because we're going to add lots of unique little touches. We call it the Hobbit House."

A kitchen counter spanned the length of one wall, under a wide window looking out into a petite garden, with spaces for a small refrigerator, stove, sink, and dishwasher yet to be installed. A spiral staircase, with a banister carved and painted into a garland of vines and flowers, swept up to a second story bedroom and large bathroom, with a balcony looking out over the dunes.

Kate stepped onto the porch, holding her hat against the wind, "This could certainly be a quaint little romantic hideaway."

"I'm sure a beautiful young woman like you and a partner would enjoy it," smiled Sloan. He continued without hesitation, "My wife's out of town tonight and I was wondering whether you had plans for dinner?"

Kate blushed, "Actually, I'm supposed to catch up with an old friend but I appreciate the invitation."

"Perhaps another time?"

"Perhaps."

Kate pulled out of the circle drive and headed north on the beach road, blind to traffic and driving on instinct. The weird coincidence of finding a glorious painting by an artist named Jessie Cotton on the same day she was scheduled to meet his nemesis, Tate Sloan, in a town completely removed from their history, was unsettling at best. She never quite concluded the ongoing conversation with her spiritual self but life had a habit of jolting her consciousness out of complacency with bizarre situations that forced her to accept perplexing revelations. Jessie vanishing into a blizzard was one of those and today was shaping up to be another extreme example.

Sloan proved to be ruggedly handsome, far more intelligent than she anticipated, and charmingly sleazy. She was astonished that he propositioned her, considering he married that blond bombshell straight out of Oklahoma. What was her name? Mavis, Mavis Simonson, daughter of The Simonson, hence the Simons and Sons construction at the development. The scandal rags carried blissful stories for months about the 'perfect couple', blessed with looks, money, and fame. After a while, rumors of scandal and friction started appearing but nothing ever came of it.

Suddenly, her eyes focused in on the breaking wave in the window of the gallery. She had absolutely no memory of driving back from SunnyBreeze. There, in the corner, was the signature of Jessie Cotton.

A tiny bell tingled as she opened the door and a frail man appeared from behind an antique desk, with a shock of white hair, dancing blue eyes behind thick, round horn-rimmed glasses, and the grin of an elfin wizard who knows more about life's secrets than we might ever imagine and, there seemed a good chance, he might bestow a bit of wisdom in the next few moments. He smiled, "I'm Derek Rangle, how can I help you?"

She held out her hand, "I'm Kate Crocket and I was admiring the painting in the window, it's beautiful."

"I think if Jessie doodled on a paper napkin, I could sell it! He's certainly a local treasure."

"Tell me more," said Kate, gazing around the room and spotting at least two more landscapes by the same artist.

"He's probably not well-known anyplace else, because we sell his work as fast as he can produce it. There aren't any extra pieces to send away to galleries in other cities."

"Does he paint landscapes exclusively or other subjects too?"

"Most of his paintings are of local scenes and things he finds in nature. He's somewhat of a recluse, except for one month each summer, when he runs the 'Art's Important' program for the underprivileged kids. He had more than four-hundred children in last year's class."

"He teaches them all how to paint?"

The old man laughed, "No, it's expanded into all forms of art from drawing to sculpture, as well as photography, dance, band and orchestra, and probably more that I've forgotten. He's got a bevy of volunteer instructors helping out."

"That sounds like quite a program."

"Jessie's quite a man."

"I noticed the little shovel and pail in the painting. Does he have children?"

"No, I doubt he was ever married."

Kate walked over to look at another exquisitely effortless painting of sandpipers racing the surf on the beach, executed with a few strokes that convinced the eye that the water and the birds were moving together in a dance of nature's own rhythms. His signature was in the right-hand corner.

"How much are you asking for the breaking wave?" inquired the journalist.

"I've got it marked at eight-thousand, because I know how long it took him to paint it. 'The Sandpipers' was painted in an hour or two but 'Breaking Wave' took months. He reluctantly let me see it in his studio while he was working on it, but he wouldn't let go of it until he was satisfied."

"It is beautiful."

"If my house wasn't already full of his paintings, I'd buy it myself," laughed the proprietor.

"Is he local?"

"Well, I've represented him for eight or nine years, I guess, but he's never mentioned what came before and I've never asked. Florida's like that."

She reached into her purse for her wallet, "I know this is a strange request but I knew a Jessie Cotton in college and I lost track of him. I'm wondering whether they could be one and the same?"

She flipped open her billfold and pulled out a tattered team photograph of Jessie in full uniform, holding his red helmet on his hip. Rangle smiled and reached into a cubby in the desk to retrieve a sales flier with a black and white photo of Jessie's cockeyed grin.

Kate gasped, "Oh my, that's him!"

"Do you want me to call him for you?" inquired the old man.

"I...I...I don't know," stammered Kate. "It's a long story."

"I understand," said Derek, "but I try very hard to respect his privacy."

"Oh, I wouldn't want to intrude."

His dancing eyes crinkled behind the round glasses, "Yes, you would. Although I really don't know anything about you or your relationship with my friend, I couldn't miss your very honest and emotional reaction." He paused, "You need to contact him."

"I...I...I appreciate that."

He scribbled on a piece of paper and handed it to her, "You can decide what you want to do on your own but don't you dare tell him that I gave you this information."

"I promise," replied Kate, a tear welling in her eye, "and…thank you for being so understanding."

Rangle chuckled, "Although it seems highly improbable, I was young once too, my dear."

~

The shiny red rental was looking somewhat battered and bruised, shrouded in dust and mud from the construction site, with bloodstains on the passenger seat, and all from her travels of less than twenty-four hours. Her flight back to Atlanta was scheduled for the following evening, after an interview with Milton Fore to see the renderings and photograph some scale models at the architect's office. She had yet to check up on Benny but almost running over him in the dark was just the first of the strange cascading coincidences that completely obliterated her ability to concentrate on the assignment.

Kate unlocked the car door and climbed into the driver's seat. The ignition buzzed, as she inserted the key, but she made no attempt to start the engine. Slowly, she unfolded the crumpled stationary and stared at a telephone number and an address, with a little note scribbled at the bottom in a handsome script, 'Life doesn't offer second chances very often.'

"*A second chance for who?*" She gazed around the shops lining the circle, her eyes absently following little eddies of tourists, wandering this way and that. What could she possibly say on a blind telephone call? "*Hi, this is Kate. You ran away ten years ago and I'm still pissed.*" Her lips curled into a sad smirk, "*No, that would not do at all.*"

"*Poinsettia Avenue,*" she muttered, pulling out the city map to inspect the index. Her finger traced down Forty-One and across to a small road that appeared to drop right into Dolphin Bay. "*If I'm reading this right, he's got to be at the very end of that road.*"

The car found its way across the bridge and south on the Tamiami Trail, her mind stumbling and fumbling with what she might say, if and when she came face-to-face with him. Maybe she should say nothing and gauge his reaction, rather than blurting out something stupid like, *"Oh, hi! I was just in the neighborhood..."*

She parked the car at the end of the lane, where a pair of driveways split, one to a large manor house and the other down a little hill to what might once have been a large garage or stable, transformed into an artist's studio with wind-chimes, sculptures, and stained-glass panels in the windows of a little entry to the right. Jessie used to sketch with a soft pencil on a pad he carried around but, as far she knew, he never took an art class at the university or revealed the incredible talent displayed in his magnificent paintings.

What was she doing here, sitting in a car, staring at window boxes overflowing with lush tropical flowers? How did she stumble onto the love she lost so long ago, while on assignment to interview his rival? What could she possibly say that would make any difference after so many years?

From the photograph, he was still handsome and surely had plenty of beautiful women in this town that would find him attractive. Her hand fumbled to open the door, then pulled it closed again, before she stepped out to pad quietly down the drive.

A black and brown German Shepherd mix bounded around the side of the house, barking ferociously but wagging her tail. Kate knelt down and held out her fist for the dog to sniff, before rubbing under her chin and behind the ears, "You're beautiful. What's your name?"

A voice from the side of the house said, "It's Gracie."

She looked up to find Jessie staring down at her. His jaw was slack, his brow furrowed in disbelief, "What are you doing here and how did you find me?"

"I hope you don't mind. I saw one of your paintings and took a chance that Jessie Cotton, the artist, might be the Jessie I knew so many years ago."

He looked away, "I'm sorry I couldn't be the person that you and everyone else expected me to be."

She marched up to him, turned his chin with a finger, and stared directly into his sad blue eyes, "I never cared whether you were some big-time quarterback or a junior varsity water-boy, as long as it made you happy."

"But…?"

"But nothing! You listened to all the gossip and read all those stupid newspaper articles cutting you down but you didn't listen to what I was saying with my heart. You chickened out and ran away with your tail between your legs. Did you ever, once, consider asking whether I might want to go along?"

"I thought I couldn't measure up, even to you."

"You're a dumbshit, you know that?"

"Yeah, I've been working on that ever since." He stammered, "What do you want from me?"

"How about a 'Hi! Nice to see you, it's been way too long. Won't you come sit down for something cold to drink and tell me what's happened in the ten years since I ran out on you?'"

Embarrassed, he walked over to open the door into a tiny sunroom filled with succulents and orchids in full bloom. She followed him into a parlor, with a kitchen to one side, divided off by a freestanding island covered with a thick slab of cedar.

He took two glasses from a cabinet and filled them with ice, then tea from a pitcher in the fridge, and turned back to her, "Lemon or lime?"

"Lime would be nice," replied Kate.

He cut two slices from a fresh lime on a well-worn cutting board and handed her the glass, "Why did you come?"

"Because…" she started, then paused, staring into his eyes. "Because I loved you and I've worried for years about what might have happened to you. I had nightmares that you ended up in an asylum, that you committed suicide, that…"

The ice in his glass tinkled in his shaking hand, "I was so lost inside, I couldn't block out the endless comments and opinions and I was punishing myself far more than they ever could. One night, I just knew I couldn't be there anymore. I had to go someplace where no one knew me. And it had to be warm."

"And?"

"Somehow, I ended up here. I don't even remember the drive, other than it was snowing when I left and it was warm and sunny when I stopped. Hell, I slept on the beach down the coast for the first month I was here, before I could find a job and a place to live."

She looked around the room, spare, save comfortable furniture, several of his paintings, and stacks of books piled in front of an overstuffed bookcase. "It's a warm house."

"Come on, you'll like the studio," he said, strolling through a doorway into a long galley, that spanned the garage space, with skylights illuminating stacks of paintings leaning against the walls surrounding two easels with partially finished canvases of gulls attacking a school of tiny shiners, flipping and jumping out of dark rippling water, and a still pond in the jungle.

Kate walked slowly around the room, taking in one painting at a time, "You are truly gifted. These are beautiful!"

"It's just what I find out there," he replied, gesturing towards the bay. "While I was sleeping on the beach, I discovered the true beauty of nature and I've been trying to capture it ever since. It became my calling."

"I'll bet it's far more fulfilling than throwing touchdowns for a stadium full of screaming fans," said Kate, lingering over roiling surf under towering thunderheads, fired by a setting sun peeking beneath the storm clouds.

He sat on a stool covered in the splatter of drips and drabs in a thousand colors, "When I left Madison, I really thought all of that mattered. It took me a long time to understand that none of it had any lasting meaning for me or anybody else. It was just a game that made a lot of money for some people, while others lost their sure bets, but now nobody even remembers how it all went down."

"You do."

"Which brings us back to my question, why are you here?"

"Actually, if you really want to know, I'm a reporter for 'American Style' out of Atlanta. They send me all over the world to write stories and shoot pictures of outrageous resorts and ridiculous private residences. I'm here doing a story on SunnyBreeze…" she paused, "and your old foe, Tate Sloan."

"Yeah, I saw him in town one day but haven't made the opportunity to get reacquainted."

"I met with him this morning, for a tour of the project, and he still comes across with that aw-shucks-good-old-boy shtick that he was using when he was at Oklahoma, but, behind the act, I have no doubt that he's a very sharp businessman. Every time he smiled that Hollywood smile, I wanted to check my pockets to make sure he wasn't lifting something."

"What do you think of the resort?"

"I think it's going to be pricey and exclusive but, if they follow through with what he's proposed, it will also be clever and beautiful."

"I have a slightly jaded opinion about all of this because I treasure the wild places and the creatures who inhabit them. His crew came in and scraped two miles of habitat off the key and they're going to replace it with concrete, Bermuda grass, and ornamental palms that aren't native to this environment." He waved his hand, "And I can guarantee that housing more than a hundred yachts will pollute the little bay and drive away all the wildlife in no time flat."

"You seem very protective of the ecosystem around here."

"C'mon," he said, walking back through the kitchen and out onto a little patio, under a canopy of ancient trees, overlooking a little dock bobbing gently in the water. He pointed to a lawn chair, "Sit."

She sat down facing the bay, framed by Banyan trees, lacy pines, and arching palms.

"Now, close your eyes and tell me what you hear."

Kate closed her eyes and listened. At first, she was drawn to the whine of a motorboat fading into the distance, but gradually she focused closer and closer, hearing a chorus of bird songs volleying through the trees, a bee buzzing around nearby, a pair of crickets calling to each other, wind rustling pine needles, and…quiet. "It's so…peaceful. I feel as if I'm having a private concert of birds singing for the pure joy of singing."

"That's why I paint," said Jessie, quietly. "That's the only way I can find that inner peace."

She opened her eyes, "Then your life is a success."

He grinned, "I don't think I'd go quite that far. Let's just say that I've found my niche but I have a lot to learn about living with other people. I'll admit that I'm pretty much a recluse, until I'm forced out into public."

"Don't you have any friends…or girlfriends?"

"My best friend is a ten-year-old named Johnny Warmington. We go fishing together any afternoon he doesn't have soccer practice."

"What about Gracie?" smirked Kate.

"She's definitely the best girlfriend I've ever had, present company excepted."

"Beautiful, loyal, friendly, and ready to defend you as needed."

He stared into her beautiful amber eyes, "That sounds sort of like you."

She blushed, "That was a long time ago."

"I'm sorry I ran out on you…" he paused, "it's just that I had to learn how to live within myself, without coaches or teammates or fans or any of that…just me. After spending my entire youth practicing and playing for the team, it was kind of scary trying to figure out who the real Jessie was."

"You survived and you figured out what you're supposed to be doing with your life."

"Did you?"

She walked across the deck to pet Gracie, "No, no I didn't. I married a guy I met after you left, but I knew from the start that it couldn't last…and it didn't. So, like you, I took this job and moved to Atlanta, where I knew no one, and I started over too."

"How's that working out?"

Kate straightened up, "I'm really good at what I do."

"I would have expected nothing less, the question is, did you find happiness and fulfillment?"

She gazed out at the water for a long moment, "No, I don't think I did."

"Why?"

"I work hard, make a decent living, get to travel to some of the most beautiful places on the planet, and have an active social life, but none of that gives me the…juice that I used to feel, when we were younger and living in dreams, when tomorrow could be anything we could imagine."

"It's still there."

"That's easy for you to say."

"No, actually, it's not," replied Jessie, taking her in his arms to kiss her tenderly.

She leaned back, then rested her cheek in his shoulder, "There's something that I have to tell you."

"What?"

"I guess it must have been the night you left Madison, I went by your apartment, through the worst of the blizzard, and let myself in and I knew, instantly, that you were gone. The heat was turned way down, the water valves were turned off, and all of your things were missing, except a notepad with a pencil sketch of me…smiling."

"I thought maybe things would be better for you…"

"You asshole!" She leaned back, "I sat in that cold dark room, weeping for hours, because you and every dream that mattered had vanished. It was as if none of it ever really existed. You were just a phantom and our love was a fantasy that I made up in my imagination. I'd never really felt alone before and it scared me. I haven't felt whole since that night."

"I'd repeat my apology but that won't change what happened or what you felt. I never stopped loving you. I regretted leaving but I knew that I had to figure out how to live with my own demons." He kissed her forehead, "How are you feeling right now?"

She snuggled close, "Scared that this will vanish too."

Chapter Five

Sammy Ball parked the Volvo in the carport and toddled around to let himself in the front door but Cammy was not waiting in her usual spot. She was sitting in Benny Young's lap on the porch.

He opened the glass door before he realized that the left side Benny's face was swollen and bruised. "What happened to you?"

"I got hijacked by some renegade racist cops, who beat the crap out of me, then turned me over to some big scary guy, in an abandoned house somewhere, who said that we need to stop organizing against the city or whole families are going to start disappearing."

Befuddled, Sammy slumped into a chair, "There's a little voice inside my head that's screaming, 'Danger, danger, be very careful!' but there's another part of me that's thinking that this is the twenty-first century and we're supposed to be getting beyond all that."

"I can guarantee, there's a whole bunch of Southern white crackers who didn't get the memo."

"I know," said the little man, quietly, "but we can hope and pray that someday mankind finds a way to live as one people, before we annihilate the whole damned population."

Cammy nuzzled up under Benny's chin, "I believe in what we're trying to do but I'd be lyin', if I didn't say those cops and that hulking brute scared the shit out of me. He threatened you and the rest of my family and I just can't take that chance. Hell, I can't even go to the police!"

"Who's going to protect us from our protectors?" mused Sammy. "I think the bigger question is, who's so afraid of us that they'd go to these lengths? And who has the power to keep all this quiet?"

"My first vote would be the Klan."

"I have no doubt that the Klan still exists, except now they wear expensive suits, wave Bibles, claim to represent true God-fearing Americans, and spout carefully crafted bullshit that attempts to make hate and racism sound patriotic. They're in it but there's a bigger power behind this reaction to working folks wanting a modest pay hike. That's coming from way high up in the food-chain."

"Then it's gotta be the mayor or someone in his office," replied Benny.

"I think it's probably someone behind the mayor, who's making a whole lot of money by maintaining the status quo."

"Then we need a list of his campaign contributors."

"That's a good start but there are still lots of ways to mask contributions, so the name we're looking for won't necessarily show up on that list."

"I don't have access to that kind of information through the maintenance department, anyway," said Benny.

"I do," replied Sammy, with a crooked little smile, "and I can cross reference every property in the county."

"We need to be careful, man. You know they'll be watchin' both of us."

"We also need to figure out who the snitch is, inside the group. Someone tipped off the police officers that picked you up."

"They weren't police officers, they were pigs," snapped Benny. "And I'd love to get my hands on them in a fair fight and, then, the asshole who set me up. That motherfucker's gonna get his due."

~

Kate found Jessie, folded newspaper under his arm, sipping on a mug of coffee and staring at the painting of the pond in the jungle, "What's missing?"

"Well, obviously, you," smiled the painter. "Did you sleep well?"

She yawned and stretched, "Lovely, thank you."

He turned back to the painting, "This is a scene that Johnny and I share as one of our secret places."

"Why is it special?"

"Because we go there to feed marshmallows to George, the alligator, and his family."

"Really?"

"Yeah, I really don't remember how we connected alligators and marshmallows but we float into this little pond, Johnny claps his hands three times, and George bobs to the surface. Then the wife and little one show up. They chomp on the marshmallows and seem to understand that we mean them no harm."

"So, what's missing is the gators?"

He pulled her in front of the canvas, pointing, "George needs to be here, with the other two back here. The problem is that it's kind of dark and scary in there and I need to figure out how to create a believable glow to draw the eye into the center."

She stepped back, "It seems like the light is coming from behind the forest on the right, so maybe you float some shafts of warm soft sunlight through the trees?" She raised a knuckle to her lips, "I'm sorry, I really don't know anything about art."

"No, I see exactly what you're saying and I think you've solved the problem."

"Cool," said Kate, softly, wrapping her arms around his neck for a gentle kiss. "I was afraid of what might happen, if I found you, and afraid that something very special might be lost forever, if I didn't."

"I'm glad you did."

"I need coffee. I have an appointment with the architect at eleven and I need to make a call, can I use your phone?"

"Sure, it's in the kitchen. Oh, and would you put Gracie's bowl down for her? She goes out to do her thing but she likes having me present breakfast for her."

"You two seem to have worked out your relationship and your routines," said Kate.

"Yeah, Gracie proved that I'm trainable."

She found a mug on the counter and poured a cup of rich dark coffee from the carafe on the stove, when Gracie pranced in, looking up at her with an inquisitive tilt of her head, as if to say, "Am I going to have to train you too?"

Kate knelt down to pet her and place her bowl on the floor, "Here ya' go, girl, enjoy your breakfast."

Gracie cocked her head the other way and consumed the grain at a steady but unhurried pace.

Kate found the number scribbled on her pad, barely legible, considering it was written in the dark and her hands were still shaking from her encounter with Benny. She felt a bit guilty, for not having followed up the previous day, but nothing about yesterday was normal in any way.

She dialed and the phone rang three times, before a female voice answered, "Hello?"

"Alva? It's Kate Crocket. I brought Benny home the other night and just wanted to check in to see how he's doing?"

"Oh, thank you for bringing him home. Those bastards beat the crap out of him and there's no one to make it right. We can't go to the cops or anyone else in 'law enforcement' and he said they threatened the rest of the family. I've got three kids to worry about."

"I'm sorry. Have you talked to a lawyer?"

"No, I don't know any lawyers who'd be dumb enough to take on the case of some stupid nigger, who got beat up by the cops for being a smartass. It happens all the time down here!"

"I live in Atlanta and we've got the same problem there."

"Someone's gotta do something about it, once and for all! Every time I pick up the newspaper or turn on the news, some pig shot another young person of color for being in the wrong place at the wrong time and nothing more. Hell, I'm even seeing cars driving around town with that damned battle flag flapping from their antennas."

"I understand what you're saying."

"It ain't just the city workers who are suffering, this neighborhood is full of working people, most of us have two or three jobs, but every other house on my block is in foreclosure, because no one can make a living. If they call a strike, the whole damned city's gonna show up."

"Just the tip of the iceberg?"

"Yeah, and it's bigger than the one that sank the Titanic! I've been hearing rumors that there's a bill in the legislature to fund camps out in the boonies, for folks whose houses got foreclosed and they've got no place to live."

"That sounds like debtor's prisons from centuries ago."

Alva sighed, "Considering how bad it is for some of my neighbors, I believe that could be true."

"I'll see what I can find out," said Kate. "How's Benny recovering?"

"He's probably walking around with a concussion but I can't keep him down. He went off to talk to his people about the walkout they were planning. I pleaded with him to stay out of it but he's not one to cower and hide."

"No, he seemed like a decent, honest, hard-working guy to me," said Kate. "Listen, I have to go back to Atlanta tonight but let me give you my number. I'd really like to talk to him sometime, when he's feeling up to it."

"He really appreciated your kindness, Miss Crocket. Me too."

"Just doing what's right. Got a pencil?"

"Yeah."

"404-555-7615."

"Got it."

"Okay, take care of yourself, those kids, and your brother…and know I'm thinking about you."

"Thanks. You have a safe trip."

"Bye."

She hung up the phone and noticed Jessie leaning against the door jam. A tear trickled down her cheek.

He held up his empty mug, "I didn't mean to intrude."

She hugged him and poured coffee from the carafe, "'I was rollin' down Highway Forty-One', as Dickie Betts of the Allman Brothers used to sing, two nights ago and stopped for gas. Somehow, I got turned around on a side road and almost ran over a man who was lying at the edge of the pavement. I stopped the car and found that he was bound and had been badly beaten. He said he got jumped by two police officers and taken to an empty house, where he was roughed up and threatened by a very large man, before they dumped him up near Federton."

"Does trouble follow you around?"

"Not usually. Anyway, I drove him to his sister's house and was just checking on him."

"Why would the cops want to beat him up?"

"I think he said he works as a landscaper for the city, but no one on the payroll has had a raise in seven years and they're all struggling just to make ends meet. I guess they were planning a strike of all city workers and someone didn't like the idea too much. His sister told me that all the working-class families are having the same problems."

"This could turn into a big fat kettle of worms, real quick," replied Jessie, sipping from his mug. "I teach underprivileged kids during the summer and we have to expand every year because more and more kids qualify."

"Yeah, the lovely man at the gallery told me a little bit about your summer arts program."

"Well, I'm kind of tied in to that community and everyone's aware that this racial undercurrent occasionally bubbles to the surface but simmers incessantly, just under a vicious boil. The vast middle-class of our parent's generation is rapidly sliding into poverty. The jobs numbers might be improving but far too many people are being forced to accept part-time, no-benefits employment slinging hamburgers or cleaning rooms, just to have some money coming in, because there are no other jobs to be had. Even the industrial manufacturing companies only offer part-time, no-benefit jobs. I need to talk to your friend."

"It makes me sad that the whole country is going through the same thing. When are we, as a nation, going to stand up to poverty, bigotry, and racism and put an end to it, once and for all?"

Jessie grinned, "The problem isn't really with the color of a person's skin, the problem is that ignorant people are afraid of anything and anyone who isn't exactly like them. Hate binds them together and the more enemies the merrier...black people, brown people, immigrant people, the Federal Government, and anyone who isn't from these parts or doesn't believe in the twisted religious nonsense their preachers are spouting...and well-cultivated fear drives them to act on those irrational emotions. It's 'us' and 'them' and everything that's wrong in the world has to be their fault."

"Merge politics and religion, add an economic hiccup with a drop in employment, and you've created a primordial soup that's destined to explode. We see the oppression all around us but, I guess, we're too smug to realize that we could be next."

"There's a story that needs to be written."

"It wouldn't surprise me to find that story unfolding right here, in the very near future." She kissed him, "And, somehow, I have a suspicion that you're going to be right in the middle of it."

"It's a better cause than tossing footballs to make fans cheer and tons of money for the gamblers, with no benefit for the players."

~

Jessie followed Kate up the Tamiami Trail to the airport, deposited her rental, and carried her bag into the terminal. They stopped short of security to kiss, long and slow. He whispered, "I'm glad you decided to hunt up an old friend."

"I don't want this to end," replied Kate holding him close.

"We're just getting started," laughed the artist. "Go file your story and, the next time you have a break, come back."

"I will…and I'll call you tonight, when I get home."

"Happy trails," said Jessie, with a final kiss.

She passed through the scanners, waved, and disappeared down the concourse. Jessie strolled out through the lobby and across the drive to the parking lot, to climb into the bus. He inserted the key and sat there, staring across rows of cars, parked in endless orderly lines, to an extra bold EXIT sign, with a pulsing orange arrow, pointing to freedom on the open road, after a small toll.

Once he escaped his past life, he had no desire to go back, but he always regretted running out on Kate, the one person who cared about the damaged human hiding inside the quarterback. His initial reaction, when she first appeared in the driveway petting Gracie, was heart-pounding shame. He was embarrassed by his selfish immaturity, while his heart was bursting with joyous astonishment that this precious phantom from the past, who held the key to healing his soul, was resurrected from painful memories best left in that dark cubby in the back of his brain.

He got out of the VW bus and walked back into the airport, to find a pay phone. He reached into his pocket, to retrieve a folded sheet of paper with the phone number in her distinctive script, and dialed. After the third ring, a woman's voice answered, "Hello?"

"Hello, my name is Jessie Cotton and I was wondering whether I might speak to Benny Young?"

"Are you Jessie Cotton, the artist?" inquired the voice.

"Yes, Ma'am, I am."

"Oh, my three children attended your camp for the past two summers and they just loved every minute of it. My only complaint is that I can't seem to keep enough supplies around here for them to work with."

"I take great joy in working with the kids and I'm glad they've continued to create. I hope you'll send them back next summer. I try to teach them that you can make art out of anything."

"I don't mean to be uppity, but why do you want to speak to my brother?"

"Well, first, what's your name?"

"I'm Alva, Alva Thompson."

"Nice to meet you," replied Jessie. "I believe you know a woman by the name of Kate Crocket? She told me what happened and gave me this number."

"Well, he's gone to talk to his little buddy."

"What little buddy?"

"The guy who's got everyone stirred up, Sammy Ball."

"I know him, do you know his address?"

"I can look it up, hang on a minute." The phone went 'clunk' on a wooden table and he could hear pages fluttering, before she returned, "Here it is, 2150 Alameda. That's over on the west side of the highway."

"I'll find it and thanks for your help. I'm sure we'll be talking again soon," said Jessie.

"You watch out what you're getting your white-self into, Mr. Cotton, this has already turned ugly. It ain't just the city workers, it's all of us."

"That's why I want to help."

He hung up the phone, trotted out to the parking lot, and paid the toll, before heading south on Forty-One. The little bus turned on Twenty-Second and pulled over in front of the third house down on Alameda. Jessie hopped out and walked around to the entrance of a charming little stucco bungalow, with cedar beams and wood shingles on the roof, that looked out through a forest of palm trees to the bay and the keys beyond.

He knocked twice and the door creaked open a crack, then more to reveal a diminutive Sammy Ball staring up at him incredulously. "What are you doing here?"

"I heard the story of Benny Young. Can I come in?"

"Sure, I'd be honored,' said Sammy holding the door open.

Jessie noticed his painting, 'Reprise', hanging above the couch, looking rather lonely on an otherwise unadorned beige wall. "What a cool little house and the view is incredible. I'd love to paint it at sunset sometime."

"I'm lucky to live here. Won't you join us on the porch?"

Jessie followed the little man out to meet Benny Young, who got up painfully to offer his hand. "I'm pleased to meet you and sorry about what you've been through."

The young black man settled back into the lawn chair, "I appreciate your sympathy but how did you know about any of this?"

"An old friend, Kate Crocket, looked me up and gave me the brief version of the story."

Sammy interrupted, "Can I get you anything?"

"No, I'm good, thanks, but I do want to understand what's going on."

Both men started to speak but Benny said, "You tell your part and I'll tell mine."

"Fair enough," said Sammy. "Long story short, most city employees, even senior workers, get paid less than minimum wage and none of us has had a raise in seven years. A group of us got together to talk about how to raise awareness and create some action to solve the problem. Our conclusion was that a one-day strike might start the ball rolling in the right direction and the publicity would provide some protection for everyone."

"That protection can't happen, until we get the press involved. I'm proof of that," added Benny.

"Has anyone gone directly to the mayor?" asked Jessie.

"No, but requests have been sent through every department and the response is always the same, there's no money in the budget," replied Sammy. "I have stacks of plans for developments that have gone up in the past few years and ought to be paying huge taxes to the city. Where's all that money going?"

"That's a good question," said Jessie. "How many people are directly involved in this?"

"Maybe a couple of dozen," said Benny. "We were supposed to contact as many people as we could for another meeting on Wednesday but, after what they did to me, I'm pretty sure everyone else will be too scared to take a chance."

"Have you got an attorney involved?"

Sammy replied, "Someone was supposed to be looking into that but I haven't heard one way or the other."

"I guess the next question is, what do you guys want to do about all of this?"

The men glanced at each other, before Benny said, "I want to kick someone's ass, several someones."

The little man took a sip of beer from a bottle and grinned, "This tyranny is going to continue against what must be hundreds, maybe thousands of people, who are doing their best to make this city function - from the trash collectors, to the landscapers, to the office workers, cops and firemen and the staff at the hospital. We, and just about every other worker in the city, are struggling just to pay our bills and put food on the table. Adding what those thugs did to Benny, I think everyone should stand up and make the citizens understand what's really going on here."

"There's strength in numbers," said Jessie. "If enough people show up, the cops won't be able to get out of line."

"So, how do we get the word out?" asked Sammy.

"First, I'll design a little notice that you can pass around to all the workers but I'll need to know the where and when."

"We had the last meeting at the VFW but someone, either from our group or an employee who works there, ratted us out. That's the only way the cops could have known anything about it."

"Then we'll need to find some other place that's private," said Sammy.

"There's an empty storefront next to my friend's gallery out on St. Michael's, maybe we could borrow it for an evening. Could you guys rustle up some chairs?"

"Sure."

"Okay, I'll get the flier together and call a friend of mine over at Channel 7. I also know someone at the paper, maybe we can get some coverage." He looked from one to the other, "Are you guys sure you want get into this?"

"Yeah, man, let's rock these bastards," said Benny.

He pulled his little camera from his jacket pocket, "I want to take some pictures of you, for evidence, if we need it."

"Have at it, brother," said the battered man, sitting up straighter and looking defiant.

Jessie shot a few frames, "Okay, now, cool it with the look. Give me the scared kid, who's looking over his shoulder every time he walks down the street."

The squint around Benny's eyes softened and his jaw went slack. Click, flash, click, flash.

Sammy said, "I'm nearing retirement but if I have to go, I'd rather go out swinging."

"Game on," smiled the former quarterback.

~

Jessie taped a sheet of paper to the drawing board and set up the crop marks with a T-square for a little tri-fold pamphlet that could be passed out discreetly, not only to city employees but underpaid workers throughout the county. *"Maybe, the best protection the strikers could have is mass.*

The cops could crush a couple-hundred protesters but they might be hesitant to attack thousands."

The phone jangled and Gracie perked up from her perch next to his chair. He picked up the handset, "Hello."

"Jessie, it's Kate. I made it home safe and sound but, somehow, my beautiful little apartment seems kind of cold and empty. My trip to your lovely city was seventy-two hours of emotional chaos but I don't think I'd change much of it, even if I could."

"I miss you too," smiled the artist, rubbing Gracie's ear. "Gracie agrees."

"She's so sweet. I have to admit that I'm envious of your relationship with her."

"I think we saved each other."

"What's happening on your end?"

"Well, I just got back from getting to know your friend and I'm designing a little flier they can hand out for their meeting."

"I knew you'd get sucked in," laughed Kate. "How's Benny?"

"Hook, line, and sinker, especially after seeing your guy. I took pictures because he looks worse than I did after the Orange Bowl."

"Yeah, now, you see why I had to try to help him. The passenger seat in the rental was all bloody when I turned it in. I was afraid they'd think I murdered someone or something."

"Well, I haven't had much time to really think about all of this but it strikes me that this problem isn't just city workers, it's the whole lower-middle class, and I'm wondering whether we could expand the scope a little bit to draw attention to the dirty little conspiracy that's driving these hardworking people into desperation and poverty?"

"Now you're trying to piss off not only the city fathers, but every employer in the area."

"Maybe that's a good thing," replied Jessie.

"Maybe that could get you smack dab in the middle of a giant quagmire! This is dangerous stuff, especially when the folks who think they have some ecclesiastical right to run everything, get pissed off."

"We went to the University of Wisconsin, we know how to organize a protest."

"Yeah, our students are famous for standing up for a worthy cause in a big way."

"And tearing up State Street, in the process," laughed Jessie. "So, what's so different about this?"

"Not much, really. This is silent oppression but no less deadly than bombs being dropped on innocent people thousands of miles away," mused Kate. "What you really need is publicity to build sympathy in the community."

Jessie smiled, "What we need is someone who can write a series of stories…"

"I'm here not there."

"So, maybe you offer a more honest perspective than some local reporter, who's in someone's pocket. Listen, the editor of the local paper is an asshole and probably sympathetic to the powers that be but the owner, Tabitha Hall, is a patron of mine. She's bought a half-dozen of my paintings and contributes a major portion of the working funds for the kids' art camp every summer. I bet I could get her to use her position to get your stories on the front page."

"I'd have to spend some time there, working on background."

"I could probably find you a place to stay."

"Let's think about all of this overnight. Besides, I'm out of here on Thursday to cover another grand opening in Charleston and have to get the story to my editor by the first of the week. Then I've got a week off."

"Done."

Mavis removed her reading glasses and sat back in the oversized chair in the conference room of the newly completed corporate suite at the back of The Commons complex. The large window behind her overlooked the grand boulevard sweeping down to the marina, flanked by regimented arcs of royal palms. She looked up at Ripley Tanger, frumpy designated headmaster of the new school, and hulking Jimbo Combs, "I think your concept for the curriculum is brilliant and I agree that community service should be an integral part of the program."

"It makes sense to concentrate our efforts on younger children, before they enter their teenage years, when they're still open to ideas and concepts that will form a philosophical foundation for establishing their place and their responsibility in determining the future of civilization," said Tanger.

Combs added, "While we make every effort to present history, science, economics, and all the rest with complete and unadulterated accuracy, the sequence of their coursework will lead them to not only comprehend the future, but embrace their part in its creation."

"What blows me away is the breadth of subject matter. This is about as close to a classical Victorian education as you can get," said Mavis.

Tanger smiled, "Everything from ancient history and classic languages to art, music, upper level mathematics, economics, the sciences, current events, and social media. Today's educational track is narrowly focused and unidirectional. Students are forced to choose a major before they've had an opportunity to sample the vast variety of subjects they might want to pursue. We want these young people to think on multiple levels, see problems from a variety of perspectives, and find solutions that provide the most favorable outcomes."

"They must be passionate about their missions in life or all of our efforts will be for naught," said Combs. "I teach people all over the world how to be confident and secure within themselves but the one thing that I can't teach them is how to be happy and content with the here and now."

Mavis grinned, "Happiness is not about stuff."

Jimbo roared, "Spoken by someone in your position, that should be laughable, but I understand exactly where you're coming from. Every generation teaches their children to expect more from their world than the parents might ever hope to achieve in the present. At some point, that expectation becomes completely unattainable and we wonder why so many people are frustrated and unhappy?"

"Because their goals are and always will be beyond their grasp. That's like trying to run up the down escalator," said Mavis. "No matter how fast you run, you're always moving backwards."

"Well put," laughed Tanger. "I've assembled a list of candidates for teaching positions and I'll start the interviews as soon as possible. I've also started acquiring sample texts for each course in the curricula and I would suggest that we plan a review in about four weeks."

"Agreed," said Mavis. "I spent yesterday afternoon with the architects and the final plans for the school are very near completion."

"Did they incorporate our changes?" asked Combs.

"Yes, almost all of them, including transmitters in every room. Once we approve the final drawings, they'll start pouring foundations immediately."

"Bravo!" said Ripley Tanger. "If they can stay on schedule, we might be able to welcome our first class by the beginning of September."

"I'll make sure it's a priority," said Mavis, standing. "You know, I appreciate all that you're doing."

Jimbo Combs knew how to mask his desires by controlling every situation but Tanger, a rather mousy intellectual and perfect for his position, fumbled a sheaf of notes to mask the bulge in his pants, as he shook her hand a moment too long.

After they left, she grabbed a golf cart to drive down the sweeping concourse to the marina. Carpenters were erecting hundreds of houses and whole neighborhoods were blooming in every direction. They were followed by electricians, plumbers, sheetrock installers, and finish crews, who moved with military precision.

She found Tate and Rupert Dent standing at the top of the marina complex, which was being built into a small mountain that had been sculpted into an organic layer cake of facilities. The 'Bait and Tackle Shop' overlooked the docks with a snack bar and elaborate pool behind, the sports bar and discotheque occupied the second level and opened onto an adult pool, and 'The Clambake', a five-star seafood restaurant, was perched on top, looking out on the bay.

She pulled up behind the men and Tate walked over for a hug. Dent offered a hand to help her out of the cart.

"I can't believe how high we are," said Mavis. "The view's going to be fabulous from the restaurant."

"That's why we designed it this way," replied Rupert. "Guests, seated on the veranda, will be enchanted by the environment and the ambiance."

"Let's hope the menu proves worthy," laughed Tate.

Mavis pointed across the water, "Who owns that land over there?"

"I don't know but we can find out," replied Dent. "Why do you ask?"

"It's just scrub jungle now but, if we bought it, we could make it into a scenic park, which would be much nicer to look at."

"I'll see what I can find out."

"Great!" smiled the beauty. "Either of you gents interested in some lunch?"

"As a matter of fact, I'm starving and I heard that the chefs from the Dolphin Run are serving samples out of the catering kitchen."

"Oooo, that sounds wonderful. Let's go check it out!"

Rupert shook hands and said, "I've got to meet with Milton Fore about these changes, so I'll catch up with you later."

"Thanks for your help," said Tate, turning to Mavis. "How'd your meetings go?"

"Things are cooking with the school. The outline for the curriculum is really good and Tanger's interviewing teachers and selecting textbooks. Jimbo Combs is taking a sabbatical from his church to work full-time on the re-education program and hopes to have a working draft in the next couple of weeks." She hugged his arm, "But the best news is that Fore thinks they can have the structure finished in time to welcome students next fall."

"That's terrific," said Tate. "Rupert just told me that we're more than two weeks ahead of schedule and he thinks the pace will continue accelerating, as long as we can dodge bad weather."

"Let's pray for sunshine."

"He also said that the inspectors have been showing up more often and they're wanting to sign off on pretty much everything."

"I have no doubt that the construction folk are doing everything exactly to code but we shouldn't be getting any harassment from the city, as long as they're getting their checks."

"I have no reason to believe that we've missed a payment, because I delivered the last one myself, but I'll make sure that's all straight with the mayor."

"Good, we don't need anyone slowing down our progress."

~

The Directors stood, as Mavis strolled into the room with a big smile and hugs all around, "Gentlemen, I appreciate you for being here."

Marvin Standler, kissed her cheek, "We're putty in your hands."

"I just carry around my own floorshow!" laughed Mavis. "Please be seated."

Everyone took a chair around the granite conference table. A waiter poured coffee and left the room.

Mavis stood, "I'm pleased to report that construction at SunnyBreeze is actually ahead of schedule and, if the weather cooperates, we should be welcoming our first guests in the spring."

Polite applause.

She continued, "We're considering three other properties for our next resort and I should have more detailed information the next time we meet. In addition, the architectural plans for the school complex have been finalized and construction will commence immediately. I reviewed the curricula with our Headmaster, Ripley Tanger, and I was more than impressed by the breadth and depth of the coursework. Our students will have a diverse intellectual base and the skills to put that knowledge to practical use. My hope is that this might become the model to rejuvenate public education from a mad rush to mediocrity to preparing young people to become responsible corporate citizens. They are the future."

"Agreed!" yelled Erwin Nash.

"I believe we've made a good beginning," said Sloan, "but I'm curious about what you've accomplished, since last we met?

Standler glanced around the room and stood, "I'm pleased to report that the planning group has identified one-hundred and fourteen initial inner-city projects, where conditions are conducive to installing eco-friendly, secure housing communities with all the core necessities, like a grocery store that sells real food, a fully staffed clinic and pharmacy, schools and job-training, and room for green space and a community garden. Residents will be chosen from applicants for positions at our nearby manufacturing or distribution centers and priority will be given to those who demonstrate ability and need. Planning is underway for development of several of the most promising sites."

"Bravo," said Mavis. "Each of these communities offers a chance to study how people adapt to the designed environment, but more important, how they take possession and make it their own. We'll understand a lot more, by the time you expand the program into the second phase."

"This is completely opposite of my normal mode of operation. My business is about taking things apart, to mine the most precious bits and pieces for a fat profit. I liken it to thieves stripping down a car for parts," laughed Marvin. "This, on the other hand, involves envisioning how people live from their bedrooms to their work environments and how they integrate everything in between. We have a flock of academics and designers working off the Japanese model of a lifelong bond between worker and employer, with some conceptual improvements."

"That whole standard works for a portion of the population but there has to be room for the mavericks, creatives, and the artists," said Harvey Sacks. "If we intend to remake society, we need to provide for the free-thinkers or we'll be fulfilling the warning of '1984'. Let the book burning begin!"

"I agree," said Timmons. "There are folks who need to live in the wilderness, they couldn't survive in a city for more than a few days. Same goes for farmers, ranchers, and fishermen too."

Ned Flint wiped his nose with a handkerchief, "Forgive me, I must be allergic to something in the air. Anyway, the problem with the concept is that there will always be exceptions and there will always be people who do not choose to participate, no matter what you offer, no matter how brutal the coercion."

"Let's not lose sight of the real purpose for our efforts," said Mavis. "The economy is failing and millions of people are falling into poverty. That's where we start, the inner cities and communities that have lost all hope. Where we can't install a factory or whatever, we buy out small businesses or whole industries and let the former owners use their expertise to run the enterprise at peak performance. Everybody wins."

"There are plenty of 'us' who are dead set against everything we're trying to do," said Nash. "I'm already hearing flak from associates, who have heard rumors of our little club, and they're all screaming that I'm becoming a bloody socialist!"

"I hate to break it to you, brother," laughed Standler, "but you have!"

"I think we should keep our plans hush-hush," said Mavis. "It would be far too easy for the naysayers to launch a publicity campaign to condemn our efforts and muck up our progress."

"Let's hope they fear the reverse, our public relations people exposing the campaigns they've bought and paid for over the past couple of decades," said Timmons. "Nobody wins a dirty-laundry war and everyone looks stupid and incompetent, but we need to account for the fact that we're competing with a very tight, well-financed confederacy, who are hell-bent on destroying the middle class, so they might resurrect feudalism."

"The only way to defeat them is to lure their supporters to our cause by proving that we can deliver," said Mavis.

"We're creating a closed financial system that will have to function in consort with the open markets around the world, while maintaining stability for all those citizens who choose to participate." Sacks looked around the room, "I'd guess that, if you tallied up all the industries and holdings represented by our little group, we already control a fair percentage of the world economy. If you add those who are sympathetic to our intent, it's that much more, but even with all that influence the question remains, if we stick our fingers in the dyke, can we actually save the world from impending implosion?"

Mavis' tone was cold, her eyes focused, "I think the better question is, what will happen if we don't?"

Chapter Six

A strong fish plunged deep and Johnny's reel whined, as his line ripped across the bow. Jessie dropped his rod on the bench seat and cranked the putting outboard to follow the prize catch. The boy kept tension on the tip of his rod and reeled a few turns with each change in direction. The duel went on for twenty minutes before the stubborn fish zipped under the boat. The artist cut the engine but the line went limp and Johnny tumbled into the bilge water sloshing around the bottom of the boat.

Jessie reached to help him up, "Are you alright? That was an incredible battle, I'm sorry it got away."

"That's okay," replied the boy, drying his bottom with a towel. "You taught me that catching something might be the prize but it's the fight between the fisherman and the fish that makes it fun."

"That's true," laughed Jessie. "We've already got a nice grouper and a couple of snapper, let's head down and see what's happening with SunnyBreeze."

"I'm almost afraid to look," said Johnny, pulling the rope to start the engine and head south. He slowed, as the dingy cleared the mangroves. The two-mile desert was populated with dense clusters of homes sprouting from the area around the central complex to cover every corner of the property not already paved. Landscape crews installed mature royal palms and groves of pines, followed by sod machines unrolling endless spools of St. Augustine grass. "Those houses are so close together, they might as well be connected."

"And none of those trees grow here on their own."

"I'll bet birds won't even come in for a visit, there's no cover and nothing to eat except maybe chinch bugs in that grass."

"You're probably right," said Jessie, shaking his head in disgust. "Let's see what they've done with the marina."

Pilings for the docks were lined up like a regiment of white sentinels marching out into the bay and the sweeping walls of the complex were stacked three stories tall. Jessie admired the architect's vision, if not his placement. "That's almost good looking."

"Yeah, but it doesn't fit with anything else on the key," replied the boy, turning the boat around. "Hey, what are those stakes on the other side?"

The artist pulled out the binoculars to scan the shoreline, "They're more surveyor's stakes."

"Which means they're planning to destroy that mangrove too? When's it enough?"

"I don't know but, if they do develop that piece of land, our favorite alligators are going to be looking for a new place to live. Let's go check on them."

The runabout eased up the shallow channel and barely slipped into the pair of pools, when both fishermen started gagging at the stench from the carcasses of three rotting alligators floating upside down against the far shore.

Johnny screamed, "You murderers! You killed our friends!"

Jessie wrapped his arms around the sobbing boy and wept with him.

"How'd they get in here anyway?" wailed the boy.

"There's a fisherman's path a couple of hundred yards south. I found it when I was looking for a location to paint."

"If someone doesn't stop them, they're going to kill off everything."

The following morning, the bus pulled into the long circular drive in front of towering columns, planters overflowing with flowers, and three-storied peach-colored Mediterranean-style buildings overlooking a grand amphitheater and a band shell, textured and painted to resemble a gigantic scallop.

Jessie parked and marched through hustling construction crews to find the corporate offices at the top of a staircase at the back of the complex. He entered ornate double doors to find a blond receptionist behind a swooping curve of mahogany.

"How can I help you?"

"Is Tate Sloan in?"

"He is, but I'm afraid he's in an executive meeting."

Jessie hesitated, "Interrupt that meeting and tell him Jessie Cotton is waiting in the lobby."

"I'm afraid I can't interrupt. If you'd care to wait, they should break for lunch in an hour or so."

"Either you pick up that phone and do as I've asked or I'll start tearing doors off their hinges, until I find that son-of-a-bitch. Do I make myself clear?"

She picked up the receiver and Jessie had to wonder whether she was dialing Tate the Snake or the police. The blond placed the handset back on the cradle and looked up, bewildered, "He said he'll be right down."

Within moments, a heavier but still fit Sloan emerged from a side door with a big smile, "It really is you! How are you?"

"I'm pissed and we're going to have a little chat."

"You're not still moping about the Orange Bowl?"

"That's ancient history but what you're doing to the ecosystem on this key is another matter. Now, do you want to talk privately or shall I start hanging dirty laundry out to dry?"

The toothy smile disappeared, "Come up to my office. Can I get you anything…coffee, tea, a stiff shot of something?"

"No thanks."

Tate opened the door and led Jessie up a broad flight of stairs to a lavish office with a wall of windows overlooking The Commons to the dunes. "Won't you have a seat?"

"Thanks, but I think I'll stand."

"What can I do for you?"

"Do you have any idea of the damage you're doing?"

"We're building one of the finest resorts in the world. That's what we're doing."

"You're destroying the mangroves and chasing off the wildlife that's inhabited this key for millennia. Now you're starting to gobble up the land on the other side of the bay."

"Yeah, we're going to develop it into a park."

"Well, your guys murdered three alligators that were friends of mine, in a little pond over there, which pisses me off, and, oh yeah, that's illegal and immoral. They're a protected species."

"I heard you disappeared but I'm not surprised you ended up hanging out in the jungle with gators."

"You were always quick with the quip but lacking in character," replied Jessie, struggling to maintain his composure.

"What do you want?"

"I want you to ditch your plans for the other side of the cove."

"Why would I do that?"

"Because it's the right thing to do. The wildlife around here is way more vital and important to this area than your profits. If your guests want a taste of nature, why not show them the real thing instead of all this plastic fantastic bullshit you've put in around here?"

"Well, for starters, liability. If one of your friends decided to chomp on some little kid for lunch, we'd have a big problem."

"Do you honestly believe that the local population of critters is going to move down the coast just because you say so?" asked Jessie incredulously. "You're trespassing on their turf not the other way around."

Tate grinned, "Call it progress."

"I'll call it bad taste and shoddy construction built by a fool."

"Well, there's no chance in hell that we're going to stop construction, because you don't like our style."

"There's a better way to accomplish your goals without destroying the habitat and replacing it with plants that don't even grow here."

"We're creating everyone's vision of a tropical paradise."

"Over my dead body."

"If you say so," laughed Sloan. "You were a loser back in the day and you still are."

"And you're still an asshole who never had much respect for anything or anyone that didn't buy into your narcissist nonsense." He turned to leave, "This meeting is a courtesy and a warning. You haven't heard the last of this."

"I've got busloads of lawyers, if you want to play, but I promise to keep you tied up in court until I've sucked every last dime out of your future and, by then, I'll have what I want anyway. There's no way you can win."

"Watch who you threaten, you might regret it."

Jessie was waiting at the gate with a hug and a kiss, when Kate arrived at the airport. "I'm glad you're back."

"I'm glad to be back but, from the sound of your voice, I'm betting there's a bit more in there than you're just glad to see me."

"There is," said the artist. "I haven't seen you in years and you can still nail me in the first ten seconds of a conversation."

"I'm rusty, I used to be able to get it just from your body language."

"Do you have a bag?"

"Just one."

They strolled down the corridor, picked up her suitcase, and headed out to the bus. "I stocked up the fridge and cleaned up the house."

"Does this mean you're glad to see me?" smirked Kate, hugging his arm.

"Yeah, on so many levels."

"So, what's up?"

"Well, the deeper I get into all of this, the more stories I hear from ordinary working people who are on the verge of losing everything they've worked for, people who wonder how they're going to put food on the table, let alone keep a roof over their heads…and it isn't just a few here and there. It's almost every neighborhood east of the highway."

"I take it the rich folk live between Forty-One and the bay?"

"Prime real estate."

"Now that you mention real estate, I asked Tate Sloan whether they were using any local contractors out at SunnyBreeze and he said that all the construction was being handled by Simons and Sons, which is owned by his father-in-law."

"Doesn't surprise me. I had a little tête-à-tête with him this morning. It didn't go well."

"I'm surprised you even talked to him."

Jessie grinned, "He didn't leave me much choice. They've staked out the land on the other side of the bay for a 'nature park' and their surveyors shot our friendly alligators, just because they could."

"I thought they were protected," replied Kate.

"Bastards can claim they felt threatened," sighed Jessie. "The bigger picture is that they're going to destroy another big patch of jungle and who knows how many critters in the process. It's got to stop someplace."

"So, you confronted him?"

"Yeah, I thought about just punching him out, on general principals, but I'm saving that for some appropriate opportunity in the future. He threatened to bog me down in lawyers, if I get in his way."

The reporter smirked, "He didn't go to the University of Wisconsin."

"Until you showed up, I was perfectly happy with my simple life of painting and fishing in the afternoons with Johnny. Now I've been drafted into creating some sort of social justice and there's no escape, until I figure out how to get all these different pieces into play. We're going to have to be really clever to get through this whole thing clean."

Kate burst out laughing, "We?"

"You're here, so you're in," replied Jessie. "I'm starting to get this foggy vision of how things might pan out but I definitely need your input and your talents as a writer. I spoke with Tabitha Hall and she might be mega-rich but she's still got a conscience. As far as she's concerned, this is her town and all the citizens are her people. She said that if she approves of your work, she'll make sure it gets a spread on the front page."

"No pressure there. We need to start with a point of view, a way to tie all of these parts into an emotional tapestry that makes people want to get involved but, in the end, there has to be a solution…a way to solve the problems and a path to binding the community back together."

Jessie looked at her, "My summer program, 'Art's Important', the whole city gets behind that."

"There you go! Let's start with Benny and the city workers and expand out from there."

"They're meeting tomorrow night in an empty storefront out on St. Michael's Circle."

"I want to be there."

"Fine, but you're going to have to meet my friend Johnny first. He's coming by after school."

"I'm looking forward to it."

Johnny eased the little boat into the slip, tied it off, and got slobbered with Gracie kisses, when he tried to climb onto the dock. They trotted up the winding path to the terrace, where he found a tall blond woman writing in a notebook. "You must be Kate. You're beautiful."

Kate blushed and extended her hand, "Thank you for the compliment and I am most happy to make your acquaintance."

Jessie appeared with a tray bearing a pitcher of lemonade, three glasses full of ice, and a plate of cookies, "Oh, I see you two have met. What do you think?"

Johnny blurted out, "You didn't tell me she's beautiful."

The writer grinned, "I think I'm going to like your friend."

"Well, now that we've got that settled, anyone for some lemonade?"

"Sure."

"How was school today?" asked Jessie.

"We got to watch a couple of films about the solar system and galaxies. It's kind of hard to believe there's so much stuff out there and how far away it is."

"I was always impressed that anyone could figure out how far away those stars and galaxies are and which direction they're moving, and

I still don't understand how anyone could measure anything in light years," said Kate.

"If you measured it in miles, it would take a roomful of blackboards just to write all the zeroes," added Jessie, passing glasses.

"Yeah, it's just a shortcut for counting really big numbers," said the boy. "I kind of like the idea that we're all made of stardust."

"Really?"

"Yeah, everything around us is made of stuff that spewed out of an exploding star billions of years ago."

"That is kind of amazing," replied Kate.

"Mrs. Johnson is going to try to get the class together some night to look through a real telescope."

Jessie grinned, "Jupiter and Saturn are both visible in the southeast in the evening, they'd make good targets."

"Do you like math and science," asked Kate.

The boy beamed, "They're really hard but they're interesting. I'll bet people like Kepler and Einstein thought really big thoughts."

"I think people like that learn to ask big complicated questions, first, and then go looking for the answers. If you keep working at it, you'll understand what they found. Then, when you look at the stars, you can work on the next puzzles that need to be solved."

"That's the difference between having a job and having a career. You take a job to earn money but you embark on a career because that's your purpose in life," said Jessie. "I started out playing football and studying economics, before I figured out that I'm supposed to be capturing the beauty of nature on canvas and protecting it from land developers."

Johnny looked down at the ice cubes in his glass, "I'm still mad about what they did to George and his family. I don't understand why anyone would do that."

"There are lots of ignorant people in the world, who don't know any better. That doesn't excuse them but, sometimes, people do stupid things," said Kate, glancing at Jessie. "I'm sorry you lost your friends."

"Me too, getting to feed them and spend time with them was kind of an honor," replied the boy. "Jessie said that you're a writer, what do you write?"

"I write articles about fancy houses and big resorts, like SunnyBreeze, for a magazine in Atlanta." Kate smiled and sipped her lemonade, "It's a job, not a career."

"So, if you don't like what you do, why do you do it?"

"I like to write and I'm really good at it but I don't particularly like the subjects that I write about, so, I'm going to write some articles about how lots of people around here are having a hard time making ends meet."

"Yeah, my mom talks about how hard it is to pay the bills sometimes, and I wish I could help her."

"You work hard in school, that's your job," said Kate. "Be really good at it and that effort will pay you back in life, I promise."

"I've got to head back," said Johnny. "Mom wants my homework finished before dinner."

"I'm tied up tomorrow but how 'bout we go fishing on Thursday?" asked Jessie.

"Sure! I saw a school of blues on the way over here and the dolphins are back."

"They're following the shiners," replied the artist, "and that means there are more fish feeding in the bay."

The boy shook Kate's hand and Jessie followed him down to the dock, untied the lines, and dropped them into the boat, "So, what'd you think?"

"I like her a lot and she sure is pretty."

"So, you approve?"

"Yeah, but you're going to have to share her with me!" laughed Johnny, as he yanked the rope to fire up the little Johnson motor. "I'll pick you up after school on Thursday."

Jessie waved, as the boat drifted out of the slip and turned down the bay, "It's a date!"

~

Derek Rangle was leaning against the store window, with his arms crossed and a scowl accentuating the creases in his face, which resembled an aging bulldog to begin with. Jessie pulled the bus into a parking slot his sales agent was saving, amid several-hundred people milling around the Circle waiting for the empty storefront to open for the meeting.

The gallery owner shook Jessie's hand and kissed Kate on the cheek, "I'm pleased to see that our confidence turned out so well."

The writer looked at Jessie and grinned, "Turns out, he's the same guy. Only now, he's better than he was before."

"I'm glad we agree but I do have a bone to pick," replied Rangle, gazing around at the rather unsavory crowd. "I would appreciate it, if you would consider another location for your next gathering. I'm afraid they'll drive the tourists away."

Jessie patted him on the shoulder, "The tourists will be back tomorrow and this lot will be long gone. Consider the inconvenience as your contribution and civic duty and a tiny compensation for all the money I've made you."

Kate held up her notebook, "My story can ignore you or I can make you into one of the founding fathers of this social movement. It's your choice."

"But...I...?"

"Okay, I'll leave you out of it," laughed the journalist.

Rangle held out the key to the empty storefront, "You're responsible for damage."

"Relax, these people want a piece of their oppressors not your drywall."

"Fine," replied Rangle, stepping into his gallery, latching the door, and flipping over a brass 'Closed' sign.

Jessie unlocked the shop and flipped on the lights. People of every size and description rushed in to set up rows of folding chairs and several more plugged in coffee pots and opened boxes of cookies still warm from the oven.

Kate joked, "All we need is some brats and brews to crank this up a notch or two!"

"We're not ready for marches and protests."

"What no riots?"

"How about a frank discussion instead?"

Kate pouted, "You're no fun at all."

Benny and Sammy pushed through the mob and the little clerk said, "I'm thinkin' your fancy flier worked some magic."

"I think it just gave all these folks an excuse to vent their frustrations," replied Jessie, inspecting Benny's wounds. "You're looking better. How are you feeling?"

"I'm getting stronger and I'm really happy to see Kate. You saved my life."

Kate blushed and gave him a hug, "I'm just glad that you're up and about and I'd like to help, if I can."

Sammy tugged at Jessie's sleeve, "You should know that there are two squad cars parked at the entrances to the Circle."

"Yeah, I saw them when we came in and I'm hoping they're not stupid enough to barge in here."

Before he finished the sentence, Trapper Johnson, the Dolphin Bay Police Chief, and Harry Conn, the City Health Inspector, marched through the door and the chatter in the crowded room dropped to murmurs. Johnson presented his badge, "You got a license for a public gathering?"

"This is not a public gathering," replied the artist, holding up a small poster for a new gallery at this address. "This is my sponsor party."

"That's just plain...horse-hockey and you know it," snarled the chief.

"No, it's not," said Derek Rangle. "I own this property and we can entertain anyone we choose. Even someone of your limited sophistication and, I must assume, complete ignorance of the arts, has to be aware that Jessie Cotton is renowned for his landscapes and solely responsible for educating thousands of children at the 'Art's Important' camp every summer."

"Are you serving refreshments?" inquired the Health Inspector, eyeing the coffee and sweets.

"We've had them catered in for this event by these fine ladies, who happen to be professional cooks at the Sand Dollar, where I know both of you dine on a regular basis."

"What is it that you want?" asked Kate.

Johnson tipped his cap and stared at Benny for a long moment, "Just making sure that no laws are being broken and the peace is being maintained."

"I can assure you that this is and will be a peaceful assembly of art lovers," said Rangle.

The Chief and the Inspector turned to leave, "Just make sure that none of this riff-raff gets loose on the street."

With the nimble agility of a seasoned quarterback darting through a hole in the line, Jessie bulled his way in front of the two men to block the door, "Everyone in this room is a citizen of this town, people who have jobs and own property. They pay taxes and your salary, for that matter, so they deserve your respect and your protection and you can be damned sure that an assault on any of them will be documented on the front page of tomorrow morning's paper. Do I make myself clear?"

The two men pushed passed him and out the door without responding.

Marilyn Cooper, manager of the kitchen at the Sand Dollar, brought a cup of black coffee for Jessie, "I wish I had a picture of that man's face when you told him off! His skin turned beet red, his eyes bugged out, and he kept moving his jaw around, like he was trying to keep a wad of racist crud from blurting out, where everyone could see."

"I don't care who he thinks he is, everybody deserves to be treated with respect," replied the artist, sipping the coffee. "Marilyn, this my friend Kate. She's going to be writing some newspaper articles about all of this."

The cook offered a cup to the reporter, "Just tell the truth, honey, that's all we ask."

"Amen to that," said Benny.

Jessie grabbed a spoon and tapped his coffee cup, "Ladies and gentlemen, if you'll take a seat, we can get started."

The crowd settled into chairs, now randomly scattered around the room, and stood three deep around the perimeter. "I'd like to thank every one of you for having the courage to come out tonight. There are people in this community who don't want things to change. They don't want people to gather to discuss problems or to suggest, let alone demand, solutions. Benny Young is testament to that and he'll have a chance to tell his story in a few minutes.

I look around and I see lots of familiar faces. I've taught your kids at 'Art's Important', or we've helped each other out somehow, or bought something from one another, or just passed in the grocery. I'm a refugee from the frigid north, who found a little piece of paradise in Dolphin Bay and made it my home. I'm determined to protect my sanctuary from tyranny from within or the invasion of shady developers from someplace else, who destroy the natural beauty to put up shoddy construction and charge the snowbirds outrageous prices, which drive up our taxes.

My point is that there are a lot of things going on in our community that need to be addressed in an open and honest manner. That's why we're here, to talk. Not to make trouble, not to intimidate or coerce anyone, just to get the discussion started."

Sammy Ball perched on the edge of a table, "This originally started as a worker's group grumbling about earning far less than a survival wage and, from the turnout tonight, it's pretty obvious that it's not just city workers who are struggling."

A chubby woman in a pink floral blouse stood up, "There are a lot of us who can't find full-time jobs. I work out at the Hardesty plant and they only give us thirty-five hours a week, so they don't have to provide benefits and they aren't afraid to remind everyone that, if we aren't satisfied with our employment, there are plenty of folks lining up outside to take our places."

"It's the same all over," added a balding man wearing his wisdom in deep age lines, etched into his face. "Unless you're white collar, there's no jobs that pay enough to live on or provide any security for a family. They've got us over a barrel."

Jessie held up his hand, "What if no one showed up?"

"They'd fire us all!" yelled a tall girl with thick glasses in the back. "They'd just find other desperate people to take our places."

"Look around, we have a couple of hundred people here, who are all facing the same problems, and you're just the first representatives of a huge portion of the workforce. If every one of you convinces your co-workers to join our cause and they tell their friends and neighbors, we could multiply hundreds into thousands and, with enough press, turn a tiny protest into a movement!"

"Yeah, but look what happened to Bennie," said his sister, Alva.

His face was still battered and bruised but he stood proudly, defiantly, "I don't know that y'all know me, I'm Benny Young and I'm employed by the city to maintain the landscape on all the public properties. After a year of thirty-five hour weeks plus unpaid overtime, they pay us one dollar over the minimum wage. There are no raises or bonuses or advancement or paid vacations. That's it, there is no more money available for the workers and, if you want to keep your job, you keep your mouth shut.

We got together to talk about all of this a few weeks ago and the next evening I was jogging down the street, when I was jumped by two uniformed police officers, who beat me unconscious and drove me to an empty house somewhere. When I came to, a huge guy roughed me up some more, scared the crap out of me, and threatened my family, if I continued to cause trouble'.

Well, I'm scared to death and I might be a nobody, but I'm not going to stand for some racist asshole threatening my nieces and nephews. I intend to cause a whole lot of trouble! Our city is corrupt and racist and it starts at the very top. The only way we can protect each other is by expanding this campaign to involve every working person who's getting screwed."

"Amen to that, brother," shouted a burly biker with elaborate tattoos swaddling each arm.

A slender Latino raised his hand, "My wife's got the cancer, I'm working three part-time jobs, and trying to raise three small children to be decent people. I gave up sleep a long time ago because, no matter how hard I work, no matter how I scrimp, I'm further behind today than I was yesterday and I don't see any chance that it's going to change."

"Yeah," said an elderly woman waving a cane, "have you been to the grocery lately? Prices keep going up but the pay stays the same, so I get to choose between eating and taking my medicines. My boss takes off every afternoon for golf and drinks at the club. He couldn't care less about my diabetes."

A proud man in a threadbare suit rose slowly from a metal folding chair, his spine barely unwinding into an unyielding hook, "I think I speak for a fair number of people in this room, when I say, be thankful to have a job, any job. I could tell you a hundred stories of honest hardworking folks, just like you and me, struggling to just barely get along; when some little hiccup forces whole families to lose everything and end up living in a cardboard box under a bridge. It happened to me and it can happen to you!"

"Hell, I told my plant manager about a group of guys, who were taking some expensive materials out the back door," said a slender young man, with blazing black eyes and thick dark curls. "Next thing I know, there's a squad of cops with dogs searching my locker and they come up with a couple of ounces of cocaine! I've never done coke in my life but, by the time I got bailed out of jail, they'd confiscated all my belongings as evidence, including my car, got me kicked out of my apartment, my driver's license suspended, and my bank account frozen. All for telling the truth to the wrong guy."

Sammy waddled over to the man and shook his hand, "I think your story represents the plight of everyone in this room. We're all struggling against a confederacy of assholes, just to stay alive, and the only way things are going to change is to stand together and say, 'Enough!'"

"We've solicited the help of Leonard Andrews, Attorney-at-Law, and Evan Thudbury, a Certified Public Accountant. They've offered to work pro-bono and advise us on our rights," added Jessie. "I want everyone to understand that this only works, if we stick together and avoid giving the opposition any reason to escalate this into a confrontation. We are a peaceful, nonviolent movement or we are nothing at all."

Murmurs grumbled through the crowd and heads nodded their agreement.

Hank Miller stood up, "We've tried to get a meeting with the mayor or the Chair of the City Council but they put us off with excuses."

Kate responded, "Mr. Andrews and Evan Thudbury have submitted a request for the City's financial records for the past five years."

"Fat chance you'll get it," came a call.

"Actually, under the Open Records Act, they have no choice but to supply us with the requested documents," replied Andrews. "They are public information."

"Then they'll string it out," said an old codger in a maroon windbreaker. "Won't do anyone no good, if they turn it over five years from now."

"Actually, any citizen can request a copy of the budget and the financial expenditures," said Thudbury. "After all, it is your tax money that's being spent."

"When can you offer an opinion?" asked Kate.

"I should be able to come up with some general observations by your next meeting. In what, two weeks?"

"We can arrange that," said Jessie.

"Alright, then," said Sammy. "That's the place to start."

"I think we should collect everyone's contact information, where they're employed, and a short paragraph on why they're here and what talents they might offer to help the group," suggested Kate.

"Great," said Jessie. "Let's plan on another meeting in two weeks. We'll let you know if it's not going to be here. Otherwise, same time, same place."

Kate turned to Benny, "How are you getting home?"

"Alva's going to drive."

"Aren't you worried?"

"I know those bastards are watching but that's not going to stop me."

"How 'bout we follow you home and we'll get Mr. Andrews to follow Sammy back to his place, just to make sure everyone gets home safe and sound?"

"Fine," said Alva. "I'm all for what you're doing but those white-trash pigs scare me shitless and I don't like being scared."

Jessie put an arm around her shoulders, "Maybe it's time to stop being afraid."

The biker with the tattoos ambled up to the group, "How 'bout my friends and I give you an escort?"

"What friends?" asked Benny.

The biker held out his hand, "I'm Eddie Glover. I've got a bike shop over on Congress and I'm here to support the cause, because I grew up poor and too many of my friends and family have done everything right and still don't have any hope for anything better."

Benny shook, "Glad to have your help and your acquaintance."

Eddie hooked a thumb over his shoulder to five friends mooching cookies from Marilyn Cooper, "I'm thinkin' six of us oughta be enough."

Kate grinned, "Angels appear at the most opportune moments."

"You might include yourself," said Jessie.

"I'd like to get some one-on-one stories, before everyone disappears."

"Go for it."

An hour later, the bus followed a caravan of two bikers leading Alva's Chevy, two in front of Sammy's Volvo, and another pair holding back two police cars, all moving at exactly one mile-an-hour below the posted speed limit. When they hit the highway, three motorcycles escorted Sammy's car north, trailing one police car, and the remainder of the parade headed south.

"They really are paranoid, aren't they?"

Jessie shook his head, "I think information is being collected."

"Let the intimidation begin!"

"Are you sure you want to get in the middle of this, it could be even more dangerous than we thought?"

Kate held up her notebook, "Yeah, the more I hear, the more I believe in what we're trying to do but we're going to have to invest in more notebooks. This one's already stuffed and I've got plenty for at least the first two articles but I need a photo."

"How about Benny? That might be the best protection we could offer, if he's part of the first piece?"

"You might be right, I'll call him when we get back to your studio."

"Actually, I've got several shots of him right after he was attacked, on a roll in my camera. We could send it to the paper to be developed."

"Done." She turned to stare out the window.

"What?"

"I spent some time talking to a homeless woman who was too ashamed to stand up during the meeting, because she and her kids are living out of their car in one of the camps. I want to go see it."

"We can do that."

"No, I mean now."

"But…" He glanced in the mirror, "We'll need to ditch the cops."

"They'll be turning east to Alva's house, maybe we're not threatening enough to warrant an escort?"

The caravan stopped at a light and Eddie pulled up next to the bus, leaning to yell, "I'm sending Nomad with Bennie and I'll follow you."

Kate crawled over Jessie, "I want to visit the pauper's camp under the east end of the bridge at Pelican Turn. If I'm going to write these stories, I need to understand what these people, our people, are going through, when society turns its back on them."

Alva's car pulled through the intersection, followed by the police car and Nomad's bike. Glover shook his head, "Alright, follow me."

The Harley rumbled down Forty-One, then west on the causeway to the bridge. They pulled off on the service road and idled between cars and trucks jammed haphazardly in the grass along either side of the pavement; a barrier protecting a sprawling village of tents and shanties fashioned from construction scraps and cardboard. Orange flames leapt from crackling bonfires, illuminating hundreds of hungry people milling around large steaming pots that would provide the communal evening meal.

Kate pointed to the second fire, "There she is, see the woman with the purple shawl holding the baby?"

Jessie tapped the horn, to signal Eddie, and pulled just off the shoulder of the road. "I don't know what they're cooking but it sure smells good."

"Come on, let's go check this out."

"I'll tell Eddie to go on, if he wants to."

"Cool."

He walked over to the biker, "Kate wants to hang out and interview this lady, so you can take off, if you need to."

"I told Benny I was going to hang at his place tonight but I'm gonna make sure that you two lovebirds get tucked safely into your own crib, before I head over there."

"Well, then, come join us."

The two men waded through a diverse crush, blind to ethnicity or background, color or creed, or former status in the real world, for that matter. From fragile geriatrics turned out of nursing homes to despairing parents with hungry children, they shared the common curse of being trampled and abandoned by circumstances beyond their control. Neither could mistake the hope and terror clashing in the eyes of every despondent pilgrim they passed, furrowed brows could not release, during passing acknowledgements, conveying the mutual heartbreak and panic of determination fading into desperation and defeat. The challenge of survival snuffed trivial dreams dimming into some withering apparition.

Kate was talking with a tall brunette woman, cradling a gurgling baby with dancing blue eyes, when they emerged from the crowd. "I'd like you to meet Gretchen Mowery and her son, Ted." She pointed to two youngsters playing checkers near the fire, "That's William and Betty, her other two children. Gretchen, I'd like you to meet Jessie Cotton and Eddie Glover."

Gretchen bowed slightly, avoiding direct eye contact, "I'm pleased to meet you and thankful that you're trying to help."

Eddie crooked a calloused finger to lift her chin, "Missy, you have nothing to be ashamed of and don't ever let anyone try to convince you otherwise. You're trying to take care of these kids and, maybe, you just need a little help."

Her dark eyes sparkled in the firelight, "Thank you, that's very kind."

"I'm thinkin' a little kindness and common decency would go a long way towards making things right in our world and that's why I'm trying to help out."

An older woman in a tattered pink gown wandered through the crowd carrying five or six steaming cups in each hand, crying, "Coffee, hot coffee!"

She stopped, offering a mug to Kate, "We know who you are and we're all thankful that you're trying to expose what the disgusting fat cats are doing to American workers. Just tell the truth, honey, that's all we can ask."

"That's exactly why we're here tonight."

"Then, we all thank you," she offered cups to Jessie and Eddie and wandered off into the darkness between the fires.

Kate turned to Gretchen, "So, how did you end up here?"

Waves of chestnut hair veiled her face, as she bowed her head and whispered, "It all happened so fast, I was married, had a nice little house and three healthy kids. My old man had a pretty good job out at the Hardesty plant, paid our bills, and worked his ass off to care for the family, until they laid him off, on a Friday afternoon, and he got killed in a wreck with a drunk driver on his way home, before he could tell me the bad news."

"Oh, my god."

"I didn't have a job, couldn't afford groceries or the rent, let alone child care, and it wasn't long before the slimy landlord showed up to collect. When I couldn't pay, he told me he might be able to put off evicting us for a few days, if I'd take care of his 'personal needs'. When I spit in his face, he slugged me, kicked us out, and locked the house up, with all our stuff inside. I tried to reason with him but he called me a slut and said, if I didn't get my disgusting children off his property, he was going to have me arrested for trespassing and assault. A friend brought us here and we don't have any money to leave."

Kate wrapped an arm around her, "Don't you have any family?"

"The only one left is a drugged-out sister, who lives on a commune out in Oregon someplace. I haven't heard from her in ten years. Hell, I don't even know if she's still alive."

"Do your kids go to school?" asked Jessie.

"William should be in the second grade and Betty qualifies for preschool but I can't afford the gas to get them there."

Gruff Eddie said, "Look, I don't want to sound like your scumbag landlord, but I've got a space above my shop that nobody's using. It's kinda rough but it wouldn't take much to get it cleaned up enough for you and the kids. We'd just need to find some furniture."

"I couldn't accept your charity."

"Honey, that's not charity, that's common sense. Think about it and I'll take you over there tomorrow to check it out, if you want?"

She looked into his eyes for a long moment, "Okay, you seem like someone I could trust and, besides, it can't be any worse than this."

Jessie gazed around at the hundreds of desperate people wandering about the encampment of people who had real lives, homes and jobs, hopes and dreams that were demolished by the cruelties of life and despicable scoundrels, who value profits over humanity.

Gretchen pointed, "You might want to talk to Walter, the guy with the bow tie. He brought up a complaint against his corporate manager for bribery. They didn't just fire him, they destroyed his life. And sweet Barbara, who said 'no' to a vice president's sexual demands, or Harry James, over there. His family had Five-and-Dime stores up and down the coast, until the big box stores stole all his customers, shuttered his businesses, and, for a final insult, bought up the last of his inventory at auction for eight cents on the dollar. So, when he'd paid everyone off, there was nothing left! Every person out here has a story that's sadder and more amazing than anything you could make up."

"Let's see if we can make a difference in your story," said Kate, hugging her arm. "Eddie's kind of crusty around the edges but I'm betting he's a decent man, he stepped up to protect all of us from the cops tonight."

~

At two-fifteen in the morning, the concussion of the explosion of the gas tank in his beloved Volvo 529 tossed Sammy Ball out of bed. Barefoot, wearing baby-blue pajamas, he stumbled outside and around to the driveway, to find the car engulfed in an inferno and fire licking at the roof of the house. Stunned by the ferocity of the blaze, he turned to the squeal of tires, as a dark pickup truck peeled down the street.

The stout little man staggered inside to call the Fire Department, then back to fight the flames with a garden hose but, by the time they arrived, black smoke billowed from burning tar on the gravel roof.

Firemen doused the flames with two hoses and he could only hope that the little cottage and some of his possessions would survive, including his treasured 'Reprise'. Damage to the roof and water flooding inside would force him to find someplace safe to stay and he could only hope that the insurance would pay for the repairs.

The Captain asked, "How'd this get started?"

"It was arson. The explosion of the gas tank in my car blew me out of bed and by the time I ran out here, the carport was blazing."

"We'll start an investigation. Can you think of anyone who might have a motive?"

"Yeah, the cops and the mayor."

"Why do you say that?"

"Because I attended a meeting last night of city and other workers who are organizing to protest pitifully unfair wages."

The man looked at him for a long moment, "I might be inclined to join you but I'm union and I'd probably lose my job."

"Well, I just lost my car and part of my house and I'm pissed," said Sammy, as two officers emerged from a gray police car at the end of the drive.

"You'll have to fill out a report but I'll let you know what I find out in my investigation."

"I appreciate your honesty," replied the little clerk.

The first cop tipped his hat, "Officers Stanton and Creed, how'd this get started?"

"It was arson. I heard an explosion and came out to find the car and the roof on fire. I saw a dark colored pickup speeding down the street."

"Didn't get a tag number by chance?" asked the second officer.

"We see a lot of this," said the first policeman, "and most of the time people are trying to collect the insurance."

"Hey, I'm the victim here!" replied Sammy. "So, let's keep this straight."

"Do you have any evidence? Any suspects that might have a reason to damage your property."

"Yeah, plenty of them."

"Like who?"

"Like the entire city government and their goons."

The first cop grinned and nudged his partner, "I think we might need to call an ambulance. This man's obviously disturbed or on drugs or something."

"I think you're right. I'll call it in."

"Turn around," commanded the first cop.

"Why?"

"So, I can put these cuffs on you before you start resisting arrest."

"Arrest for what?"

"Well, arson for starters," said the second guy, slamming his head against a palm tree and slapping handcuffs on his wrists. "Don't make things any worse than they already are!"

"I want my lawyer!"

The fireman walked over, "What's the problem, officer?"

"We're pretty sure this guy started the fire and we want to take him downtown to ask a few more questions."

"There is no evidence that he had anything to do with it. I haven't had a chance to investigate the source yet and my report's the only official inquiry that's required in cases like this."

"You do your investigation, brother, but this guy's coming with us."

The fireman looked down at Sammy's bruised face, "What's your name and who's your lawyer?"

"I'm Sammy Ball and he's Leonard Andrews."

"I'll call him for you. Save the only call you're going to get for someone else."

"Thanks. Oh, could you make sure that the painting that's hanging on the wall of my living room is safe. It's an original by Jessie Cotton."

"Can do."

The policemen grabbed Sammy's arms and dragged him down the gravel drive, banged his head against the side of the car, and tossed him into the back seat.

~

At four-twenty in the morning, a dark gray sedan - no lights, no plates – pulled into the gravel drive of Benny Young's neighbor and cut the engine. No one emerged from the car for precisely ten minutes, then two burly men got out and skulked across the street and around to the back of Alva Thompson's small bungalow with weapons at the ready. They were dressed in black and pulled hoods over their heads, as they stole along the narrow walk.

The neighborhood was silent, save a yelping dog three doors down, and the house was dark. They crept up the back steps and onto the small screened-porch. The second intruder eased the door closed as three stout shadows rose from a couch and lounge chair to pummel the assassins. The frustrated assailants crashed through the screening and fled. Eddie Glover's two mates, Jimmy James and Nomad, ran to their Harley's and roared after the gray sedan.

Eddie leaned through the torn screen to retrieve a Glock 17, lying in a smashed hibiscus where one of the assassins dropped it. He unloaded the pistol and called out, "You can come out now. It's over."

Benny, Alva and her husband, Harold, and the three children, Sophie, Angie, and little Bill, emerged from a small storage shed at the back of the garden.

Benny asked, "Did you catch 'em?"

"Naw, we only got a couple of licks in, before they busted through your screen and ran like scared rabbits. Nomad and Jimmy are chasing them."

Alva hugged him, "I can't thank you enough, for realizing there could be trouble and sticking around. I don't want to think about what could have happened tonight."

He knelt down to the kids, "Are you guys alright?"

Sophie patted him on the shoulder, "We were scared but I'm glad you were here to chase those bad men away."

"Happy to help, darlin'."

"Good thing Sammy's neighbor called," added Harold.

"Yeah, but now we've got to find out what happened to Sammy," said Benny. "That little guy's tough as nails but, if they could beat the shit out of me, he's in big trouble."

"That lawyer said he'd go down to the jail and check on him," said Alva, "but that seems like it was hours ago."

"Does Jessie know about any of this?" asked Harold.

"Hasn't been time to call and it's the middle of the night."

"Call him anyway," said Eddie. "That writer girl needs to be on top of this."

Jessie untangled himself from Kate and trudged to the kitchen to silence the jangling telephone. "Hello. Who is this and what could you possibly want at this hour?"

"Jessie, it's Benny."

The artist yawned and glanced at the clock above the sink, 5:02. "What's up?"

"Eddie Glover and his boys just chased two armed men off Alva's back porch and Sammy's been busted for arson. The cops claimed he tried to burn down his own house for the insurance. His neighbor told me that the gas tank in that old Volvo exploded and you know he wouldn't let anything hurt that car."

Kate appeared in the darkness and Gracie's nails clicked, as she padded across the tile floor to sit next to Jessie, cocking her head inquisitively.

"Are you okay?"

"Yeah, man, but I'm pretty sure it would have turned out bad, if Eddie and his friends hadn't stuck around."

"Angels, man, angels," replied Jessie, reaching to rub behind Gracie's ears. "Is your guardian going to stick around for the rest of the night."

"Yeah, we're covered."

"Listen, we're going to head down to the jail and find out what's going on."

"That lawyer guy called and said he was going down there too, but that was a couple of hours ago," said Benny.

"We'll let you know what we find out."

Kate's green robe and fuzzy pink slippers almost glowed in the early morning light, wafting through the window, "What's happened?"

"The bad guys have been busy," said Jessie, taking her in his arms. "First, they burned down Sammy's house and blew up his car, then the cops hauled him in for arson."

"Arson? Really? That's absurd."

"Yeah, exactly. And no one's quite sure where he is, at the moment. Andrews told Benny that he'd check it out but hasn't been heard from since."

"Shit."

"Then two armed guys tried to break into Alva Thompson's house but Eddie Glover and two of his buddies chased them away."

"This is intense," said Kate. "Should we be worried about someone trying to intimidate us?"

He kissed her forehead, "I'd count on it."

A flash of light flickered through the stained glass in the entry. Gracie cocked her ears and let out a low growl, as she started towards the door. Glass shattered and the doorframe exploded as six police officers in full battle gear, their faces covered by reflective shields, brandishing automatic rifles, stormed into the tiny house. Voices screamed, "We have a warrant to search the premises! Show yourselves!"

The dog leapt at the first man, who clubbed her with the butt of his gun. She whimpered and fell into a heap. A half-dozen flashlight beams darted around the room and focused in on the couple. "Show your hands!"

Jessie raised his hands, "What do you think you're doing, busting into my house in the middle of the night?"

Two cops grabbed him and cuffed his hands behind his back, then Kate. "Do you have any weapons in the house?"

"No, but if I did, I sure wouldn't hesitate to use them."

The other men flipped on lights to wander from one room to the next, dumping furniture and rummaging through the cupboards.

Kate screamed as the two in the studio tossed canvases across the floor, dumped over Jessie's easels, and returned with a pair of packages wrapped in red cellophane.

"Look what we found," said the first cop, handing one brick to the leader.

"What's in those?" He peeled back the wrapper and poked a little hole with the tip of a switchblade. "Looks like beige heroin to me. Search the rest of the house."

"I've never seen those before," stammered the artist.

"Yeah, that's what they all say," said another cop, shoving the couple outside to a waiting gray sedan.

Little Johnny Warmington eased the skiff into the open slip next to the Kate, tied her off, and trotted up the path to the back door. He was looking forward to fishing with his best friend and he was secretly hoping that they could spend some time alone together.

He reached to knock on the screen but the window in the door was broken and he could hear Gracie whimpering. His mother always insisted that you don't enter someone's house, unless you're invited, but he peaked inside anyway. Usually neat and tidy, the kitchen cabinets were open and empty and the floor was strewn with books, pots and pans, broken dishes and glasses, and the contents of every box in the cabinets. The whole room was dusted in a layer of salt, herbs, flour, and sugar. He could see through to the studio, where paintings and splintered frames were jumbled on the floor.

Johnny snuck inside and lifted an overturned chair to free Gracie, who had a gash across her left ear and her eye was swollen shut. He wrapped his arms around her, "What's happened? Where's Jessie?"

Gracie licked his face and struggled to stand.

The boy tiptoed through the kitchen to peer at the carnage in the studio and glittering shards of stained glass exploded across the entry. The shattered door stood open and he could see a police car parked across the driveway. Gracie limped up behind him and growled.

Johnny rubbed behind her good ear and grabbed her collar to lead her back through the carnage and out the back door. He knelt down to whisper, "I don't know what's happened but I think we need to disappear, before anyone realizes we're here."

He guided the dog down the path, lifted her into the MissU, and untied the line. He pulled the rope on the little outboard and a booming voice yelled from the patio, "Who goes there?"

He pushed the boat out of the stall, spun around and torqued the throttle to head out along the shoreline of the bay. Heavy footsteps pounded down the path and across the wooden planking and the voice screamed, "Stop or I'll shoot!"

Johnny ducked down, covering Gracie, and caught the glint of the policeman's gun, as the boat slid around the point. He stayed low for most of the run to the little rental house, backed the boat into the slip, and wrapped a rope around a cleat. Gracie stumbled onto the bench seat and he lifted her onto the dock. "C'mon, we need to get you some help and, maybe, my mom will know what's going on."

The dog looked up at him with sad brown eyes and limped up the walkway to the little gray house.

The screen door banged, as they marched through the kitchen and he yelled, "Mom, Mom, I need you!"

Bobbie appeared in the doorway, "What's wrong honey? And what's happened to Miss Gracie's eye?"

"I went to pick up Jessie to go fishing but no one came to the door, so I peeked inside and the whole house is upside down, broken doors and windows, stuff scattered all over the place. I found Gracie under an overturned chair and someone's hit her with something."

"You didn't find Jessie?"

"No."

"I'll call the police."

"No, you can't do that!"

"Why not?"

"Because there was a police car out front and the cop yelled, 'Stop or I'll shoot!', when I pulled the boat out into the bay."

"Wait, you're saying the cops are in on this?"

"I don't know what I'm saying but I'm pretty sure the cop wasn't there to protect Jessie's stuff. All his paintings were broken and torn on the floor of his studio," replied Johnny.

"Oh, this doesn't sound good at all. No, it doesn't."

"What are we going to do?"

"The problem is, we don't know who we can trust. My guess is that his gallery sponsor might be able to help. I'll call him. What's his name? What's his name?"

"Mister…Rengle or something like that," said the boy. "I met him at Jessie's, when he came by to pick up a painting."

"No, Rangle, that's it," said his mother, grabbing the phone book. "What's the gallery's name?"

"That's easy, 'Tropical Paradise'. Jessie's got his card tacked up on the wall in the studio."

"I'm glad you're so observant."

A minute later, she spoke into the phone, "Mr. Rangle, you don't know me but my son, Johnny, is a good friend of Jessie Cotton."

"Ah, yes. Jessie's very fond of your son. What can I do for you?"

"Well, Johnny went by to pick up Jessie to go fishing…only, no one was there and the house has been ransacked. Johnny said that the studio was littered with paintings, doors and windows were broken, and there was a police car blocking the drive."

"Oh, my…I feared something like this might happen."

"What do you mean?"

"I mean that our friend, Jessie, was trying to organize underpaid workers to fight for their rights and, it would seem, someone doesn't approve."

"Is he in trouble?"

"I think he is in dire straits, Mrs. Warmington. Give me your number and I'll call you, when I find out what's happened."

"It's 747-2575," said Bobbie. "If you find him, tell him we've got Gracie. She's been injured but I think she'll mend."

"I'll pass that along, if and when I find him."

~

Derek Rangle dressed and drove his vintage Jaguar across the bridge and into town. The glow of dawn seeped through the sculpted palm trees, illuminating the dew on the manicured grass into sparkling splays of liquid diamonds and the first red hibiscus opening to greet the new day on the grounds around the grandiose courthouse, which only proved that the architect, David Brenner, lacked any sense of proportion or style.

He parked at the far end of the block, beyond the line of white police cruisers, two gray sedans, a red two-seater Mercedes, and noticed that the chrome on a classic black Lincoln Continental was positively dazzling on a bright sunny morning, as he walked back to the entrance to the jail. Leonard Andrews lurched out the door, before he could reach for the handle.

"Mr. Andrews?"

The attorney looked up, "Yes?"

"I'm Derek Rangle. I own the Tropical Paradise Gallery out on the Circle and Jessie Cotton is one my artists. I received a call from Benny Young, saying that two armed men tried to break into his sister's house, Sammy Ball had been arrested, and, now, Jessie's house has been ransacked and he and his girlfriend, Miss Crocket, seem to have disappeared." He paused, staring at the confusion in Andrews cool blue eyes, "Oh, and there's a police vehicle parked in the driveway."

"I've been chasing this down for several hours and I can find no trace of Mr. Ball and Mr. Cotton has not been brought into the jail, since I've been here."

"This is something of a mystery."

"I'd call it a conspiracy, Mr. Rangle. People don't just disappear into our legal system without a trace."

"Jessie told me that Benny Young had been assaulted by two police officers and threatened for his involvement with the protest committee, before they dumped him out on a country road somewhere."

"Is he safe?"

"Yes, I believe those gentlemen on the motorcycles were staying with him for the time being."

"Well, he's still got charges against him, so they could still try to put him away."

Rangle turned to the street, "Is that your Mercedes?"

"Yes, why?"

"Well, actually, I was more interested in those matching inconspicuous sedans. Are they official?"

The two men walked around to inspect the license plates and Leonard said, "No, those are normal plates. They could be undercover cars."

"I wonder who drives them? Did anyone in uniform enter the jail while you were there?"

The lawyer pondered the question, "I noticed two officers come in about an hour ago, followed by a big burly guy in civilian clothes, who talked with them for a couple of minutes out in the hallway and then disappeared."

"Is there a judge you might consult?"

"I'm not sure who can be trusted."

"What about Tabitha Hall?"

"The old dame who owns the newspaper?"

"Yes."

"I'm afraid I don't know her. Can we trust her?"

Rangel smiled, "If there is anyone in this city who would help Jessie Cotton, it's Tabitha."

~

Andrews parked the Mercedes under the portico at the top of the circular drive of a stately, turn-of-the-century mansion - classic white columns sprouting above tall hedges and a pair of massive oaks draped with gray swathes of swaying Spanish moss. The syrupy scent of gardenias wafted on a salty breeze that rustled a stout banyan tree, twittering and chirping with the chatter of a flock of pastel parakeets.

"This is like a set out of an old movie," commented the lawyer.

"Tabitha Hall will defend tradition, until her last dying breath," laughed Rangel. "She is certainly unique in a very admirable way."

Before he could ring the bell, the massive door opened and a large black man, in full tails, appeared with a bow, "Ah, Mr. Rangel, Mrs. Hall is looking forward to your visit."

"Hannibal Davis, may I introduce Leonard Andrews, Attorney-at-Law."

"I'm pleased to meet you, Mr. Andrews, won't you please come in? Mrs. Hall will be with you in just a moment."

They stepped across the threshold into another century, with crystal chandeliers glinting above black and white tiled floors, Persian carpets, and priceless antique furnishings. All of the artwork and sculptures were period pieces by ancient masters, with the exception of two large canvases in the drawing room. Over the fireplace, a brilliant sunset illuminated a violent storm charging the beach with towering surf and howling winds assaulting battered palm trees. On the opposite wall, low lazy light filtered through a jungle to reveal a roost of coastal birds in vibrant plumage.

"Are these Mr. Cotton's work?" asked Leonard.

"Yes, two of my favorites. I actually hate selling his artwork because, if I could afford it, I'd much rather just keep them all for myself."

Andrews would have sworn that someone turned up the lights the moment Tabitha Hall's radiance glided into the room. He had seen her out in public at a distance, but in close proximity, she was tall and slender, with a mane of white hair that framed shimmering green eyes in a pale parchment complexion.

She reached to shake Rangel's hand firmly, "It's so nice to see you, Derek, in spite of the hour, and I do hope that I can be of some help."

"Thank you. I'd like to introduce Leonard Andrews."

"We've never met but your reputation precedes you, Mr. Andrews. I understand that you fight for the right causes."

"I'm afraid that's why we've come to see you, Mrs. Hall. I'm…representing a group of working people who are trying to organize for better wages from the city, as well as most of the industries in this area. These people can't make ends meet, while they're earning the minimum wage or less, even if they're holding down two or three jobs."

"I'm aware of the problem and the movement."

"A core group decided to hold a meeting to see whether there was really enough interest to have a meaningful protest," added Derek, "and hundreds, maybe even a thousand showed up."

The lawyer added, "Unfortunately…one of the young men, who started this campaign, was hijacked by two police officers, roughed up by an unknown gangster, who threatened the boy's family, and dumped in a field in the middle of the night with a warning to stop or face the consequences."

Tabitha gasped, "I honestly didn't think people still behaved that way."

"There's more," said Andrews. "After the big meeting, a security detail intercepted two armed men trying to break into the boy's sister's house in the middle of the night, after the house and classic car of another spokesman were torched and he was hauled off by the police to be charged with arson. He never showed up at the jail and the police have no record of the incident. I have no idea where he might be."

"Jessie Cotton and his girlfriend, the journalist I spoke with you about, were helping to organize the group. His studio has been ransacked and they, too, are missing," said Rangel.

Tabitha gestured to armchairs, upholstered in a bright floral chintz, arranged around a square table with a marble chessboard inlaid in the center. "Please be seated. Hannibal should be along with some strong coffee, momentarily."

Rangel and Andrews waited for her to take a seat. Mr. Davis appeared with a silver tray bearing a teapot, delicate porcelain cups, and a small platter of tempting biscuits. He served Mrs. Hall and, then, the gentlemen. "Will there be anything else?"

"Thank you, dear man, I think we've sufficient to tide us over until lunch."

Davis laughed and disappeared through the center hallway.

"Let me make some calls," said Tabitha. "I do have some connections that might prove helpful. In the meantime, you spoke of the young man who was accosted by the police. Is he available?"

"Yes, we have some people protecting him and his family."

"Considering the fact that we can't be certain who is involved in this…conspiracy, and it could only be directed by someone from the gilded society, although I'm fairly certain that our dear Mayor Kane lacks the gravitas to participate in, let alone conceive of anything this sinister. He might be corrupt but he's timid and stupid, and way too wimpy for the role. I might suggest a strategy of soliciting public sympathy and outrage through a story on the front page of my newspaper."

"That's what Miss Crocket was working on," said Rangel, "a series of exposés, based on her interviews with the working people who are being forced to fight for their survival. Do you know a reporter we can trust?"

The matron smiled, "Jessie called me about her and I am looking forward to reading her work. In the meantime, I have an ancient but still valid degree in journalism and a pretty good idea of how this should read. Bring the young man to me and we'll get started."

"That's very generous of you," said Andrews.

"I might be heir to all of this but I started out as a cub reporter, covering big stories about little league baseball teams and how many stray dogs are being held at the pound and collecting the details for obituaries. But I worked my way up and, eventually, married the boss," said Tabitha.

"Believe me, I have sympathy for these people because I'm still one of them."

Chapter Seven

"Have you read the front page of today's paper?" screamed Mavis into the phone.

"No, haven't had time," said Tate. "I've been on site since six this morning, the inspectors are inspecting."

"They won't find anything to complain about, our crew is top-notch," snapped Mavis. "The point is that, while we've been focusing on theories and projections of world-wide disaster, the working-class citizens of Dolphin Bay are about to revolt!"

"What's happening?"

"Evidently a group of city-workers started organizing and some renegade cops decided to beat the crap out of a young agitator, who works landscaping for the city. When that intimidation didn't stick, two armed heavies tried to break into the boy's house to take him out and, oh yeah, his sister, her husband, and three kids also lived there. Then they burned down another guy's house, arrested him for arson, and nobody's seen him since."

"Holy shit!"

"Here's another wrinkle, your ol' buddy, Jessie Cotton was helping organize the workers and his studio was trashed and he's missing too."

"I'm thinking it wasn't renegade cops, somebody with a whole lot of pull is running this deal and they don't want to share the spoils with the common folk."

"If the working poor pour into the streets demanding their basic rights, this could explode across the county."

"And?"

"And, we're not ready to launch the campaign, let alone contain mass protests and insurrection, and demonstrations would not go down well with our tenants."

"Things could get out of control real quick."

"You're tight with the locals, see what you can find out about all of this."

"I'll make some calls," replied Tate. "You too busy for lunch?"

"I wasn't before but I am now," said Mavis.

The line went dead. Tate replaced the receiver and sat back in his oversized office chair, staring at cheery palm fronds waving in a blue sky. "It's fourth and goal, be careful how you play this, Ace, because it could be the ballgame."

He dialed the phone and waited. Ned Flint's crisp New England accent answered, "Ned Flint."

"Ned, it's Tate."

"Lovely to hear from you first thing this morning, last night was glorious."

"Listen, I need to find out what's going on with the police hijacking the spokesmen for some phantom group of protesters in Dolphin Bay."

"Yes, dear boy, I did hear something about that through backchannels. Seems some of the underprivileged are feeling underprivileged and trying to make some noise about it. The powers that be don't take kindly to anarchy and insurrection disrupting the tourist's expectations."

"You know as well as I do, that the have-nots are going to erupt, if things don't change."

"Yes, I've attended several meetings with your wife and, I must say, she is most determined, in spite of the fact that even her tight little group, who possess endless resources, is not going to solve the problem of poverty or the disparity between the rich and the poor. It has always been this way, why should it suddenly change now?"

"Because the alternative is disaster."

"I realize that you have no reference but families like mine have weathered and profited from every financial upheaval for the past five-hundred years. When the correction comes, it will affect them, not us."

"I honestly believe that we are on the brink."

"You are tasked with completing SunnyBreeze and you would be wise to let your spouse attend to social justice. In the meantime, I'm making sure that you don't have any construction disasters or fail your inspections. You will do as you're told or I will personally deliver a portfolio of images of you looking absolutely torrid, although even your sultry Mavis might find some of the more compromising positions utterly distasteful, considering she married a hulking Adonis dripping with testosterone to satisfy her own desires."

"What photographs?"

"Oh, I'll share them with you the next time we're together. I'm sure you'll find them stimulating." The magnate moaned, "I must say, you are a magnificent specimen. Won't you join me for another night of debauchery?"

"You bastard."

Flint laughed, "I'm very confident of my lineage, dear fellow. I'm not sure we can say the same for you. Now, to answer your question, the missing agitators are being held incognito in the old abandoned jail in Fort Myers and they will be released, as soon as they agree to follow the rules of the game."

"What game?"

"The game of life, my boy. It's amazing what one will agree to, when given no other choice."

~

Alva leaned over a snoring Benny and shook his shoulder, "Wake up, bro', you've got to see this."

Benny rolled over and threw an arm over his eyes, against the glare flooding through the slats of the Venetian blinds, "What?"

"This article on the front page of the paper, you're famous."

"Famous, what are you talking about?" He sat up, squinting to read the first few paragraphs under a three-column photo of his battered face. Mrs. Hall's version of his story was accurate and it was all in there, the absolute truth. "Now everyone knows."

"It's about damned time," replied his sister, turning to answer the phone. She yelled from the hallway, "It's for you."

"Who?"

"That Andrews attorney guy."

Benny shuffled to the only phone in the house, "Hello?"

"Benny, it's Leonard Andrews, have you seen the paper?"

"I'm just reading the article. I'm proud that it's out there but I'm feelin' kind of naked."

"Well, you are now the poster child for a movement."

"What movement?"

"You might want to get your guards to escort you down to City Hall. There have to be several thousand people out here and they all want to know what happened to Sammy, Jessie, and Kate…and you."

"You're shittin' me!"

"No, son, I'm not and I think you're the only person who can address this crowd and make them understand what's really going on."

"Where are you?"

"Outside Shoemaker's Pharmacy, across from the Courthouse."

"Stay there, I'll be down in fifteen."

Andrews paced the curb, watching waves of people packing into the square from every direction. Many carried signs and placards with slogans like 'Fair Pay!' and 'Show Some Respect' or 'My Children Need to Eat!'

Someone was setting up a microphone and speakers, at the top of the steps, but he had no clue whether members of the group or the authorities planned to speak to these people. Those who came, out of curiosity or a need to express their own frustrations, were swallowed up in a seething mass of humanity fueled by pent-up anger and a common terror. The tone and tenure of the crowd noise rose into shrill shouts and rumbling demands for answers from the authorities about Benny's beating and the three missing volunteers. The working poor viewed the police force as the mayor's private army, tasked with accosting, intimidating, and abusing the innocent.

A caravan of Alva's old Chevy and three classic Harley choppers rumbled down Main Street, past two bewildered traffic cops, and parked across from the Courthouse entrance. Nomad, Jimmy, and Eddie surrounded Benny as he stepped onto the sidewalk, with Alva, Harold and the three kids.

Andrews approached, "They're setting up a sound system and a podium. I think you ought to tell these folks your story."

Benny inhaled deeply and let it out in a long slow whistle, as he took in the anxious crowd, "One thing I've got to know, has anyone heard anything about Sammy, Jessie, or Kate?"

"Nothing."

"Alright, let's go."

The bikers plowed a path through surging chaos and confusion, followed by Andrews and the Thompson's, and delivered Benny to the bottom of the steps. City Hall housed the Courthouse, the Police Department and the Jail, as well as the offices of the City and County executives. Each had their own grand entrance, burrowing into one side of the massive white box, bounded by broad walkways, bordered with profusions of flowers, planted by the landscape department, that were being trampled by thousands of shifting bodies.

He found Hank Miller, Harvey Harris, and Rex Tatum arguing. "What's happening?"

"Well, we were going to try to speak to all these people about what we're trying to accomplish," said Miller, "but we're not really sure who put up the microphone."

"It might be for some official announcement or something," said Harvey. "Considering what the cops have done to our friends, we don't need to piss 'em off any more than necessary."

"I don't care who we piss off," snapped Benny. "They beat the crap out of me and they're probably doing the same to our friends, so somebody needs to tell these folks the truth and it might as well be me."

Without waiting for his guardians, he marched up the steps to gaze out over an undulating sea of turbulence and jostling, confused and angry faces staring up expectantly, staccato shouts and a deep guttural roar died down into rippling murmurs. He tapped the microphone, "Can y'all hear me?"

The crowd cheered.

"Most of you don't know me..."

Someone at the bottom of the stairs yelled, "We all know you, brother, and we're here to find out what's going down."

Benny grinned, "I guess you might have read the story in this morning's paper?"

"We sure did!"

"Then you have to understand that we're all in the same boat...you, me, everyone who works for a living and isn't making it. We got some people together to talk about finding a way to demand a fair wage, reasonable working conditions, and maybe even some basic benefits. Do any of you have benefits?"

A few hands went up but a stout woman yelled, "Hell no, and I don't get any sick leave either. My boss'll work me 'til I keel over and then he'll hire some desperate fool to take my place!"

"Okay, let's back up. Our original group was made up of city-workers from schools, the hospital, road crews, and all the functions of maintaining this community. We've made formal requests and sent requisitions through the system and they've always been denied with one lame excuse or another. The problem is that I...and all of you...have to pay the rent, put food on the table, clothes on our children, and gas in the car...if you can afford one."

The crowd cheered, "Right on!"

"No one can maintain a decent standard of living on the minimum wage, especially when we're expected to put in overtime without pay...usually when you're needing to get to your second job or they'll get pissed and fire your ass."

"Greedy bastards!"

"We've been patient, we've done everything by the book, but we haven't received any response that showed respect for our troubles or any hope that they might be resolved." He paused and looked around, "From the looks I'm seeing, I'm betting that most of you face the same bullshit every day. Am I right?"

The whole plaza erupted in cheers and applause.

"Then this is the moment when we join together to demand change, to demand that our voices be heard, and we'll keep demanding until someone in authority is ready to do something about it, besides using violence to intimidate hard-working people. Are you with me?"

"Yes!"

He looked across the crowd and noticed police cars blocking the side streets and officers in full riot gear fanning out to corral the gathering.

A police lieutenant emerged from the heavy black doors of the Courthouse, marched to the podium, followed by two beefy cops, who shoved Bennie up against a wall and handcuffed him. "This is an illegal gathering under City statutes and you are, hereby, directed to disperse immediately or I will have our officers clear the plaza. You have five minutes to comply."

The crowd exploded into pandemonium, people screamed, bodies scattered in every direction, placards fluttered and waved like a flock of butterflies in a stiff wind, bottles and paving stones flew through the air, crashing on the steps in front of the little podium.

The lieutenant strapped on a helmet with a face-shield and reached for a radio to summon backup. Andrews ran up the steps, "What is he being arrested for?"

The frightened officer pointed to the roiling mass surging up the staircase, "Inciting to riot, to start with...then we'll add resisting arrest...and I'm sure we can find several other charges."

"You started this riot, you moron! I'm his lawyer and I demand his release."

"I don't care who you are, you can stand in line at the jail, until we get him processed, just like every other lawyer."

Tabitha Hall appeared with a photographer, snapping shots of everything and everyone involved. "I believe that the citizens of our community will take a dim view of senior police officers infringing on this young man's rights or abusing the citizens gathered here peacefully today. I have three more photographers working the perimeter and they will provide high-quality images of any violence or abuse that happens this morning. You can rest assured that the most damning of those photographs will be plastered across the front page of tomorrow's newspaper and every media outlet in the country. Do I make myself clear?"

The lieutenant hesitated, stepped back, as the angry mob climbed closer, the clamor of their fury reverberating off the walls of the building in deafening tremors.

"You will release Mr. Young and you'll have your thugs withdrawn immediately, or I will make sure that your career ends right here and now." She grabbed the photographer to shoot close-ups of the anger and confusion on his face, then leaned in close with a big smile.

He turned to the two cops, pressing Benny's nose into the white stucco façade, and nodded. They unlatched the handcuffs and backed away.

Nomad, Jimmy, and Eddie muscled between Benny and the officers.

Tabitha Hall leaned over to the lieutenant, "You can tell Mayor Bert that I double-dog dare him to show his chubby face to this crowd. They'll want to hang him from the nearest tree!"

She walked to the microphone, "Ladies and gentlemen, I am Tabitha Hall and I own the Dolphin Times."

The din of the surging madness settled into churning chaos and someone yelled, "You've got some balls on you, lady!"

The old woman's pallid cheeks went decidedly pink, for a moment, but she smiled, "I believe the fact that all of you were brave enough to come out here this morning, to support Bennie and protest the intimidation by our elected government, proves that your cause is worthy and just. Look around, everyone in this plaza is here for the same reason, to be paid a decent wage for your efforts, to be valued as citizens of this community, and to put a stop to the intimidation.

The next step is getting all of you organized, so in tomorrow's paper, you'll find a simple form for your name, address, phone number, where you work, your expertise, and we'll have ample room for brief comments or questions. Fill it out and send it the address provided and your volunteers will organize the information and get in touch with you."

"Who else is going to see that list?" shouted a bearded man with a red baseball cap.

"That's up to all of you, more than a few of you are going to have to step up to make sure this is handled professionally. If you're going to become a movement, then do it with intelligence and decorum. You're demanding fairness in compensation for your work and integrity in those who will be negotiating a solution to this problem. Treat them with honesty and respect and expect nothing less in return."

She glanced back, during extended applause, to find Benny and the bikers grinning. "This cause will not be won by loud voices or wanton violence, victory will be earned by decent, dedicated, law-abiding citizens. People willing to commit their time, their knowledge, and their talents to building an organization that will speak for everyone with one rational but firm voice. If you want to change the world, step up. None of this works without everyone being involved and committed. Thank you."

She backed into the wall of bikers and turned to Eddie, "Thank you for looking after Benny. He told me that you saved his life."

The mechanic grinned, revealing two golden caps, "Ma'am, I don't like big guys picking on little guys and I don't care whether it's on the playground or in these offices up here, I'll do what I can to put a stop to it. Someone up there needs to engage some common sense. Now that these people understand that they're all being screwed, they're only going to remain patient for so long before they revolt and who could blame them?"

Tabitha smiled, "Amen."

Benny took the microphone, "I want to thank everyone for coming out today, for proving that this is much bigger than just some manual labor guys whining about a raise. This is about the survival of our families, that's the bottom line.

I wish I could give you some information about what's happened to Sammy Ball, Jessie Cotton, and Kate Crocket. They were taken into custody, the night before last, and have not been heard from since. Our attorneys are investigating."

Shouts and jeers.

"I think we should take Mrs. Hall's advice. Let's keep this peaceful, I want everyone to disperse without pushing and shoving. Make sure you fill out those forms and send them in. Anyone who can volunteer some time to help with the clerical work, or anything else for that matter, should contact Evan Thudbury, who's right down here in front. You can't miss him, he's the only guy in the whole crowd wearing a bright pink bow tie!"

Cheers and laughter.

"We need to organize another gathering, as soon as we have your information. Tell your friends and your co-workers to join the cause. We need everyone to step up!"

The crowd started to thin out and a small mob gathered around Thudbury, who was madly scribbling names and phone numbers. Benny started to turn back to Mrs. Hall, who was staring at a sleek white limousine pulling up to the end of the walkway. The driver donned a black hat and walked around the car to open the rear door for a tall, shapely blond woman in a slinky lavender dress. The mass of bodies, wandering this way and that, seemed to part, as the woman marched up the walkway and the steps to Tabitha Hall.

"Mrs. Hall, my name is Mavis Sloan. My husband and I are the project managers for SunnyBreeze."

Tabitha held out her hand, "How may I help you?"

"I believe I have information that might be helpful in retrieving your missing persons."

Andrews stepped in, "I'm Leonard Andrews, attorney for these people. Any information would be appreciated."

Mavis leaned close, "I believe they're being held in the old jail in Fort Myers but, after this gathering, there's really no point in detaining them. I wouldn't be surprised if they weren't released almost immediately."

"Or they could just disappear," interrupted Benny. "Witnesses."

"I don't know who is or was holding them. I was only told where." She glanced at Tabitha, "I can't reveal my sources but I believe them to be reliable."

"If you'll excuse me, I'll have someone check that out," said Andrews, rushing down the steps.

"I understand the dilemma," said the newspaper woman, "protecting the source is as vital as getting the whole truth."

Mavis took the old woman's hand, "Thank you for understanding."

"Thank you for volunteering your information, it might save some very important lives."

142

"All lives are important."

"You're not what I expected," said Hall.

"I get that a lot," replied Mavis. "I don't apologize for my shape or my intelligence."

"Nor should you."

"There's something that I'd like to discuss with you in private, when you have the time."

"I noticed that you have a rather large car, would you consider giving me a ride home?"

"Certainly."

The driver tipped his hat as Tabitha slid across the back seat, marveling at the sleek sophistication of the expansive interior. Mavis sat next to her and tapped a panel, which opened to reveal a champagne bottle on ice and delicate crystal flutes, "Could I offer you a drink?"

"Thank you but it's a vice I was forced to give up many years ago."

The driver settled behind the wheel and turned to ask, "Where to, Mrs. Sloan?"

Mavis glanced at Mrs. Hall, "Hampton House on Seagrape Circle."

"Yes, Mrs. Sloan."

"Take the scenic route and would you close the window, please?"

"Yes, Mrs. Sloan."

The window divider rose to seal the passenger compartment and Mavis turned to Tabitha. "I think we both know that the protest this morning was just the tip of the iceberg. The whole world is getting ready to explode into class warfare, unless something drastic happens in the very near future."

"On that we agree."

"A group of very prominent, old-money people have joined together to form an exploratory think-tank that is actively working on a viable alternative to anarchy, that would benefit the lower classes and, perhaps, save our society."

"Why would the sinfully rich care one way or the other?"

"Because, without the working class, there is no economy. Wealth has no meaning, when the upper classes have to hide behind great walls and armed guards. We're already there and it will get worse. The only way to protect what we have is to tame this beast before it becomes uncontainable."

"What are you proposing?" asked Tabitha.

Mavis grinned, "Basically, socialism on a grand scale. We already own most of the international corporations that are running the world at the moment, so why not take it another step and own everything? Then we could offer everyone a job, a safe and decent place to live, quality education for their children, real universal health care, lifelong security, and a stable economy."

"But…the upper classes won't support that for a minute. They're much too worried about clinging to what they have."

"They would, if the choice was the complete destruction of their perceived notion of social and economic equilibrium and the income that pays their bills. Think about it, if the lower classes were to revolt and anarchy took over the western world, there would be no market for goods or services, the economy would crumble and rampant inflation would finish the job. No one profits from that. Hell, we both know plenty of fascist families who are pouring gobs of money into gerrymandering and extreme right-wing candidates, supposing that, if they destroy the structure of our society, they can own everything. Hate to tell them but, whatever's left, isn't going to be worth much."

"That's an extreme supposition."

"That's what's coming, if something doesn't happen fast."

"What do you have in mind?"

"We're working on a plan to pave the way for several giant corporations to run everything and that mandates a program to re-educate the populace to value and accept the coming changes, in exchange for peace and security."

"And?"

"We have test projects ready to roll out in seventeen cities and more online, each a self-contained little community, but we need more time."

"How do you expect me to help?"

144

"By assisting these people in finding a reasonable and acceptable short-term solution, before this local protest takes on a life of its own."

"I'm not sure that you or I or the President of the United States could accomplish that," replied Tabitha. "These people are desperate and, if something doesn't change in a hurry, there's no future for them, they'll fall off the edge."

"That's my point, isn't it? There's a chance we can avoid complete disaster, if we all work towards the same goal."

~

Jessie and Kate were handcuffed, muscled into the back of a police cruiser, where black hoods, damp with ether, were tugged over their heads. They awoke, chained to chairs in a dark musty room, squinting into the glare of a flashlight held by a burly man with a deep voice and the bulk of an offensive lineman for the Chicago Bears.

"Do you have any idea how much trouble you're causing?"

"Helping people, who are struggling to survive, is not causing trouble," snapped Kate. "Who the hell do you think you are?"

"I'm the guy who's going to decide whether you walk out of here, Sweetheart, and at this point, it could go either way. Do you get my drift?"

"I'm not intimidated by you!"

The amber light traced across the ceiling and a crushing blow knocked Jessie to the floor. The beam erupted on the artist's bleeding cheek.

"Jessie!"

"What we have here is a failure to communicate. So, I'll communicate and you'll listen."

Delirious, Jessie struggled through a tangle of rattling chains to right the chair.

"Protests are bad for business. Our economy depends on tourists buying into the fantasy of spending time in paradise - renting rooms and apartments, eating in restaurants, going to bars, looking around at housing options, and dreaming of retiring here someday."

"You can't starve a whole segment of the population out of existence," said Jessie. "These people have been abused for long enough."

"Yeah, does whoever's behind this realize that he won't have anyone to build houses or mow his lawn or wait his table at a restaurant or harvest the food in the fields for that matter?"

"I think you ought to concentrate on making sure that the movement dissolves, like one of our afternoon storms turning into puffy white clouds rolling inland, or I'll enjoy proving that your girlfriend can die of ecstasy."

"Touch her and I'll find you, no matter where you hide!" shouted Jessie, rattling the chains binding him to the chair as he tried to lunge at the huge man.

"You're in no position to threaten me with anything," snarled the inquisitor. "Do you need another dose of humble?"

"What do you want?" screamed Kate.

"I want you to put an end to this. There's no reason innocent people need to suffer but I'm afraid my people won't take 'No' for an answer."

"Screw you," said Kate. "You're not going to keep an enormous portion of the population from standing up for their rights. They've been betrayed and this is just the beginning of a massive revolt. Once it starts rolling, there'll be no stopping it. I'd suggest that you and your 'people' better get out of the way."

"That's your opinion, Missy. Unfortunately, it's not what my people want to hear from you. You'll be spending some time with your friend, Mr. Ball, in the cooler. Maybe, the three of you can come to an agreement on how to resolve this problem before your time runs out."

~

Hours later, Kate whispered, "You guys okay?"

Jessie reached through the bars on the adjacent cell to just touch her outstretched fingers. "I have no idea of what's coming next."

"I wouldn't call this my idea of a romantic getaway," giggled the writer. The cellblock was dark, save the faint glow of a window blurring across the damp floor from the far end of the hallway, there was no power, and the dank still air was thick with musk and mold. Each dingy cell had a steel cot, with bare springs and no mattress, fixed to the wall, a broken toilet, a small sink, and no running water. "Are you okay, Sammy?"

The little clerk, battered and bruised from his 'interrogation' by the brute, mumbled, "You two might want to keep it down, it's past time for them to bring us some food."

"I keep hoping that the next time the echo of footsteps clatters down the hall, they won't be delivering our last meal," said Kate, stretching to squeeze Jessie's fingers.

"If they were going to kill us, they'd have done it by now," said Sammy. "The question is, what are they going to do with us?"

"Actually, between us, we've only seen three faces, the two cops and the intimidator," said Jessie. "Most of the bunch who ransacked my house were wearing helmets and masks, so these cops might not even be on the force. They could be from some other city…"

"Or just henchmen dressed up in uniforms," added Kate.

"Either way, there's no bustin' through these bars," said Jessie. "They might be rusty but they're still solid."

"Hell, I might agree to do what they ask in exchange for something to eat!" cried Sammy.

The faint glow reflecting on the grimy floor faded to black and a second night of darkness consumed the dingy cellblock and potential tomb. Hours passed, no food arrived, and conversation withered into lonely deliberations of consequences and fate. Kate flinched, her entire being torn between hope and terror, as a door creaked at the far end of the hall.

~

Andrew's young cousin, Kevin Wilson, killed the lights, as he pulled his Mustang into the weeds growing in the parking lot of the old decaying jail in Ft. Myers. He grabbed a flashlight and eased into an open door on the side of the building. A large rat scurried into a crumbling stack of boxes, old files, and debris piled in grimy mounds, as the light tripped across three battered chairs around a small round table covered with empty beer bottles, a greasy carton of chicken bones, and an overflowing ashtray. "Well, someone's been here."

A cold sweat leached across his forehead, on realizing that this was all good fun, until some real cop or PI showed up with a gun to find out who was wielding the weird wandering lights, flickering inside the derelict building. The boy skulked through the office, jarred by the creak of the rusting metal gate to the cellblock. The first three doors stood open, the cells empty, but a woman's voice called out, "Who's there?"

He aimed the light at the fourth grated door to find a very small man, in torn and soiled blue pajamas, shielding his eyes. His face was battered and bruised but he fit Lenny's description of Sammy Ball. "You wouldn't be Sammy Ball, would you?"

"Yes, my boy, I am," replied Sammy. "You'll find Jessie and Kate in the next two cells and we'd very much appreciate it if you would get us the hell out of here!"

Kevin swept the light across Kate and Jessie, holding up hands against the glare, "Do you know where they kept the keys?"

"No," replied Kate, "but I heard them jingle before they came into the cell block, so they might be hanging on a hook or a nail out there somewhere."

Wilson sloshed through the slime and heaved the rusty door open to scan the office. He swept everything off each desk and the clerk's counter but found nothing. He shoved the chairs away from the table and picked up the ashtray, newspaper, and found a ring of keys under the soggy chicken carton. "Eureka!"

He ran back and jangled through the dozen keys, until one turned in the lock in Sammy's door. He moved to Kate, who was wearing a tattered bathrobe and grimy pink slippers, and then Jessie, who asked, "Who the hell are you?"

"I'm Kevin Wilson, Lenny's cousin. He asked me to check this place out and see if there was any evidence that you'd been here."

"I'm pretty sure he'll like what you found," said Kate, taking his arm. "Let's get out of this dilapidated dungeon.

Kevin led the parade out of the cellblock and killed the light as he peeked out through the doorway into damp salty darkness. His eyes darted around the perimeter of the property, before he hurried them to the Mustang, cranked the ignition, and tore out of the parking lot and along the highway to a shopping center with a pay phone outside the entrance.

He fumbled quarters into the machine and dialed Lenny. The line crackled and his cousin answered, "Hello?"

His body trembled with an adrenaline rush and his words tumbled out in a flurry, "Lenny, it's me, Kev. Listen, I checked it out and that abandoned jail is rank, man, like gross prisons in old movies, but they were there, I'm positive."

"How do you know?"

"Because, they're standing right beside me, man."

"No shit? Lemme talk to Jessie."

The artist took the phone, "Thanks for sending Kevin to bail us out, we've been sitting around in that slimy hellhole for way too long."

"It's good to hear your voice. There are a lot of people worried about you three."

"It's nice to be missed - but better to be freed."

"Are you alright?"

"They roughed Sammy up but we'll survive, if we can find something to eat in a hurry."

"Didn't they feed you?"

"They brought us some crappy fried chicken yesterday but we haven't seen anyone since."

"Listen, I'll get Kev to bring you back up here, but you missed a fairly massive protest at the Courthouse. Benny's story has been all over the paper and your kidnapping is a big part of it."

"Is he okay?"

"Yeah, he's fine. Actually, I think he's too famous for anyone to do him any harm, but he's got Eddie and his friends chaperoning."

"Cool."

"I hate to say it but the only reason that you're alive is that whoever is running this thing got cold feet, because of the publicity.

Otherwise, I'm pretty sure no one would ever find your bodies in the everglades."

"I have to confess that thought crossed my mind, along with the question of what did they hope to accomplish?"

"We'll have to figure that out. Lemme talk to Kev and I'll see you about dawn at your place, if that's alright."

"Good a place as any, they've already trashed it." He handed the receiver to Wilson.

"Hey man, you did great. Bring them up to Dolphin Bay and I'll send you a hundred bucks in tomorrow's mail."

"Yeah, sure, the check's in the mail," laughed the amateur detective.

"No shit, cousin! Have I ever screwed you out of anything?"

"Well, no…"

"Actually, I'm just messing with you, I'll pay you when you get here…but your passengers better be safe and sound."

"Deal."

~

"Hey, Kev, do you have any money? I'm starving and I didn't get a chance to grab my wallet, when they arrested me for burning down my own house," said Sammy.

Kevin pulled out his wallet and thumbed through a scant few bills, then opened the ashtray to retrieve a jingle of change. "Twenty-three dollars and sixty-eight cents." He turned the ignition, "and barely enough gas to make it to Dolphin Bay."

"Hell, I'm so hungry, I'd even eat McDonalds," said Kate. "It's cheap and it'll tide us over for a couple of hours."

"I'm along for the ride," said Jessie, hugging Kate in the back seat. "Just find us food."

Wilson hopped on Forty-One and turned into a burger stand a few miles north. He looked over at Sammy, who looked like he'd escaped an asylum by trudging through a swamp, then at Kate, in her bathrobe and nasty slippers, and Jessie, who could pass for homeless, "Do you want me to go in and get it?"

Kate piped up, "I'm filthy and I need a real bathroom."

"I sure hope they don't have a dress code here," laughed Jessie. "Let's go."

Everyone piled out and trooped into the glare of fluorescents and the aroma of grease. The hostages peeled off to use the facilities and returned to chow down on hamburgers, fries, and shakes under the dumbfounded stares of two teenage employees, who looked as though they were considering calling the cops.

"I still don't understand why they just left us there," said Sammy, leaning back to rub his tummy. "It would have been cleaner, if they'd off-ed us."

"You folks didn't get to see the protest, it was all over the news. Several-thousand people converged on the Courthouse in Dolphin Bay and Benny gave a speech. But Tabitha Hall, who owns The Dolphin Times, kind of took over and told some uppity policeman to get his thugs off the square and challenged the mayor to come out to explain the mysteries to the crowd. He declined," said Kevin. "Everyone knew you'd been kidnapped or arrested or something and no one was leaving until they got some answers."

"That's amazing," said Kate. "Kind of reminds me of the old days in Madison."

Jessie grinned, "Those folks know how to throw a protest."

"Everyone read about the anti-war riots in Madison. Were you kids involved?" asked Sammy.

"We could only be convicted of participating, not instigating," replied Jessie.

"Along with a hundred-thousand fervent brothers and sisters," added Kate. "It was a different time; a time when you got involved because it was the right thing to do."

"It was the only thing we could do, to end the war and save our own asses!" laughed Jessie.

"I never imagined that people would come together like that for a righteous cause in my lifetime," said Kevin, "but they proved me wrong."

"So, Benny and the crowd saved our butts?" asked Sammy.

"I saved your butt," laughed Kevin.

"We could have starved to death in that hellhole, if you hadn't come looking for us," said Kate.

"I wouldn't be surprised to find a welcoming party waiting for you, when we get to Dolphin Bay. If everyone's finished, let's hit the road."

The Mustang purred up Forty-One through Punta Gorda and out along the misty two-lane, barely higher than the inky marsh water and menacing mangroves crowding either side of the highway. Glaring headlights illuminated a slender silver strip, a rapier plunging through the darkness to the first glimmers of morning and the promise of civilization. The adrenalin rush wearing thin, Kevin struggled to focus on the lane markers flicking under the car in a blur, until a flash in the rearview mirror roused his attention.

He shook Sammy's leg, "Wake up, we've got someone coming up fast."

Jessie turned in his seat to spy a bright pinpoint of light that rapidly spread into two beams racing closer in a hurry. "That doesn't look good."

"I don't like the vibes," said Kevin, pressing the accelerator to the floor. "Everyone buckle up, we're going to find out what this ol' girl's got under the hood."

Kate turned around, "He's still coming."

Kevin was an avid stock car fan and studied the tactics that the drivers used to slow down or spin out a competitor, who was threatening a lead, when they ran at the dirt track up the coast or the networks showed the races on television. Other than getting his license, he had never taken a driving lesson in his life but, when the headlights filled the rearview mirror, he swerved into the left lane, then zipped right and hit the brakes to let the gray sedan slip past. Wilson caught a glimpse of two men in the front seat and the passenger was turning to point a gun out the window.

He whipped across the centerline, snagging the left rear bumper, and hit the throttle to spin the phantom car into the ditch.

Jessie yelled, "Don't stop, keep going!"

"You scared the shit out of me, kid, but that was some terrific driving," moaned Sammy. "I think I need a bathroom, can we go home now?"

Kevin grinned and checked the gauge, "We might have enough gas to make it, just barely."

~

A small army of friends were hauling broken furniture and boxes of shattered china out of the cottage, when the Mustang sputtered down the drive. Benny, Alva, Andrews, Eddie, and his buddies, as well as Gretchen Mowery and her kids, gathered around to applaud the ragged crew that crawled out of the car.

Benny hugged Sammy and took off his jacket to cover the little man, whose torn and soiled pajamas barely covered his pale pudgy flesh. "Man, I can't believe you're back. I got a taste of those bastards and I was worried about you."

He reached to turn Ball's chin back and forth, inspecting bruises and lacerations, "You'll heal but it's gonna take a while."

"Ah, I knew the brute wasn't going to kill me, before he hit me the first time," he grinned. "I don't remember the second blow, I was out cold."

"You're lucky to be alive, brother."

Gretchen hugged Kate, "I couldn't believe you disappeared just hours after we met. I worried that maybe you'd been cursed somehow."

"Weird coincidence but if you're here, then something must have changed."

"Yeah, Eddie got us moved into the apartment. A chic condo it ain't, but it's clean and warm and he's rounded up a little bit of furniture. Best part is it has a shower!"

"So, there is hope for tomorrow?"

"Yeah, I actually felt that, for the first time, when I took the kids back to school yesterday."

Kate hugged her, "Now, we have to find ways to help all those other folks in the camp to find their next step."

Andrews patted his cousin on the back, "You don't know how proud I am of you, for saving these guys."

Jessie interrupted, "You don't know the half of it. They tried to run us into the swamp, out in the boonies, on the way back. Kevin handled this Mustang like a stock car racer at Daytona and spun them into the ditch!"

"They would have succeeded, if he hadn't had his stuff together," added Kate. "You can chauffer me anytime and anywhere!"

Kevin lit up a sheepish grin, "It's been my pleasure."

Jessie gazed around at the growing mound of debris, "Did they leave anything intact?"

"They pretty well trashed everything," replied Leonard. "Rangel's in the studio taking inventory."

Everyone followed the artist into the bungalow, where Bobby Warmington and several moms, from the soccer team, were sweeping up shards of glass strewn from the tiny porch to the back door. The artist raised his fist to his lips, surveying total destruction of the few objects that comprised his worldly possessions.

Bobby hugged him, "I'm so glad they found you. Johnnie's been beside himself, since he found you missing, this place destroyed, and cops guarding the driveway."

"Oh, my, I forgot about our date to go fishing. Is he okay?"

She wet the corner of a rag to wipe the blood from his cheek, "Yeah, he's on the bus to school but I know he'll be relieved to know you're safe."

"I'll catch up with him this afternoon."

"He's been imagining the worst, ever since the cops chased him off the property with guns drawn."

"I'm sorry to have frightened him and I'll try to explain it to him as gently as I can," said Jessie, with a hug. "Where's Gracie?"

"She's at our house and she's healing from a blow to the face. Her eye's still swollen but the vet said she'll be okay."

"Thank you, I was worried about her." He turned into the studio, where he found Rangel seated on the floor, sorting through a pile of torn canvases. Derek looked up, tears streaming down his cheeks, "I'm so glad you're back but...they destroyed years of your work!"

The artist knelt to hug his promoter, "It's paint and canvas and we both know I can produce these in my sleep."

"But these were so beautiful."

"There will be more but I think I want to pursue a new direction, something with more connection to what's really happening in the world, rather than just pretty pictures of scenes that only exist in my imagination."

"No, they're a stunning exaggeration of nature's wonder but that's how we want to remember it, isn't it? Lush and wild and magnificent; maybe touched by humans but extraordinary and humbling in spite of it."

"People forget to cherish all that we have," replied the artist, ruffling through a dozen ragged fragments. "We live by Mother Nature's blessing."

Andrew's held up pieces of canvas, "These must have been beautiful. You know, if you applied your talent to telling the stories of these terrified people, it could be very powerful."

Rangel stood up and brushed himself off, "I agree. Don't stop the work you're doing but start illustrating the plight of far too many people in this country. We'll sell your landscapes to rich tourists and use the money to promote your new work."

"That's quite a change in attitude," said Jessie, hugging his mentor. "Weren't you the guy who had his nose out of joint about all the riff-raff sullying the front of your gallery?"

"Yes, I admit it, but I'm allowed to learn, to view things from a more considered perspective. I spent a lot of time worrying about you these past few days. Not only are you my best-selling artist, you are my friend and I have every respect for the man you've become, since we first met nearly a decade ago."

He kissed the old man's bald forehead, "I love you too! Now let's get all this crap out of here, so I can get back to work!"

Rangel turned to Kate, admiring her once fuzzy pink slippers, "Tabitha Hall has been writing and running stories every day in the Dolphin Times. She would very much like to meet you and, I can assure you, she would appreciate an account of the past few days, as soon as you can manage."

"I'll get right on it but I have one question first."

"What's that?"

"What color are the local police cars?"

"White with green lettering on the sides," said Andrews.

"Thanks," grinned the journalist.

"Why do you ask?"

"Because the car that took us to Fort Myers was gray."

Benny interrupted, "You know what, I think the car that stopped me on the street, the night I got beat up, was gray too."

The lawyer rubbed the stubble on his chin, "I'm fairly sure none of the neighboring counties have official cars that color but there were two gray sedans parked outside the jail, when Rangle and I were trying to find you."

"Which means the guys who hijacked us probably weren't from around here. They were private hires," said Kate. "I think we need to talk to Mrs. Hall today."

~

Hannibal Davis opened the front door of Hampton House with a broad smile, "Am I correct in believing that all of those missing are now accounted for?"

Derek Rangle turned to Kate, "Allow me to introduce Kate Crocket, writer and freed hostage."

Davis bowed, "I'm very glad that you're safe. Everyone in this city was worried about you."

"Well, most of them," laughed Kate, gazing at Jessie's painting over the fireplace in the next room.

"Won't you please follow me?" He guided them across the black and white tiled floor beneath sparkling crystal chandeliers, glittering off deep mahogany paneling that sheathed the expansive entry with the grace and grandeur of a time long passed.

The lady of the house appeared in the drawing room, as they entered, and walked directly to Kate, staring into her deep amber eyes, "I'm Tabitha Hall and I'm so glad that you were rescued."

"From what I hear, your work probably gave our captors cold feet."

"I have the good fortune of owning the voice; so, yes, I've done what I can. I know the readers want to know your story."

"That's why I wanted to talk with you, before I started writing," replied Kate. "The local police might have been involved but I don't think it was their guys, who invaded Jessie's house and took us hostage. I think they were hired by someone to do the dirty work."

"When Kate mentioned that the police car was gray, I remembered the same thing when I was 'arrested'," added Benny.

"But none of the municipalities around here have cars that aren't mostly white," said Leonard. "I think Kate's on to something."

"I should add," interrupted Rangel, "that Leonard and I noticed two gray sedans parked outside the jail, the morning after you were taken. Someone inside that building knows who's behind this intimidation."

"So, the question is, who has the most to lose if the protest grows into something much bigger?" said Kate.

"Oh, there are a lot of very wealthy residents of the area who would very much like things to remain as they've always been," replied the matron. "I could start with our mayor, a weasel and stand-in for his wife, who's the real power behind the throne. Her daddy owns the largest construction company on the southwest coast and most of the politicians. I could also point to the owners of countless manufacturing facilities or the big resorts, who don't want to pay decent wages to their employees and really don't want the disruption to interfere with the tourists' illusion of paradise."

"There might be an easier way to whittle it down," said Kate.

"How's that?"

"Who owns the derelict jail in Fort Myers? The land's got to be worth a fortune."

"That should be easy to find out," said Leonard. "Could I use your phone?"

"Certainly, there's one in the hallway," replied Tabitha.

Kate turned to the publisher, "There's one more thing that I've been wondering about."

"What's that?"

"Benny's sister mentioned rumors about a bill, before the legislature, to build camps to house the dispossessed, sort of tropical debtor's prisons. Is there any way to find out if that's true?"

"I'll look into it and let you know what I find."

"I visited a homeless camp under the bridge at Pelican Turn, where hundreds of people are stranded in hopelessness. This bill strikes me as the government's institutional version of the same nightmare."

Andrews returned, referring to a small notebook, "The title was assigned to a 'Fort Myers Development Company', which is a dummy for 'Southwest Properties', which has a post office box in a strip mall in Naples and no telephone."

"Find where that trail leads and we'll have a better idea of who's running the counter-insurgency," said Kate.

"Do you have enough to write an initial article? I can reserve three columns on tomorrow's front page, if you can have it ready by midnight."

"I haven't slept for days but, if I could read your stories for the background I missed, I'll have the first article finished in time."

~

Delveccio knocked gently on the study door in the Calhoun's palatial and isolated mansion on Highland Point, overlooking Caxambas Bay south of Naples. Mrs. Calhoun opened the door with a slight bow and practiced smile that made no attempt to conceal her contempt for the 'plebeians' in her husband's employ, "Come in."

The bodyguard followed her across the enormous room, paneled and beamed in beautiful, rare, and certainly illegally harvested woods with

158

massive windows on three sides framing magnificent views out over the water and the islands to the Gulf. JD was seated in a chaise next to a roaring fire in a massive hearth of smooth round river rocks hauled in from Colorado.

He leaned to whisper but Calhoun waved his hand, "You can speak freely."

Delveccio straightened up and nodded to Mrs. Calhoun, recognizing the evolution in her status within the ranks of the inner circle, from trophy wife to consigliere. "Our guests were rescued and driven to Dolphin Bay, as you requested. Unfortunately, their trip was without incident."

"Am I to understand they had a safe journey?"

"That is correct."

Intimidation displaced impatience in the developer's old gray eyes, but Sonia inquired, "And our private police force?"

"Two of them were involved in an accident in the Everglades, before dawn this morning, but the vehicle has been recovered and they should all be back in Alabama by now."

"I'm sure they were frustrated at not completing the assignment?"

The guardian hesitated, "No professional likes leaving loose ends."

Calhoun's eyes bored into him, "Could they identify any of you?"

"I'm the only one they might recognize."

The old man nodded, slowly, "I appreciate your dedicated service but, with all the publicity, we will be pursuing another strategy to tamp down the hubbub. You will be taking over security at the Santa Cruz office for the next few months. We've been getting a lot of flak from tree-hugging environmentalists and a few members of the City Council have yet to sign on to support our proposals. I'm sure you'll find a way to convince them of the quality of our work and the benefits that this project will provide to the community for years to come."

Sonia's mock smile disappeared, "The jet is waiting at the airport. Have a safe journey."

The brute hesitated, the overdeveloped muscles in his neck tensed, and the corners of his lips curled into a grimace. Violent options flashed through is mind, simple enough to assassinate a sniveling but lethal boss and his arrogant wife, but the consequences of betrayal might prove far more distasteful than the bitter flavor of submission. Several secret sessions at the Mayo Hospital, over the past few months, hinted at the old man's waning vitality. "I am at your service."

Chapter Eight

Johnny jumped off the school bus, dropped his books in the kitchen, and hugged a wiggling Gracie. "C'mon, your dad's home!"

They ran down the steps, climbed into the MissU, and motored along the bay to dock in the slip next to the Kate. Gracie pranced in place, waiting patiently for the boat to be tied up, and then raced him up the path and in through the torn screen door of Jessie's bungalow.

The artist called, "C'mon in, Johnny."

The dog skidded across the linoleum floor and crashed into Jessie's legs, dancing and leaping for a pet and a kiss. The boy ran to hug his friend, "I was so worried about you."

"I know and I'm safe and fairly sound. Your mother told me that you were the one who found us gone and I sure want to thank you for doing the right thing and telling your mom. Her phone call to Mr. Rangel probably started things rolling and ended up getting us freed."

The boy brushed the wound on Jessie's cheek and started to cry, "It didn't make any sense and I was scared. Why would the police take you away and tear up your house? You wouldn't do anything wrong."

"I was scared too but you didn't let that stop you from being brave and doing what you could to help Gracie and I'm very proud of you."

Johnny looked around at the empty room and through the doorway into the pile of trash on the floor of the studio, "Did they wreck everything?"

Jessie grinned, hugging a wiggling Gracie, "Yup, pretty much, there wasn't much to salvage. Guess I'll just have to start over."

"Can I help?"

"You bet. I want to go back to the little pond where George and his family used to live, just to get a sense of it so I can paint it again. I had one version almost finished but I'd like to try again."

"Can we fish while we're out?"

"Of course!"

Jessie could taste ocean salt on a stiff westerly breeze, as Johnny guided the little skiff to hug the lee side of the key into the little bay. He sat on the little bench seat facing the boy, "I'm really proud of you for figuring out what was happening and telling your mom. You probably saved our lives."

Johnny grinned, "I was really scared, because I couldn't figure out why the police would want to bother you or why they would trash your house?"

"I don't think they were real police. I think someone hired them to pretend to be police officers to intimidate us into abandoning our efforts to help our neighbors survive."

"But they beat you up…"

The artist grinned, "I guess I've never told you that I was the quarterback for the University of Wisconsin football team that played, and lost, the National Championship in the Orange Bowl a long time ago. I got knocked down a lot, so I'm kind of used to that kind of pain."

"Doesn't make it right."

"No, it doesn't, but I'll tell you what's admirable and that's all these people coming together to stand up for what's right and true. They're all poor and desperate and they might lose their jobs just for participating but, from what I hear, they were out in force at the Courthouse. How could I possibly walk away from helping them?"

"You couldn't, that's not who you are."

"Thanks. How are things at home?"

"Oh, they're alright. My mom took us over to take tests at the new school and I actually liked the lady who showed us around. She didn't seem snooty at all."

"That's good, what are the facilities like?"

The boy grinned, "It's still under construction but there's going to be a giant gym and playing fields."

"So, now, you'll have more information to work with, if and when it comes time to make a decision."

"Yeah, you're right."

"How's your mom?"

"Oh, she got a job at SunnyBreeze cleaning houses and she's pretty excited about it."

"That's great, she's a special lady and she deserves a better job and better pay."

"How come you didn't tell me about playing football?"

"That's a long story but, for the moment, let's just say that I'm really proud of you every time I watch you play soccer and, even though football seems kind of romantic and macho and all that, kids get hurt all the time. Not just banged up, but really hurt, and I don't want that to happen to you. Okay?"

"Okay."

The mangroves opened into SunnyBreeze and the progress was dramatic. Thickets of houses blossomed across the once-barren landscape at an astonishing pace. Great cranes lumbered along curving asphalt streets depositing mature trees into perfectly round holes, huge machines rolled out miles of green sod, and crews installed thousands of flowering shrubs with mechanized efficiency. Few, if any, of the plantings were native to the west coast of Florida but, given enough care and water, most would survive for a while. The moonscape was being transformed into a completely artificial tropical paradise ready for occupancy.

"Wow, I can't believe how fast they're building houses," said Johnny.

"Yeah, they'll probably start having tourists in the next month or two. It's kind of hard to believe that they scraped away the mangrove forest and replaced it with ugly houses and trees that don't grow here."

"I liked it better before."

"Me too," replied Jessie with a grin. He pulled out his lunch box and offered a peanut butter sandwich and a cup of lemonade. "The one thing the bad guys can't destroy is peanut butter."

Johnny wiped a dollop from his lip, "Good thing."

"Hey, I've got a question for you."

"What's that?"

"What color was the police car that you saw in my driveway?"

The boy cocked his head, "It was gray. I kind of wondered about that, because police cars in Dolphin Bay are white and green."

"That's right, which means they probably weren't local cops."

"If they weren't real, who were they?"

"I'm not sure we'll ever know but we've got some people looking into it."

"I can't believe I didn't pay attention to that at the time. I just assumed it was a cop car and figured they were undercover or something."

"It's funny how your mind works when you're stressed. You deal with the situation but you don't have time to register lots of details that you're taking in, until later. Your brain is recording lots of stuff and stashes it away in your memory bank, until there's time or reason to sort it all out."

"I guess."

"No, really, it happens all the time to almost everyone. It's the body's way of protecting us from overload; by forcing us to concentrate on the task at hand, while the gray matter takes care of the rest.

I'll give you an example. When you're driving the ball down the field, you're concentrating on your footwork, and where the defenders are, and what direction they're running, whether one of your mates is going to open up a lane, and how far you have to go before you can take a shot…but you're not thinking about being out of breath and your lungs feeling like they're on fire, or that cute girl in the first row of the stands, who only cheers when you're doing something spectacular, or that the sock inside our right shoe is rubbing a blister because there's a little fold. Everything is focused on your next step and the one after that."

"Yeah, I see what you mean."

"After the game, you might remember how you wanted to fall down and take a deep breath, or see the girl, or you might take your shoe off to rub the blister. You knew all those things but they weren't relevant to what was happening."

The boy laughed, "What pretty girl?"

"How old did you say you were?"

"Ten and three-quarters."

"Yeah, you're too young for that." He gazed across the little bay at the first luxurious yachts docked in a forest of white pilings south of the fluid lines of the aqua marina draped around the manmade hill, terraces emulating long slow waves rolling into the beach at sunset. Towering palms bordered a wide boulevard sweeping down through stylish neighborhoods, to split into a circular drive and parking for the multi-story marina complex or a shaded avenue along the length of the quay.

Johnny pointed across the bay, "Looks like they haven't destroyed that side yet."

"Let's go check it out," said Jessie. "I've definitely seen enough of this."

The little engine whined and the boy brought the boat about to hug the opposite shore to the inlet. He slowed and eased into the narrow channel, "We haven't been back, since the bad guys shot George and his family."

"I know and I still feel bad that we didn't do more to protect them."

"We didn't know," replied Johnny, "or we would have done something."

"Do you have any idea of how proud I am of you?"

Johnny blushed, "I just do what you and mom taught me to do."

"And you just keep right on doing what feels right," said Jessie. "Have you noticed that there aren't any surveying stakes in here?"

"Yeah, maybe they've given up on destroying nature."

"Let's hope. I talked to old man Little, who owns all of this, and he was kind of dazzled by being offered big money. I asked him what he'd do with all that cash, if he sold out to SunnyBreeze, and he said he'd probably just put in the bank, because he's too old to travel and too young to waste his final years on a golf course."

"So, what's all that mean?"

"I hope it means that he values the land and the critters and the tradition more than money he doesn't need."

The boat squeezed into the little pond. No dark eyes bobbed to the surface but the birds of the forest provided a joyous song to soothe sad memories. He pulled a little camera from his pocket and fired off six or eight frames at varying exposures and then a few of the smiling boy, "You know, I've always thought that this place is absolutely beautiful and I was working on a painting of it, that got destroyed by the cops, so I want to do another one with George and his family looking out from the shadows. We ought to remember the fun we had feeding them marshmallows, I think that's what they would have wanted."

"Weird to have alligators for friends."

"Why? Gracie's one of our best friends and no one thinks that's weird."

"You know what I mean."

"Yeah, I do and I'm glad we get to share these memories with each other forever."

"Me too."

~

Mavis marched into Tate's office, "I tried to convince Tabitha Hall to help quell the riots, before they become a national movement."

"And?"

"I think she's sympathetic to what we're trying to accomplish but she's a journalist, who will report the facts without withholding anything."

"What happened with the kidnap victims?"

"I passed your information along to Mrs. Hall and I got a call, a little while ago, that the prisoners had been freed. You were aware that one of them was Jessie Cotton?"

"No shit? You mentioned that he was missing."

"Evidently, he's acting as a coordinator for the protestors."

"I guess it doesn't really surprise me but that guy keeps coming back like a bad penny. Hell, he came through here a while back, threatening me because the surveyors shot three gators across the bay and he doesn't want us tearing up any more tropical forests."

"I noticed that nothing's changed over there."

"I don't know who he got to, but the property owner tripled his price and backed out of the deal."

"Let's let it ride for a while and, maybe, I can convince the owner to come around to seeing my vision for a recreation and educational jungle park for the guests and our students. In the meantime, Cotton's on the right side of this argument and maybe a voice of reason to keep things from getting out of hand."

"Good thing, we've got the owners' opening next month and we don't need them being distracted by protesters marching all over paradise. Besides, there's too much that needs attention before the first guest shows up."

"I took our directors to lunch at the Dolphin Run and it was fabulous! The room is absolutely stunning, the food was wonderful, and the service was exceptional. If we can duplicate that level of attention in all our services, we're golden."

"How's it going with the directors?"

"Those, who actually believe in what we're trying to do, are dedicated to getting the first test operation up by the end of the month. We found an abandoned high school complex in Philadelphia and we're transforming classrooms into apartments. If everything goes right, we could have all seventeen pilot programs up and running in six months...but I'm not sure we can stay ahead of the frustration that's bubbling to the surface all over the country."

"Just stay ahead of the craziness and you've got a chance of pulling it off."

"I sure hope you're right."

"What's happening with the school?" asked Tate.

"Tanger's lined up most of the teachers and they're going through indoctrination with Reverend Combs. We've already got two-hundred applications and we haven't even made a formal announcement."

"I guess I should know but, with all the other details I'm working on, I guess I just missed it."

"Missed what?"

"What's the final name of the school?"

Mavis grinned, "The New School at Dolphin Bay."

"I like it. It's got a positive perspective and a sense of forward thinking."

"How's it going with Flint?"

Tate hesitated, "He's kept the inspectors at bay and he's helping to fine tune the training of the staff. We know the level of service to expect and he knows how to communicate that expectation to the personnel."

"In spite of the organized chaos, having the owners stay in their own condos should help to smooth everything out. I have no doubt that they'll provide instant feedback, if anything isn't up to their standards and expectations."

"We've got a small army dispensing their preferences for china, linens, towels, kitchenware, and all the rest."

"At least they provide the furnishings."

"This is going to be a month of parties and festivities. We've got major talent lined up every night, the clubs are booked, and the hospitality crew has contests and events, luaus and family movies, and enough programs to keep everyone busy twenty-four/seven." Tate walked around the massive desk to take her in his arms, "I can't believe we've been on this quest for more than two years and we're finally within sight of the finish line."

"This is only the pilot project and, as soon as we've got this one running, it's on to the next two. Are you still up for that?"

"As long as we do it together." He leaned to kiss her but she backed away.

"We're a winning team and we'll keep on winning."

"Is something wrong?" asked her husband.

"I'm feeling something different in you but I'm not sure I understand what."

"We've both been under a lot of pressure to make all the puzzle pieces fit and function seamlessly and we're going in different directions to get it done. I'm fairly sure that I've been distracted."

"I'm sure that's it," replied his wife, with a kiss to his cheek. "The markets are down and the investors are nervous, so I'm off to Miami for the next few days, calming and soothing the restless and impatient."

She turned to leave but his voice called out, "We need to make some time for us, it's been too long."

"I know. When all this is finished, I vote we go away someplace quiet and romantic."

"Wasn't it you, who mentioned having kids?"

"I did suggest that, didn't I? I guess we'll know when the time is right."

He waved his hand, "I don't want all of this to get between us."

"I think we've both got tunnel-vision to see this thing through, we'll make time."

"I'm going to hold you to it."

Bobby Warmington and a group of housekeepers followed her new boss, Milly Savage, into a sprawling six-bedroom mansion, decorated in Art Deco furnishings and angular contemporary artwork, with massive windows framing a view over the dunes to the glittering Gulf beyond. The women were paired up into teams, that merged with other teams to form the optimal and most efficient use of woman-power to return trashed condos to their former pristine splendor. This unit had been dressed out to reflect the lifestyle of six twenty-something bachelors, who spent a week barely sober enough to proposition every woman in the resort.

"Ladies, this is an extreme mess and the new guests will be checking in less than four hours. Team One will take the kitchen, Two and Three can handle the bedrooms and bathrooms and collect the linens to be sent out. Teams Four and Five will collect trash and recycling, vacuum, dust, and mop the living areas, and inventory and restock the bar. Nothing less than perfection is acceptable. Once we begin occupation, you will be expected to complete six units a day, every day. You have ninety minutes. Go!"

Bobby and her partner, Janey Holliday, donned rubber gloves and tackled the kitchen, lining up three bins to collect food waste, paper, glass and plastic. Janey hauled the recycling bins out to the collection container hidden in a blind cavity behind the garden walls and returned for more, while Bobby scraped and loaded piles of dishes and glasses into the first dishwasher and started on the second.

"I can't believe people would spend a whole week and not even rinse a plate or a coffee cup. I thought the rich people were supposed to have some class."

Janey laughed, "It's been my experience that the more money they have, the worse they behave."

"Amen to that," replied Bobby, dumping greasy pans into soapy water. She turned with a grin, "They have people like us to clean up their mess."

Savage clicked her stopwatch at eighty-six minutes. "You ladies are terrific. You beat the deadline by four minutes, this place is spotless, and I'm really proud of you!"

The women beamed. Getting paid more than the minimum wage, with increases dependent on quantity and quality, made them want to work hard but being appreciated made them feel that they were part of the SunnyBreeze team.

She glanced at her watch, "I believe it's time for Conference and then we'll let each team tackle a cottage."

They marched on an undulating ribbon of pink faux pavers snaking along Hibiscus Boulevard, past the thatched shops and restaurants on the dunes, then down Seahawk Way, twisting through little neighborhood clusters, lush with trees and green textures. The brilliant colors and enchanting scent of flowering plants were designed and placed to promote the sense of seclusion and privacy in a little village, with the population density of a large city.

Janey leaned to whisper, "I'm not sure I buy into all this mumbo-jumbo they're drilling into us at Conference. It feels like they're trying to brainwash us."

Bobbie glanced around to locate Mrs. Savage, "I'd be careful how I phrased things like that, if I were you."

"Well, you're my best friend here, so, what do you think?"

"I think our training was designed to make every employee feel fortunate to have been selected to be a part of a professional team, trained and prepared to produce the perfect experience for our guests. I don't know about you, but I'm making more than I made holding down two jobs before. I've got kids, who need my attention and never quit eating, and I'm thankful that they're being considered for the new school."

"So, they're not just pulling your chain, they've got the whole family in the noose?"

"We both work hard to earn our pay and you don't have to believe everything they're saying, but it doesn't hurt to listen." Bobbie straightened up and walked faster.

Janey trotted along to keep up, "I moved into the employee apartments yesterday and they might be new but the construction company used the cheapest materials they could find. I could push a finger through the wooden doors, the plumbing leaks, and the whole place stinks of chemicals. They claim we're getting a deal on the rent but, after looking around, I'm afraid to live there."

The winding way wound through a pine forest to a large gate in a tall pink wall, that admitted employees to the worker's compound, where every function of the complex was coordinated and many of the staff were housed.

The women joined hundreds of workers, all dressed in black and white, streaming into a gigantic hall, where rows of chairs faced a stage under a banner bearing the motto, 'EXCELLENCE IS NO EXCEPTION!' and tall screens flashing portraits of happy animated workers.

Bobbie wandered through a spacious cafeteria, serving hot meals day and night, to grab a cup of hot coffee, with a little cream, and settle in for a momentary pause.

The subtle din of people moving around the enormous space was crushed by cheery pop-rock classics cranked up to deafening decibels. Jackie Hopper, Director of Employee Training, and all the group leaders bounced onto the stage, dancing and enticing everyone to get up and move their bodies to shake off the stress and fatigue.

After five strenuous minutes, the music faded and Hopper greeted the crowd with a gigantic smile, "I'm so glad all of you are part of this family! Give your neighbors a hug!"

The crowd obliged, hugging the desperate and determined souls around them.

"I've talked with every single one of our fabulous leaders and they're all reporting that everyone is doing a fantastic job in these final frantic days of training and preparation. We're all really proud of you!"

Cheers and applause.

"Our first guests will be arriving on Saturday and I have no doubt that they're going to be knocked out by the level of service and attention we'll provide. We've tried to prepare you to fulfill just about any request or solve any problem, but I'm absolutely sure that things will pop up that none of us could have foreseen. So, what's the proper response, when you don't know what to do?"

The crowd responded in unison, "If you would be kind enough to give me a moment, I'll consult my supervisor."

"Splendid! You all have ear-buds and microphones, so don't be afraid to take charge of the situation and ask a question or offer a solution, for that matter. We've got your backs and we're all part of the team that makes SunnyBreeze more than just a resort because…"

The crowd chanted, "…our sole responsibility is making sure that every guest's dreams and desires are fulfilled beyond their expectations."

A low, moaning tone reverberated through the hall, as he spoke very softly, "I know that we're all exhausted, so stand up and let's see if we can banish the poisons and replace them with dynamism and vitality!"

Tired workers rose reluctantly.

"We're all proud to be part of this incredible concept that will alter the very perception of exclusive resorts forever. We get to be the keepers of this magnificent facility, that's about as close to paradise as human hands can create." He turned to applaud the team leaders on the stage, then the crowd, "Let's give a round for our awesome management team, who know how to pull the levers to make all of our systems work flawlessly, and we applaud our team, because you are the frontline, who will make this a magical experience for our guests. You are the heart and soul that defines the character and provides the effervescence in the spirit of SunnyBreeze."

Soft ethereal music floated above deep vibrations rumbling through the floor, gently soothing tired muscles and weary joints. "So, stand tall, shoulders back, close your eyes and take a long…slow…deep breath…and hold it for a moment. Now, let it out very slowly, expelling all the bad air, until there's nothing left. Now, inhale slowly, fill your lungs completely and, then, slowly release it. Continue to five."

The workers obeyed.

"You've received in-depth instruction from the finest coaches and instructors in the industry, who've shared decades of experience and wisdom to make sure that every one of you knows, not only, how to do your job expertly but why our techniques are crucial to delivering a gratifying and lasting impression. You've suffered through grueling training and practice scenarios, with admirable patience, persistence, and humor. You know you're ready, we know you're ready, and, with your dedication to perfection, you'll ease our guests into wonderland with brimming enthusiasm.

All together now, recite with me, 'I'm filled to overflowing with the energy of my convictions, I'm just beginning my journey to achievement and fulfillment, and I am blessed to be a part of a congregation that serves a greater purpose, that lifts me up to seize my potential and see the path to my future. I'm the best me I can be and I've only just begun!'"

"Now, open your eyes and stretch."

"Hug your neighbor."

Smiling workers embraced, knowing that they were finally nearing the culmination of training.

"We realize that you're working far more hours than your normal workweek will require and we appreciate the effort that you're putting out to make this a spectacular opening. This place is nothing without all of you! You are SunnyBreeze!"

Cheers.

Janey leaned to whisper, "They'll never give us more than thirty-five hours a week, so they don't have to offer benefits."

Bobbie replied, "Will you stop that?"

"Okay! Everyone, we're all in this together! On three! One, two, three! SunnyBreeze!"

An enthusiastic roar erupted and faded into crowd noise.

"Take a few minutes to grab a bite to eat and then get moving! The guests are coming, the guests are coming!"

The employees cheered and applauded and wandered out of the enormous cavern. Janey sauntered to the cafeteria and Bobbie headed over to check in at the housekeeping wing, where she found Milly Savage waiting impatiently at the entrance. The nurturing humor that danced in her blue eyes was replaced by a cold hard stare, "May I have a moment?"

"Of course."

Savage pushed through the crowd and marched along a hallway to her office. Bobbie followed and her boss closed the door.

"I understand that Mrs. Holliday has a dispute with our methods and I must ask whether you share her opinion?"

"I'm sorry but I don't know what you mean."

"She's been overheard complaining about the training."

"As far as I know, she's as thrilled to be working here as I am. This opportunity means everything to all of us. This job replaced desperation with hope."

"I appreciate that but you must understand that the list of qualified applicants, who want your job, is long. You'll be getting a new partner this afternoon."

"But what about Janey?"

"She'll be on suspension for a week, during which time she'll have the opportunity to adapt to our philosophy…or find other employment."

Bobbie stared at the floor, "As you wish."

"It is not my wish to have any need to discipline an employee but none of this will work, if even one person tries to buck the system. We all share the responsibility to put the guests before everything else and, in the process, build a thriving cooperative community based on trustworthy relationships within our ranks."

"I understand."

"Fine. We'll meet in the training room in fifteen minutes."

Bobbie turned to open the door but Savage said, "Don't interact with Mrs. Holliday, she's being escorted off the property, and don't be late. There's no time for sentiment."

"Yes, Ma'am.

~

It was late, by the time Bobbie got home from work. Her mother, Beatrice, managed to feed the children and tuck them in for the night, with one of her dreadful stories of pixies and goblins and terrifying creatures chasing children through the night. She grew up listening to them and still had occasional nightmares.

Her mother peeked out of the kitchen, as Bobbie hobbled through the front door. "Here let me take your coat, you look so tired."

"I *am* tired."

"Well, I saved you a plate of chicken and mashed potatoes, if you're hungry."

"Thank you, I'm starving. They charge too much for the food in the cafeteria but we're not allowed to bring our own," replied Bobbie, leaning into the hallway, listening for stirring children. "Sounds like all's quiet on the western front."

"I never have any trouble with them, they're wonderful children."

The daughter sat down at the table and took a bite of fried chicken, chewing slowly, savoring the crispy crunch and salty flavor. "That might be because you told them the story of Hattie the child-eating goblin, who might come for them in the night, unless they're sound asleep."

"Well, yes, there was some discussion…" smirked her mother.

"That story still gives me the willies!"

"How was work today?"

Bobbie took a sip of iced tea, "Grueling. We're three days from opening and the training is unrelenting and the preparations endless."

Beatrice leaned back and stared, "There's more to it than that, I can see it in your eyes."

"I never could keep much from you," replied her daughter. "They suspended my partner for complaining about the indoctrination and my boss basically told me that, if I want the job, then I better stay away from her, for the time being."

The old woman stiffened, "They can't tell you what to do on your own time or who to associate with!"

"They can and they have!"

"I know you need the money to raise these kids but you have to remain true to yourself."

"I'm in too deep. I can't go back to my old jobs and I'm afraid that, if I quit, they wouldn't consider the kids for the New School. They deserve a shot at a good education."

"That friend of Mr. Cotton's, Kate Crocket, called this afternoon. She's writing a series of articles for the paper on the working people of Dolphin Bay and the struggles we're all facing. I think she'd like to interview you, the working mother. I got her number."

Bobbie's eyes crinkled into an ironic grin, "I'm employed and earning good money, so I don't think I should complain."

"Considering what you've told me, maybe mum's the word."

"Amen to that."

"Oh, I almost forgot, this came for you from the school," said Beatrice, handing her an envelope with the logo and return address for The New School at Dolphin Bay.

Bobbie bit her lip, hesitating before tearing the flap to read:

Dear Mrs. Warmington,

We are pleased to accept your son, John D. Warmington, into our fall semester.

Unfortunately, we are unable to accept your daughters, Cara and Stacy, for this session but we hope that you will submit applications for the spring term.

We look forward to the opportunity of working with you to ensure your son's success at The New School at Dolphin Bay. Please contact our Admissions Office to set up an appointment to discuss the details and requirements, as well as setting a schedule for your son's orientation.

Sincerely, Tatum Green, Director of Admissions

She handed the letter to her mother, "I really don't know what to make of this."

Beatrice scanned the letter, "Well, that's wonderful for Johnny."

"But not for Cara and Stacy. How can I send one and not the others? That's not fair."

"Would you deny him this opportunity?"

"Well, no…but the girls…"

"But nothing. They're offering him a chance to advance beyond what they're doing in public school. He's bored to tears and at least a year ahead of his peers and we both know it."

"You've got a point," replied Bobbie, picking at a bowl of coleslaw with her fork. "But how do I explain that to the girls? I'm too tired to make these decisions tonight and I've got to be back there by eight in the morning."

"Let's put you to bed," said Beatrice, taking the plates to the sink. "Just don't let what might be an opportunity, for that wonderful little boy, slip away."

Bobbie hugged her mother, "I promise I won't but, right now, I need a shower."

~

The armory was packed past capacity with thousands of raucous supporters, cheering and chanting impatiently, until Benny and the three hostages climbed onto the stage. The response shook the building to the foundation for more than five minutes, before Benny raised his arms above his head and yelled, "Enough!"

The deafening din slowly dwindled to restless murmurs.

Benny smiled, "I knew you could do it!"

Shouts and whistles.

He turned to his friends, "I'd say we've survived their best shot and now, it's our turn!"

The audience erupted.

"I just talked with Leonard and Evan, a few minutes ago, and more than five-thousand people have signed up to join the campaign and more than half volunteered to help out in one way or another! You folks are amazing!"

Cheers.

"What started out as a little protest has developed into a movement that can change our world and maybe everyone else's too, if we all stick together!

I'm sure you'll all join me in welcoming back the heart, soul, and conscience of the group – Sammy Ball, Jessie Cotton, and Kate Crocket!"

The four exchanged hugs, to thunderous applause, and Jessie took the microphone, "Thank you, every one of you, for standing up for us. I'm pretty sure you saved our lives!"

Kate shouted, "You believed in us and we believe the rights you've been denied!"

Sammy held his short arms high, "We've come up with a suggestion for a name for our movement. Considering Jessie's annual summer program for the kids is called 'Art's Important', we thought we might call ourselves 'All People Matter'.

The audience cheered.

Tabitha Hall marched from the wing through the clamor to the simple podium and waited for the crowd to calm. "A great deal has happened since last we met on the steps of the Court House!"

Raucous applause.

"First, I have to thank so many of you for sending in your forms and your honest and thoughtful comments. I also want to thank Cheryl Forrest and her crew for organizing those responses into a database and responding to as many as they have." She pointed to the office crew at the front of the stage. "I'd like to mention the absolutely stunning articles that have appeared in the Times these past few mornings by our own Kate Crocket!"

The writer blushed and the crowd roared.

"We're trying to get organized, while keeping pressure on the powers behind the scenes with a blizzard of articles, editorials, and information, but I understand how difficult life is for so many of you. I know it's hard but I have to ask that you to have a little patience with the steering committee, as we build other teams, from volunteers in the files we've collected, and delegate responsibilities. In the meantime, I can promise you that we will propose a countywide one-day strike to draw attention to our cause. We will propose a date when we next meet in two weeks, right here."

The enthusiasm in the assembly's approval rattled the windows.

"I'll ask again before we disperse that, if you have a talent, if you have some spare time, if you care about the outcome of this movement let us know! Volunteer! Talk to these wonderful people at the front of the stage. Tell your friends and neighbors and bring them to the next meeting. We're only going to succeed if everyone is involved!"

Applause.

"If any of you haven't had a chance to read Miss Crocket's articles, we have free copies of the most recent editions of the Times at the back of the room. Thank you all for coming and we'll see you in two weeks!"

She turned to Benny, Jessie, Sammy, and Kate, "Did I cover everything?"

"Yeah," said Benny with a hug. "It's better having you up front, because you keep everything businesslike. If any of us got started, these people would be marching down the street looking for someone to lynch."

"Maybe we should let you announce the date for the strike," said Tabitha. "I'm a reporter but you're becoming a politician!"

Jessie clapped him on the back, "Better you than me, brother."

"Hey, I never set out to get elected to anything. I just want folks to get paid a fair wage, so they can pay their rent and raise their kids."

"We might never prove that the Dolphin Bay cops were actually behind our kidnapping but we know they were involved," said Sammy. "So, it might be time for real people to run for the City's highest office and you'd be great."

"I don't know nothing about running a city," replied Benny. "So, let's concentrate on what needs to come next, okay?"

"Okay."

~

The intercom buzzed and Jenny, the receptionist, said, "Mr. Flint on line two."

"Thank you," said Tate, clicking the blinking button. "Ned, how are you?"

"I've been missing you, my boy, but I understand that opening day is fast upon us. Are we ready?"

"I think, with your help and guidance, we're as prepared as we can possibly be. I'm absolutely positive that the guests will be blown away."

"I hope you're talking figuratively rather than literally."

"I checked the weather and there's nothing on the horizon, at least for the next few days."

"Would that we could program the weather."

"Amen."

"Trust your staff to handle the minor problems and allow them a little time to put all that we've taught them into practice. Given the opportunity, I'm confident they'll excel far beyond our expectations."

"Your guidance made that possible," said Tate.

"If you're not on your wife's short leash, perhaps we could have dinner at my villa, say Sunday evening?"

"Unless something dire comes up, I'm fairly sure that I'll be a bachelor that evening."

"Not if I have anything to say about it! I'm having palpitations just thinking about the possibilities."

~

Attendants guided an endless procession of luxury cars through the broad circular drive, under a colonnade of Royal Palms soaring over long curving planters stuffed with hibiscus and tropical color. Guest representatives, dressed in pastel shirts, emblazoned with the SunnyBreeze logo, over white slacks and white tennis shoes, greeted every new arrival with efficiency and humor. They directed the new residents to personal liaisons, who were prepped as coordinators for specific residences, with full knowledge of the owners and their families, having memorized their preferences and priorities from the questionnaires that accompanied each builder's contract.

Abby Thomas, a pale cherub with a shock of orange hair, leaned into the driver's window of a shiny black Mercedes wagon, with a huge smile, "Welcome to SunnyBreeze, Mr. and Mrs. Huffington! I'm Abby and I'll be helping you get settled in. If you'll follow my scooter, I'll lead you down to your villa in Ocean View."

She hopped on a pink Vespa and buzzed north out of The Commons, turning into the dunes three blocks down. She parked the scooter at the top of the drive of a pale yellow four-bedroom lodge surrounded by a vibrant magenta hedge of Bougainvillea, sweeping beneath gnarly oaks and a stately Banyan tree shading a curving walkway to a pair of teak doors with brilliant brass fittings.

Abby beamed, as the Huffingtons emerged from the Mercedes, and reached to shake each of the children's hands. "You must be Harper - and April - and Travis. You won't believe how cool your rooms are! You're going to love it here, there's so much to do!"

She turned to Abe and Frieda, "I can't wait to unlock your little piece of paradise but, first, I want each of you to close your eyes and tell me what you hear."

The family obliged and April said, "I hear a flock of birds cruising behind those trees over there."

Travis grinned, "I can hear the sound of the surf and I can smell salt in the air, so it can't be far away."

Frieda sighed, "I hear something that's hard to find in our world."

"What's that?" asked her husband.

"Quiet."

Abby laughed, "That's one of the marvels of this development. There are hundreds of families moving into their new vacation homes today, but all I hear are the sounds of nature. C'mon. Let me show you around."

She unlocked the door and handed the keys to Mr. Huffington with a grin, "I know you're going to love everything about this place."

The family trooped into an adobe atrium cooled by palms and fichus, ferns and orchids reaching to skylights, two stories above a flagstone floor that stretched around the house to the shady garden. The magnificent entry was warmed by a flight of parakeets and canaries fluttering through the foliage, singing songs of welcome. A massive great room felt slightly masculine, with plush leather furniture and a huge stone hearth wrapping a fireplace and a six-stool bar, beneath a wide staircase spiraling up to the balcony and four bedrooms on the second floor. Another broad arch opened into a bright airy kitchen, with commercial appliances and a long rustic table set in an alcove surrounded by a wall of windows, offering a vignette through lush plantings to the secret retreat.

Frieda Huffington set her purse on the counter, "This is lovely. I can't wait to cook a meal in here."

Abe smiled and, almost imperceptibly, the tension in his shoulders relaxed.

"There's a modest grocery in The Commons but, if you want to take a night off, there are more than a dozen restaurants three blocks down. They offer everything from pizza to the finest French cuisine and plenty of seafood. You can even have them cater meals here."

"How far is it to the beach?" asked Travis.

"Follow me," said Abby, marching up the stairs to a bank of windows overlooking the dunes and the Gulf beyond. "Is that close enough for you?"

The children cheered, "This is fantastic! How fast can we get our stuff brought in, so we can change and go to the beach?"

"I can have a porter here within a few minutes, if you want some help bringing your bags and personal belongings in from the car."

"That would be splendid," said Abe, extending a hundred-dollar bill cupped in his hand, "I am more than pleased with our new home and I hope you'll extend my congratulations to Tate Sloan."

Abby pocketed the bill with a smile and switched her communicator to 'Call'. "I'll pass that along, just as soon as I order up a porter."

~

Milly Savage stationed four-woman teams in fully stocked vans, every few blocks throughout the complex, to assist guests and Harvey Millsap had crews of maintenance experts at the ready in case of minor emergencies but there were no angry or distressed calls to the front desk, rather frustration at not finding the bar stocked with their favorite libations, because they neglected to fill out the form, a porn channel in the media lineup, or free bottles of lotion and shampoo, terry robes, and slippers in the bathroom.

One inebriated female guest wondered whether it would be possible to repaint the walls, in the great room of her chalet, a slightly peachier tone of beige, before her in-laws arrived on Friday?

Sara Brighton, an astute operator who handled the call, replied, "But Mrs. Creighton, have you seen that color at sunset? It's absolutely stunning! You might want to hold your decision until you see how that tone just glows this evening."

The woman stammered for a moment, said, "Thank you," and hung up.

Tate stood in a second-story window, watching a small army of energetic young people guiding the parade of guests through the gauntlet, isolating their assignments with enthusiasm and humor to lead them to their personal Shangri-las.

His fears and emotions about Ned Flint aside, the old master's training program, combined with Reverend Comb's persistent inspirational encouragement, transformed common laborers into a cadre of disciples dedicated to producing perfection. Two years of toil and hustle was rolling out to happy customers.

He reached for the phone and dialed. A secretary answered, "Howell Foundation."

"This is Tate Sloan, I was wondering whether my wife might be in your offices. She was scheduled to meet with Marvin Standler this afternoon."

"Let me check with his secretary."

The opening strains of soft jazz soothed his impatience, for the few moments before the woman returned, "I'm sorry, it seems that they've gone to the project site. May I have your wife return the call, when they return?"

"Certainly," replied Tate, "and thanks for your help."

He dropped the handset into the cradle and stared out the window at the controlled mayhem rolling through the circular drive. SunnyBreeze was the first project that he and Mavis had planned and executed from concept to completion but this moment of triumph, the birthing of a living breathing entity effervescing with life, felt empty and lacking without her.

Cynthia Jones, Activities Manager, scheduled a welcome barbeque in The Commons this evening, with a good-time country group playing through the dinner and the latest hit family film showing in the band shell at twilight. The clubs at the marina offered a hot cover band, a trio of comedians, and dueling pianos in the poolside bar, and every restaurant on the property was booked into the wee hours of the morning. The pulse of SunnyBreeze was coming to life and, for the next month, waves of owners and their families would transform the development into a thriving community.

Tate took great pride in cleaving this little slice of wonderland out of swamps and mangroves but the latest projections, for the revenues it would produce, were absolutely staggering. Mavis might be off on her crusade but he felt no guilt in wallowing in the glow of this success for the weekend.

~

Marvin Standler offered his hand to help Mavis step out of the limousine to inspect the tasteful entry sign at 'Providence', a sprawling urban shopping center, abandoned since the paying clientele and upscale shops moved to a safer neighborhood decades ago. Clever architects and expedited construction renovated the site into a vision of future urban housing. A cluster of shops and entertainments occupied a portion of the original structure but almost half was converted to classrooms for re-educating the new tenants and their children, and the rest remained to be developed as the residents found needs that might enhance the community. Twisting wings of stacked prefab apartments grew from the central complex like the appendages of an insect. Vast parking lots were dug up and replaced with rolling hills covered with trees and peaceful gardens, spaces for growing vegetables, pools, and athletic courts. Everything was connected by sweeping pedestrian and bike paths curling through the landscape.

Mavis shielded her eyes against the afternoon glare, "I like the hammered steel effect. It feels industrial but something more than that…maybe inviting? It makes me want to see what's on the other side of this entrance."

"That's exactly what we were after, the impression that this is a really cool place and everyone who lives here takes pride and ownership in the entire property."

"I can see how all of this, between here and the main building, used to be paved over but, now, it's like a mature park that's been here forever."

"Our patrons will have access to everything they might need on site and we'll have shuttles running back and forth to the factory, which is only four blocks away. So, for the most part, our employees will be spending more than ninety percent of their time within our ecosystem and, given patience and persistence, they will become true believers," said Standler, opening the door to the car.

Lush plantings, a cheery fountain at the center of a broad circular drive, and an enormous glass entry seemed more appropriate for a resort than worker housing.

Mavis looked around as they entered the building. "I don't see any parking lots."

Marvin pointing to a residential wing wandering out into the landscape like children's blocks stacked haphazardly, "The basements are two stories of underground parking, so there's no need for cars lined up on the street."

"Clever," replied the beauty. "When will the residents move in?"

"They've already been selected and our planners are working out who will live where."

"What's the criteria, seniority or expertise or what?"

"The size of their families," laughed Standler.

"Really? That's so…I don't know, Utopian!"

"It makes absolute sense that families with lots of kids need more room than newlyweds."

"How many apartments are there?"

"When the final wings are finished, we'll have housing for almost a thousand workers and their kin."

"I can't believe that our idea is coming to fruition at the same time SunnyBreeze is opening."

"That's today, isn't it? I'm surprised you aren't down there helping out."

"I think this is more important right now." Mavis looked away, "I watched that enormous crowd in Dolphin Bay ratcheting up to riot, only to be pulled back by some very cool heads, and the premise for all of this became very real. We need to accelerate our program because, once the protests begin, they'll spread all over the country. There are millions of desperate people ready to rise up and demand a piece of the folks who created this mess and, once it starts, there'll be no turning back."

"When you first started talking about all of this, I agreed with your prediction but I thought you were fairly naïve to think that you could actually make a difference."

"And?"

Marvin's steely eyes softened, "You've convinced me that we're headed for a convulsion that will make the Great Depression look like a minor inconvenience. Maybe it's a little bit of guilt, maybe it's just common sense, but either way, getting out in front of all of this seems desperately logical."

"Thanks," replied Mavis, taking his hand. "I've doubted myself and my motivations, since my father pointed all of this out to me several years ago."

"That just shows how much faith he has in your abilities and your judgment. This wouldn't be happening without you driving it forward."

She waved her hand around the beautiful and inviting interior, "Or someone like you making it real."

"I doubt there's much I wouldn't do for you," replied Standler, removing his cowboy hat to kiss her.

Chapter Nine

Gracie pranced out onto the patio followed by Kate, who stumbled while attempting to balance a full cup of hot coffee and stifle a yawn.

Jessie looked up from her article on the front page of the Dolphin Times with a grin, "'bout time my favorite girls rolled out of the sack. Good article."

"That's why I get to sleep in," replied Kate, sitting to gaze out through the trees to the water, the quiet graced with birdsongs. "It's so peaceful here."

"It's pretty easy to get too comfortable in my little hideout. I hate to admit that, when I'm in the proper state of mind to produce a lot of work, I become a cranky antisocial hermit."

"You're a complicated man but I've recognized that part of you since the day I met you."

"What's that?"

"So, focused, you can't see what's right in front of your nose."

"Like what?"

"Well me, for example."

"I already apologized…"

"Even when you were playing ball, you zeroed in on what you needed to do and everything and everyone else could get in line until you'd finished. Nothing's changed."

Jessie nodded in agreement, holding up the paper. "I think you're hitting your stride. I was truly moved by the story of the family losing everything, because the wife got cancer and the husband lost his job and his meager insurance. That's what this whole thing's about, people getting crushed by reality."

"And there's no backup, no help, and no hope," replied Kate, mischievous amber eyes peeping over the rim of the half-empty cup. "Leonard and Evan provided a breakdown of the City's finances, so tomorrow's story is going to present the evidence and ask the question about where's all the tax money gone?"

"That should raise some hackles!"

"At least a few. It's the beginning of the buildup to the next meeting and then the strike. We have to make this movement seem completely reasonable to the retirees, who are living comfortably on their perilous pensions."

"Yeah, we both know it's going to be huge but it doesn't have to be intimidating to the rest of the population. It would be better to give them a reason to be sympathetic."

"We only want to intimidate those who have something to hide," laughed Kate.

"Everyone's got something to hide."

"Including you."

He laughed, "Guilty as charged and paying my penance, ever since I left Madison."

She reached to take his hand, "I'm glad we found each other again."

"Me too, but I'm feeling a little bit guilty for dragging you into all of this turmoil."

Kate moved to sit on his lap and kissed him, "After what we've learned and those bastards put us through, I'd be behind this even if you weren't here. So, don't make it complicated. I'm here because I still love you and we're in the middle of this together."

He kissed her passionately, interrupted by Gracie nuzzling against his leg. He rubbed behind her ear, "Oh, so you're jealous now, huh? You know you're my best girl and always will be."

Kate leaned to pet the dog, "I'm second fiddle, girlfriend. You were here first."

Gracie whined and licked her hand.

"So, what have you got on for the day?"

"I'm taking Johnny over to his orientation at the new school and then I've got to meet with Benny and Sammy about security arrangements for the meeting."

"I'm sure you'll take the time to look around, while you're there?"

"Of course."

~

Johnny was quiet on the ride across the causeway and Jessie finally asked, "Are you nervous about today?"

"Yeah, I guess I don't know what to expect," replied the boy.

"Well, from what your mom told me, I think they're going to introduce you to the campus and the code of conduct they expect everyone to abide by. You might get to meet some of your teachers and a counselor, and I'm pretty sure you'll have plenty of opportunities to ask questions."

"Do you think I'll have to take any tests?"

"I don't know, they might test you just to determine where you fit in. If they do, don't worry about it. Just do your best."

"What if it's not good enough?"

Jessie pulled over on the side of the highway, just north of the SunnyBreeze boundary. He reached over to pat Johnny on the back, "Listen, you're bright, intelligent, athletic, funny, and my best friend. So, as far as I'm concerned, you're just about perfect. But no one's really perfect, because, hopefully, we keep learning and getting better and this is an opportunity for you to learn a lot of new things in a big hurry. Don't be intimidated and don't try to pretend to be anything but exactly who you really are. Just be open, absorb not only the information, but learn how to combine all those different bits of knowledge into a more complete understanding of the world around you. Just be yourself and you'll do fine."

Johnny blushed, "Alright."

Jessie grinned, "C'mon, we both know that you're up to this. The question is, are they?"

The bus motored along the winding road at idle speed through dense clusters of housing, softened by lush plantings that were already beginning to wilt. Hundreds of sunburned tourists wandered through the village of restaurants and shops perched on top of the dunes and migrated across the road into The Commons. Herds of children zipped through slow traffic on brightly painted rental bicycles and hopeful teenagers hauled short surfboards to the beach. Unfortunately, or, perhaps fortunately for their parents, the surf at Dolphin Bay rarely grew large enough to support body surfing, let alone riding a board, unless a large storm was approaching.

"Wow, they sure built up these dunes, they're huge," said Johnny. "And there must be a pizza parlor somewhere in there, because it sure smells good."

"They make it easy for the tourists to spend money on entertainments, that's the secret to this whole operation."

"What do you mean?"

"Keep the guests on the property and make it hard to go anyplace else to spend their money. I've been clocking it and we've gone twelve miles since we passed that grocery by the bridge, which means it's easier to walk down the street to a restaurant than to drive all of the way to the store and back and then fix a meal. These people are on vacation and most of them don't want to mess with anything that requires any effort on their part. They expect to be served and they have the money to pay for it."

"That's weird."

"No, it's human nature that allows resorts like this to cash in on their laziness and gullibility."

"I guess."

At the southern end of the property, a small tasteful sign, 'The New School at Dolphin Bay', pointed to a narrow lane lined with wispy purring pine trees that veiled a very modern complex of buildings nearing completion, surrounded by groves of mature oaks flanking brilliant green playing fields.

"This looks like a cool campus," said Jessie.

"I guess I'm about to find out," replied Johnny, sliding out of the seat. He pulled at his red tie, "I'm definitely not going to enjoy wearing this rag around my neck all day."

Jessie straightened it and kissed him on the forehead. "You look great and it's a uniform, just like the one you wear when you play soccer. It means that you're part of this team."

"I still don't like it."

The artist whispered, "You might have guessed, I don't like ties either but I was always part of a team. C'mon, let's go."

They walked up the path to enter the sleek modern building through a pair of tall weathered doors, that might well have opened into an ancient cathedral in a previous incarnation. Streams of sunlight flooded a brilliantly white interior space, with the reception desk at the far end of a colonnade of inverted tapered columns, supporting stout beams and an arched ceiling, all of it softened by soothing potted palms.

A smiling woman, in a blue skirt and a gray jacket, appeared and extended a hand to Johnny, "You must be John. I'm Mrs. Westbrook and I'll be your counselor this year."

"Pleased to meet you," replied the boy bashfully.

She turned to Jessie, who held out a hand to shake, "I'm Jessie Cotton, Johnny's friend."

"I'm an admirer of your work. In fact, our designer hasn't made a final decision about artwork for this entry and I suggested they consider your paintings, not only for the spectacular colors but the tension you create between earth and sky. They could prove inspirational to our young charges."

"Well, thank you. I appreciate that. You should have them contact Derek Rangle at the Tropical Paradise Gallery."

"We'll need to keep John for a couple of hours, if you could come back to pick him up?"

"I'd be glad to," replied Jessie, patting Johnny on the back. "We'll have some lunch on the way home."

Johnny and Mrs. Westbrook watched Jessie walk through the starkly modern hall to exit through the heavy wooden doors. The councilor caressed Johnny's shoulder, "You're lucky to have a friend like that."

"I know," whispered the boy.

"Did you observe the antique doors?"

"Yes, they made me feel small and…young."

She smiled, "That's quite observant of you. The symbolism represents the fact that everything is built on all that came before. Human beings are problem solvers and every generation of our distant ancestors found solutions to the challenges they faced in the world around them. Our society and everything we enjoy is the product of their intelligence, patience, and diligence. None of this would exist, if not for their efforts. Hopefully, the young people who pass through those doors come seeking wisdom and knowledge."

Johnny nodded.

"The reason that I share this insight is that our goal, as an institution, is to expose our pupils to a broad range of studies, to prepare you to lead our world into the future. You'll become acquainted with ancient cultures and languages, study the latest scientific theories, world history and politics, and learn to appreciate the splendors of the arts."

She smiled down at him, "If you'll work to master each and every course, I can promise that you'll achieve many things that other children your age might only dream about."

Johnny grinned and marched after the tall woman, the staccato cadence of her spiky heels echoing down a gleaming white hallway to her office.

"I understand that you're a soccer player?"

The boy blushed, "Yes, I am."

"We intend to have competitive teams and I hope you'll help us out."

"I'd be glad to."

"Good." She picked up a file, "I've been looking through your records and you've done very well in school and it looks as if you're at the head of your class."

"My mom makes us work at our homework and won't take any excuses for bad grades."

"You're a fortunate young man, you have a wonderful mom and a best friend like Mr. Cotton."

"I do feel lucky to have special people in my life."

"Well, I'd like to introduce you to another special person, our motivational guru, Dr. Jimbo Combs."

A giant black man, dressed in a white suit and a broad smile, strode into the room and reached to envelop his tiny hand. "I'm Jimbo Combs and you're Johnny Warmington, I'm pleased to meet you and excited to have you join our team."

"Didn't you play basketball?"

"Yeah, I did but you're kind of young to remember back that far."

"I remember my dad talking about you, when he watched basketball on TV, saying that no one could defend like Jimbo Combs."

The Reverend laughed and patted him on the back, "We've only just met and I like you already."

Johnny smiled, "That's what he said."

The huge man sat on the edge of a stainless-steel windowsill before a view of a statue of a boy setting a bird to flight in the middle of a glistening fountain, "Have a seat, there's something I want to talk about with you."

The boy sat on a hard, contoured chair, dazzled by a world famous celebrity making time to talk with him.

"I look around at our world, at the things that are happening in our world, and I wonder why we can't find solutions to the problems we face. Things like pollution and starvation and wars and oppression aren't going to be resolved, just because we wish it so. It takes dedicated and intelligent people to join together, with a common purpose and the will to act on their convictions." He paused and smiled at the boy, "And that's why we intend to train the children, who will graduate from this institute, to be prepared to take an active role in guiding our world into the future."

"That sounds like a really big job," replied Johnny.

Combs laughed and patted him on the knee, "You wouldn't be here if you weren't very bright, talented, and athletic, so I'm guessing that you like to do things that other people don't get to do."

"That's kinda true."

"That's what this school is all about, lots of hands-on experience to go with your bookwork and enough adventures to scare your mother to death."

"Like what?"

"Like scuba diving and, later, sky diving, nature studies out in the bush, human studies in the cities, and self-study in our meditation regimen. We want to develop the whole person to be the best that you can be in a wide variety of skills but, in order for our efforts to be successful, we must be assured that you will dedicate yourself to accomplishing the tasks that will be assigned to you, to the very best of your ability, first time, every time."

Johnny grinned, "My mom has a note that my dad wrote to me, before he died, and one of the things he said was that you'll never regret doing your very best…and I haven't."

The huge man smiled and reached to shake the boy's hand, "I think we have a deal."

~

The old bus turned into a neighborhood of carefully integrated blocks of pastel homes, surrounded by colorful plantings, jammed together as visual screens. Straight-line winds during a tropical squall would thin the vegetation in a hurry, the lack of sunlight might take a little longer. The houses were set at odd angles to the curving street, providing an illusion of privacy, and pedestrians and bicycles could avoid traffic by following shady pathways meandering through the complex.

He eased from one little neighborhood to another, noting that all roads descended towards the marina on the bay, like the fingers of a palm frond. Endless docks were jammed with boats, from luxurious ocean-going yachts to sleek cigarette racers, and the wharf was awash with boaters and anglers flaunting the latest fashions from the shops in the tastefully modern three-story complex undulating around an artificial mountain. An enormous bait and tackle shop occupied the bay-level, while the first balcony fronted bars, restaurants, and trendy shops, and the top was reserved for The Clambake, certainly a showcase seafood restaurant, and a large neon sign invited revelers into a club called The Cat's Cradle. Glimmers reflected behind the building from a large pool adjacent to an open Tiki-bar, under a thatched roof covered in splays of imitation palm fronds, with bikini-clad waitresses providing snacks and drinks to patrons at dozens of tables under colorful umbrellas.

The engine sputtered, as the bus idled at the base of the grand boulevard sweeping up to The Commons, a hulking mass perched on a manmade ridge sandwiching Midnight Pass Road, renamed Hibiscus Boulevard over these two miles, between the dunes. The peachy stucco finish shimmered with hues of gold in the late morning sun, radiating a soft halo silhouetting a golfer on a putting green against the shadows of dense foliage. Jessie turned to face the bay and realized that the engineers had designed the property into wedges and this parking lot was the base of a funnel, channeling rainwater into the bay. Considering massive contouring hollowed out the natural rise on the bayside of the key, to build the ridge, if the ocean decided to push through again, once the dunes were breached, the tide would meet little or no resistance.

A Mercedes honked and Jessie puttered up the drive and around the concourse to park facing the pink band shell. He hopped out and wandered through a stream of sunburned tourists, in flip-flops and tennis shoes, gaudy clothes, and broad-brimmed straw hats, to an old-fashioned ice-cream parlor with a soda fountain and chrome bar stools. Mothers were chiding children balancing dripping ice-cream cones, a young man was flipping greasy burgers on a sizzling griddle wafting a mouthwatering aroma, and a cocker spaniel wandered around the restaurant licking up sweet puddles on the floor, like a friendly beige mop with short legs.

A perky young lady, wearing an iridescent pink SunnyBreeze tee shirt and a frothy smile, said, "Welcome to The Pirate's Parlor, where you'll find a treasure trove of goodness in everything we serve!"

"Could I get a glass of iced-tea with a lot of ice and a slice of lemon?"

"Sure you don't want to try our double-chocolate mocha shake, it's delicious!"

He took a seat at the counter, "Thanks, but I don't want to spoil my lunch."

"Iced-tea it is!" Shaved ice tinkled into a globular soda glass and she poured amber tea from a silver pitcher, wedged a slice of lemon on the edge of the glass, and added a straw.

"What do I owe you?"

"Are you a guest?"

"No, just a curious tourist."

"Then, that'll be a dollar."

"Is it cheaper for guests?"

"No, but I can just put it on their tabs, instead of dealing with money."

"That's convenient."

"Saves them having to carry cash, especially at the beach."

"You do have a point. Thanks for the drink," said Jessie, handing her two dollars and taking his glass to sit at a small round table outside in the shade, where he could watch the parade of temporary residents wandering through the shops looking for ways to waste more money on gaudy overpriced merchandise.

He glanced across the drive to the bus and noticed two older couples admiring the oxidized paint, aging corroded chrome, and expanding rust patches. One man lifted his Green Bay Packers ball cap to brush back thinning gray hair, "This brings back memories of driving one of these old beauties clear across the country to the west coast and back with a couple of buddies. It took forever but, I'll tell you what, she never quit on us, just kept going and going. Think we only had to change the oil once, on the whole trip, and that was only because it smelled so bad. I sure miss those days."

His wife elbowed his ribs, "You drive a big black Cadillac, with all the comforts of our living room, and I'm betting you wouldn't last five minutes in this old tub now! The seats are hard, the air-conditioning never worked, and these girls had a hard time getting past fifty miles-an-hour downhill with a tailwind. I'm pretty sure whoever owns this rusting hunk of junk would trade you even right now, if you really want to, but I'm riding with the guy who's got the comfortable wheels. Take your choice, me and the Caddie or dreams that you're too old to remember?"

The other couple laughed, the man chortled and replaced the Packers hat, and they wandered away.

Jessie sensed hard-soled shoes scuffing the pavement, amid hordes of people, barefoot or in soft shoes. The irony of meeting Tate made him grin. "I've gotta say, you've done a hell of a job creating a gigantic Hollywood set to fool the tourists into believing they're basking in paradise."

"I'll take that as a compliment," replied the former quarterback, easing a still fit frame onto a small stool at the tiny table. "I don't know whether anyone told you, but I found it odd, or maybe only fitting, to be tasked with pinpointing your whereabouts, during your recent vacation."

"No, I didn't know but I guess 'thanks' are in order."

"No need. In spite of our rivalry, you would have done the same for me or anyone else, for that matter. That's just who you are."

"I guess I should take that as a compliment. Now we're even."

"Listen, in spite of being an entrepreneur, I admire what you're trying to do with the protest movement and you should know that my wife has organized a committee of some of the wealthiest people in the country to take control of the economy and rebuild the middle class. They're opening seventeen completely self-contained miniature cities to house a workforce employed by a nearby factory or production facility."

"You're kidding?"

"No, I'm not. If they can stay ahead of the protest movement, they might be able to turn the tide."

"What's in it for them?"

"Survival."

"I'd like to talk with her."

"She'll be back next week and I'll tell her about our conversation."

Jessie cocked his head, "You already know that the big protest is scheduled for two weeks from Monday, don't you?"

"Yeah, I've heard rumors."

"Then the answer is 'No', I won't make any effort to slow this beast down, unless it's a matter of protecting our people from violence or harm."

Tate rubbed his chin, "I've heard rumors that the folks, who tried to intimidate you and your friends, are still unhappy with the prospect of a protest march disrupting their tourist dollars."

"They should be worried about solving the problems that these people are facing. The easy way to end the movement is to take care of their workers, treat them as human beings, and pay them a fair wage. Simple."

"You know and I know that management sees the profit potential of every employee in a basic equation – how much does this worker cost the company and how much do they produce above breakeven? The investors expect that calculation to lean heavily in their favor."

"They don't make a dime, if the factories aren't churning out product," said Jessie. "The weird thing about this group is that it isn't just the underpaid and underappreciated workers, it's all the desperately oppressed, unemployed population that needs a decent job too. So, I don't think management will be able to fill the absent slots with scabs, because it's their fight too."

"As I said, I'm a sympathetic realist. I love what Mavis is trying to do but I have to admit that I have my doubts about how this is all going to play out." He waved his hand around the shops, "All these people honestly believe that their income will continue increasing forever and they couldn't care less about people who can't live on minimum wage."

"I know they're only going to understand when the products and services, that they've come to expect, aren't available. When cities and hospitals and grocery stores and gas stations cease to function because the people, who do all the invisible jobs that make everything work, go on strike. Then and only then can the re-education and the reordering of society begin."

Tate reached a hand to shake but Jessie did not respond. Without missing a beat, Sloan offered his business card. "Here's my card, I'll tell Mavis to call you."

The artist took a last sip of tea and stood, "Tip to the wise? Get your landscape crew on watering all these expensive plantings or they'll all be dead inside a month."

He gazed around at the columns of palm trees and flowering hibiscus.

"All the leaves are beginning to wilt, the flowers are shriveling, and, once they go, you can't revive the plant." He started to walk away but turned back to his slightly panicked rival, "I wish I could say it's nice seeing you again."

Ten minutes later, he was standing in the starkly beautiful lobby at The New School, which would definitely benefit by having one of his large oceanscapes hanging behind the reception desk. Mrs. Westbrook appeared out of a hallway to deliver a smiling Johnny, wearing a slightly-too-large green blazer. "We had a lovely visit and I think that young John is going to fit in just fine."

"I'm glad to hear it," said Jessie, looking at the boy. "Did you have a good time?"

"Yeah, this place is fairly amazing, the building is incredible plus they've got a soccer field and a football field and a giant pool."

Mrs. Westbrook said, "We'll be sending John's course list and additional information to Mrs. Warmington within a week or so."

"Great, I'll let her know."

She reached to shake Johnny's hand, "It's been a pleasure getting to know you and I look forward to working with you this coming school year."

"Me too," replied the boy.

They pushed through the front door and Johnny started pulling at his tie, "You won't guess who I met."

"Who's that?"

"Jimbo Combs, Reverend Jimbo Combs, actually."

"Really?"

"Yeah, I got to talk with him for a while and he's really cool. He's the motivational counselor for the school."

"What did you talk about?"

The boy paused, then looked up, "Stick-to-it-ive-ness."

"Okay, wise guy, explain."

"Basically, they want to teach the students about how everything in the world fits together but they need us to commit to working really hard to learn the lessons."

"That shouldn't be much of a problem for you," said Jessie.

"I told him about a note that my dad wrote to me, before he died, and it said that you'll never regret doing your very best…and I haven't."

"I think that's about the best advice a dad could offer his children."

"He wrote it but you taught me how to expect that from myself."

"I'm flattered," replied Jessie, with a grin, "and I'm glad that you enjoyed today. I really hope that this new chapter in your life turns out to be a golden opportunity. You deserve it."

"Thanks, I think I do too."

~

Alva guided Jessie to the screened porch, overlooking a tidy garden at the rear of the house, to join Benny and Sammy. "You three remind me of the musketeers and I'm pretty sure you'll cause just as much trouble!"

"We're the good guys," laughed Benny.

"No, you've always had a talent for putting yourself in the wrong place at the wrong time. Hell, you couldn't even go jogging without tripping over a couple of fake racist cops!"

"Sister, you're looking for trouble."

"I'm just teasing. Actually, I'm really proud of everyone who's involved in this whole thing and I'm damned sure thankful that y'all are still alive. Now, sit yourselves down and get to work and I'll bring something cold to drink."

Sammy laughed, "I guess it's too early in the day for a cold brew?"

"You got that right!"

The three men sat on comfortable lawn chairs around a round wooden table and Jessie asked, "What's happening with your house?"

The little man's blue eyes peered over reading glasses perched on his pug nose, "Well, that Fire Department Captain, who helped me out on the night of the fire, filed an extensive report stating that, in his opinion, the fire was started by an unknown arsonist using rags, torn from a yellow terrycloth towel, as a wick in the gas tank of the Volvo. The remnants of the rag were found on the lawn near the end of the driveway and, upon further investigation, it was determined that there were no other yellow towels on the property. All of mine are blue."

"Well, that's good," said Benny.

"Yeah, it lets me off the hook and, this afternoon, two of Dolphin Bay's finest showed up to ask some questions about whether I had any suspects in mind. I mentioned the goon who beat the crap out of me, for starters, and told them about the fake cops who hijacked us."

Jessie shook his head, "I guess it doesn't matter, if they already knew about what happened and who did it, there isn't much they can do to stifle the truth. Too many people know."

"Kind of what I figured," said Sammy. "Plus, if they are on the up-and-up, they need to know, so I can collect on the insurance to start the repairs and get myself another car. Either way, I didn't see that there was much to lose by just being up front about it."

"I agree," replied the artist, "but we've got to assume that those same forces are not going to be happy when thousands of angry workers shut down the town and take over the plaza."

"You know, we need to have some scouts out surveying that whole scene right now, so we know every entry and outlet, every place that snipers or trouble-makers could hide, where the chokepoints are, and how to evacuate everyone in a hurry, if need be."

"I think you're absolutely right," said Jessie.

"So, do you have anyone in mind?" asked Sammy.

"Yeah, there's about a half a battalion of retired military folks, living in this neighborhood, and I can guarantee they'll jump right on it."

"What about our bikers?"

"They're already looking out for all of us and they'll be acting as our personal bodyguards on the day of the march," said Benny. "Eddie said that he expects about fifty guys to be available that morning to escort our folks into town. I know they'll be looking out for anyone who tries to stir things up."

"We need to have this whole thing nailed down or we're asking for trouble."

"There's one other kind of trouble, we ought to be paying attention to, and that's the weather."

"Yeah, it'd be a bummer to have all these folks marching in the rain," said Sammy.

"Well, I noticed a low-pressure system brewing down near Saint Lucia on the weather last night."

"Damn, just what we need bad cops using a hurricane as camouflage!"

"We need to look at this from every angle, because I don't want one person to come away with a stubbed toe, let alone anything worse," said Jessie.

"Amen to that," said Alva, setting a tray of icy glasses on the table. "If you're going to do this, do it right. Too many good people are depending on you."

~

Mavis marched into Tate's office without a smile, "I thought you had this opening under control."

Her husband stood and stepped around the desk, "When did you get back?"

"About long enough to check the logs on the front desk and notice that we've had fourteen calls in the past twenty-four hours about strange fishy odors coming from the floor drains in the Mansion houses along the bay and a half-dozen about the cable service fritzing out over on the north end. What are you doing about it?"

"I've got Harvey Millsap looking into both problems, as well as several complaints about appliances failing. We've also had a few calls about a deep voice that seems to be coming from inside the walls. That's why we invited all the owners to spend some time in their lovely new homes, before we start renting them out, so they can identify the problems that need fixing. This is the dry run, before the real onslaught of tourists starts next week."

"Just so you're on top of this," replied Mavis.

"The restaurants and clubs are packed seven nights a week. They're turning twice the projections and the retail is more than that," smirked her husband. "How'd it go for you?"

"A thousand workers and their families are moving into Providence in Philadelphia and the transformation from abandoned shopping center to thriving mini-metropolis is as astonishing as what we've accomplished here. Only they did it in six months."

"That's terrific! What about the other projects?"

"We're hoping to have all seventeen open and occupied by the end of the year and the committee's identified thirty-two more."

Tate stepped closer to hug her, "I've missed you."

"And I've missed you too." She returned his kiss but backed away, "We've just had so much going on and it's all coming to a head right now."

He leaned against the desk and folded his arms, "I ran into Jessie Cotton the other day and we had a reasonably friendly conversation."

"And?"

"I told him a little bit about what you're trying to do with the foundation and he said that he'd really like a chance to talk with you…and they're planning a general strike for a week from Monday. Rumor has it that they'll turn ten-thousand demonstrators out on the square and shut the city down. With Tabitha Hall in the middle of it, you can bet that it'll receive nationwide coverage in newspapers and on television."

"I'm betting there are a lot of folks who won't take too kindly to that."

Tate looked up, "Including me. We don't need the distraction, when we're trying to accommodate our first full slate of guests."

"If we've designed our services properly, they'll have no reason to leave the property and they can remain blissfully oblivious to what's happening in town."

"That's wishful thinking, if I ever heard it…and I usually don't hear it from you."

Her high heels clacked on the terrazzo floor, as she moved to stare out the windows overlooking The Commons, watching sunburned guests wandering around the shops with their SunnyBreeze charge cards at the ready. "I'm absolutely committed to making this work but I'm equally involved with finding a solution to this coming nightmare. I guess I'm realizing that, no matter how fast we work, we'll never stay ahead of the desperation that the working people are suffering. They deserve to be heard."

"You can be as sympathetic as you want but I made a commitment to open this resort and milk it for everything it's worth, so we can program the next two or three. Our clientele can afford to ignore the demonstrations and we have the perfect secluded escape to shield them from reality in absolute luxury."

She turned around, "Somehow, keeping their Dom Perignon at exactly forty-six degrees doesn't mean much, when you compare it to the struggles of a single mom raising three kids on minimum wage or less."

"We might push the help to provide an exceptional level of service but, you know as well as I, we're paying them at the top of the scale. We've had a couple of problems with renegades, who don't want to buy into Jimbo Combs' indoctrination, but no one has complained about their salaries."

"At least I'm proud of that."

"Look, I don't know what's changed over the past few months but, as far as I know, we're still married, we're still lovers, partners against the world, and we're going to succeed together. If any of that's changed, I need to know."

"It all changed, when we prostituted ourselves to make this project fly, so we could make scandalous gobs of money."

"No, so we could make our own money!"

She waved her hand, "All of this is about greed. We and our investors expect a spectacular return, anything less will constitute a failure."

"That's the plan, always has been."

"Well, maybe that's not enough, anymore. Maybe there has to be something more than just taking money from people who don't have any concept of its real value or how lucky they are to have security. Maybe having more than you need is more a curse than a blessing. Maybe helping those who need help is more rewarding than taking advantage of those who don't."

Tate stood tall, "Look, between now and our grand opening on Friday night, I need you to focus on making SunnyBreeze shine. Let's do the work, play our parts as the glamorous couple hosting their holiday in paradise, and sneak away for a few days alone together, when things are up and running."

Mavis kissed him on the cheek, "You'll have my absolute attention."

"Great."

She turned and marched out of the office, down the hall, past her secretary, and slammed the massive door to her office.

~

Al Delveccio rang the bell and waited. Presently, the door opened and Sonia Calhoun flashed her professional practiced smile, "Al, it's so good to have you back! Won't you come in?"

Mesmerized by the rhythm of her hips, he followed her into the clubroom. The boss was seated in a lounge by a roaring fire, in spite of a ninety-degree temperature outside, with a light plaid blanket covering his legs.

Delveccio bowed, "It's good to see you."

"We're both surprised that I'm still alive, aren't we?"

Sonia sat down next to her husband and the bodyguard stood at ease.

"Can I offer you a drink?" asked Calhoun with a wave of a bony hand. "Sonia get the man something to drink."

"I never drink when I'm on duty, Sir."

Calhoun chuckled, "Considering your reputation as a ruthless professional, I don't find that surprising."

"Considering you had me flown back from California, I might suspect that you have an assignment."

"That I do," said the old man. Piercing eyes peered out of gray sockets buried in a translucent mask barely covering blue veins in a gaunt face, thin parchment ready to crack and flake away, leaving only withered muscles binding ivory bones. Even then, the assassin would be wary of an amoral depravity, capable of unleashing cruelty and violence at the slightest provocation, even from the grave.

"We're going to have a protest march on City Hall up in Dolphin Bay on Monday. I want you to organize your associates to disrupt the festivities, cause as much chaos and mayhem as possible, and make it look as if the ringleaders are directing the violence."

"Are we talking about the same bunch, who refused to cooperate before?"

"Exactly."

The bodyguard grinned, "I'm happy to be back in the Sunshine State, Sir, and I can guarantee that our Alabama volunteers will be eager to lend a hand."

"Let there be no doubt that the folks at the front of the parade are responsible for the violence and the riots that follow. I want the public to turn away from their televisions screens in revulsion at the carnage produced by this mob of ungrateful freeloaders. If you play this right, the authorities will arrest the directors in front of the cameras and the ignorant masses will disperse in disgust and frustration."

"That might be wishful thinking," said Sonia. "These people are fighting for a very personal cause and they're not going to quit, until they win or they're dead."

The old man chuckled, "I guess it's their choice, isn't it?"

Chapter Ten

The perky weatherwoman on the television pointed to a low-pressure system arcing northeast towards the west coast of the Florida peninsula. "Our latest projections show this storm picking up strength from the warm waters of the Gulf, building to hurricane force winds over the next forty-eight hours, and coming ashore someplace between St. Petersburg and Fort Myers by Tuesday."

"We recommend that people evacuate low-lying areas and that everyone begin making preparations for a category-two and, possibly, a category-three storm. We might get lucky and dodge a bullet but all the data we're collecting suggests that surging tides and winds, in excess of one hundred miles-per-hour, will cause major damage all along the coast. Be smart and be prepared."

Kate squeezed Jessie's hand, "I think you ought to postpone it until the storm passes."

"We've got folks coming from all over the South and I'm not sure that we could build this kind of momentum again."

"I agree, it's kind of now or never," added Benny. "From the maps on TV, it looks like we'll be about twelve hours ahead of landfall. Maybe the weather-gods will hold off just long enough for us to get through the speeches."

"Everyone's so ready, we can't hold them back," said Sammy, "even if it gets kind of damp."

"Hell, we're going to have major network coverage and bad weather might just work in our favor."

"What do you mean?" asked Benny.

"From the viewers' perspective, these people are so desperate, they'll march through a hurricane just to make their point."

"Makes sense," said Jessie, "but how 'bout we change it from a march to a rally. It'll be way easier to control a stationary crowd in the square."

"Okay," said the writer, "I'll write the story and get Tabitha to put the word out in tomorrow's newspaper but you guys had better have a plan 'B', in case the weather-gods don't cooperate. How are you going to get thousands of people out of harm's way, if the shit hits the fan?"

"I've got retired Major David Martin working on security and he's got a hundred guys ready to move. I'll ask him to expand the scope of their mission to include evacuation."

"Done."

~

Tate lifted the receiver of his private line, "Tate Sloan."

Ned Flint's slightly nasally accent inquired, "How are you, my boy? I've missed your company."

"I'm sorry, I've been tied up, but I'm pleased to say that we have a full house and all systems seem to be functioning without a hitch."

"Oh, I'm jealous, I do so enjoy being tied up."

Tate grinned, "SunnyBreeze is a first-class destination, in part because of your training program, and the obscene profits that we're going to make will not begin to repay your contribution."

"How's your lovely bride?"

"She's in Detroit for a couple of days opening another village."

"Lucky her, missing the storm," said Ned. "I get so anxious when they're coming in. I suppose, I could fly off to the Hamptons until it passes but I'd much prefer to hunker down and ride it out, if you could slip away to protect me? I don't think I can face this alone."

"I can't leave the property during a potential crisis but there's no reason you couldn't stay here. I could put you up in the Hobbit House, the most enchanting honeymoon chalet in the complex."

"Only if you'll stay with me."

"Fine, I'll have the staff stock the cupboards and freshen the linens."

"Just make sure that we have plenty of cold and very expensive champagne to sooth my anxieties. I get so needy when I'm afraid."

"What do you need?"

"Hmmm, is it need or want? I want your strength, to bolster my cowardice, but I need your pulsing vitality to satiate my other primal yearnings."

"That's a nice way of putting it."

"Don't wear any underwear. I want you to be accessible, when I can't restrain myself any longer."

"Think we'll make it through dinner? I'll have the Dolphin Run cater something special."

"I'll behave myself, until the help has been excused, but I know I'll be anxious for them to depart from the first moment I see you."

"I'll look for you Sunday afternoon."

"Thank you, dear boy, you've saved me months of therapy."

Standler handed Mavis a frosted flute of Crystal Champagne, as the limousine slipped through the Detroit-Windsor tunnel and into the city. "You'll love the new site. We've renovated an old factory into a virtual wonderland."

"I saw the photographs you sent," said Mavis, touching glasses. "This has to qualify as turning a sow's ear into a silk purse on an industrial scale."

Marvin laughed, "At least we didn't have to kill the pig."

"How many will it accommodate?"

"Fifteen-hundred families and we're renovating another plant next door, so we'll be hosting twenty-five hundred by Christmas."

"And they're all employed at the distribution facility?"

"Every one and we're recruiting and training spouses too."

She took his hand, "I can't believe this is coming together."

"Just not fast enough?"

"The rally in Dolphin Bay is scheduled for Monday and, from what my sources tell me, they'll have thousands of marchers and plenty of heavyweight speakers, so it'll get national coverage for sure."

"That doesn't help us."

"Not if the movement gets rolling and things get out of hand."

"What are you going to do?" asked Marvin.

"I've got a private jet waiting at the airport, so I can slip back into town overnight and walk with the dignitaries. If we're going to lead the masses out of the coming disaster, we need to be right in the middle of it."

"The cameras aren't going to miss you, even if you wear a trench coat."

She stuck out her chest, "And I have the perfect little outfit for the occasion."

"I'll bet you do," smiled Standler. "The question is whether you have the perfect little outfit for tonight?"

"I thought we were here on business," replied Mavis, with a coy smile.

"I'd love to make you my only client."

"I'll have to see what surprises might be buried in my suitcase."

The driver motored down a tree-lined cobble street with a wide walkway in the shadow of an imposing wall of black steel plates interspersed with stainless steel light poles that curved into shepherd's hooks supporting simple shop lamps in vibrant red, yellow, purple, blue, and green. He wheeled the car around a broad roundabout overflowing with flowers, through the security gates and a dense greenbelt of mature trees and shrubs. The soaring entry recalled the chrome-plated front grills of vintage Detroit luxury cars and the outer walls of the main factory were dressed in a vibrant rusty red that peeked through gaps between large squares of brushed stainless reflecting the colors and tones of the landscape and the sky.

Mavis gazed around, as she stepped out of the car, "You've done it again! This feels secret and private and futuristic."

"It is in every way," replied Standler. "We've incorporated the latest advances in computers and electronic control systems, so the residents can customize the environment around them to respond to their presence. Once the system recognizes your preferences, it will react wherever you go, adjusting lighting, temperature, artwork, background music, or anything else that you want to program into your private genie."

"That's astonishing, especially when you consider these people are one step out of destitution."

"We want them to be citizens of the new age, we want them to be capable of contributing to our movement as soon as possible and, while they're learning to use these systems for their own comforts and amusements, they'll also be training themselves to do far more complex tasks for us."

"Did some of this come from Jimbo Combs?"

Marvin laughed, "Of course, in spite of his 'religious' status, he's one of the most delightfully deceitful human beings I've ever met. It's part of a program he's been working on called Legacy Self-Transformation, where the individual is supplied with tools and knowledge and subconsciously tasked with creating the person they know they should be. Reverend Combs believes that ninety-seven percent of his subjects will successfully refurbish the mentality of the poor pitiful loser to become enthusiastic and self-sufficient champions of the cause."

Huge sheets of glass parted to allow entry to an enormous atrium illuminated by giant skylights, with a forest of enormous palms and Fichus beneath twenty stories of balconies sweeping through the building, unbraided strands of steel ribbons rippling in a breeze.

"We can house five-hundred families in this main building and an equal number in two satellite concourses which surround pools and athletic fields. We converted the corporate office building to house the school and stripped down the maintenance barn and turned it into a funky shopping mall with all the necessities, so, once again, our tenants will spend a great majority of their time inside the corporate field."

"This is beautiful and brilliant and I know that we're going to be successful in changing the lives of so many people but I'm terrified that we won't have enough time to make a difference."

"Maybe you should look at it from another perspective."

"What's that?"

"That we've already brought several thousand into the fold and, no matter what happens in the rest of the world, we'll bring in tens of thousands more before the end of the year. This is a project that will accelerate as it rolls along, in spite of the economy going crazy, because it's completely self-contained. We will help all we can."

In spite of her outward bravado, Mavis felt small and humble, dwarfed by the enormity of the building and the magnitude of the challenge, and leaned close, "Thank you for believing in me."

~

The Gulfstream dropped out of a turbulent cloud deck and turned into gusty southerly winds on approach for landing just after dawn. The sleek jet powered through the blinding squall, until wheels touched tarmac and the pilot announced, "Welcome to Dolphin Bay, the time is five-thirty, the temperature is eighty-two and it's raining. Our radar indicates that the first bands of storms, spiraling out from the eye of Hurricane Dot, will begin arriving in earnest sometime around noon. Latest weather forecast suggests that the center of the storm will come ashore north of Fort Myers sometime late this evening or early tomorrow."

An attendant produced a large black umbrella and escorted Mavis down the steps and into a waiting SunnyBreeze limousine. The driver tipped his hat and turned to lean over the seat, "Where to, Mrs. Sloan?"

"The Commons, please."

"Straight away, Ma'am."

The headlights fired streaking raindrops into molten embers, bouncing across the pavement in wayward waves rolling to the curbs. The limousine plowed down highway Forty-One, turning to creep across the causeway at Pelican Turn above raging whitecaps ravaging the bay. The driver headed south on Midnight Pass Road through clouds of salty mist and a blizzard of sand whipping off the dunes, the howling wind bending palm trees to bow in submission, fluttering fingers of frantic fronds reaching for an anchor, mayhem scored to the tempo in the thunder of surf pounding the beach in a relentless tantrum.

Mavis buttoned her light jacket against the damp chill of dawn's dull gray glow muffling the colors and textures in a haunting haze, reducing paradise to blurry shades of charcoal struggling to survive the looming threat of nature's fury. *"Pray the engineers were right and she unloads her wrath on some other beach."*

She noticed two of the soaring Royal Palms toppled across the promenade on the far side of The Commons and water pooling in the amphitheater beneath the band shell. The driver wheeled around the circle to pull under the portico, jumped out, and rushed around to open the door, reaching to help Mavis out. "Will there be anything else, Mrs. Sloan?"

"Yes, I need to check in and then I want you to take me into Dolphin Bay."

"There's supposed to be a big protest this morning."

"I know, that's the point."

She marched through the lobby, past an empty reception desk, up the stairs and into their apartment. There were no dishes or glasses in the sink in the kitchen and no Tate sleeping in their bedroom, so she changed into a snug weatherproof hot-pink jumpsuit and matching boots, leaving her black heels lying in the bathroom.

The boots tramped down the stairs and across the lobby to the reception desk. The secretary kept a log of the movements and contact numbers for all the principals and managers. The number for Tate was listed as The Hobbit House, her favorite honeymoon cabin on the property. She flipped back a page to find a note that the Hobbit House had been reserved for Ned Flint by her husband the previous afternoon.

"Bastard!" hissed Mavis, slamming the book on the counter before marching across the quiet lobby, through nature's raging fury, and into the back seat of the white limousine. The driver shook the droplets off his hat and brushed the damp from his coat, before climbing into the front seat. "Where to?"

"Hampton House on Seagrape Circle, please."

Twenty minutes later, the wind and rain tapered to an annoying drizzle and Hannibal Davis welcomed Mavis into the foyer. "Mrs. Sloan, won't you please come in out of that terrible weather?"

"I was hoping I might join Mrs. Hall in the march this morning, if it's still on?"

"Oh, I don't think they could hold these people back with a full-on hurricane. An approaching storm is just an inconvenience!"

Tabitha descended the old staircase slowly, with grace and dignity, "I'm not particularly surprised to see you but, I must say, your outfit is made for television!"

"If you can't lick 'em, join 'em! I believe the program we're instituting will make a profound difference but there's no denying the cause or these people demanding their rights and an end to the cruelty of those who oppress them."

"This is a war that will be fought on many fronts, from the boardrooms to the streets, from anarchy to social engineering, there is no single solution to a problem that afflicts far more than half the population."

"And nothing will happen, until disparate voices join into a chorus that shatters the status quo."

"Well put," said the matriarch. "I just learned something new, you should know."

Mavis tilted her head, curiously, "You mean besides tens of thousands of people risking their lives to march into a hurricane on principle?"

Tabitha chuckled, "Well, besides that, we have allies that we never knew existed."

"Like who?"

"Like a group of people in the little town of Cameron, Oklahoma, who took down an election scam that turned out to be funded by a notorious ministry, backed by those extreme right-wing families, we were talking about a few weeks ago. Oklahoma froze the mid-term elections, while they disqualify more than a dozen candidates and bring charges against a small army of conspirators from across the nation."

"That's incredible."

"It gets better."

"How?" asked Mavis, incredulously.

"Federal elections in eight red states have been postponed, because so many candidates are completely unqualified and most of their campaign finances are supplied and controlled by Future Freedom, a nationalist PAC in California, that's a front for those same families. Congress is imploding and the Justice Department is investigating."

"Their circle remains unbroken, in spite of being exposed, and they'll succeed in countless elections across the county. It seems obvious that they're packing Congress, in anticipation of determining the victor in the next presidential elections, to implement their traitorous agenda."

"Lord help us, if they win."

~

Jessie's battered bus crept along Palm Avenue, three blocks from the plaza. Every street was jammed with cars and pedestrians. He finally found a space in the lot behind The Roxie, the last of the city's old-time movie theaters.

"Sammy was right, even Hurricane Dot isn't going to hold these people back," said Kate, brushing the fog from the window to watch swarms of colorful hoodies and raincoats under bobbing umbrellas marching through the parking lot in the pouring rain. "You've got to make sure that everyone makes it out of here, before the real storms come in."

"Weather lady said things should stay relatively calm until after noon." He checked his watch, "That gives us four hours and, even stretching it, our program won't last more than three."

"I sure hope they've got everything set up."

"We tasked Hank Miller with being stage manager. The illusion of authority makes him feel like a big shot and keeps him out of everyone else's hair."

Kate kissed him and pulled up the hood on her parka, "Let's get going."

They trotted across the parking lot and out through the lane to the square. A relentless tide of bodies gushed out of every side street, merging into a churning human amoeba oozing around a stage built on top of two flatbed trucks decorated in red, white, and blue. Stacks of speakers blasted John Lennon singing, 'Give peace a chance…' above the deafening drone of thousands of voices.

Jessie stopped to gaze around the plaza. Uniformed police officers were stationed around the entrances to the City Building and pairs of police cars, with lights flashing, blocked all traffic in or out of the square. From the way they were parked, he wondered whether they were there to protect the citizens or to seal the exits, if things got out of hand. Several small groups of uniformed officers roamed the periphery of the crowd. Armed spotters peered down, scanning the human mass from the rooftops, and one could only hope that they were Benny's military guys.

Eddie's bikers, wearing their colors and dark sunglasses, stood out as menacing sentries securing the stage and kept two meandering lanes open out to the street with gruff growls and intimidating gestures. Television crews manned cameras, swathed in plastic, covering the stage and reporters roamed through the crowd with handheld units. A pair of production vans were parked directly across the square from the stage to broadcast the event to the entire nation.

Kate leaned close, "There's an electric edginess in this crowd."

"It feels like determination."

"I hope you're right, 'cause if it goes the other way, we've got big trouble."

They found Benny and Sammy behind the stage in a heated discussion with Hank Miller.

"Ready to crank it up?" asked Jessie.

"Yeah," said Sammy. "Butthead is stuck on the original schedule but we want to put Tabitha up first, to welcome the crowd and introduce the speakers."

"Who showed up?" asked Kate.

"We don't have time to get them all in," laughed Benny, consulting a clipboard wrapped in a plastic bag. "We've got Dr. Harold Cochran of American Justice, Lincoln Jones from the Rainbow Coalition, Samuel Mays who started the 'Shine a Light' Foundation to expose lies and corruption of our elected officials, and a dozen more. Plus, there's a whole slew of actors, actresses, and even some famous musicians, who want to use the stage for a benefit concert tonight, if the weather holds out."

Miller added, "I heard the mayor wants a few minutes."

"Yeah, I'll definitely put that asshole at the top of the list," snapped Benny.

"Well, the City did provide security."

Jessie grabbed Hank's shoulder and pointed, "Do you see those police cars? They're set up to keep vehicles from going out, not coming in."

"Oh."

"What about us?"

Sammy grinned, "I think we ought to get Tabitha to introduce us, so we can get the crowd going and move on to some of the speakers. Then maybe finish it up with Tabitha revealing our plans and showing people how to get involved in creating solutions to these problems."

"Yeah, they need to feel like they've become a vital part of something much larger than just a few folks, who are having a hard time getting by."

"They're going to want to go out and burn down the city, if we don't handle this right," added Kate. "We have to give them hope that things can change without violence and insurrection."

"Let's hope we can hold it to a dull roar," replied Jessie, scanning thousands of faces jostling in surges and eddies. Voices and words blended into a chaotic chorus but the eyes made no attempt to hide their frustration or mask the desperation and injustice that replaced pride and security. There was anger but he sensed a strong communal energy flowing between total strangers, who grasped a mutual plight that demanded camaraderie and unity.

Hannibal Davis, sporting a top hat and tails, pushed through the crowd behind a wedge of Eddie's bikers. He carried a large umbrella to shield Mrs. Hall and Mavis Sloan from a downpour driven by a gusty gale. The newspaper heiress wore an Edwardian cloak over tweeds and riding boots but her companion's sensuous curves were embellished by her pink superhero costume, certainly inspiration for a futuristic erotic cartoon for an audience with a latex fetish.

Benny hugged Tabitha, as if she was a close relative, and leaned to whisper above the roar. "You're on first, because they admire the calm assurance of the voice they hear in your editorials in the paper every day."

"I'm fairly sure that Kate's stories are the reason that so many people are participating. There are still swarms pushing in from every side street."

"We're going to want to move this right along, because there's no guarantee that the weather's going to hold. We've got twenty more speakers than we anticipated and there sure isn't room on the schedule."

"I'll keep it short and to the point."

"When you're done, we'd like you to introduce us and we'll do a few minutes of history, then we'll bring on the dignitaries to fire things up, and end with the plan and a push to get people to sign up and help out."

"I talked to the committee last night and we've got almost eight-thousand members and donations are coming in from across the country. I'm afraid this might turn into a movement."

"Mass poverty is a worldwide challenge," said Mavis, whose pink jumpsuit radiated an electric glow in the gray mist. "This is just the tip of the iceberg."

Jessie moved closer, "I'd really like a chance to talk you about your program, when this is over."

"I'd be happy to chat and, if there's time, I'd like to talk to them," replied the developer, pointing to the crowd. "We're opening our facilities as fast as we can and there are more coming online in the next few weeks. If we had enough time, we could make a big dent in the problem."

"I admire what you're doing."

Hannibal Davis held the umbrella over Tabitha, as she marched up the stairs and approached the small podium to thunderous applause that rolled through the plaza and streets beyond. "Ladies and gentlemen, I'm pleased and astonished that so many of you braved this dismal weather to show your determination to make our voices heard."

A heavyset man with a thick white beard yelled, "We ain't gonna let a little rain get in the way of our future!"

The throng cheered.

"Because the weather is so dreadful and there is every expectation that it will deteriorate in the next few hours, we will do our best to present our information and our distinguished guests, as quickly as possible, and send you good people on to the safety of your homes.

Before we get to that, I would like to take a moment to express my pride in the courage and determination that are at the very core of this organization. The point of this general strike is to encourage the employers in our community to show some respect for the contributions of the workers, who show up every day to put in the time and effort that results in a profitable bottom line. Without all of you, none of the suits would have a job!"

Massive cheers.

"I take great satisfaction in the fact that we, all of us, have conducted this campaign with dignity and respect. You're not asking for anything extraordinary, but you are demanding that your diligence and honesty be rewarded with a fair wage, reasonable benefits, and the opportunity for advancement. I would hope that your bosses are paying attention to the national press coverage because, if they don't respond affirmatively to this protest, we will begin shutting down at least one business a week, until they do, and we'll start with the largest and work our way down from there."

Rousing applause.

"Our list includes every enterprise that employs workers, including municipalities, not-for-profit foundations, and corporations. None will be excluded.

Before I introduce our first speakers, I would like to say that our demand for dignity and respect means that we have to act like responsible citizens, during our gatherings and in our interactions in the workplace. We, none of us, gain anything through confrontation. Negotiations will only be successful, if we are professional in our approach and willing to listen to what the other side has to say. Counter-proposals mean that both sides are listening and, hopefully, willing to work towards a resolution that benefits everyone. Just as we strive to represent you in the best possible light, we expect you to act responsibly, because each of you represents all of these other people. We are all in this together!"

The roar of the crowd seemed to slow the raindrops into elongated silver beads, a shimmering sheen suspended in the wind for a moment.

"I would ask everyone, who has not signed up to join our movement, to stop by one of the kiosks that were erected at every intersection and become a member. We need your voice, your dedication, and your talents!

Someone doesn't like what we're doing and their intimidation included beating one of the founding members and the kidnapping and torture of three others."

Boo's and jeers.

"I'm pleased to report that all four have recovered and they've been working diligently with our staff to prepare for this day. Let me introduce Benny Young, Sammy Ball, Jessie Cotton, and Kate Crocket!"

The horde erupted with raucous cheers and relentless applause, as the four bounded up the steps and across the wet plywood deck that had been secured to the surface of the flatbeds. Each hugged Tabitha in turn and Benny took the mike with a big grin, "I can't believe y'all showed up in the spite of this incredible storm. What's wrong with you people, didn't your mama teach to get in out of the rain?"

A slender black woman with a bright blue Afro yelled, "There's no place we'd rather be!" and the crowd went crazy.

Jessie leaned in, "We were kidnapped because of our dedication to all of you, but now, I want to thank all of you for showing your dedication to us and each other in return. We're all in this together and we'll stick together, until we get a reasonable resolution to our demands."

Sammy added, "Every one of you is just as important as the suits in the front office and we're going to keep hammering away at this, until they realize that they have only one option...showing some respect for the people who actually make things happen!"

Kate stepped up, "Many of you have been following my stories in The Dolphin Times and I'm pleased to see so many of the people that I wrote about here in the crowd today. Every one of those stories represents the terror and misery shared by hundreds or thousands of you. Look around, everyone in this enormous crowd is suffering the same indignities, the same injustice, the same bigotry and discrimination as you have. None of you and, certainly, none of us can solve these problems alone. We have to depend on each other and, from the turnout, I'd say our solidarity is going to have the desired effect."

The protesters clapped and cheered but Jessie was interrupted by a loud explosion and the crinkle of sheet glass shattering at the far end of the block. Another blast erupted on the opposite side of the plaza and plate glass shop windows clattered to the sidewalk in three or four other spots around the plaza, before the frightened crowd began to move in reaction to the ruckus.

The calm, almost rhythmic, motion of the mass of bodies vaulted into frenzy, as the communal sense of comradery disintegrated in chaos and confusion. Cheers melted into terrified screams and panic replaced enthusiastic smiles, as bodies surged away from the explosions and towards the side streets that were blocked by police cruisers.

Benny scanned the rooftops for any sign of Major Martin or his lieutenants. The retired military volunteers were using scopes in an attempt to identify and follow the agitators, who were breaking windows, setting off small explosives, and fading into the flow of bodies.

Harvey Harris, of the city motor pool, charged across the stage to hand a walkie-talkie to Benny, "It's for you."

He held the radio to his ear, "This is Benny."

"David Martin here, I'm getting reports that the sabotage is being conducted by a squad of stocky middle-aged guys with buzz-cuts."

"Who are these guys?"

"I'm thinkin' ex-special forces and, from what you told me, I'd guess they might be the same bunch who kidnapped you and your friends. They're definitely not locals."

"Has there been any looting?"

"Absolutely none. In fact, people who were on the scene are guarding the shops that have been trashed. The bombers cause a commotion and disappear into the crowd, as another disturbance starts someplace else."

"Can we nab any of them?"

"The city police have been driven back by the stampede but we've got teams taking up positions around the square."

"Then track the bad guys!"

The radio hissed, as a huge bolt of lightning crackled across the sky, "Can do."

Jessie grabbed the microphone, "Don't panic! Stop running and listen! There is no danger to you! You can stop the troublemakers!"

"That's easy for you to say, sucker," screamed an elderly lady, with curly blue-gray hair sprouting from an old-fashioned gingham bonnet. "You're safe up there above the crush."

The artist ran to the edge of the stage and reached down to grab her but she toppled over in the turmoil, her screams lost in the frenzy of bolting bodies and trampling feet. He jumped into the melee but lost his footing in the jostling mob, battered by shins and knees, as he tumbled over the shrieking woman. He wrapped his arms around her frail body and rolled towards the blue bunting suspended from the deck of the truck, flashing on the many plays where he ended up under a defensive pile, while attempting a busted quarterback sneak.

Tabitha Hall's voice echoed around the plaza, "Ladies and gentlemen, please, stop and listen. The very people who want us to fail sent their storm troopers to disrupt this protest. If you panic or there is destruction of property, they win!"

Eddie and two of his friends shredded the paper banners to retrieve Jessie and his fallen dance partner from beneath the truck and hauled them behind the stage. The artist rolled off the victim, noticing a trickle of blood on her lip, "Are you alright?"

Impish blue eyes twinkled and she wrapped her arms around his neck, "Being battered and bruised is a small price to pay for rolling around with a real man for the first time in thirty years!" She pulled herself up and planted a kiss on his lips.

Jessie lifted her to her feet, "Are you sure you're alright? We could get the medics in a hurry."

"I'm fine, sonny. I came here pissed off at the big guys for taking advantage of so many good and righteous people, then I felt a communal energy in this crowd that I haven't felt since the Sixties; then panic, when the explosions went off and everyone started pushing and shoving, and finally sensual overload, when you jumped in to save me. What more could an old woman expect from one day?"

He kissed her on the forehead, "I enjoyed it too. Now, you stay out of trouble, I've got to help get things back under control."

Rough Eddie escorted the little lady to a tent, where the guests and speakers were sheltered from the rain, and Jessie ran up the steps to the stage. Small charges detonated with clouds of gray smoke and the clatter of glass crashing to the pavement a block to the left, followed immediately by another on the far side of the building.

The surge of bodies twisted away from each blast, splitting into swirls spinning, searching desperately for an exit and cover from torrential rain. Stiff gusts from the southwest sent hats, umbrellas, and loose articles of clothing tumbling through the crowd. People closest to the stage seemed to settle, as they realized the carnage was occurring around the storefronts across the street from the plaza.

Sammy spotted a burly man, with dark curly hair and black eyes, wearing a burgundy poncho, and moving against the tide of bodies. He pointed and yelled to Benny, "Is that the guy who beat you up?"

Benny scanned the crush of terrified protesters, "Son of a…if I could get to him, I'd kill him myself!" He picked up the radio, switched channels, and said, "Major Martin, do you read me?"

The walkie-talkie squawked, "Roger."

"The ringleader is wearing a burgundy slicker and he's moving west about fifty-yards from the front of the stage. See if your guys can grab him."

"Roger."

Tabitha thundered through the PA speakers, "Stop where you are and look around. The perpetrators are stocky, military types with very short hair. If you spot one of these people, we want to know about it immediately!"

The roiling movement slowed and a mob, down near Second Street, started hooting and pointing after a running man in a light blue shirt and a black stocking cap. An armed militiaman on the roof followed the suspect through his scope, passing information over his radio, until the suspect disappeared around the corner on Flamingo Road.

Another group chased an escaping agitator, on the west side of the square, who jumped into a waiting gray police car that sped away with lights flashing.

Once the protesters realized that the threat was gone, they swarmed back to the stage waving fists and shouting about revenge. "Let's burn 'em out!"

"Yeah, let's start with the pigs who wouldn't protect us!"

"How do we know they weren't in cahoots?"

Tabitha turned to Jessie and grinned, as Benny took the microphone, "So…now you see how easy it is for the bad guys to make us look bad? All these cameras, set up around the square, recorded the destruction of property and panic in the crowd. That's not what we want the world to see!"

"Let's burn down the factories!"

Benny held the walkie-talkie to his ear, listening for a moment. "I've just been told that six bad guys escaped in a gray police vehicle, driven by the dude in the burgundy hoodie, who seemed to be directing the crew, and our esteemed local officers are in pursuit."

A resounding cry went up through pounding rain blowing horizontally.

Mrs. Hall took the mic, "We have more than twenty people who would like to speak to you but, considering the weather's turning for the worse, I think we should conduct our business before we get to the speakers."

"Right on!"

"Because the very core of this organization grew from the frustrations of city workers, we will expand our one-day strike to a week for anyone employed by the city of Dolphin Bay. If our elected officials refuse to negotiate in good faith, we will extend the strike and add the Hardesty Companies the following Monday. If both entities refuse to resolve this problem, then we will add the next largest company, and the next, and the next, until they finally capitulate."

The crowd cheered and applauded.

Sammy took the microphone and sat on the edge of the stage with his short legs dangling over the heads of the protesters. "We started our little group in frustration at not being heard, not being valued or respected by our city bosses. I doubt that anyone who was involved in those initial meetings had any idea about how many other people in our community were suffering the same frustrations, the same disrespect, and a shared terror that we might not be able to provide for our families."

Murmurs and light applause.

He stood awkwardly, pointing to the television cameras. "This isn't just about the city workers anymore. This isn't just about the impoverished workers in the city of Dolphin Bay. This is the beginning of a movement that will sweep across this country, forcing the elite to recognize the value of our contributions and compensate us accordingly."

Cheers.

He swept his hand across the crowd, "This isn't just about us anymore, it's about an entire class of people and I'm very proud to be a part of what all of you are about to do for this country!"

Most of the panicked protesters had filtered back into the square and the mass of humanity erupted in response.

"We're about to rebuild the middle class!"

Lightning crackled across the sky and deafening thunder rumbled through the city, as the heavens opened, fierce winds whipped the plaza, and the impassioned crowd was forced into retreat.

Chapter Eleven

Ned Flint stepped back from the rattling windows overlooking The Commons, as a battering blast toppled two towering Royal Palms into the pool, overflowing the amphitheater to run down the circular driveway onto the beach road, feeding a river rushing between the houses in the gully behind the dunes. He tottered across the gray carpeting and pulled open the bar to pour two fingers of Scotch from a crystal decanter. The aging playboy tossed down the shot and poured another, turning to Tate who was yelling into the phone, "What do you mean, they've gone?"

He listened and then exploded, "You mean the entire management team left the property? Who didn't run?"

Before he slammed the receiver on the cradle, Jenny Rose, the receptionist appeared at his door. "What?"

"Can you find me some assistance? The phones are ringing off the hook with guests freaking out about power outages, leaking ceilings, rivers racing down the streets, flooding down by the marina, and wind knocking down trees all over the property. Mrs. Thompson, over in The Barbados Complex said they tried to leave but Midnight Pass is impassable north and south."

"I'll see who I can find," replied Tate, "but contact the guests, they can evacuate to the Conference Center. It should stay high and dry and we've got room for everyone. If there are any staff left on the key, tell them to assist in any way they can."

She turned to leave, "Can do."

He called after her, "Are any of the restaurant people still here?"

Jenny peeked back inside the doorway, "I think the cooks and bartenders bailed but I can find out."

"We'll need to supply food for a crowd."

Ned's hands were shaking, "I'm terrified."

"Oh, pull yourself together, man. The worst that can happen is the whole property falling into the ocean, in which case we'll die together."

He walked over to stand next to Tate's chair, "Hold me."

The phone jangled and Tate answered, "What?"

Mavis voice sounded far away, "I'm at Tabitha Hall's house. I tried to get back to SunnyBreeze but the bridges are closed and the roads are out. What's happening there?"

"I'm glad you're safe," replied her husband, brushing Ned's pawing hand from his shoulder. "The amphitheater is now an Olympic pool, trees are falling down all over the property, we're getting lots of calls from guests complaining about water seeping into their units, there are raging rapids rushing down the access streets to the marina, and the entire management staff took off, when the storm started coming in."

"Oh shit."

"Yeah, oh shit! This could turn into a disaster in a New York minute. I've directed everyone to move to the Conference Center, which is the highest point on the property but Jenny Rose just told me that all the cooks and bartenders took off too, so I'm not sure how we're going to feed everyone."

"I stopped through there to change this morning and I should have stayed to help. I'm sorry."

"Are you okay?"

"Yeah, the same bunch who kidnapped Jessie Cotton and his crew, infiltrated the crowd at the rally to set off small explosions and smashed store windows to make it look like a riot. The crowd freaked but security chased the bad guys away. Fortunately, most of the protesters got the gist of the program, before the heavens opened and everyone fled for cover."

"I saw a little bit of it on the news, I'm glad you're okay." He paused, "Listen, don't fret it, I'll find a way to keep everyone safe until this is over."

"I'll figure out a way to get back there, as soon as I can."

The other line rang. "Gotta take this, be safe and I'll see you soon."

"You and Ned stay safe," replied Mavis.

Tate whispered, "I love you," before the line went dead.

~

Bobbie Warmington and Janey Holliday bundled the Turner family off to the Conference Center in their Mercedes, through the Spring Creek neighborhood and then Pelican Way, which were still clear of downed trees.

Bobbie said, "I sure am glad you got your job back, I missed you."

"I've learned my lesson, head down, mouth shut."

"Might be safer for the time being. Let's clear out what we can."

They lugged all the movable furniture to the second floor, stuffed towels under the French doors to the garden to stifle a steady stream of water flowing across the kitchen, and unplugged everything except the refrigerator.

The lights flickered as they locked the front door and slogged to the covered golf cart through a brutal gale, spinning raindrops into daggers and debris into missiles. They were both soaked before they zipped up the side panels and rolled on to the next occupied residence.

Janey turned to Bobbie, "Don't these fools have any common sense? They've all been told to evacuate but they're riding it out."

"We've been through enough hurricanes to last my lifetime and I've got a feeling ol' Dot wants to be famous, if not deadly."

"Just so it ain't us, sister, just so it ain't us."

"Amen," replied Bobbie, rolling the little cart around a gray sedan in the driveway to park close to the front door of the blue six-bedroom villa. She pulled up the hood on her yellow slicker and leapt over a gushing stream running along the pathway to press the doorbell. A bolt of lightning sizzled through the trees, stalked by growling thunder rumbling through her tired body, as the door cracked open and a young woman with a stylish blond pixie cut peered out. "Didn't you get a call to evacuate?"

"Well, yes, but we didn't think they meant right now."

"If you want to be alive in the morning, I suggest you get your things together and hightail it up to the Conference Center as fast as you can go. It's the highest point on the property and Midnight Pass is closed north and south. Most of the roads are running rivers and blocked by downed trees. If you don't go right now, I can't guarantee your safety."

The door swung open, revealing a muscular man with cold dark eyes and short curly hair. He stared at her for a long moment but did not invite her to step in out of the storm. "We'll be leaving immediately."

Bobbie turned to point, "Take Poinsettia Drive to the top of the hill and turn right onto Oak Road but watch out for running water on the cross streets. It's going to get worse in a hurry!"

The woman started to say, "Thank you" but the door slammed shut.

Johnny's mom jumped into the cart and zipped up the plastic cover. "That was weird and the guy was creepy. They were totally clueless and didn't seem to understand the danger."

Janey giggled, "Maybe they have something to hide, do you think they were having an orgy?"

"I think they guy who appeared at the door was downright scary. The way he looked at me, I felt like he wouldn't hesitate to hurt me, if I said the wrong thing."

"Guess the front office doesn't do much background checking; if the guest has the cash to pay the rent."

Bobbie pressed the accelerator and headed up the hill to a bungalow on the west side of the ridge, their second last stop. "I need to use a phone to check on the kids."

"If these folks have already left, we can use our pass key to get in."

Lightning crackled through swirling thunderheads, dumping torrential rain on shrieking winds. Bobbie stamped her foot in a puddle and two black water snakes slithered into tattered hibiscus plants next to the entry. Janey knocked twice before opening the door with her service key. "Hello, is anybody here? SunnyBreeze housekeeping, is anybody home?"

There was no reply. They closed the door, wiped their feet on the matt, and shook the moisture off their rain gear, before walking through the living area to the kitchen. A knitting bag on the couch, a couple of news magazines and a paperback edition of 'Dr. No' on the arm of an easy chair, the weather radar spinning 'round and 'round on the television, which was turned down to a whisper, and a stack of dirty dishes in the sink indicated that a party of three left in a hurry.

Bobbie picked up the phone and dialed her home number. The line crackled but, after three rings, Beatrice answered, "Warmington residence."

"Mom, it's Bobbie. Are you okay?"

"Yeah, we're all battened down, still have power and water still comes out of the tap. We've got whitecaps on the bay and I've seen three or four boats floating by! How 'bout you? I bet it's crazy out there."

"We've got one more house to check to be sure the guests have moved up to the Conference Center, then we get to help out up there. Midnight Pass is closed north and south and one of the maintenance guys told us that the surf's trying to top the dunes," replied Bobbie. "How are the kids?"

"They're fine, watching some nature program on PBS."

"Good, give them a hug for me and I'll call you back when we get up to The Commons."

"You be careful, sweetheart, we all want you to come home safe and sound."

"That makes five of us."

They turned off the lights and unplugged the appliances, locked the front door and climbed into the cart to wind along Oak Road, which was littered with shrubs and tree limbs. Rivers flooded down meandering cross streets to the marina and the gale was blasting holes in the walls of neighboring houses with a barrage of ceramic roof tiles.

"If this gets any worse, there won't be any SunnyBreeze tomorrow," said Janey.

Bobbie slammed on the brakes, as an alligator waddled across the road, desperate green eyes glowing in the dim lamps on the front of the cart, and peered down the hill through the lashing trees to the dunes beyond the main road, "Oh, my God…"

Enormous waves crashed over the sand barriers, exploding through the shops and restaurants along the beach. Beachfront houses crumbled and the debris piled up to form a dam just south of the entry to The Commons, channeling the water into a lake behind the amphitheater. Great sections of the pavers on Hibiscus Boulevard were peeling away under pounding surf cleaving a new inlet across the key.

Janey gasped, "I don't think we'll be getting out of here anytime soon."

"If at all," replied Bobbie, pressing the accelerator to the floor.

She parked the golf cart in a covered alcove behind the Conference Center, where four giant generators hummed in unison. Janey leaned close, pointing, "That means the power's gone out."

"Probably the phones too."

"Let's find someplace dry."

They fought a fierce wind to struggle up the stairs to the loading dock and pushed through the employee's entrance, shaking off their slickers, borrowing a few towels from the kitchen to soak up some of the moisture from their hair and clothes.

"We'd better find someone in management, if there's any left," said Bobbie, banging through double doors into the conference hall. She stopped, gazing around the enormous room, where nearly a thousand guests and workers huddled against the storm. She spied Tate Sloan talking with kitchen staff and marched in his direction.

"Excuse me, Mr. Sloan, might I have a moment?"

He stared at her identity badge for a moment, "I'm sorry I haven't had the pleasure, Mrs…Warmington, is it?"

"Yes, I'm in charge of one of the cleaning teams under Miss Savage."

"I'm afraid Miss Savage left the property."

Janey piped up, "How come that doesn't surprise anyone?"

Sloan pursed his lips and turned back to Bobbie, "How can I help you?"

"Well, we've just come from clearing out the last of the guests down in Pelican Way and, on the way back, we noticed that the surf has overtaken the dunes. All of the shops and homes along the beach are being destroyed, the debris is forming a dam, and the pavement on Hibiscus Boulevard is coming apart."

"Oh, my God!" exclaimed Tate. "It's happening again."

~

Gracie danced around the kitchen, nuzzling Jessie and Kate, who were trying to shed wet clothes and find towels. The artist knelt, "Come here girl, I know we've been gone too long and this awful storm just won't quit."

She ducked her head under his arm and lifted her nose to lick his chin. "We're all safe together, sweetheart."

The phone jangled and the lights flickered. Jessie and Kate exchanged a glance, before he picked up the receiver and, after a moment, said, "Hey Johnnie, how are you? Are you all safe?"

"Well, we're with my grandma and Mom's working at SunnyBreeze but, other than a phone call a few hours ago, we haven't heard from her. The news reports say that Midnight Pass Road is closed, the bridges are shut down, and I'm worried."

"Have you tried calling the main number?"

"Yeah, but all I get is a voice saying, "Your call cannot be completed, please try again later."

"Tell you what, I've got another number. Let me try and I'll call you right back, okay?"

"Okay."

Jessie hung up and pulled out a soggy wallet to extract a business card with SunnyBreeze logo embossed in brilliant yellow.

"What's up?" asked Kate.

"That was Johnny. His mom's stuck at SunnyBreeze and he's worried."

"I don't blame him. Being out on a key in this storm sounds like a really bad idea."

"Yeah, I've got Tate's number, so, let's see if we can get through."

He dialed the number and, after several rings, a quivering voice answered, "Hello."

"Who's this? I was calling for Tate Sloan."

"This is Ned Flint. Tate's dealing with the guests, who have been evacuated to the Conference Center."

"Is it possible to talk with him?"

"I don't think so."

"Why?"

"Well, because I'm totally petrified, the lights keep flickering on and off, this whole building is shuddering, and I've been told that the highway is closed north and south. I'm not sure that any of us is going to get off this key alive."

"Okay, take a deep breath and tell me what's happening outside."

"The wind's taken down most of the trees, the surf's made it past the dunes, and the storm's demolishing houses. There's debris floating in rivers and flying through the air."

"Go get Tate, right now. I'll wait."

"But…" stammered Flint.

"No but's…if you want to get out of there alive, I need to talk to Tate, before things get any worse."

The receiver clanked on the table and, ten minutes later, Tate said, "Hello."

"Tate, it's Jessie. What's happening out there?"

"I'm afraid the storm's trying to cut through the key and taking out most of the development in the process. There's no way to get these people out of here."

He squeezed Kate's hand, "It's that dire?"

Tate hesitated, "Yeah, I think it is. It's fourth down and I've got my back against the goal line against a savage defense."

Jessie was quiet for a minute, "Listen, I've got a crazy idea. How many boats do you have tied up in your docks?"

"Why?"

"Just give me a number."

"Hang on."

Jessie could hear papers shuffling before Sloan came back on the line, "I've got forty-two boats in dock."

"How 'bout rope?"

"What have you got in mind?"

"Just answer the question, does the bait and tackle shop have a bunch of rope?"

"Yeah, they're completely overstocked," replied Tate.

"Okay, I'm going to get some guys together. I'll need keys to all those boats and a couple of miles of rope. Can you get someone to get that organized on your end?"

"Yeah, but what you are going to do?"

"We're going to build a floating bridge across the lagoon and guide your people across to safely."

"You're out of your mind."

"Yeah, I know, but it's your only chance, so get your shit together and I'll organize my guys."

Kate grabbed his arm, as he hung up the phone, "Are you out of your mind? You can't go out in this storm, let alone in a boat!"

"Johnny's mother is over there, along with a whole bunch of people who don't have a clue about hurricanes, including Tate Sloan. There really is no other choice."

"I'm not likin' this."

"I'm not either but I have to see if I can convince Benny and Eddie to gather a bunch of volunteers to help out and I need to call Johnny back."

"You're not going anywhere without me," said Kate, wrapping her arms around his neck. "You ran out on me once and I'm not giving you the chance to do it again. I'm coming along."

"You are one pushy broad, you know that?"

"Yup, that's why you love me. Make your calls."

He dialed the Warmington's number and Johnny answered.

"Johnny, listen, I think I've got a plan to get your mom off the key."

"How?"

"I'm going to build a bridge across the bay."

"In the middle of this storm? What are you going to build it out of?"

"The boats that are tied up at the docks at the marina."

"That's brilliant. I'm coming too," replied Johnny.

"No, you're not, it's too dangerous!"

"Either we go together or I'm going to hop in the MissU and head over there right now."

"Damn it kid, I don't want you getting hurt."

"I'm a better pilot than you are."

"In fair weather."

"In any weather. Come get me or, I swear, I'll head out without you."

"Okay, we could probably use two boats anyway. Give me thirty minutes, I've got to line up some volunteers and then I'll head over to your place. Bring every life jacket and all the rope you've got."

Gracie danced and pranced around the back door, yelping at Jessie, who was gathering supplies for the trip. "I know you want to go but the storm's getting worse and I've got enough to worry about without having you in the boat."

The dog stopped and cocked her head, staring intently.

"You really think you should go along?"

Bark, double bark.

"I guess, if we're all gonna die, we might as well go down together."

"I'm nervous enough about this adventure, without you making wiseass comments."

"I'm sorry," said Jessie, binding three life jackets together, "but this isn't an adventure, it's a rescue mission. There are hundreds of people stranded right in the storm's path and no one else is going to step up to help. Do we really have any choice?"

"Why do you do that?"

"What?"

"Break it all down to its simplest form, where there can be no argument?"

"That's what quarterbacks are trained to do, take charge. Do we have everything?"

"Well, a great big heavy watertight boat with a huge engine would be a start."

"Have faith in the old girl, she's named after you."

"I guess that's a good omen," smirked Kate. She walked over to hug Jessie, "Just in case we don't make it, I want you to know that I'm really glad that I found you."

He kissed her, "Me too."

The wind whipped huge old trees to bow to the ground, palm fronds into slashing swords, and rain pelted everything with liquid darts racing horizontally. Jessie and Kate crouched low and scampered down the path to the dock. Gracie ran across the decking to the shelter of the storage locker to shake off the water soaking her coat.

The artist rummaged through the closet and produced several more life jackets and three coils of stout rope. He tied a tarp from the windshield to the cleats on the stern and stashed the supplies inside before he cranked the engine.

Kate pointed to the waves exploding across the bay, "Do you really think we can get through that?"

"Johnny's house isn't too far, so we'll only have to cross over once to get behind the keys for some protection."

"This is not my idea of a hot date!" yelled Kate over the roar.

"At least you can honestly say that our dates have never been boring."

"True that."

He hauled Gracie off the dock, set her under the canvas, and strapped an orange life vest around her chest. She curled up on some blankets in the bow, watching every move. Kate untied the lines and scrambled aboard, amid the violent clang of gunnels slamming against steel rails, as Jessie backed the runabout out of the stall. Winds and waves pounded the boat from every direction and the engine screamed, as they hugged the shore around the bend to approach the little dock behind the Warmington's rental house.

Johnny charged down the concrete stairs to the dock and waved.

Jessie pointed at the MissU and tossed a line. "Let's tow her! Tie her off and then we'll pull up to the dock so you can climb aboard."

Beatrice appeared on the deck above the dock screaming, "Johnnie! Johnnie! What are you doing? You can't go out in this storm! Your mother will kill me if anything happens to you!"

The boy ignored his grandmother, knotted the rope to the bow cleat, and untied the spring rigging that held her in place. The MissU bobbed and banged against the supports under the dock, as he shoved her out of the slip into a violent chop. Jessie edged the Kate closer and closer, in a slow-motion struggle against the cross wind, until Johnny crawled under the canvas. Kate hugged him and Gracie lurched from her perch to nuzzle against him. "Grab on to something, the chop is vicious."

Jessie wrapped an arm around Johnny, "We'll get your mom home safe and sound." He pulled away from the dock and aimed across the gale at the narrows that opened into the Little Bay. Mighty winds whipped the tarp and waves crashed over the bow, the engine whined but the Kate fought through the storm to relative shelter from the brutal blast, in the shadow of the key.

"Was that your grandmother up by the house?" asked Kate.

"Yeah."

"You did ask permission, didn't you?" asked Jessie.

Johnny looked down at the water sloshing around the hull, "No."

"You didn't even tell her where we're going?"

"No, 'cause I knew she'd say 'no' and we'd have a big fight and I'd have to disobey her."

"Great, I'm in the doghouse with your grandma for getting you involved in saving your mother!"

Kate braced herself into the seat, as the bow rose and slammed into the next wave, and glanced up at Jessie, "You'd better make this work or die trying!"

Lightning crackled and thunder rumbled above a haze of droplets, demon daggers discharged into the wind by the surf pounding over the dunes. The boat struggled against churning tides rolling white caps across the channel in a deadly game of dodgeball that drove the little boat towards the shallows.

Johnny bailed water with a bait bucket and peeked through a gap in the tarp to check on the MissU, which was being pummeled by the waves and riding low in the water. "How far do we have to go?"

"I think we just passed the slough where George lived, so we should be coming up on it," replied Jessie, wiping the condensation from the windshield.

"Good, 'cause the MissU is half full of water and she's going down, unless we get somewhere calmer than out here."

"The bay gets skinnier just this side of the marina, so I'm hoping it will be just a tad more calm. Otherwise, I don't have a clue how we're going to keep all those boats from floating down stream."

A light flashed in the distance and vanished in the storm's gray veil, before it flashed again. The sweeping curves of the marina appeared through the fog on the right and the blinking light guided them into a slip. Jessie tossed lines to two men in yellow slickers and crawled onto the wharf, "Thanks for guiding us in."

A bear of a man extended a hand, "Harvey Millsap, Head of Maintenance, and this is Rory Hodges. Mr. Sloan said to do whatever needed to be done."

Two sets of headlights blinked on and off, on and off, on the opposite shore, and Jessie waved, as he pulled Gracie onto the dock and removed her life-vest. "Okay, here's the plan, we need to bail out our second boat and start floating our crew over to this side, then we're going to back these boats out of the slips and tie them off in alternating pairs, like links in a chain, so your folks can crawl across. Start with the biggest and work to the smallest."

"Are you out of your mind?" yelled Harvey Millsap. "That's tens of millions of dollars in boats."

"Yeah, it's probably a crazy idea, but I'm fairly sure they're all going to be tinder by tomorrow anyway and, unless you've got a better plan, I'd say we better get crackin'."

Millsap wiped the condensation from his glasses, "There's probably a thousand people up in the Conference Center and the surf's trying to cut at least one channel right through the key, so, we're with you."

"Okay, we'll untie our second boat, get it bailed out, and start hauling guys over from the other side. You get all the keys in the right order and every yard of rope and life vest you can lay your hands on."

The Head of Maintenance clapped Jessie on the back and the two men jogged through blinding rain to the bait and tackle shop. Kate and Johnny dragged the MissU into the next slip and tossed buckets of water over the sides.

"I'm going over to pick up Benny and his friends to help move boats. Those two are getting the keys, life preservers, and lots of rope. The guy said there are around a thousand people up in the Center."

"How are we going to get that many people across?"

"I don't have a clue but we don't have any other options, so let's make this work."

The artist hopped into the Kate and backed out into a roaring gale that hurled the little boat sideways across the lagoon. He pumped the engine and spun the boat around to back into a rough landing on the sandy shore. Four men tromped down the bank, waded through pounding surf, pushed the little boat free, and climbed under the tarp.

Benny flipped back his cowl and grinned, "I figured I owed you big time brother, I just wasn't expecting you to try to collect quite so soon."

"How many guys have we got?"

"Oh, 'bout twenty, but there's probably another hundred coming."

Jessie hugged him, "Do all of you know how to handle a boat?"

Eddie's friend, Twigs, raised a hand and said, "No, man, haven't a clue. Anything on wheels, I've got 'em covered; vehicles that float on water, not so much."

"Okay, you stay here and organize our volunteers. I can take four at a time and another boat will be coming across that can probably take three. We're going to commandeer all those yachts over there, string them together into a bridge, and march a thousand people to safety."

"I'm thinking someone better go find some major transportation for these folks," said Twigs.

"Great," said Eddie. "Send Jammer to make the calls. He knows everyone who knows anything about transportation."

"Okay. Twigs, send another guy down and get things organized over here. I'll be back for more, as soon as I drop these guys off."

Twigs was replaced by a wiry little guy named Hughie and Jessie set off, bobbing and weaving through choppy waves, blinding rain, and battering wind. The motorboat veered hard to starboard as Johnny and Kate blew by in the MissU and Benny tapped him on the shoulder, "Was that that kid you hang out with?"

"Yeah, man, he's probably the best pilot on these waters and he's just coming up on eleven years old."

"No shit! I'm impressed that he'd even be out here."

"His mother works out at SunnyBreeze and she's stuck up in that lodge with all those other people," replied Jessie, pulling into the slip.

"That makes him a hero," said Eddie.

"That's why I hang out with him."

Bernie, Eddie, and two other bikers hopped onto the dock and trotted over to talk with Millsap, who handed out keys and pointed out the first two boats. His partner took the other two bikers to secure a midsized yacht to the piles, while Eddie fought the currents to back a magnificent cruiser into position to be lashed into place by a motley band of soggy volunteers. Benny followed with another and, one by one, the line crept farther and farther from the docks, as more and more hands joined the struggle.

The approaching storm was driving ocean water through the inlet, raising the tide in the bay and a blistering wind pushed the tail of the line downstream. Jessie tapped Millsap on the shoulder and pointed to two sleek racers, "Have you got keys for those?"

He flipped through his ring to retrieve the keys, "Yeah."

"They've got huge engines, let's use them like tugboats to keep our line straight."

"Go for it!"

He handed a key to Johnny and pulled the straps on his orange life jacket tight, "You think you can handle this?"

The boy turned his back to the storm and grinned, "Wanna race?"

"No, I want everyone to get through this alive!"

Jessie backed out of the slip and fought crosswinds and a vicious chop around the tail of the growing bridge to set lines from the middle. Johnny hauled a pair of ropes from the second to last boat and angled north. Jessie pointed to the racer and motioned Johnny forward to even up the line, they gradually pulled the entire column against a raging gale and buffeting waves. Slowly, more yachts were tethered into a writhing, crashing multi-million-dollar escape jetty, until Benny wheeled a three-decked liner around to beach her stern first. Headlights bobbed and flashed through the jungle on the east side of the narrows, as the final two boats were lashed to thrashing palm trees.

A fleet of white Suburbans arrived at the marina from the Conference Center to disgorge terrified guests. Kate greeted the Cohen clan, who piled out of the first van, a family of six, including an infant. She leaned close to the father and yelled, "I know this is crazy but we're going to walk you across this bridge of boats. We've got transportation on the other side to take you to shelter."

The man's eyes darted from his children to the bounding boats to Kate's face, "Isn't there another way?"

"The storm's getting worse and this is the only escape you've got. This is your chance to save your children from certain disaster."

Their flimsy raincoats flapped in the gale and the mother clutched the baby to her chest, shaking her head, as she stared at the string of yachts banging and clanging against each other in a violent conga line of imminent death and certain destruction. "We're not taking our kids across that!"

Gracie trotted over to the hesitant father, growling and shifting back and forth to shepherd him towards the first cruiser. The poor man backed across the dock, terrified of the storm, the bridge of boats, and this vicious dog threatening to take a chunk out of his leg. He grabbed two of his children and clambered aboard, with help from Sammy and

Nomad, handing them off to two other volunteers, who buckled them into life jackets. Slowly, a chain of bodies began to cross the gyrating barrier to splash up the little beach into yellow buses parked in the mangroves.

Millsap guided seven feisty senior women up the improvised stairs to the first boat. Kate caught the next Suburban, which ferried the Nelsons, an extended family of twelve, with six children, from the relative calm of the overcrowded Conference Center to the terror and chaos of a natural disaster. She yelled to an older man, "We're going to guide you across this bridge we've built."

"You'll understand if I'm terrified for all these children."

"Don't worry, we have people to help you all the way across."

The mother was trying to corral three little ones, when a violent gust flipped open the smallest girl's raincoat and pitched her across the pavement into the cove. Before the humans could react, Gracie leapt into three-foot waves to grab the toddler and, after an excruciating pause, hauled her to the surface.

Millsap wound a rope around his arm, tossed the other end to Kate, and jumped in after them. He rolled on his back, pulled the girl onto his chest, and wrapped an arm around the dog, as everyone on the wharf pitched in to drag them to the dock. Violent waves crashed against the jetty, heaving them close to the ladder, then hauling them back out into open water. Kate leaned over the ledge to grab the little girl, as a large breaker washed Gracie onto the pier, but Millsap crashed headfirst into a concrete piling and disappeared in a blinding wash, his yellow slicker bobbing to the surface, then vanishing in the swirling turmoil.

Kate yanked the rope but the loose end flipped into the air and snapped like a bullwhip in a violent gust. Millsap's partner started to go in after him but Benny restrained him, "You aren't going to save him, man. He's gone."

Rory let out a wail and Benny wrapped an arm around his shoulders, "I know he was your guy but, if he was here, he'd be telling you to get your shit together, because we've still got hundreds of people to save and the eye of the storm hasn't even arrived yet."

Hodges straightened up and wiped the tears from his eyes, "That guy was a son of a bitch but he was our son of a bitch."

"Make him proud," said Benny, as an endless line of vans pulled through a rushing river.

~

Tate put every available employee with a driver's license behind the wheel of a vehicle and loaded them with guests bound for Jessie Cotton's phantom bridge. The drivers of the first Suburbans returned to inform him that the motley crew on the dock were using a vicious dog to force hesitant refugees across a ramshackle bridge of expensive yachts but none turned back.

Two hours into the evacuation, the crowd in the Conference Center was beginning to dwindle and Jenny Rose appeared out of the crowd to whisper, "The phones have been out for hours but I've been watching the weather and the eye of the storm is heading directly for us and should be here within the hour."

Tate shook his head, "We'll get thirty minutes of calm and then all hell's going to break loose. We need to get these people across the bay before that second wave hits."

The receptionist gazed around at the anxious faces, "You might just make it."

"Let's hope."

"There's one more thing."

"What's that?"

"I've been watching the dunes, when there's a flash from a big bolt of lightning, and I'm pretty sure that it's carving a channel through the key. The waves are breaking on this side of Hibiscus Boulevard and it looks like it's aiming to cut right through The Commons."

"Shit! Who says lightning can't strike twice in the same place?" Tate straightened up, "Listen, can you keep these people moving for a few minutes. I have to check on Ned Flint."

"I thought you sent him away hours ago."

"No, he's hiding out upstairs. I'll be right back."

He charged up the stairs and found an inebriated Flint cowering under his desk. He reached down to retrieve him, "C'mon out of there, so I can send you to safety."

"I thought you'd abandoned me," slurred Ned.

"I can't believe it! We're facing an apocalypse and you're drunk!"

"I thought you and everyone else had gone."

"No, I've been trying to send a thousand people across a temporary bridge and we're finally beginning to see the end. Tell you what, the storm's going to break for about thirty minutes and I want you to go during the lull."

"I won't leave without you."

Tate smiled and wrapped his arms around the trembling man, "I can't leave until everyone else is safe, including you. Now do as I say."

Flint kissed him hard on the lips, "I wouldn't mind dying in your arms."

"No, we're both going to live but just like the captain of a ship, I have to be the last to leave. Now, come on, we're wasting time."

Ned stumbled towards to door but Sloan held him upright, and they descended the staircase to the lobby and into the Conference Center. Jenny Rose was about to send a crew of seven burly men and a younger woman with short blond hair off in the next van. Tate walked up to the group, "Excuse me, would you mind taking our friend under your wing, until you get across the bridge?"

An imposing man with cold eyes and dark curly hair inspected Flint. His voice was gruff and raspy, "Is that old wimp drunk?"

"I'm sure terrified would be a better description."

Before he could answer, the blond woman grabbed Ned's arm and said, "I'll look after him, don't worry."

Flint looked up at Tate, with pleading eyes, and pawed his arm, "Promise me you'll get out safely."

Sloan squeezed his hand and the thug grunted, as Jenny cracked the door open, leaning to restrain a brutal torrent charging whitecaps through the breezeway that were lapping at the top of the wheels of the idling Suburban.

Tate gazed around the room for a rough count and turned to Jenny, "Looks like we're down to less than a hundred. Go gather any employees you can find and, maybe, we can shut this thing down, before the second half of the storm arrives."

"I'll check the building."

"Hurry!"

Even with a pair of massive engines, Jessie struggled to maneuver the long slender cigarette boat against a fierce southerly gale and rampant tides but the bridge seemed to be holding for the moment. He peered across to Johnny and waved. The boy waved back and the artist sliced a finger across his throat and pointed to the string of boats. He cut the engine and leapt to release the lines from the cleats at the stern, as a brutal blast blew the bow around to face the second boat.

Johnny heaved the ropes over the side and raced back to the wheel but a fierce flurry of breakers broadsided the sleek racer, lifting bow into the air. Johnny tumbled over the transom into the water and the boat pivoted on her stern, toppling over upside down with an enormous splash that merged with rain and ocean spray into a glistening haze streaking across the bay.

Jessie shrieked, "No!" and gunned the motors to come around next to the overturned vessel, searching desperately for the boy. A blast of wind crushed the bow into the overturned hull but he caught a flash of orange beneath the stern, slammed the throttle to idle, and jumped between the boats. His life jacket prevented a dive under the stricken boat, so he released the clips, took a deep breath, and dove under the thrashing waves. He surfaced in an air pocket beneath the capsized hull, which was bouncing on raging breakers and slamming Johnny's unconscious body from port to starboard and back again.

He grabbed the life vest and checked for a pulse. The boy was alive but barely breathing. "I hate to ask you to hold your breath but I've got to get you out of here."

He wrapped his arms around the boy, cupped Johnny's mouth and pinched his nose, and hauled him under the gunnels, just as the first boat rode up and over the second with a mighty crunch of shattered fiberglass. The stern shifted and spinning propellers chewed ragged chunks from the hull, as Jessie pulled the boy under and stroked hard for the bow of the upturned power yacht.

Ferocious waves pounded the artist and his charge, trapped between the violent undulations of the flotilla and the jagged tangle of splintered hulls and snarling props of the advancing racers. He flipped Johnny on his back and kicked with all his might into a gap between two magnificent cruisers creaking and grinding in the ferocious chop.

A silver ladder splashed in the water and Eddie reached down to grab the boy and haul him over the stern. Jessie clambered onto the yacht, as the shattered racers plowed into the crevice with a vicious crunch, to find Sammy and Eddie performing CPR on Johnny's limp body. The boy coughed, rolled over to vomit, and sat up. Jessie dropped to his knees to hug him, "Are you alright?"

"Yeah, I think so," replied Johnny, his face pale, his body wracked with tremors from shock and fatigue.

"I was afraid I was going to have to answer to your grandmother," laughed Jessie.

The boy turned away to cough up a stream of bay water, "Our only defense is to bring my mom home alive."

Sammy wrapped them both in damp towels, "Word just came down the line that they're going to start sending employees across, as soon as the last guests are clear."

"Damn good thing too, because our boat bridge is about to beat itself to death," added Eddie. "I don't think wind can blow any harder than this!"

The howling storm and raging surf suddenly died, the sky cleared, and stars appeared at the top of a hollow column of charcoal clouds spinning into the heavens. Johnny gazed around, confused, but Jessie said, "It's the eye! We're in the center of the storm!"

"Get ready to get clobbered from the other side," said Sammy.

"Let's get Johnny across and I'll head back to the dock to make sure everyone is clear."

"I'm going with you," protested the boy.

"You've probably got a concussion, so you're going to shore," said Jessie. "You've done more than your share and I want to be sure that you're safe on one of those buses, when I find your mother or I'll have both of your ladies chewing on me forever."

Rex Tatum appeared, guiding a petite blond in a blue parka, who was helping a frail man stumbling and fumbling from one groaning yacht to the next. They were followed by a posse of stout men in rain gear, fashioned from black garbage bags that covered their torsos but left their arms exposed, following another in a burgundy parka with the hood closed to cover everything but dark piercing eyes.

Sammy glanced up from attending Johnny, as the procession passed, and looked after them, "Did any of you notice those folks who just went past?"

"No, why?" replied Eddie.

"Except for the girl and the old man, they were seven burly guys, and that guy in the burgundy parka reminded me a whole lot of the guy who was running the bombers on the plaza today."

"No shit?"

"I know we're all exhausted but I'm pretty sure I'm right. Those might be the guys who kidnapped us and started the trouble at the protest."

Eddie picked Johnny up, "Alright, tell you what; Jimmy James and I will take the boy across and put him on a bus, then we're going to isolate those bastards and see what happens."

"Do you want some help?" asked Jessie.

"You've got enough to do and, besides, if they are the guys who kidnapped you, you might lose control and do something stupid. If we beat the crap out of them, who's gonna care?"

"Nobody," laughed Jimmy James.

"Hey, man," said Sammy, "we're the good guys, remember? We've got tons of volunteers out here doing righteous work, saving the rich folk from certain death, and we don't need a splotch on any of the good publicity we'll be getting for the rally and all of this. We're leading a movement and we need to act like we know what the fuck we're about." He looked down at Johnny and blushed, "Excuse me."

"You're right, man," said Eddie. "So, who are we supposed to turn them over to? According to Andrews, your attorney guy, they've got someone working the inside of the police department."

"Then hand 'em over to the FBI," suggest Jessie.

"The FBI ain't going to come out in weather like this," argued Jimmy James.

"They kidnapped you guys, why don't you kidnap them back, until you can give them to the FBI?" asked Johnny, with a mischievous grin.

"There you go," said Jessie. "And besides, our guys control who gets on which bus."

"Tell you what, how 'bout we make them disappear for a few hours of fun on the school bus from hell, until the storm's over?"

~

Jimmy James handed Johnny down from the last half-mangled Chris Craft on the beach to Eddie, who carried him up to a yellow school bus jutting out of a trail plowed through the soggy jungle. The doors swung open and he climbed in to set the boy on the top step, "I want to make sure young Johnny gets home safe and sound."

"You've come to the right place," replied Hannibal Davis. "I'm checking everyone in and assigning seats on the next transport out of here."

"What are you doing here?" asked Eddie, recognizing Mrs. Hall's houseman.

Davis smiled, "Well, Mrs. Hall and Mrs. Sloan both wanted to come out here to help but I refused to drive them, so, as a compromise, I volunteered to lend a hand, if they would stay at Hampton House until the storm passes."

The biker clapped him on the back, "You're the man! Listen, this is Jessie's friend, Johnny. He's been injured and might have a concussion."

"Take him over to the second bus, we've got two doctors helping out."

"Great," replied Eddie. "Hey, did you notice that last group of folks who came through, bunch of burly guys in garbage sack rain gear and a little gal leading an old guy along?"

"Yeah, they didn't even seem to be relieved to be on dry land."

"Where'd they go? I need to speak with them."

"I sent 'em to the second bus, until the next transports get back. We've been sending them to town in pairs, in case someone gets in trouble with the weather or flooding or whatever. Safer that way."

"Are there any spare buses?"

"Why?"

"Well, because I might want to escort them out of here myself. They could be trouble."

"There's that short bus over there," replied Davis, pointing through the window. "It only carries fifteen, including the driver."

"Got the keys?"

The biker covered Johnny with a towel and carried him back to the next bus, where he found Jammer and Twigs. "I need to talk with you guys but I've got to get Johnny to the docs first. Can you hang out for a minute?"

"We're already soaked, what's a little more?" asked Jammer.

Eddie carried the boy into the bus and set him down on seat, where a doctor was treating a woman with a cut on her arm. He looked up, "How can we help?"

"Think the boy might have a concussion and shock from exposure."

A slender woman, with garish red hair sprouting from beneath a black hat with a flat rim, sat down next to Johnny and asked, "What's your name?"

"Johnny Warmington."

"Where do you live?"

"23 Crested Heron Road."

She pointed a penlight into his left eye and moved it back and forth, then repeated the test on his right eye.

"Why are you out here?"

"To save my mom, who works out on the key."

She looked up at Eddie, who grinned, "He's been running boats back and forth across the cove since this whole thing started. He's a real hero."

The doctor put an arm around Johnny's shoulders, "I don't think you've got a concussion but you are kinda beat up, so how about you let me try to make you feel better?"

"Okay."

Eddie glanced at the waiting crowd at the back of the bus and patted Johnny on the back. "I'll be back in a minute. Do as the doctor says."

The biker trotted down the stairs and gathered his guys in a huddle. He handed the keys to Jammer and Twigs trotted off in another direction.

Eddie climbed back onto the bus and sauntered to the back, singling out the man in the burgundy parka. "Excuse me."

The man turned with a scowl.

"I was told to collect you and your party. There's a bus waiting."

"Great," replied the man, marching down the aisle, out into a moment of relative calm, and onto the bus that pulled up.

The girl guided an older unstable man after the others but Glover stepped into the aisle, "I'm sorry, Ma'am, but you'll have to wait for the next bus."

"But I'm with those people."

"Sorry, we'll get you out of here as fast as we can and, besides, it looks as if this gentleman should be on a bigger, more stable bus."

"Okay," said the blond. "Just so we all get to the same place and soon."

"No worries, darlin'. I'll make sure you're first on the next bus."

He ruffled Johnny's ginger hair and trotted down the stairs into the mud. Twigs handed him a sawed-off 12-guage and followed him onto the short bus, where the seven hefty men were sorting out seating in the cramped little van. Eddie stood at the front and pumped the shotgun, "Gentlemen, we will be escorting you out of this jungle but, much as I'd like to hand you bastards over to the FBI, I'm afraid we won't have that opportunity until the storm passes, so we'll have to create our own amusements to pass the time. My associate, who's standing in the back will be by to collect any weapons that you might be carrying and, please, don't play the fool. Given just the slightest provocation, I will not hesitate to take out the whole bunch of you assholes right here and right now."

The men glanced from one to the next, until the burgundy parka reached under his jacket and held up a Beretta by the barrel, staring contemptuously at Eddie and Twigs. "Do as the man says."

Jammer collected four more guns and took the driver's seat. He started the engine, flicked on the lights, and rolled out of the clearing. "Everyone buckle up for safety!"

The captives were tense but silent, ready to spring, given the chance but the two scatterguns proved calming. Large drops of rain splattered on the windshield and gusts of wind pitched palm fronds and debris across the trenched path. The bus sloshed through the dense jungle for more than a mile before sliding out on a deserted stretch of asphalt and heading east into the Everglades.

"This ain't the road to town, where are you taking us?"

Eddie grinned, "Well, you stashed our friends in a derelict jail and abandoned them. They would have died of starvation or worse, if we hadn't found them. Did they ask where you were taking them or did you just drug them, so you wouldn't have to answer stupid questions?"

The leader turned away without a response and reached under his jacket. Twiggs pressed the shotgun against his temple and said, "You don't really want me to pull the trigger, now do you? Hand it over."

He held up a small revolver and the biker took it.

Jammer plowed through the storm for thirty minutes and turned south on a flooded gravel road that gave way to a muddy path that twisted through the marshes for another half hour, until he came to a clearing. The bus stopped in the middle of the open patch, battered by catastrophic winds, massive lightning strikes, deafening thunder, and tortuous rain. He shut down the engine, collected the pistols into a cloth bag, ripped the wires from the ignition and opened the door.

The burgundy parka asked, "What now?"

Eddie pointed the shotgun, "Well, we could just take you outside and blow your asses away but, after consulting with the people that you brutalized, we decided to let you cool your jets, until we send the Feds back to put you in the pokey, where you belong."

"And how are you getting out of here?"

Headlights flashed through the back window and Twigs pointed, "We called a cab."

Glover looked the man in the eye, "I would suggest that you concentrate on how you're going to survive this storm and don't even think about coming after us, because I'd love to even up the score without the cops getting involved. Oh, and this is one of my favorite spots to picnic, it's thirty miles to the nearest road and the mosquitoes shouldn't be too bad until the rain stops, but there's plenty of snakes and gators roaming around. I can guarantee they're faster than any of you, in case you decide to run for it."

The three bikers stepped off the bus, sloshed through the muck to climb into a silver Land Rover, and drove off into the storm.

Chapter Twelve

Jessie clambered across the grinding boat bridge and down onto the dock, where Kate and Benny were organizing a van full of employees to start the harrowing pilgrimage to safety, and knelt to nuzzle a soaked Gracie.

Kate trotted over to hug him, "Where's Johnny?"

"I guess you couldn't see from here but a huge gust of wind flipped his boat and I had to go in after him. He got banged around a bit but he's going to be okay. I sent him across with Eddie and one of his pals."

"Couldn't be in better hands."

"Speaking of which, did you see a bunch of stout guys, dressed in garbage bag rain gear, go through?"

"Yeah, they were the odd group. They looked like aging offensive linemen. Everyone else has been couples or families."

"Sammy thinks they're the guys who kidnapped us and set off the explosives at the rally."

"You know, the guy in the burgundy parka seemed kind of scary...and familiar, now that you mention it. Gracie started barking and growling as soon as they got out of the van, and she was really aggressive when she herded them onto the bridge."

"She's always about two steps ahead of me, I'm surprised she didn't take a bite out of one of them. Eddie was going to handle them until he can contact the FBI."

"I'm not sure which guy I'd be more scared of...the asshole who slugged you or Eddie pissed off!"

Jessie grinned, "I like Eddie a lot but I sure don't need to see his dark side."

"Yeah, me neither but he did step up to help Gretchen and her kids."

"Those guys have some balls, hiding in plain sight."

"It's actually kind of brilliant. I sure wouldn't have thought to look for them here."

"Yeah, me neither," replied Jessie. "How's it going?"

Kate pointed to the vans parked along the quay, "We're finished with guests and I think these Suburbans coming down might be the last load or two of employees."

"I wonder whether Johnny's mother's gone across?"

"I haven't seen her."

Another van pulled up just as a swirling column of clouds passed overhead, gusty winds picked up from the northwest, and the heavens opened the taps with a deluge. Twelve women in SunnyBreeze yellow slickers leaned into the gale and staggered across the wharf.

Bobbie Warmington marched over to lean close, "Where's Johnny?"

"He's safe on the other side," yelled Jessie.

"He's supposed to be at home!" snapped the exhausted and frantic woman.

"He volunteered to try to rescue his mother and ended up saving a thousand people besides you."

"And I'm sure you didn't have anything to do with it."

"I couldn't stop him. He was planning to take the MissU out by himself."

"He is kind of bullheaded."

"He's also a hero," added Kate.

Another woman joined them, as Benny guided the other ladies up the makeshift stairs to begin their journey across the bridge, which was creaking and arching in the opposite direction. A blast of wind and rain whipped over the dunes to hurl whitecaps across the bay at ninety miles an hour.

Bobbie said, "This is our receptionist, Jenny Rose."

Jessie asked, "Where's Sloan?"

"He said he was going to check to make sure everyone's out and he's got a Suburban to drive down here…" She paused and looked up at Jessie, "But I'm not sure he will."

Bobbie leaned close, "He better get out of there soon, because the ocean's getting ready to carve a new inlet right through The Commons. Another few hours of this and there won't be anything left."

Jessie hugged Kate, "I've got to go make sure he's out."

"Why? You don't owe him anything!"

"If I did anything else, I wouldn't be who I am…I'd be like him."

She kissed him passionately, "I'll wait for you."

"No, you won't. You and Gracie are going to guide these ladies across and take everyone you find along the way to safety. I'll be along as soon as I kick his ass down the hill."

Kate held him for a long moment, her strength and determination withering under the terror in her amber eyes, "I lost you once and I don't want to lose you again."

"Me neither," replied Jessie, kneeling in the swirling waters to hug Gracie. "I want you to go with Kate and Bobbie and I'll meet you on the other side."

She cocked her head and whined.

"I know you want to help me but I need to know that all of you are safe, so, just this once, do as I say, okay?"

She licked his cheek and trotted across the wharf to climb up the makeshift staircase. Jessie grabbed the keys from the driver and plowed upstream through a raging river rushing down to the marina.

He parked under the portico and climbed out of the van into a torrent of debris flushing through the narrow passageway with a vengeance. He waded to the double doors but hesitated, overwhelmed by the snarl of waves crashing on the circular drive, where ravenous breakers had reduced the enormous band shell to a tangle of jagged fingers reaching desperately from a churning tidal pool. Whatever remained of Midnight Pass Road resided fifteen or twenty feet under the surf. The tide would start dismantling the massive columns and the building within minutes not hours.

The wind slammed the door closed, as Jessie stumbled into the lobby, which was dark, silent, and empty, save piles of abandoned clothes and suitcases scattered around the exit. He jogged down a corridor to a deserted reception room and climbed the granite stairs to the corporate offices. A desk lamp on Sloan's desk cast an orange wedge across gleaming terrazzo, pointing directly at Tate, who was standing at the window, watching hell gobble up his dream.

Without turning, he said, "You're a damned fool for coming back but you always were a goody-two-shoes kind of hero."

"I wanted to make sure you got out."

"I'm not going. There's no point."

"Of course, there is, every one of your guests and employees is safe on the other side of the bay and we can be too, if we hurry."

"As I said, I'm not going." He turned around and flipped a football to the former quarterback. "That was the game ball, which warrants the question of whether you ever wondered how we made you guys look like fools in the Orange Bowl?"

Jessie tossed the ball back, "I just assumed we had a bad day and you had a spectacular one."

"That's a bit naïve, don't you think?"

"What do you mean?"

"I mean our folks laced your water and Gatorade with downers and, although I didn't know until later, ours with amphetamines."

"It did seem like you guys were flying, while we were slogging through mud."

The Okie quarterback threw a soft spiral, "We didn't win that game, we stole it. By all rights, you should have won going away, but there was too much money riding on it and the guys who run the books don't lose money…ever. I should know, they paid me a really nice salary that covered everything my family needed for more than four years, while I tossed a football around and made up stupid one-liners that sounded catchy on television. Hell, I didn't show up for a class during the fall semester and still got B's."

"You've known all these years?"

"Yeah, I did and I didn't even feel guilty about it, because I knew I wasn't really the guy that everyone adored, the hero or the legend, and I kind of figured that you weren't either…until I did some research and found that you bagged your scholarship and disappeared right after the game?"

"Actually, I left Madison in a blizzard, headed for anywhere warm, where no one knew me, and ended up here. I slept on the beach for the first month or two after I got here. Guess I needed time to at least identify my demons and figure out what I was running from."

"I've seen some of your paintings and they're amazing. You might have been fighting depression but you sure found something magical on that beach."

Jessie heaved the ball hard, "So, I went through years of doubt and torture, because you bastards cheated?"

"Yup and I ended up marrying the rich girl, who I actually thought I loved, while spending gobs of her daddy's money and playing my part in the 'perfect' couple for all the magazines and television shows. It was all hype, I just had to be who they expected me to be and, to tell you the truth, I knew from the beginning that I wasn't in the same league as my wife. I've always felt like someone was going to expose me for being a good ol' country boy from the sticks of Oklahoma, who had no right to be jetting around with the super-rich, living in mansions, driving exotic cars, and living extravagantly."

"You played the part well."

Tate handed the ball to Jessie, "Turns out I was just a pawn, a frontman for the girl with the money, and, odd as it might seem, considering what all the scandal sheets say, I'm gay."

"Really?"

"Yeah, I never had a clue…until recently."

"I don't even want to know but isn't whoever you're involved with worth living for?"

"I'm fairly sure that I'm just an amusement to be cast aside, when he's finished with me."

"So, this is what's behind the All-American hero bit, a mushy crybaby who's ready to give up when life finally hands him a real challenge?"

"Look, there's no love left in my marriage, my affair is just that…an affair, and this place was my creation. I put everything into making it a world-class destination." He pointed out the window, which was bowing and quivering under crushing wind gusts, "There's nothing left to salvage and I'm sure the lawyers are gonna have a field day after Mother Nature gets finished."

Jessie slammed the ball into Tate's chest, "Tell you what I think, I think you cheated me out of an Orange Bowl triumph and years of sanity, I think you cheated yourself out of being a real hero by buying into your own bullshit and fucking up the opportunity to build an extraordinary life, but I'll guarantee you're not going to cheat anyone out of whatever comes next."

"What do you mean?" stammered Sloan, fumbling the ball.

Jessie grinned, leaned back, and landed a perfect right cross on Tate's chin. The pigskin bounced across the room, as the Okie crumpled to the floor. His rival hefted him onto his shoulder, staggered down the stairs, across the lobby, sloshed through waves crashing through the portico, and tossed Sloan into the back seat of the Suburban. "You're damn sure not going to keep me from being who I need to be."

Rushing streams erupted from side roads, melding into raging rapids rushing along the winding boulevard to the marina. The floundering Suburban floated down to the docks, amid flowering shrubs riding fence panels and rootless denuded palms torpedoing crumpled patio furniture but sparing a little girl's pink pram, bobbing along in the flow. Jessie jumped out and ran around to drag Sloan out onto the flooded tarmac. He slapped Tate's face several times before his eyes blinked open. "Now what?"

"I'm going across that bridge before it disintegrates and you're coming with me."

Tate turned to scan the flailing procession of splintered yachts, "No, I'm not."

"Look, you don't get to be a martyr, so get your shit together. I'm out of shape and sure as hell don't have the strength to carry you, so do us both a favor instead of me having to kick your ass all the way across. I've got people to live for and so do you."

Sloan shook his head and leaned into the gale, "Fine, be the hero. Let's go!"

They staggered through a buffeting southwesterly squall and up a stack of crates to crawl onto the heaving deck of the first mangled yacht.

Sloan snagged a cleat to avoid washing into a great gash, ground into the fractured fiberglass by incessant impacts against the pilings, as a massive wave crashed over the stern. The chain of crumbling cruisers bowed north up the channel on a furious incoming tide and several were riding low, hammered by an unrelenting frenzy of savage breakers.

Jessie crouched low and scrambled off the bow onto the bounding remnants of a magnificent ocean liner, that once visited the most prestigious ports in the world but found its final calling as a tottering escape for more than a thousand desperate souls. He turned to haul a petrified Sloan between pitching rails, through a once luxurious lounge paneled in mahogany with teak accents and gleaming gold fixtures, and over a broad slippery transom onto a dilapidated sloop. They waded through a tangle of lines binding a shattered mast and twisted boom, impaled through the windows of the cabin and grinding a gaping hole in the hull of the next boat.

Vicious winds whipped the chain of yachts, snapping ropes and wrenching cleats and fittings from their moorings, adding to a barrage of deadly shrapnel firing through the storm. Jessie leapt from the bow of a fishing boat onto the stern of a schooner, as the bridge exploded with a thunderclap of broken timbers and mangled splendor. He tumbled to the deck and scrambled to reach for Sloan's hand, as brutal waves swamped the trawler and dragged her shattered skeleton out into the tempest dancing madly across the bay. The artist grabbed a coiled line floating in the bilge water sloshing back and forth in the well, and heaved it through crushing winds to the Oklahoma quarterback, who made no attempt to catch it.

Sloan scaled the rising bow of the sinking vessel and yelled through the deafening roar, "It's my time! You're the real hero, go save yourself!"

Cotton screamed, "No!" but wicked winds dragged the ragged chain of battered boats back across the lagoon towards the marina. Pounding breakers shredded pipedreams into a slashing snarl of rigging, binding deadly shards of wreckage into a serpent's tail whipping through churning currents.

The enormous sailboat listed to starboard on a massive swell exploding over the stern and Jessie clamored over the cabin, as the mast splintered with a mighty crack and toppled across the bow, with lines and stays lashing the bridge of the next battered boat. He leapt onto a crumbling cabin cruiser, as the sloop keeled over, her broad deck catching the gale to haul the snarled string of shattered yachts back to shore. The artist raced through blinding rains across the devastated hulks of a dozen million-dollar vessels, until he clambered onto Benny's three-story liner which broke loose from the beach in the thrashing tide. The ravaged fleet of mangled dreams dragged props and hull through the sand, with the deafening groan of dying desires melding into the chaos of the storm.

Just as he stumbled onto the aft deck, the stern slammed into a rocky outcrop and tossed him over the rail into bounding breakers hammering the mangroves. A titanic tidal surge swept him through savage seagrape, cruel cordgrass, and scrawny cypress, saw-teeth slashing the slicker and his flesh, until he washed up under the front wheels of a yellow school bus.

Barely conscious, his muscles incapable of helping or hindering desperate hands rolling his body through the muck to drag him up the stairs. Benny dropped him into a seat and Kate wrapped her arms around his neck, whispering, "You're alive."

Benny sealed the door, cranked the engine, and slammed the transmission into reverse, "'bout time you showed up, sucker. Five more minutes and we'd have had no choice but to leave your scrawny white butt behind. I've already backed this ol' girl up twice."

"Why?"

Hannibal Davis pointed out the windshield as the bus rolled backwards, "The ocean's busted through, there's a new inlet where SunnyBreeze used to be."

Gracie rested her head in his lap, as Jessie pulled himself up to stare through wind and rain, where the headlights illuminated ocean waves rolling across the bay, "Oh my god…I heard it and felt it but I didn't have time to realize what was happening."

Gracie climbed onto his lap to lick his face, as he slumped into the seat.

Kate whispered, "Where's Sloan?"

"He didn't make it."

"I'm sorry, what happened?"

"Long story but I had him halfway across, when a surge unraveled the bridge and he floated off across the bay. I tossed him a rope but it was too late."

Kate wiped mud from his face with a towel, "If someone wrote this into a novel, no one would believe it."

"I'm not sure I do," replied Jessie, shaking with cold and exhaustion, blood dripping down his cheek from a laceration on his forehead. "Did everyone get out? Where's Johnny?"

"Yup, all accounted for," said Hannibal, offering a dry blanket, "even the bad guys."

He hugged Gracie, "Oh?"

"Word came down the line that the bus they were traveling on took a wrong turn and had engine trouble someplace out in the middle of the swamp. Eddie figures it's going to take the FBI's expertise to find them, when the storm finally passes."

He looked into Kate's gaze, "Only slightly better accommodations than we enjoyed on our little vacation."

"Serves them right," laughed the reporter, "and what's coming next will be even sweeter."

The tires whined over the sodden track through the jungle and Jessie cuddled with Gracie and slumped against Kate, his exhausted body limp, his soul sapped by sorrow and relief.

$\sim$

Hushed voices and quiet movement merged into distorted echoes bounding through the roar of the storm and visions of Johnny falling over the transom of the flying racer, terrified people scrambling through madness and fury, the fear in Kate's eyes, deadly gales and boiling tides tearing the chain of boats into jagged fragments, and Sloan, just out of reach, drifting away into a roiling gray oblivion.

He opened his eyes and struggled to focus on Johnny's smile, "You're back!"

"Where…?"

"You're in the hospital. You're kinda scuffed up and you got your bell rung."

"But the doctors say that you should be better in a few days," added Kate, leaning to kiss his bandaged forehead. Jessie started to sit up but she pushed him back into his pillows. "Sit, stay!"

"Yes Ma'am."

"What day is it?"

"Wednesday night," replied the boy, looking up at the clock, "almost Thursday. I was worried about you."

He took the boy's hand, "I know how you feel. I was desperate to find you, when you took that dive off the cigarette boat."

Johnny blushed, "I didn't have time to be scared, it just went out from under me."

"I think we both got lucky." He hugged the boy and turned to Kate, "What'd I miss?"

"Well, while you were napping, the storm blew through, carved destruction through Orlando and Jacksonville, and then headed out into the Atlantic. The city's a mess but there were only four deaths – an elderly man died of a heart attack and two women drowned when their house collapsed into the bay. Oh, the FBI sent a team down from Tampa and they finally found the missing bus this morning with seven miserable refugees ready to give up for food, fresh water, and something for the bug bites."

"What about…?"

"Sloan?"

"Yeah."

"The ocean cut three new inlets through the key, so the only way to get out there is by boat."

"And?"

"All the guests and employees of SunnyBreeze are accounted for, except Sloan. The sheriff sent a search party but they haven't found him. They did find Harvey Millsap's body, the maintenance guy, who helped us set up the bridge. He and Gracie went in the water after a little girl and he crashed headfirst into the seawall, after saving the kid and the dog."

"That's too bad, he was a real hero. Where's Gracie?"

"She's with my mom," said Johnny.

"Good. How bad is SunnyBreeze?"

Kate hesitated, "From the reports I've heard, there is no SunnyBreeze. The storm stripped the island from the beach to the bay."

"Wow, the power of nature is incredible."

"I think you should do a painting," said Johnny.

"I think that's a good idea," replied the artist. "Say, how'd it go with your mom and your grandma'?"

The boy blushed, "Well, mom couldn't be too mad, I mean we did save her and a whole bunch of other people, but I got the lecture anyway. Then I got it again from grandma, except she was chasing me around the kitchen with a broom!"

"Good thing you can run fast."

"The downside is that neither one of us has a boat, so they think we can't get into any more trouble for a while."

"We'll see about that! I guess, if the New School got wiped out, you'll be going back to your old school?"

"I don't know what's going to happen but Mrs. Sloan came by to check on you and she said they're looking for a building they can use for a temporary school and she wants more local kids too."

Jessie glanced up at Kate, "What aren't you telling me?"

"She heard that you tried to save Tate and wanted to thank you."

"And?"

"She wants to have a meeting, when you're feeling better."

"No point in being at cross purposes," replied Jessie.

"I think she wants to coordinate the entire movement – the protests and strikes, the work that she and her foundation are doing to house and employ the homeless, and a re-education program to help the unemployed to climb out of poverty."

"She's got the money and the connections."

"I'm glad you approve but you'd better get yourself better because, whether they find a body or not, Tate's funeral's next Tuesday."

He laughed and hugged Johnny, "Leave it to Tate Sloan not to show up for his own funeral."

~

Selby Simonson, a living legend in oil and gas, ranching, and large-scale construction, escorted his daughter and Tate's mother, Betty, down the aisle of St. Pius Cathedral, following Father Moorland, an aging Anglican with a taste for fine port and an eye for beautiful women. A maudlin pipe organ spewed a depressing dirge and Mavis whispered, "Tate would have preferred the Rolling Stones."

Simonson and Betty smirked, as they took places along the first pew. Sloan's mother dabbed her eyes with a lace hanky and said, "I actually think he'd resent all of this, in spite of you two living in fantasyland."

"Yeah, he'd prefer having a few brews, telling some outrageous stories, and remembering the good times."

"That's my boy," said Betty, turning to Alfy, Tate's younger brother, and the three sisters – Missy, Sharon, and Carole. "You look terrific! Tate'd be proud of all y'all!"

Mavis blew a kiss to Tabitha Hall, who was seated with Hannibal Davis, Jessie, Kate, Benny, and Sammy, and glanced across the aisle, where Ned Flint sat alone, holding a handkerchief to quivering lips. She stood, smoothed her slinky black dress, adjusted the veil of a broad-brimmed hat, and sashayed over to sit next to him. The tears in his eyes overflowed and she clenched his hand. "We both loved him, so why don't you come sit with us."

Embarrassed, he avoided her gaze, "Considering everything, I couldn't sully his reputation."

Her laughter echoed around the chapel, "Honey, after all the fantastic magazine stories, all the lies that way too many people actually believed, there's no chance of that. Now, come on, you've earned a place in this very strange family." She stood up, took his hands and guided him across to sit next to Tate's mother, while the minister waited patiently, inspired to his own damnation by her every move.

A late procession of investors and board members wandered down the aisle to pack the pews before the congregation settled down and the last endless note from the organ rumbled around the gray stone walls. A single shaft of sunlight illuminated the Reverend, a beacon in the gloom of the massively majestic and spiritually oppressive space, "Now, if everyone is ready to begin?" He paused, gazing around the crowd, "I think Tate Sloan would be pleased to see so many loyal fans in the stands…"

The audience laughed.

"In fact, Tate's most famous game was a contest for the national title in the Orange Bowl, Oklahoma against number-one Wisconsin. Oklahoma won that game and, if I'm not mistaken, the quarterback for the Wisconsin team is the man who made a valiant effort to save Tate during the storm. He's with us today, Dolphin Bay's own Jessie Cotton."

Applause and cheers recoiled around the inside of Jessie's skull, as the crowd stood. He felt he was viewing a Salvador Dali hallucination of towering elongated bodies looming over a deep well and flashed on the turmoil whirling across the bay, splintered lashings unshackling a donnybrook of damaged yachts thrashing the bridge into shattered fragments, and Sloan evaporating into the fury of the storm.

Kate squeezed his hand and Reverend Moorland's words echoed through the chapel, "Part of his charm was that he wasn't afraid to tell his own story. He was a scruffy kid, who grew up poor on his daddy's ramshackle ranch in the sticks of Oklahoma, played eight-man football in high school, and earned a scholarship to the University of Oklahoma, where he broke all kinds of records as the winningest quarterback in school history. He married his sweetheart and partner, Mavis, and together they built a fledgling oil services company into an industry giant. Then they developed SunnyBreeze, which opened last spring to sold-out bookings and articles of praise in the New York Times, Travel, Home and Garden, and American Style. Yet another triumph in a lifetime of achievements that defied all odds!

So, it shouldn't surprise anyone to learn that Tate, with the help of Jessie Cotton and a troop of volunteers from the protest rally, evacuated everybody on the key, that's more than a thousand guests and employees, before attempting to escape himself. He might have been a lot of other things but, when the chips were down, he stepped up to go far beyond his obligations. You might call that bravery, I call it character, because underneath everything else, the glitter and the glamour, the fame and the fortunes, Tate was still that scrawny good-natured kid, who carried a value system gleaned from his meager but righteous roots.

Mavis, Betty, Alfy, Missy, Sharon, and Carole, we share your pain and sorrow. I believe that there's an empty place in the human landscape, where a very public man, who was loved and revered…" He paused to admire the black heels and stockings as Mavis crossed her long legs, "A man, who had everything to live for, would sacrifice his own life to save all those who were depending on him. He was the captain, who went down with a sinking ship, and there are more than a thousand people who are thankful for his intelligence, his grace, and his valor.

Had he died of normal causes, the world would be mourning the loss of a shining star, who charmed and entertained us, thrilled us with astonishing athletic abilities, and built an empire…but we would have missed his most important trait…a hero, who valued other lives more than his own."

The hum of murmurs wafted through the crowd. "Let us pray."

Jessie sat on a stool before a very large white canvas in his studio, which was almost as clean and empty as the day he finished construction, save thousands of drips and drabs in a rainbow splattered on the floor around his easels and plywood covering the shattered windows on either side of the front door. Two or three paintings survived the invasion, the tattered remains of the rest were hauled away to the dump by overzealous volunteers, eager to erase reminders of the kidnapping. He could see each image, each stroke, the awe and wonder of magic light illuminating the beauty of nature, and he was determined to revisit those scenes along the way, but the work would be different now.

He closed his eyes, his mind reeling through fleeting glimpses of the gruesome storm in lethal shades of gray, occasionally broken by brilliant flashes of blue lightning and hammered by deafening thunder…but textures and vibrant colors were veiled behind a cruel monochromatic haze. The smell of salty mist lingered in his nostrils, the taste smothered the flavor of every meal, and the vision of his suicidal nemesis, floating away on the splintered bow of a sinking ship, invaded what fitful slumber he could manage.

Frustrated with the silent seclusion of his depression, Kate kissed his cheek, "I'm worried about you and I don't want to leave when you're in this…state, but I don't have any choice."

"I'll get through it," replied the artist.

"The question is whether we'll get through it."

Jessie turned, "I lost you once and I don't intend to make that mistake again."

"Then you have to get through this. You did everything you could to save hundreds of people, who would surely be dead, but you lost one in the process."

"You know it's more than that."

"Of course, and we should mourn his death, but he'd be pissed, if he knew that you're down in the dumps and completely non-functional. You let him do that to you once before, remember?"

He stared at the mosaic of paint splatters on the floor, "The only thing I can compare it to is the frustration of waking up just before you reach the end of a dream. Tate was standing on the bow of a sinking cruiser, as it faded into the storm, just out of reach, and there was no fear or desperation in his eyes. He had accepted whatever fate had in store for him."

"Then you have to accept your destiny, that your life will be different now, that your priorities and obligations have been altered by your experience, and that you've taken another step in becoming who you're supposed to be."

"Life before and life after?"

"Exactly…and I expect to be in the middle of it."

"I'm glad."

"Then get your shit together. I have to quit my job, before they fire me, and clean out my apartment. I'll be back by the weekend with a truck that will need unpacking."

He hugged her, "Be safe and come back to me."

She kissed him, "I will…because, I love you."

Gracie trotted in the door as Kate left and rubbed against his legs. "It's just you and me for a few days, girlfriend. Think we remember how to live on our own?"

The dog tilted her head, as if to say, "I spent years training you, I hope you remember your part."

He knelt and hugged her, "I'm grateful to have you as my friend."

She picked up a grimy tennis ball, "Then come toss a ball for me!"

They wandered out through the kitchen to the bare patio and Jessie lobbed the ball down the hill. Gracie pranced through fallen palm fronds and several large branches, wrenched from the aging oaks and the banyan trees, searching for the yellow ball. The steel structure supporting the open slip of the dock was fractured during the storm, allowing crumbling Styrofoam blocks, supporting a strip of planking and part of the roof, to drift away and then crash back into the storage locker on each successive wave. *"Time to call old man Perkins to come by and weld it back together, before it gets any worse."*

Gracie trotted up with the ball in her mouth but her ears perked up and she focused on something behind him. He turned to find Mavis Sloan peering over the gate. "May I come in?"

Jessie unlatched the bolt and Gracie sniffed at her black pants suit, "I don't mean to intrude."

"It's fine, how are you holding up?"

"I hate to say it but Tate and I lived full-tilt on every level and, although there are some things we might have done better, I don't think either of us could regret much of it. We got to share a spectacular fantasy together, a grand performance for all the world to see. What they didn't see was how hard it was to maintain that illusion and how damaging all the negative press can be on a relationship."

"Not all it's cracked up to be?" asked Jessie, setting up lawn chairs.

"Exactly, I think we both knew that, at some point, there'd have to be a very public split, if either of us really cared about the love we shared or any hope of maintaining our respect for each other."

"If you had scripted this whole thing, you couldn't devise a more appropriate ending, Tate disappearing in a storm after saving a thousand people?"

"The world always saw him as a hero."

"Well, I had every reason not to like the son-of-a-bitch but I tried, very hard, to keep him alive."

"I know and that's why I've come by…to thank you, because most people wouldn't have risked going back to get him."

Jessie blushed, "It's okay, he would have done the same."

"Actually, I think, at this end of his life, he would."

"Can I get you something?"

"Sure, anything cold and wet," replied the striking blond. "What's your dog's name?"

He started for the kitchen door, to grab a small table, "That's Gracie and she's my best friend."

She leaned to rub Gracie's cheek, "The best kind."

The artist returned with a tray bearing two glasses of iced tea, a plate of lemon slices, and a bowl of sugar.

"Thanks, this is perfect." She took a glass and twisted a slice of lemon, "So, how are you recovering?"

"I'm getting there but I'm realizing that it's going to take longer than I'd like."

"You aren't the agile young quarterback anymore."

He grinned, "I really hate to admit that, even if my body's been telling me since before I quit playing."

"The Orange Bowl was your last game?"

"Yes, I dropped out of school…out of life, for that matter, a month after the game, somehow ended up sleeping on the beach down the coast and took up painting to make some money."

"And now you're up to your eyeballs trying to save a whole class of people. How'd you get into this?"

"Long story but, once I got started, there was no turning back."

"I know exactly what you mean. I was a spoiled brat but I was smart enough to become the student of a wise father and he taught me to consider all the ramifications of any business deal. Obviously, it's supposed to make money but what happens to the worker bees, who actually make it happen? If you want them to contribute their best, then you have to ask what's in it for them?"

"And?"

"And, when we started brainstorming SunnyBreeze and researching economic trends, all the evidence of a complete and total financial collapse, sort of, tumbled out and landed in my lap and I couldn't ignore it. By the time we pitched our backers, I made everyone aware of the impending threat and I offered them the chance to buy in to it, to control the disaster, instead of riding it over a cliff into chaos."

"I doubt that rich folks give a damn about all these desperate people, who used to hold a valued place in our society, before they were laid off or replaced by robots and banished to second-class citizenship."

"You're right, what they care about is saving their own asses from a revolution that will destroy their investments and their lifestyle. So, I offered them a plan to build a new economy by employing and housing masses of workers in the industrial hearts of major cities and a surprising number of them got behind it. We've opened seven centers, signed up, trained, and employed almost fifteen-thousand people, and we've got another two-dozen projects under way, with more on the drawing board. Oh, and Reverend Jimbo Combs heads up our training program."

"That's incredible." He grinned, "My friend, Johnny Warmington, was really impressed with him, after his interview for the New School."

"Yeah, Jimbo was captivated with your young man, too." She paused, "It didn't take long to realize that I was naïve to believe that we could get ahead of the curve. We'll never change the course of history, unless we can find a way to get people across the country and across the world, for that matter, to stand up and fight for their rights and their future."

Jessie sipped cold tea, "And…?"

"And, what you've started here in Dolphin Bay is becoming the model for rallies and protests across the nation. I don't know whether you've been watching the news but you've become an icon."

He grinned, "I don't have a television, since the fake cops destroyed the house and my studio."

"Well, I heard the FBI has them in custody."

"Yeah, but they're pros, so they won't talk. They'll do their time, knowing they'll be well paid by someone, when they get out."

"They don't have to, I know who was behind it."

"Who?"

"J.D. Calhoun, a construction magnate, who builds resorts and big condominium projects, that compete for our clientele, up and down the west coast of Florida. He was pissed that my father's company was doing the construction in his backyard and he wasn't getting a big enough slice of it. He's a big shot around here, but he's just a minor player in a much larger fraternity of nationalists, who are hell-bent on destroying the government and owning the economy."

"So, the dissolution of the middle class is just another step in the plan?"

"Yup, it does make sense, doesn't it? Sad part is that there's really no reason to go after our bastard, because he's old and diseased. The inside poop says his heart's going to give out before he can be brought to trial."

"Too bad, I'd like five minutes with that guy."

"Well, I might have a little tidbit to soothe your frustration."

"What's that?"

"I don't know whether you've heard, but we've got allies."

"What allies?"

"Have you seen the stories about the Cameron Conspiracy?"

"No, I'm clueless. Sounds like one of those spy movies."

"Well, some brave folks in Cameron, Oklahoma, exposed a sham Congressional candidate. The young kid's daddy was trying to buy him an election, in conjunction with a whole crew of shady characters, who were trying to throw contests across the state, stacking the deck with evangelical numbskulls, who would vote to enrich their sponsors. They shut down the elections."

Jessie grinned, "Cool."

"Gets better. Once the Feds got wind of it, they discovered the same crap going on with lots of candidates in other states, on every layer of elective office, from national all the way down to city and county.

Contests in at least eight red states are being investigated; elections were postponed at the last minute and new primaries will be organized."

"Maybe the little guys will finally grasp the reality, that the Republican Party has been playing on their ignorance and bigotry, for decades, rallying the hate to entice them to vote for hand-picked candidates, who have no intention of voting for any bill that would benefit working-class citizens, but I'm not countin' on it." Jessie shook his head, "I wish I could believe that our little campaign might become another cog in the wheel that's going to crush fascism, with real democratic freedom for the folks who deserve it most."

Mavis's face lit up with that magazine cover smile, "I'd like to propose that we join forces, you and your people run the front end and I'll supply the financing and get my folks to accelerate our program. It seems pretty obvious that, after everything that's happened, we need to create an organized political movement and you're already a recognizable spokesman."

"I think Benny's perfect for the job." He grinned, "With that smile, does anyone ever say 'No' to you?"

"Not very often."

"What's in it for you?"

"First, I think what we're trying to do is going to evolve into the template for how employers and employees interact in the future. Rather than an adversarial temporary relationship, think of it more as a big family, where squabbles are resolved internally for everyone's benefit. So far, it's an enormous research project and we're already learning how to improve our concept but we'll never get the chance, if the world falls into chaos."

"That doesn't answer my question."

She tilted her head and popped that smile again, "Honey, we own oil wells, pipelines, refineries, ocean tankers, enormous developments and cattle ranches, and corporations that I've never even heard of. Hell, my old man owns the only Rolls Royce dealership in Texas, just to have a certified mechanic fix his car, so I don't need the money. I need the satisfaction of seeing this through because, for a change, it's the right thing to do, and, oh yeah, I don't quit until I get what I want. Are you with me?"

Jessie smirked, "Do I have any choice?"

"Not really. Tabitha, Kate, Benny, and Sammy are already on board. We've scheduled a meeting at our headquarters in Houston for a week from Monday and the folks from Oklahoma, as well as leaders from the west coast, the rust belt, and all the other struggling regions around the country, will be there. I'll have a private plane here to fly all of you out there and back, think you could make it?"

"What's the agenda?"

"This is a huge challenge and it's going to be a long slog, but we need to pull all the different groups under one umbrella with a common purpose and a mutual message. We'll introduce you to more than a dozen Senators and Representatives, who are sympathetic to the cause, and our PR department will have some names and concept designs for inspection and discussion."

"What's wrong with 'All People Matter'?"

"Nothing, I like it a lot and I admire your talent as an artist, so help us put together a public relations package that will draw our people into the organization." She pursed her lips, "I used to be able to convince Tate to go anywhere in the world, if I promised him an outrageous meal."

"What are you serving?"

"I don't know but I promise it'll kick your taste buds into high gear."

He reached to shake her hand, "That's called bribery."

"Yeah, works every time!"

An hour later, Bobbie Warmington's worn station wagon rattled down the drive and Johnny jumped out to knock on the door. Jessie and Gracie trotted around the side of the house to hug the boy, "How are you?"

"I'm good. How 'bout you?"

"Well, I think I'm starting to feel a little better, now that you're here." He leaned in the driver's window to give Bobbie a peck on the cheek, "How are things?"

"Hell, I'm back to looking for another job but I won't complain. We're all safe and I'm proud that we helped all those people. I just have to pray that things are going to work out somehow."

"I'm positive they will, because you're a special lady. In fact, if things keep growing, I'm sure we could find you a job with the movement."

"That'd be a gift from heaven. I never intended to spend my life cleaning up other people's messes."

"I don't blame you. I'll see what I can do."

"Thanks."

Johnny pulled a tackle box and a couple of rods out of the back of the wagon.

"I guess we're still on probation?" inquired Jessie.

Bobbie looked up at him, "You boys broke every rule in my book but ended up doing the right thing, so, considering you destroyed your own boats, plus a whole bunch of other people's expensive yachts, I think you two get to fish off the dock for a while, so I know you're both safe."

"Alright."

"Good, because I'm not going to take any sass from either one of you! I'll be back to pick up Johnny at five o'clock."

He kissed her cheek again. "We'll be easy to find."

He grabbed a tackle box and they started back to the house, when the mail truck pulled up and Clancy Barnes, the neighborhood carrier, stepped out to hand Jessie a bundle of envelopes. "Looks like you've become a popular guy. I'm going to have to charge you extra, if I have to carry more mail to your house."

"I'll gladly pay," laughed Jessie, as the truck rolled up the driveway to the main house. They walked through the entry into the kitchen and he dropped the mail on the counter. The corner of a red post card peaked out of the beige and white pile and he pulled it out.

The photo showed Memorial Stadium at the University of Oklahoma in Norman packed with a sea of crimson and cream. He flipped it over to read simple block lettering, "Now I understand why you had to escape." It was unsigned and there was no return address, but the postmark was from Senders Creek, Oklahoma.

The Characters

SunnyBreeze – idyllic community on the south end of Breezy Key created for wealthy tourists by Tate and Mavis Sloan, providing 'elite' vacation housing and every amenity in a safe, exclusive environment. Beautiful houses are built for investors, by Simonson's corporate construction company, on land leased from the 'corporation' on a ten-year basis, with the idea that they would be torn down and replaced periodically with updated units to generate recurring returns

Tate Sloan – from Senders Creek, Oklahoma, eldest of five children of a farmer who ran a small herd of cattle on a tiny spread. Tate got a scholarship to OU for his ability to pass a football sixty yards and led the OU football team to a National Championship. Graduated and married Mavis.

Chester Sloan – Tate's father
Betty Sloan – Tate's mother
Alfy Sloan – Tate's younger brother
Missy, Sharon, and Carole – Tate's sisters

Mavis Simonson Sloan – Former OU cheerleader and sorority girl, trained by her father, Selby Simonson, to be far more cunning and ruthless than her husband in their business enterprises.

Selby Simonson – Mavis' father - tycoon who made his first fortune using other people's money to punch holes in the Texas dirt, until he made a massive strike. Branched out to own pipelines, refineries, a fleet of ocean tankers, a giant real estate development and construction company, private jet rentals – whose clients are added to an ever-expanding list of potential partners, and the only Rolls Royce dealership in the state of Texas.

Chen Chen – very old Chinese assistant to Simonson, runs all his personal business, including the house, and is Selby's only confidant. Their relationship goes back to the war, when Chen saved Selby's life and took responsibility for his well-being. Helped raise Mavis.

James Robert Combs – 'Jimbo' – semi-evangelical conman with an enormous congregation, built from massive mailing lists stolen from every major religion – Baptists, Methodists, etc. Donations built a gigantic glass temple in Tampa that can seat 10,000 true-believers with facilities to broadcast 24/7 across the globe. "Religion is an entertainment business."

Jessie Cotton – Junior quarterback for the Wisconsin team that lost the National Championship, dropped out of school and disappeared from public view to live out his life as a landscape painter in a little bungalow with a view of the barrier islands across Dolphin Bay, along Florida's west coast.

Gracie – Jessie's Shepherd/Dobie mix

Johnny Warmington, 8-year-old, who lives nearby with his single mother and younger sisters, loves to go fishing with best friend Jessie, and has an innate connection with animals and nature in the bay. Blue eyes, ginger hair

MissU – Johnny's boat

Bobbie Warmington – Johnny's mom

Cara and Stacy - younger sisters

Beatrice Rowlins – Bobbie Warmington's mother

Kate Crocket – Jessie's college girlfriend and, now, lifestyle reporter for 'American Style' magazine in Atlanta. Tall, willowy, horsy, thick blond hair, piercing amber eyes, pretty without being glamorous

Marvin Standler – CEO of Brinksman Investments, charming and lecherous snake, famous for leveraging buyouts to wring every last penny out of a company, before dumping the remnants and the debt for the vultures

Ned Flint – hotel and shipping magnate, provides expertise in management and guest relations

Bernie Baker – eighty-five, made his fortune in waste management in the Northeast. Last of his generation, opinionated, old-school, oblivious to real world

Duffy Timmons –timber magnate, more comfortable in the forest than the board room

Harvey Sacks – CEO of the country's second largest financial group, Harvard graduate, and certainly the class of the group, inherited money, distinguished presence

Erwin Nash – Created Primary Pharmaceuticals to market his arthritis drug, 'Rhythmus', currently bringing a genetic coding device to market, has several PhD's, more money than most developing countries, and ego to match. Youngest in the group.

Jeffry Marsh – inherited wealth, slum lord, purchased three dying movie studios and made another fortune in porn

JD Calhoun – aging builder and real estate tycoon in southwestern Florida and power behind the political scene, gray eyes. Always accompanied by his bodyguard.

Al Delveccio – Calhoun's bodyguard, massive, observant, and threatening, dark eyes and curly hair

Sonia Calhoun – JD's wife, Brazilian bombshell - beautiful, educated, and sophisticated

Rupert Dent – chief engineer for SunnyBreeze

Milton Fore – chief architect

Mayor Bert Kane – Dolphin Bay

Nina Calhoun Kane – the mayor's wife & daughter of JD Calhoun

Police Chief – Trapper Johnson

Harry Conn – Health Inspector

Sammy Ball – tiny clerk in the Planning Commission's archives, bushy gray eyebrows, green eyes

Cammy – Sammy's tabby cat

Rex Tatum – janitor at high school Sammy Ball's neighbor, plump Irishman

Hank Miller – original organizer of city workers

Harvey Harris – mechanic for the city motor pool

Benny Young – landscape maintenance for the city

Alva Thompson – Benny's sister

Harold Thompson – Alva's husband

Sophie, Angie, and little Bill – Thompson children

Derek Rangle – art gallery owner - a shock of white hair, dancing blue eyes behind thick horn-rimmed glasses, and the grin of an aging wizard

Leonard Andrews – attorney

Evan Thudbury – accountant

Eddie Glover – motorcycle shop

Jimmy James – biker

Nomad – biker

Tabitha Hall – aging heiress who owns the newspaper, The Dolphin Times. Tall, slender, mane of white hair, green eyes and pale parchment complexion.

Hannibal Davis – Tabitha Hall's houseman

Gretchen Mowery – homeless woman living in the camp under the bridge at Pelican Turn with her three kids - Ted, William, and Betty

The New School at Dolphin Bay

Ripley Tanger – Headmaster at The New School

Tatum Green – Director of Admissions at the New School

Mrs. Westbrook – Counselor at New School

Milly Savage – Director of housekeeping at SunnyBreeze

Janey Holliday – housemaid at SunnyBreeze with Bobbie

Harvey Millsap – head of maintenance

Cynthia Jones - activities manager at SunnyBreeze

Abby Thomas – greeter for first guests at SunnyBreeze – a pale cherub with a shock of orange hair

Abe & Frieda Huffington – owners of a residence in SunnyBreeze

Harper, April, & Travis – Huffington children

Jenny Rose – SunnyBreeze receptionist

Major David Martin – retired Marine – in charge of rally security

Reverend Moorland – pastor at the funeral

About the Author

Rick Stiller is a novelist, an award-winning commercial photographer, an educator and advocate, and a Master Gardener.

<u>Nellis Gray</u> explores bigotry and racism, while <u>SunnyBreeze</u> exposes the economic disparity between ultra-rich and the rest of the population. The third book in the series, tentatively titled <u>The Forge</u>, predicts the rise of a renegade tyrant intent on gratifying the goals of a fanatical fraternity of tycoons, who have conspired for decades to destroy our rights, liberties, hopes, and dreams for ultimate power and absolute economic domination.

If you enjoyed this story, please post a five-star review on my Amazon page and like my 'Eric T Stiller – Author' page on Facebook.

Novels by Rick Stiller

Fiction

Dealer

The Redemption Series
Nellis Gray
SunnyBreeze

Young Adult

The Morgan's Knot Serial Fantasy

Morgan's Knot
Island of the Children
Ice Island
Islands of Concrete and Steel
Islands of the Mind
Islands in the Sky
Islands of Dark Miracles

Visit: www.rickstiller.com for more of his books,
photographs, and music and www.morgansknot.com for
the latest on the Morgan's Knot series.